RESCUED

ALSO BY MARIA MURPHY

For the Love of Martha

Rescued

MARIA MURPHY

POOLBEG

Published 2017
by Poolbeg Press Ltd
123 Grange Hill, Baldoyle
Dublin 13, Ireland
www.poolbeg.com

ISBN 978-1-78199-862-5

Lines from 'An Old Woman of the Roads' by Padraic Colum used by kind
permission of the Estate of Padraic Colum

Printed and bound by CPI Group (UK) Ltd, Croydon, CR0 4YY

www.poolbeg.com

About the Author

Maria Murphy, poet and author, lives in County Kildare with her husband and two sons. Lured by her passion for the sea, she often returns to her home county of Cork. Therefore it is no surprise that this, her second novel, is set in the beautiful surroundings of West Cork.

Her debut novel *For the Love of Martha* was published by Poolbeg in 2015.

Acknowledgements

I wish to thank the following people, who helped me with my research by patiently answering my questions in person, over the phone or by email. It was a pleasure to talk with you. Any inaccuracies are all my own doing!

So, thank you to: Gay Brabazon, Michael Kelleher, Aedín Johnston, Brian Moore, Philip O'Regan (Skibbereen Heritage Centre), Stephen O'Sullivan (Mizen Signal Station), and Nic Slocum (Whale Watch Ireland).

Thank you to Clíona Ní Shúilleabháin and the Estate of Padraic Colum for kindly granting permission to use the first verse of his poem 'An Old Woman of the Roads' at the start of this novel. It is much appreciated.

Thanks to all my family, especially to my husband, Kieran, for his constant support and encouragement, for his calm presence and ability to make me laugh when I need it most, and to our two wonderful sons, Sam and Luke. (And of course, to Rufus, my sister-in-law's gorgeous dog, who was the inspiration for Shep.)

Thank you to Neil Donnelly and Theresa Murray O'Meara for reading the first draft and for giving me their valuable feedback.

A very, very special thank-you to my friend David Bedwell for that one sentence he uttered which planted the seed for this whole story.

Thank you to my editor, Gaye Shortland, for always seeking more.

Thank you to Paula Campbell and all at Poolbeg Press.

And finally, a huge thank-you to all the readers of my first novel *For the Love of Martha*. I hope you enjoy this one too.

For Kieran, Sam and Luke

Oh, to have a little house!
To own the hearth and stool and all!
The heaped-up sods upon the fire,
The pile of turf against the wall!

From 'An Old Woman of the Roads' by Padraic Colum

Chapter 1

May 1889 West Cork

He saw the dark shape of land out of the corner of his eye, but he was too exhausted to raise his head to look properly. Tiny spears of rain hit his face. The plank of wood he lay across moved closer to the shore. Now that safety was in view it was as if all vigilance and strength finally had permission to leave him.

He slipped into unconsciousness.

Slowly he woke to the touch of fingers on his chest. Heat coursed through him, warming him to the core. The sand was damp and cold beneath his palms but the heat kept flowing.

A young woman was leaning over him, her long red hair lit by the morning sun.

She was staring intently at her hands which were placed on his chest.

"Who ...?" He tried to speak but it came out as a croak.

"*Shh*," she said softly. "You are safe now."

She sat back on her haunches, breathing evenly.

He looked up at the blue sky and listened to the sea, calmer now, after the storm, the lapping of gentle waves a comforting sound. Yes, he was safe, he had been rescued. Or maybe it was all a dream?

He looked back at the young woman and gripped her hand. She nodded and smiled. Tender fingers brushed a clump of hair back from his forehead. He had never seen anyone so beautiful. Never. She was dressed in ordinary country clothes – plain dress and shawl – but he knew there was nothing ordinary about this woman. She got to her feet and extended her hands towards him. He grasped them and felt her gentle strength haul him to his feet.

He looked into her open smiling face and tried to speak. Again all that came out was "Who?" but this time it sounded not as a croak but almost as a prayer, a prayer of thanks for being alive.

"Come, I will get you some dry clothes."

She walked away quickly and he followed, observing her tall, slim shape.

He glanced around at the sandy cove, perplexed at how well he felt. His body didn't ache and his head was quite clear. Surely he should be exhausted after the battle he had fought with the sea? It was as if the woman had taken all that away, but the idea was preposterous. He shook his head.

He looked around him, studying the land across the bay, trying to figure out which part of the coast he had been washed up on. Up ahead, smoke drifted from the chimney of a small cottage. Beside it a donkey grazed in a field and a small hill rose up beyond it. No other houses were visible. It had an air of peaceful seclusion.

Passing through a gate in the low wall, he heard the buzzing of bees. The woman walked ahead of him to the open half-door, then stood on the threshold where, with a movement of her hand, she invited him to go in. He walked straight into the kitchen and she nodded to the fire. He went and stood with his back to it while looking around the room. The smell of freshly baked bread teased his nostrils and his stomach as his eyes fell on a loaf of soda bread on the table.

The cottage was humble but well kept. There was a wooden armchair at one side of the hearth and a rocking chair on the other, a couple of stools and a table in the centre of the room. A dresser stood against one wall, an assortment of dried herbs hanging from the top of it. Beneath them on the dresser stood a row of earthenware jars and a pewter jug full of wild flowers. Over the door was some kind of cross woven from rushes. The deep sill of one small square window held a bowl, jug and candle. On the opposite wall, he was surprised to see a shelf holding a small collection of books. Not a sight commonly seen in cottages like these. His eyes widened as he saw among them Dickens, Brontë, Austin and Swift. That might explain why she seemed so much more sophisticated than the average countrywoman – most of whom could hardly read at all.

He watched her with interest as she turned now from the dresser and passed him a cup of water. He had a savage thirst so drank it in one go.

"You need to get into some dry clothes," she said.

She disappeared through a door beside the fireplace, and returned a moment later with a pile of clothes.

"Here," she said. "These were my father's. They should fit you, I think." She passed them to him, and added a linen towel. Picking up a basket, she went outside.

Hastily he stripped off his sodden shirt, trousers and undergarments which were beginning to stiffen with the salt, then rubbed himself down with the towel.

He thought about the woman who had brought him here. She intrigued him. He quickly put on the spare clothes which, though rough and a little worn, felt good. He tucked the flannel shirt into the trousers. There was even a set of braces and he snapped them into place before putting on the heavy knitted gansey.

He knew he must look like a fisherman and wondered what his friends would say if they saw him like this. But the thought was only fleeting because at that moment he didn't care what they thought. He was dry and alive and very curious about his rescuer.

A knock on the door had him calling to her to come in.

She looked him up and down. "Not as fine as your own clothes and a little short on the legs but otherwise good enough."

He felt himself blush, something he hadn't done since he was a boy.

To cover his embarrassment, he moved over to her. "Can I help you with that?" he offered as he reached for the basket she was holding. It had some herbs in it.

"Thank you," she said.

He placed it on the stout wooden table.

"You were worth saving since you have such good manners," she said with a smile. "Now sit by the fire and get yourself warm."

He did as he was told, feeling peculiar about the ease with which he was taking instructions from her and she just a peasant woman. But the ring of authority in her voice brooked no argument. She brought a blanket and placed it on his knees.

He wanted to say that he had been warm from the moment her hands were on his chest, but it had been such an unusual sensation he couldn't make sense of it and felt awkward about asking her to explain it.

He propped up his shoes near the flames to dry them. The wet clothes she hung on a line strung across the corner of the room.

He felt his body beginning to relax. She had a presence which seemed to fill the room, and soothe him at the same time. He had never been aware of someone in that way before.

With a fluid motion she tied an apron around her slim waist. She began to prepare some porridge. As she put it to cook over the fire, he caught her scent, a subtle fragrance of roses and some other flower he couldn't name. It was light and fresh. He wanted to keep inhaling it, but she moved back to the table where she removed some flowers and herbs from her basket. Before doing anything with them, she moved past him again, to light a taper from the fire. With it she lit a candle on the windowsill despite the brightness of the sun outside.

She tied a piece of string around her full, wavy hair to hold it back at the nape of her neck. It gave him full view of her high cheekbones and creamy skin. She looked over at him and her warm, glowing eyes made a sigh escape from his lips.

"Your throat must be a little rough – I'll make you a hot drink to soothe it," she said.

Her voice was as soothing as any drink she could make, he thought, but he was having trouble swallowing so he didn't object. The scent of the candle wafted over to him. He was pleasantly surprised that it was the scent of beeswax and not the unpleasant odour of a tallow candle which he would have expected in such rustic surroundings. But then he had heard the bees on the way in.

Tearing some leaves from the assortment of herbs she had brought in, the woman crushed them between two stones before transferring them to a teapot. She added some dry herbs from one of the jars on the dresser.

Coming over to the fireplace again, she leaned past him to get the kettle. Returning to the table, she added boiling water to the teapot, and gave it three stirs, then let it steep for a while before pouring the liquid into a cup.

Although wanting to ask where he was, he found the question

slipping away. He could sit there all day and watch her. To him her movements were sensual and hypnotic. Dipping a spoon into a jar, she took out some honey, twirling the spoon around once, then twice, before lowering it into the cup and stirring slowly. Then she cut a couple of slices of the soda bread and spread butter on it with even strokes. She took the bubbling pot of porridge to the table, spooned it into two bowls and added honey to them. The aroma made him realise that he was famished.

She passed him the hot drink then brought the plate and bowl over and placed them on the stool beside him. Taking her own bowl, she sat in the rocking chair opposite him while he cautiously sipped from his cup.

It was very pleasant and immediately eased his throat. His eyebrows rose questioningly.

"It's the honey," she said. "It's sweet and curative, especially mixed with those herbs."

After a few more sips, his throat was soothed enough to try the porridge.

It tasted wonderful and a very male sound of satisfaction rumbled low in his throat.

She laughed – a soft gentle sound that lit up her eyes and brought an answering smile to his.

With a nudge of her foot, she set her chair rocking back and forth while she ate, studying him. When he was finished the porridge he moved on to the bread. When everything was gone, he spoke.

"Thank you for your kindness," he said, his voice sounding much improved to his own ears. "Where am I exactly? I set out in a rowing boat yesterday evening." He paused and laughed. "Well, I think it was yesterday. Is today Saturday?"

She smiled and once again he was transfixed by the curve of her lips and the light in her eyes.

"Yes, it is. The storm blew in very quickly from the northwest yesterday. Tell me what happened to you."

"I had only intended being out for a short while. I was restless after dinner and took out my friend's boat – from Sheep's Head just a little west of Durrus – but I didn't pay attention to the changing weather."

He saw the slight shake of her head.

"I know," he said, "it was foolish. Before I knew it, the waves were whipping up around me and I think the tide must also have been on the turn because I was unable to make any headway back. I was pushed across the bay towards the Mizen peninsula." He took another drink before continuing. "This is Mizen, isn't it?" He looked at her questioningly and she nodded. "I was being taken closer and closer to the rocks despite rowing as hard as I could. The boat hit then and pitched me into the water. The waves were breaking on top of me and it took all my strength to keep above the surface. I saw the boat being smashed against the rocks and I was sure I was due the same fate, but I must have got caught in a different current, because I was borne south along the coast instead. Fortunately a plank of wood from my boat drifted that way too and I grabbed on to it. My head was pounding at that point. I think I must have received a blow to it because I don't remember anything after that." He paused. "The tide must have washed me up here sometime during the night."

She nodded and, distracted by a lock of her hair falling free, he forgot his desire to know where he was and instead wanted to know more about her.

"What's your name?" he asked her suddenly.

Her eyes darted to his and she looked at him for a long moment. Just as he thought she wasn't going to answer, she said, "Ellen." She lowered her eyes to the fire then looked up at him again. "And yours?" The question was almost a whisper as if she felt she shouldn't be asking.

He didn't know why this would be so, but that was how it seemed.

"Blake," he said truthfully, then added "Stephens", a surname he picked spontaneously from the air. It had just struck him that she might be one of his half-brother Arthur's new tenants – he had recently bought some land on the Mizen peninsula. If so, he didn't want her to know of the connection.

A yawn suddenly overcame him and he put his hand to his mouth to cover it.

"It's time for you to go," she said.

He blinked a few times at the abruptness of this but didn't argue. Bending forward, he put on his wet shoes.

She stood up and waited for him to stand too.

Reluctantly he did so, his limbs feeling very heavy. Her scent filled his senses again as they faced each other in front of the fire. He almost swayed towards her.

"I hope many blessings follow you on your way, Blake," she said softly.

"Ellen?" he said, searching in his head for the question he felt he needed to ask. At last he remembered. "Where exactly is this? I still don't know where I am."

She shook her head. "No more questions now. I'll take you back to Durrus and you can make your way to your friend from there."

Gathering his wet clothes, she rolled them into a ball, and made for the door.

He followed her, unable to protest. Something seemed to be dulling his brain.

Reaching up, she took a man's cap from a hook and passed it to him.

He put it on.

Her shawl she took from another hook and threw it around her shoulders. She opened the door and he followed her outside.

Wordlessly, he helped her hitch a donkey to a cart, but his movements were slow. She got up on the bench in front and took the reins. He recognised the Sheep's Head peninsula across the bay but failed to identify the exact area facing him. He heaved himself up beside her, the fog in his head thickening more. They had only gone a few yards across a field when he felt himself sinking into sleep. His head drifted towards her shoulder and all went black.

Chapter 2

Shortly after dawn, Ellen had gone down onto the seashore to collect driftwood for the fire. The storm had passed during the night. The previous evening she had relished its power as she stood braced against the wind. The roar of the waves had exhilarated her as they crashed and thundered in their white, surging magnificence. This morning they just whispered and gushed, sending white foam fingers scurrying onto the sand.

She liked going onto the beach after a storm because something of interest often washed up. However, she had not expected a person, but that's exactly what it had brought. A man lay there, the receding tide still lapping at his feet. He wasn't moving.

About to rush forward, she hesitated as an uneasy feeling came over her. She stood still. There was something about the scene before her that was tugging at a memory. But try as she might, it remained elusive. She pushed the feeling away and was compelled to move forward by the knowledge that someone needed help.

On reaching him, she dropped to her knees on the wet sand without a thought for her skirts and heaved him over on to his back, noticing the fine quality of his clothes. This was no local fisherman who had been caught in the storm. He was a stranger to her. In a glance she saw it was a pleasant face, without a beard or moustache, though there was a slight stubble on his strong jaw.

To check if he was breathing, she swiftly dampened her cheek by rubbing it against his wet shirt, then put her cheek near his nose. Feeling the soft caress of air she sighed with relief. But he was extremely cold and she had to act swiftly to help him. A life would not slip away if she could prevent it.

Rubbing her hands together rapidly three times, she looked up at the sky. She invoked God's healing. She could feel heat surge in through the top of her head, down her neck, into her arms, burning like fire in her hands. Placing them on his chest, she felt the heat pass from her into him.

Soon he stirred and opened his eyes. She smiled with joy, for life was a precious thing. Sitting back, she silently gave thanks while watching him.

Raising his head, he stared at her. His blue eyes were bright and intelligent. Something swelled inside her, making the breath catch in her throat. The moment seemed to hold a wealth of significance, but she didn't understand why. She healed people all the time, but this felt different. She held his gaze.

His hair seemed dark but she believed it would be fair when it was dry. Impulsively she brushed a lock of it off his forehead, before standing and helping him up. He had a strong frame beneath his fine linen shirt. When he stood he was a good bit taller than her.

She led him up to the cottage. It was a while since there had been a man in the house and it felt strange. While he changed into dry clothes, she went to the garden to give him some privacy. Rounding the corner of the cottage, the memory she had tried to grasp earlier hit her forcibly, rooting her to the spot. She remembered every detail as if it was the day before, but it had been fourteen years earlier, when she was only thirteen years old. As she stood there, one hand braced against the wall, the scene replayed vividly in her mind.

It had been a blustery autumn afternoon when she had been inside the cottage putting some turf on the fire. Her grandmother, Nora, was on her deathbed and Ellen's mother, Kate, was tending to her.

Ellen heard her granny cry out.

Kate appeared at the bedroom door.

"Ellen, come in quickly! Granny wants to see you."

She slipped past her mother and stood beside the bed. Her granny seemed very agitated, plucking at the blanket with her fingers. Ellen took her hand in her own.

"I'm here, Granny. What is it?"

"Ellen," she croaked, "I see a man lying on the strand, thrown up by a storm and you, all grown up, standing over him." Her grip tightened with amazing strength on Ellen's hand. Her watery eyes became piercing in their intensity. "Listen to me! He and his kin will bring trouble to you and your kin! You must have nothing to do with him. Do you hear me?"

"Yes, Granny."

"My time is nearly done here, alannah, and I can't stay on to protect you. You must mark my words."

"Of course, Granny. Don't be getting upset." Reaching out, Ellen stroked her grandmother's cheek until her agitation melted away and she drifted into sleep.

Ellen came back to the present and leant back against the wall for support, frightened. This must have been the man her grandmother had seen. And she, Ellen, had just helped him! But even if she had remembered the vision then she couldn't have left him there. Her grandmother had had the 'sight' and Ellen would never take her words lightly, so now she knew she had to get him to leave quickly and make sure he never came back. All she could hope was that it would be enough to honour her grandmother's warning and that the damage hadn't already been done. Straightening up, she hurried into the garden, forming a plan.

She frowned as she gathered herbs into her basket. What she found strange was that she hadn't instinctively had a bad feeling about the stranger, or felt fear despite his size and obvious strength. Though she didn't have the 'sight' like her grandmother had, she had very strong instincts that usually proved correct about people. Why he could mean danger for her she couldn't imagine and she regretted that he would have to go. Thinking of those intelligent eyes, she knew he would bring interesting conversation and be good company. But the moment she thought that, her grandmother's warning struck fear in her heart again. No, she would hurry him on his way – it was what had to be done.

Returning to the front of the cottage she knocked on the door. His hoarse voice sounded pleasant to her ears when he invited her to come in.

It was odd to see her father's clothes on him, but he made a handsome picture in them. Lively eyes shone from his face, and his hair was the colour of dry sand on a spring morning. He filled the gansey well with his broad shoulders. She waited a heartbeat to see if she felt any danger from him now that she had remembered her grandmother's words. But there was nothing negative in the light around him – in fact it was the opposite. He seemed kind and polite, though reserved, which didn't surprise her – he'd probably never been in a humble cottage like hers in his life. She believed he would never intentionally hurt anyone. As well as her grandmother's warning, the fact that he was obviously landed gentry and most likely Protestant was another reason to send him on his way soon. What did she know of them and their ways, other than knowing they would be intolerant of her and hers?

Yet he looked well standing there and for a moment she wondered what it would be like to have a man of her own to take care of her for a while and share her hearth.

She dispelled the foolish direction of her thoughts and the sudden, strange longing they'd brought, by quickly making a comment on his borrowed clothes, and though impressed when he helped her with the basket she made light of it. Immediately she went and lit a candle in the window for protection from any harm, as well as protection for her heart.

She made him a drink with herbs and honey and was relieved to see him drink it willingly. As he ate the porridge she had made, she studied him again. There was depth and goodness in him, but there seemed to be some sort of conflict going on within him too. She looked away to the fire and puzzled once again over how he could be a threat to her.

When he asked what her name was, she knew she shouldn't answer. A detail like that spun a tiny thread that linked two people together. Once they knew each other's names they would no longer be strangers. But she couldn't seem to help herself and she released it on a whisper. She could see him catch it and hold on to it. Looking down into the flames, she fought with herself – but again she lost. Glancing back up, she asked him his name.

Blake Stephens. She liked the sound of it and let it turn over and over in her head.

When he yawned, she knew that the herbs she'd put in his drink were working, and it reminded her of what had to be done. He would be asleep within minutes so she had to get him outside to the cart.

They barely made it. No sooner had the cart started moving when he fell asleep and his head came to rest on her shoulder. It was heavy but very pleasant. She was glad the bench had a backrest or he would have toppled over. She urged the donkey up through the fields behind the cottage until they reached a gap in the ditch and came out onto the road. She pulled his cap down a little to hide his face and turned north towards Durrus.

His hand slipped from his thigh onto the seat between them. He had long lean fingers and well-kept nails. He was gentry all right, she thought. Everything about him showed it, even his hands.

She put her hand over his and felt its warmth. Turning it over, she placed their palms together, her fingers only reaching three-quarters way up his. She was surprised to find his palm calloused, suggesting that he laboured in some way with them. Seeing a horse and cart coming towards her, she whipped her hand away and saluted the driver as he passed by. The man nodded towards Blake, and said: "Too much poitín last night?" and drove on, laughing.

The journey to Durrus would only take an hour or so. They meandered along beside fields of green or vast patches of yellow gorse that sloped away over rocky ground down to the bay. The breeze was warm and the sea, although calmer than the day before, still drove white waves up against dark rocks. Ellen's spirit was light as she revelled in the beauty of the strange light that often followed a storm

She believed she was doing the right thing by taking Blake back to Durrus without him knowing where she lived. That way, he wouldn't return and bring the harm her grandmother had warned about. She hoped it would be enough.

Starting to hum a tune, she shifted the weight of his head slightly on her shoulder.

The time passed quickly. When the first cottages came into view, she pulled the cart up at the side of the road beneath a tree.

She gently shook him awake. "Blake? We're here now."

He stirred and looked around in a daze.

She got down and went around to his side. "We're in Durrus," she said. "Take my hand."

He took it and leaned heavily on her shoulder as he got down. His legs gave way and she had to put her arm around him until he became steady. Helping him onto the grass verge, she lowered him on to it, pushing him back against the tree trunk.

He rubbed his hand over his eyes, still groggy.

She put her face close to his, her hand on his shoulder.

"I'm going to leave you now. You can hire a horse here at the farrier's to take you the rest of the way."

He squinted at her. "Ellen?"

She placed his damp clothes down beside him.

"Goodbye, Blake," she said, putting her hands on his head. "Many blessings on you."

His sleepy smile drew one from her.

"What happened on the strand, Ellen?" he slurred. "Something happened to me on the strand." His eyelids were drifting shut, but he forced them open again. "You have extraordinary eyes." He rubbed at his face to keep himself awake.

Murmuring goodbye, she removed her hands. Having looked up and down the road, she took hold of the donkey's bridle, turned him for home and climbed back up onto the cart.

On the return journey the clouds were breaking up but the day still felt cool. Ellen pulled her shawl tighter. Feeling stiff, she stretched her legs, back and shoulders. The journey home seemed twice as long as the outward one had.

A strange ache rested around her heart. She dismissed it and urged the donkey on.

Once home, she unhitched the animal. "There you go, Ned," she said, scratching behind his ears as she walked him into the field where she gave him some water. Having drunk, he hee-hawed loudly and she walked away laughing.

Inside, the fire had dwindled. She built it up and then went outside for more wood. Having gathered a large bundle in her arms, she paused and gazed at the sea which had carried Blake to her shore.

Closing her eyes, she lifted her face to the salty breeze.

"I had to help him, Gran," she said, opening her eyes and looking into the depth of the sky, "but I hope I've honoured your vision by doing what I could to make sure he doesn't return here."

Chapter 3

"Travers!"

Blake's eyes flew open as a riding crop prodded his shoulder. He had fallen asleep again.

"Where on earth have you been and why are you dressed like that? I was beginning to despair of finding you!"

Blake squinted up at his friend, who was on horseback, before looking around in puzzlement. People were passing up and down the street, some herding animals and some driving carts with baskets of produce on the back. His hand touched off the bundle of damp clothes beside him.

He jumped up as John dismounted.

"Where is the woman who brought me here?" he asked his friend, scanning the crowd.

"What woman? Is that where you've been all night – with some woman? And there we were scouring the grounds of the house, the nearby fields and woods, and farther afield in case you'd been attacked and robbed, or worse!"

Blake halted his puzzled search of the passers-by and turned his eyes on his friend, who, he saw, looked a bit rough, tired and unshaved. He put his hand on his shoulder.

"I took out your boat and got caught out on the bay in that storm. I nearly drowned. I'm afraid your boat was wrecked. I'm sorry, John."

"Dammit, man, you never take out a boat without telling someone! Exactly for that reason. We never even thought of looking for you at sea! I was equally foolish not to notice the boat missing!"

"I apologise again, John. The sea tossed me up somewhere on the Mizen peninsula where I was helped by a local woman. It was she who brought me back here but she seems to have disappeared. She saved my life, actually." As he spoke he looked around again. But she still wasn't to be seen.

"Hah – a mermaid no doubt! If it wasn't for your present attire I'd say you were drinking all night and couldn't find your way back to my estate."

Blake looked down at what he was wearing and laughed. "Not up to my usual standard, is it? God, if Arthur could see me now!"

"He'd disown you. But it must mean you're telling the truth about what happened. Did you really almost drown, Blake?" John studied his friend's face.

"Yes."

"Good God! Do you think I should get the doctor to examine you?"

"Not at all! I'm perfectly well."

"Still, I'd best get you back to the house." John put his foot in the stirrup and mounted his horse.

The sun broke through the clouds and Blake pulled the knitted gansey off before taking John's proffered hand and getting up behind him. John guided the horse through the village.

Blake thought of Ellen. He remembered every detail, every word she had said, few as they had been. He now realised that whatever she had given him to drink had put him to sleep – drugged him, in fact. Why would she do that, he puzzled. Was it just that she gave him too much of it? Or was it deliberate? Maybe she didn't want him to know where she lived. Why should it matter? It's not like he had any intention of going back there.

"So what the devil happened?" John asked, as they left Durrus and took the road out on to the Sheep's Head peninsula.

Blake told him.

"It's lucky you're alive. I hope you rewarded this woman for saving you?"

Blake immediately felt guilty. "No, actually. I had nothing to give her."

"Well, perhaps you can go back, return those rags and give her a reward. Your life is a valuable thing."

"I wouldn't be able to find my way there. I was exhausted after being in the sea and fell asleep as soon as we left her cottage." Feeling sure that he had been drugged, he wasn't sure why he was misleading John about it.

"What was her name?"

"Ellen – I don't know her surname. Ah, she was just some fisherman's wife. She'll forget the incident soon enough, as I intend to."

"Robert and David went further out Sheep's Head looking for you early this morning."

"I really am sorry for creating all this fuss, John."

Half an hour later they reached the estate and dismounted.

Taking another look at Blake, John asked: "Are you sure you're well?

"Yes, thank you."

"Go on in then and get some decent clothes on! I'll follow presently. Of my three guests, I never expected you to be the troublesome one! But thank God you didn't drown. Your brother would have thrown a fit and called me careless." John grinned over his shoulder as he led his horse off towards the stables.

"Only because Arthur would have one less person to do his bidding," Blake replied drily, then called after him: "You didn't send a messenger saying I was missing, did you?"

"God, no!"

Relieved, Blake went up the steps of John's mansion. Nearing the top, he turned as he heard other horses approaching and saw their other two friends riding up.

"Where the hell have you been?" Robert, the shorter of the two, shouted, obviously tired and annoyed after his search for Blake.

The other man, David, raised his eyebrows at Blake's attire and smiled sardonically. "Getting tired of being part of the upper class, Blake, my man? Becoming rustic like the peasants?"

Blake held up the gansey and flashed a grin at him. "Damn comfortable after a night at sea! I'll explain in due course and I apologise for the bother I've caused you. Thank you for searching for me."

Leaving them even more curious than when they had arrived, he went inside.

Greeting the butler, he requested some hot water to be sent up.

In the bedroom, he shaved and put on fresh clothes. When he was done, he sat on the bed rubbing his thumb over the rough wool of the borrowed gansey where it lay beside him, Ellen's face floating into his mind.

Suddenly realising that he was wondering what it would be like to take her in his arms, he snatched his hand from the garment and stood up. He had meant it when he told John that he would be putting the incident behind him. Yes, he had nearly drowned, and yes, the cold might well have finished him off if Ellen hadn't saved him, but that didn't mean he should give her a second thought. "Just some fisherman's wife," he murmured, repeating what he had said to John. Yet he knew he didn't believe that. One, he had got the impression she lived alone, and two, he thought Ellen would never be 'just' anything.

He suddenly remembered though that, not only had he not rewarded her, he hadn't even thanked her. He felt another twinge of guilt, but irritably pushed the feeling away, excusing himself and blaming her – she had drugged him, thus removing from him the opportunity to thank her.

Having exonerated himself, he moved to the window and stared out at the expanse of Dunmanus Bay and the Mizen peninsula across it. Ellen lived somewhere over there above her little cove in her cosy cottage. He began to wonder if he should send someone out with a reward for her. No doubt a few pounds would be a fortune to her. Even without her full name, it couldn't be that hard to find where she lived. The messenger would have to follow the coast. Blake didn't know how far they had travelled this morning while he slept but, judging from the view he had from her cottage of the Sheep's Head peninsula, he didn't think her cove was too far south of Durrus. There couldn't be that many coves like the one in front of her cottage. He could describe it, and Ellen, to the messenger and he could ask around for her. Blake imagined her standing by her door when the messenger arrived and her beautiful smile when she received the borrowed clothes and the reward.

Catching himself smiling at the image, he cursed himself, irritated now that this total stranger was so occupying his thoughts. Dismissing her from his mind again, he left the room.

Back downstairs he met John in the hall and together they went into the drawing room where the two others were already drinking whiskey. Blake gladly took the glass John offered him, and sat sipping it while comparing the grandeur of the room, its marble fireplace, French windows and richly upholstered furniture, with the simplicity of Ellen's cottage. He sat in a large wing-backed armchair, acknowledging to himself that while this grandeur was what he was used to, he had felt very comfortable in Ellen's tiny home. He quickly changed the word 'comfortable' to 'comforted' which made him frown into his whiskey.

"Go on then, tell us where you've been, you ungrateful wretch," David urged, his rangy form spread on another armchair, one booted leg carelessly thrown over the arm. "We've been searching all night and half the day for you"

"I nearly drowned at sea, my dear friends, so your worrying was warranted," Blake replied.

"Oh, I see. I didn't want to go looking for you at all," Robert admitted. "You're a grown man for God's sake! When you didn't return for dinner last night I presumed you were languishing in the arms of some woman in Durrus or maybe Bantry. But your host had a 'funny feeling'," his words dripped with mockery, "so made us search for you. I'm man enough to admit I was wrong and humbly apologise to both of you."

"Humble, my foot!" David grunted. "You're so self-obsessed you won't even let the man tell us what happened. Now be quiet!"

Robert threw him a dirty look.

Blake retold the story, this time not saying anything about Ellen. "Eventually I got washed up on a beach, one of the locals gave me those clothes you saw me in and something to eat, and then I got a lift back to Durrus."

For reasons he couldn't explain to himself, he didn't want these two knowing about his rescuer. Perhaps he knew they would make fun of the situation he had found himself in.

He glanced over at John who had a gleam in his eye. Blake ignored him.

"I thought I was a dead man when the boat hit those rocks."

He successfully kept their attention on the storm for the next while and neither one asked anything about his rescue.

"Well, here's hoping the weekend improves after all that. We came all the way down here from Limerick to share some sport with you two Corkmen, so try not to go missing again, there's a good man," said Robert. "I hope there's some interesting company at this dinner party of yours tonight, John?"

"You're a complete hedonist, Robert! But, don't worry, I'm sure you'll be provided with some very pleasant conversation tonight from the daughters of the finest families who come here to take the sea air in summer," John mocked.

Blake was relieved. He'd forgotten that the reason for this get-together was a dinner party to be held in honour of John's birthday. John's wife always threw wonderful dinner parties, with attractive ladies attending, and he would certainly welcome the distraction of it. Robert and David had badgered John into having this one because they had yet to find suitable young ladies in Limerick to tempt them into marriage and thought West Cork might turn up a beauty or two. Blake himself was open to meeting someone he could marry – he was thirty-one now and badly wanted to move away from his half-brother, Arthur, onto an estate of his own. Unfortunately he needed a rich bride to make that happen. And yet, the idea of bride-finding held less appeal today than it did yesterday.

Robert, already bored with the conversation, had turned his attention to a copy of a newspaper on a table beside him.

"What's this then?" he asked John.

"It's the *Southern Star* – a new newspaper which they've started publishing in Skibbereen. I brought it down with me last week."

Robert just grunted and opened it.

John studied the group. "Well," he said, "I'm going to cancel this afternoon's shooting trip as I don't trust anyone's aim after the night we've just spent. I suggest you all take the afternoon to rest so that you'll be able to make reasonable sense over dinner tonight. Any objections?"

The others shook their heads.

"Please join me in the study for pre-dinner drinks at six thirty."

Just then the butler announced lunch. As they crossed the hall Blake held John back, letting the other two go ahead into the dining room.

"John, I'll pay to replace your rowing boat. Again, my apologies for causing you so much trouble."

"We've been friends since we were boys – you must know I don't give a damn about the boat. I'm just relieved you're alive." A teasing gleam came into his eyes as he lowered his voice. "And I'll be eternally grateful to your mermaid for snatching you from a watery grave."

Blake grinned back at him then sobered quickly. "You know, when I was in the cottage it occurred to me that perhaps she's one of my brother's new tenants. I told you he has bought some land on the Mizen peninsula. I think he said it was somewhere south of Durrus, not too far out the peninsula at any rate." He sighed in exasperation. "Why on earth didn't I ask her for her surname?"

"Are you thinking of sending her a reward after all?"

"Perhaps."

"Good, that way your debt to her will be paid. You said she's not of our class. You wouldn't want her extracting money from you at some future date. Your brother is the biggest snob I know and if he catches wind of the fact that you are indebted to some peasant over there, possibly one of his new tenants, he won't be impressed. You don't need me to tell you that Arthur has a mean streak."

Blake could feel the frustration of being the younger and dependent half-brother rise up again inside him as it had done many times since his father's death two months earlier.

He grunted. "I know it too well. But have no fear. On the spur of the moment I didn't give her my real name when she asked. I suddenly felt ashamed of my association with my brother, aware that she could be one of his tenants, and for a crazy moment I just wanted to be someone other than a Travers." He shrugged. "I must be losing my mind – that's what living with Arthur does to me. So you see that's why getting away to visit here with you and Grace is such a welcome change. I really cannot stand my half-brother." He gave John an apologetic smile. "It's your birthday and I'm being melodramatic, but no more. We'll celebrate you well tonight." He slapped his friend on the shoulder and they went into the dining room.

Chapter 4

After lunch, Blake strolled down to the waterfront and out along a jetty which had some rowing boats tied to it.

He gazed out over the sea. Suddenly he was gripped by the images of the night before – could see again the huge waves crashing on the rocks and could hear the boat breaking up. A violent tremor shook his body and he thought his legs were going to give way beneath him. Looking at the land in the distance, he willed himself to think instead of his first sight of Ellen and how the sun seemed to set her red hair on fire. As he saw her smile again in his mind, his breathing calmed and the shaking eased. Then he remembered the heat on his chest. He should have asked her to explain it. With a frown creasing his brow, he went on unsteady legs back up the path to the house.

As he entered, John's wife Grace was crossing the hall.

"Why, Blake, you look wretched!" She rushed over and took his arm, lending her strength despite her petite size. "Come into the drawing room with me." She led him into the room to a pair of armchairs by the windows which had a view of the garden. "Now sit there, while I ring for tea and brandy."

After pulling the cord beside the fireplace she came over and sat opposite him. Warmth and concern filled her eyes.

"I'm so sorry I wasn't here for lunch. I had a prior engagement, but John told me about your ordeal last night. My goodness, if anything had happened to you, John and I would have been devastated."

He was touched by her concern as he relaxed back into the chair.

"Is it exhaustion that has you looking unwell?" she asked.

He gave a self-conscious laugh. "I'm afraid I scared the wits out of myself by going down to the water's edge just now. I suddenly realised how close to dying I'd come last night!"

Leaning forward, she patted his hand. "John says someone very kind helped you."

He knew John had told her everything and he didn't mind. She was like a sister to him. He stared out at a flowering magnolia tree in the garden.

"Yes, her name was Ellen, and she was kind, but also she was ..." He broke off, searching for the way to describe her, and then continued in a rush of words. "She was gentle but powerful all at once, and when she smiled it was as if light burst up through her and out of her eyes to sear into mine. And she was beautiful – long red hair that glowed in the sun and green eyes like the sea on a crystal-clear spring day." He laughed at himself when he saw Grace's eyes widen. "It was hard not to notice – as I said, she was a beautiful woman." He shrugged. "And I don't even know her full name so that I can reward her kindness."

Grace frowned at his last words. "She seems to have made a huge impression on you," she said kindly, "and we are all grateful to her for returning you to us. But I hope you are not intending to take that reward to her personally. John told me she might be one of Arthur's tenants. He wouldn't take kindly to you getting too friendly with her if that is so."

Blake released a long, frustrated sigh. "I hate the power my brother has over me. But, that aside, there is nothing to be concerned about. I don't intend to go back there myself but I will send a reward – if I can find out where she lives. I fell asleep on the way back to Durrus and don't know how far we travelled."

After the butler placed a tray on the table between them, Grace poured Blake some brandy and herself some tea. She studied him for a moment.

"May I ask how things are for you since your father's recent passing?"

"I miss him terribly. It has only been a couple of months but the shock of it is still with me. As you know, I was the one who found him slumped in his armchair. At least he didn't suffer. The doctor said the heart attack killed him instantly."

Grace's looked at him with compassion. "And how are you and Arthur getting on? You and your half-brother were never on very good terms."

"That's an understatement. He has hated me since the day I was born! He resented my father's second marriage to my mother and took every opportunity of reminding me that he was the first-born son!" Blake swirled the brandy in his glass. "The heart-breaking thing is, Grace – and I haven't been telling people about this – about six months before Father died, he and I were riding out together one day when he told me that I was just like him in the way I loved the land. He said he admired the progressive way I thought about things and my instincts around the stock. Those who worked for us liked me, he said, and that was the mark of a strong character. He confided in me his disappointment that Arthur had no feeling for the land or the tenants. He felt that Arthur had become extremely greedy, wanting the money the estate brought in but not caring how it was managed. I could see that for myself – he goes away as often as he can to weekend shooting parties and balls. All he's interested in is bringing in the money and keeping up his social standing among the rich and jolly." He looked up at Grace. "Father told me that though traditionally the eldest son inherited, he did not want the estate to go to Arthur, but to me."

Grace gasped.

"He said he thought that if he left it to Arthur he would run it, and the tenants, into the ground, whereas I would nurture and care for it." His voice caught with emotion and he had to clear his throat before continuing. "He said he was going to change his will, leaving the estate to me and a financial sum to Arthur that would leave him comfortably off."

"So why *did* Arthur get the estate then?" she asked, hurting for him.

Blake rubbed a hand over his face and sighed wearily. "Father obviously had every intention of changing the will but hadn't got around to doing it before his sudden death."

"But surely you can contest it on the grounds of your father's intentions and the work you've been doing on the estate all these years?"

He nodded. "I've set things in motion with a solicitor in Cork, but these things take time. Also he thinks my chances are slim because there were no witnesses to the conversation my father had with me, and Arthur is the first-born with a will leaving the estate to him as is the tradition. You know Arthur will fight tooth and nail before relinquishing it."

"But you were not left destitute surely?"

"No, he left me some money. And Arthur is happy for me to manage the estate because he doesn't want the burden of it, just the profits, and pays me well enough."

"At least he is wise enough to recognise the skills you have. But do you want to stay under these circumstances?"

"That's my dilemma. I hate working for Arthur, but I feel I owe it to my father to look after the estate, because that was what he wanted, will or no will. And of course it has been my life's work so far. And," he said, putting down his now empty brandy glass and accepting a cup of tea, "as if the Bantry estate is not enough for Arthur, he has gone and purchased some land out on the Mizen. It was land my father had shown interest in before his death. Before Father was even cold in his grave, Arthur told me that he had gone ahead and bought it for himself."

"Arthur does not take after either your father or your mother. They were both such caring, sweet people."

"I'm told he takes after his own mother, Father's first wife, who by all accounts was a cold, hard-hearted woman."

Grace pensively sipped her tea. "Perhaps you should stay open to the possibility of leaving Bantry? You might not have your own estate but you are comfortably off. You could make a good match." She looked at him mischievously. "On that subject, there's one person in particular I'd like to introduce you to tonight at the dinner party. Maybe she will be your choice. She is pretty and interesting with excellent prospects – the only child on a large estate in Skibbereen. They are staying with friends nearby for a few days."

"Why, Grace," he teased, "surely you are not suggesting I marry for money!"

"Absolutely not. It would hurt me to see you marry without love. But wouldn't it solve your problems if you fell in love with a rich heiress!"

Blake smiled then sobered. "I would be a lucky man to have what you and John have, but it doesn't always work out that way. We can't always have what we want."

Ellen's face floated into his mind and for a moment he wished she was the daughter of a fine family. But then the thought seemed so preposterous that he laughed out loud because, after all, what was so appealing about her was the difference between her and some of the tamed, and sometimes purely ornamental, women he had met in society.

"What is so amusing?" Grace asked.

"I'm sorry. Nothing, nothing at all. Please tell me about this lady."

"The lady in question is Miss Felicity Hannon, beautiful and highly educated. Her father has a vast estate near Skibbereen. I'll do my bit by introducing you to her tonight." Her cheeks dimpled as she smiled at him. "And I fervently hope you will find love *and* a means to leave Arthur's estate at the same time."

His looked at her affectionately. "You are quite the matchmaker, Grace."

"Just looking out for you, my dear," she said, eyes twinkling.

"To tonight then," he said, touching his cup against hers. "Now tell me, how are you liking your new summer residence?"

"Oh, I love it here. I like being at home in Skibbereen too of course but it's lovely to be this close to the sea in the summer months. John finds it very relaxing too. I'm glad you came over from Bantry to spend the weekend with us, despite your mishap of yesterday." A clock chimed. "Oh goodness! I need to have a word with Cook – see if everything is going according to plan for tonight. She is a bit disgruntled because the kitchen here is a little smaller than the one on the Skibbereen estate. Please excuse me, Blake."

She rose to her feet and with smile left him to finish his tea.

Later that evening the guests began to arrive and were shown into the drawing room. Both David and Robert were already in conversation with two young ladies in one corner when Blake went in. Grace caught his eye and he joined her and her group. She introduced him to a Mr. and Mrs. Williams and their daughter Elizabeth. They exchanged small talk for a few minutes and then she whisked him off to introduce him to some of the other guests. Finally she introduced him to Mr. and Mrs. Hannon and their daughter, a willowy young woman in a blue gown.

"Mr. and Mrs. Hannon, Miss Felicity Hannon – may I introduce Blake Travers?"

Blake bowed in greeting and smiled at the elegant, fair-haired beauty who stood before him. She gave him a confident, slightly flirtatious smile.

"Mr. and Mrs. Hannon, there's someone I'd like to introduce you to." Grace glanced meaningfully at Blake as she slipped past him, drawing Felicity's parents away with her.

"It's a pleasure to meet you, Miss Hannon," Blake said. "Have you known Grace and John long?"

"Not long. I've been away in France a lot. I was only introduced to Grace in the spring at a dinner at their home in Skibbereen."

Her voice had a hint of a foreign accent that was not unappealing.

"And what takes you to France?" he inquired.

"My grandmother is French, so I went to a finishing school there and spent half of each year with her since. And you, Mr. Travers, where do you spend your time?"

The gong for dinner sounded, he offered her his arm and answered her question as they moved with the others across to the dining room.

"The Travers estate is on the edge of Bantry town with lands inland to the north and south of the town." It was the truth but it was also misleading. He knew his chances with her would be nil if he mentioned straight off that his brother, and not he, owned the estate. Perhaps if some affection grew between them she might be better disposed to accept the fact that he didn't have an estate of his own.

The table was set for twenty-two people with glittering silver and glass and a magnificent centrepiece arranged by Grace herself. They took their seats.

Blake and Felicity talked easily with each other, she leaning close to him any time he spoke. Her perfume was discreet and alluring, her conversation entertaining, but still his attention wandered. His thoughts were once again drawn back to the cottage by the sea and the mysterious woman who lived there. There was no comparison between the sophisticated, cultured woman by his side now and the free-spirited, raw beauty of the woman who had saved his life that morning. And he thought, glancing around, the splendour of Grace and John's dining room was in complete contrast to the humble cottage . . . yet the homeliness of Ellen's dwelling still clung to him.

He pictured Ellen sitting by her fireside now while it was dusk outside, and a longing to be sitting there opposite her scorched through him, shocking him with the strength of it. With a shake of his head, he tried again to concentrate on the conversation going on around him, wondering if that blow to the head he had received, when he was tossed from the boat, had left him a bit fanciful.

The men retired for their brandy and Felicity's father came to speak to Blake. They soon discovered a mutual interest in the different strains of grain crops.

At the end of the conversation, Mr. Hannon remarked on how impressed he was at Blake's knowledge. Shortly afterwards they went to join the ladies in the drawing room.

Blake and Felicity reunited to play cards with a couple of others. When the evening drew to a close and Felicity's father beckoned to her, saying their carriage was ready, Blake walked her to the hall.

As the butler held out her cloak, Blake took it from him and placed it around her shoulders, inadvertently brushing her neck with his fingertips. Felicity turned to thank him with an unmistakeable invitation in her eyes.

"I hope you find yourself in Skibbereen sometime soon, Mr. Travers," she said, her voice remaining properly polite. "It would be lovely if you were to call on us."

"Indeed, I second that, Blake. I would enjoy further conversation with you," Mr. Hannon said.

"It would be my pleasure to visit," he responded. "Goodnight, Miss Hannon." He bowed politely. "Goodnight, Mr. Hannon, Mrs. Hannon."

He shook their hands and watched speculatively as they walked away, knowing that Grace had been correct: it would be a good match for him and could be an answer to prayer. Felicity was very attractive and no doubt she would have a substantial dowry, if not the whole estate some day, and he would get out from under his half-brother's thumb. That was, of course, if her father would think him worthy – he would bring very little with him to a marriage except his small inheritance and his ability to run the farming side of the estate to a very high standard. But Mr. Hannon already seemed to be impressed by his experience. It might be just enough if Felicity fell in love with him. The idea was definitely worth considering, he thought with a smile. It was time to take sensible action regarding his future, just in case fighting the terms of the will came to nothing. As he joined his friends for a nightcap, he chastised himself for wasting so much time that day thinking about the flame-haired woman by the sea.

Chapter 5

There was a knock on Ellen's door. Her nearest neighbour Séamus was standing outside. He removed his cap when he saw her.

"Morning," he said with a nod of his head.

She smiled warmly at him. As usual he was respectful, though always seemed a little in awe of her.

"Hello, Séamus. What can I do for you on this lovely morning?"

"The cow is sick and I'd be obliged if you'd come and take a look at her."

"Of course. What's the trouble?"

"Everything seems to be running through her the last few days and her stomach is tight and shrunken in."

"Just a minute."

She ducked back into the cottage and selected herbs from some of the jars on her dresser, placing them in a pouch at her waist. Then she went out to join Séamus, closing the door behind her. As they set off together, her eyes were drawn to the beach. That had been happening for the last couple of days since she had found Blake lying there. Sometimes she thought she'd imagined it, the encounter had been so strange. She had healed many people, but this had been different. The essence of it lingered with her.

With a shrug and a smile she turned her attention back to Séamus.

"How are Síle and the children?" she asked as they left the cottage behind.

Séamus's farm was a little more than half a mile away. Even though he lived on the coast they had to walk inland first around a rocky, hilly area before turning back out towards the sea. It was the rocky nature of the land surrounding Ellen's that gave her such privacy. The fields were too poor to plant on, suitable only for grazing sheep and a few cows.

They arrived at Séamus's cottage which was as small as Ellen's, but there were two adults and four children living in it. The children and a couple of dogs were making lots of noise out the front while playing some game with a stick. Ellen waved and greeted them all by name as she passed. Their clothes were worn but clean. The smallest child, Úna, ran over and hugged her around the knees. She was only three and there was great affection between them since Ellen had taken away the pain in her leg after a fall when she was two.

Ellen bent down until they were eye to eye. "The blessings of this sunny morning on you, Úna." She smiled and kissed the little girl on the forehead.

"Our cat had lots of kittens!"

"That's wonderful. Will you show them to me after I see to the cow?"

The little girl nodded her head vigorously and ran off.

Ellen followed Séamus into the field next to the house to examine the animal. Its back end and tail were very dirty, confirming Séamus's words. It lowed softly when she put her hand on its neck and began murmuring to it.

Séamus stood back and watched as she ran her hands over its back and stomach.

Raising her face to the sky she spoke an invocation quietly and rubbed her hands together three times. When she felt the heat in them, she placed them low on the cow's left side. She kept her hands there for several minutes and the cow remained perfectly still. After a while it gave a loud moo and turned its head to nuzzle against her arm.

Ellen laughed and saw Séamus scratch his head in puzzlement.

Some crows cawed loudly nearby. Ellen looked over to see some of them standing on the edge of a stone drinking-trough.

"You'd want to do what you can to keep those crows away, Séamus. See there – their droppings are going into the water. That's probably what's made the cow sick. Get the children to help you make a scarecrow, maybe. I'm going to give you some herbs to mix through hay and you must give her that for the next three mornings and nights. Give her plenty of clean water – she'll have lost a lot of it the past few days. She'll be fine, but come and get me again if you think she isn't improving."

He didn't ask any questions. He would never understand her gift but he trusted her implicitly ever since she had helped Úna.

Síle came out of the cottage and thanked her for coming to see the cow. They talked for a few minutes about the children and the weather until Úna came over to take her to look at the kittens who were feeding from their mother in the shade of a bush.

They fussed over them for a while and then Ellen got up to go.

"Thank you," Séamus said, walking with her to the lane. "Do you want me to walk you back?"

"No, not at all."

"Is it all right if I pay you with a hen? She's a great layer."

"Only if you can spare her, Séamus. You know you don't have to give me anything."

"We've a grand clutch at present. I'll drop her over after dark so that when your own hens wake in the morning they'll think she was always there and won't fight with her."

"I'm grateful to you. My own two have been a little slow with the eggs the last few weeks."

She bade him goodbye and went on her way.

When she got home, there was a boy of about twelve with a lame dog waiting for her. The dog only had a thorn stuck in his paw.

"Watch me remove it, so you can do it yourself if it happens again."

The boy watched intently while she pulled out the thorn before washing the area with warm water.

"He'll be grand," she said, releasing the dog.

The boy shyly pulled a shiny stone from his pocket and placed it in her palm then ran off happily with his dog.

Just then an elderly man came around the corner. She heard his cough before she saw him.

"Ah Dan, you're sounding a bit chesty today. Come on in and we'll see what we can do for you."

"Thanks, Ellen," he wheezed as he shuffled inside and placed a covered billycan on the table. "A drop of buttermilk for you."

Thanking him, she settled him in a chair by the hearth and went out to the garden.

"I have some radishes here for you, Dan," she said, returning.

After rinsing them she rubbed them against a stone to release the fumes.

"Hold these under your nose and breathe in the smell as deep as you can."

On his first breath he took a fit of coughing but, as he continued to inhale the scent, the coughing abated.

"I'll make you a nice cup of sage tea now too and that'll warm your chest for you. Are your own sage plants coming along all right?"

He nodded, continuing with his deep breathing.

"Good. And do you still remember how to make the tea from the leaves?"

Again he nodded.

After a few minutes she took the radishes away from him and gave him the sage tea.

His watery eyes studied her over the rim of the steaming cup. "'Tis a great gift you have, Ellen, no doubt about it."

"Sure, you can do this for yourself at home, Dan."

"Ach, but it's the knowing what to use and how to use it, isn't it? And on top of that I love the chat and the stroll over here." His eyes twinkled at her.

She smiled. "I'll give you some radishes to take home with you."

"You're a good girl, Ellen."

After Dan left she made a cup of tea and drank it leaning on the half door, looking out at the sea.

The water was calm and the small waves barely made a whooshing sound on the sand.

A sigh drifted past her lips. She loved her home and the sight, sound and smell of the sea. The tug of it now had her putting down her cup and going onto the strand.

She had always been happy in this place and luckily she had

avoided any trouble. Although it was an isolated spot, she liked the solitude it gave her and was never lonely with the sea as her companion.

Pulling off her shoes, she walked along the edge of the water, holding her skirt up a little. The water was warm and lapped against her ankles as she sauntered along.

But being here was different now. Something had shifted inside her the morning Blake had arrived. It was as if he had burst through some invisible barrier that cocooned her strand and home, leaving it wide open – open for what, she didn't know. During the past three days, his face had kept coming into her mind, making her wonder again and again what possible trouble her grandmother's vision had alluded to. What threat could a gentle man like Blake bring to her and her kin? She was only too aware of a feeling of regret that she had been forced to send him away without any possibility of them meeting again.

She looked up at the cottage which she had once shared with her parents and her sister, suddenly missing them all very much. At least, she consoled herself, her sister was living nearby in Ballinmara and she would see her that night at Johnny Dunne's wake.

Going back up the beach, she picked up a basket from outside the cottage and went to gather some seaweed.

Chapter 6

At six thirty that evening, Ellen changed into her black dress and shawl and headed to Ballinmara, the fishing village nearest to her cottage, further down the coast. In her basket she carried two loaves of bread and a jar of honey. Johnny Dunne's wake was to take place in his cottage on the edge of the village. He was an old bachelor who had farmed his holding all his life and had died in his sleep the day before.

Most of the village was already there when she arrived. She passed through the crowd standing around outside in the evening sunshine, warmly replying to those who greeted her.

Going into the cottage she looked around to see if her sister, Annie, was there. But it was Annie who saw her first and pushed her way through the crowd to hug her.

"Hello, Ellen!"

Ellen returned the hug warmly and looked at her sister who, four years younger than her, had taken after their father and was therefore fair and short. She was twenty-three now and had two children.

"Where are Mick and the children?" Ellen asked.

"They're outside. Let me take this while you pay your respects." She took the basket from Ellen.

Ellen went into the bedroom off the kitchen where the corpse was laid out in his suit, with candles by his head and his feet, and rosary beads entwined in his joined hands. Some of the villagers were gathered around him, sharing stories about him.

His face looked waxy in the light and a glimmer of a smile lit Ellen's eyes. "You're on your journey now, Johnny – may you be at peace," she murmured as she lay her hand over his.

A few minutes later the curate, Father Dempsey, arrived.

He said the prayers over Johnny. He was young and had been in the parish for over a year but kept very much to himself. Over the months Ellen had tried to engage him in conversation a few times but had found him very shy and distant. Someone offered him some ale, but he refused and left immediately.

Someone gave Ellen a glass of porter and a piece of brack.

Annie's husband, Mick, was across the room. Low-sized and wiry, he stood inside the door, with a tankard gripped in his large, rough hand. The sea had weathered him but, Ellen thought, it was also his own character which had etched grim lines into his face. While in conversation with some other men his eyes roamed the room, narrowing as they fell on Ellen before moving away again.

She resisted the urge to shudder and wondered for the thousandth time what Annie saw in him. She had married him when she was only nineteen and he was thirty. Ellen had felt uneasy around him from the start and had gently tried to persuade Annie that he was too old and perhaps not quite right for her. But Annie decided she was completely in love with him and stubbornly went ahead with the wedding. Without parents to back her up, Ellen had to step away and let Annie make her own choices.

Mick had never taken to Ellen either and was one of the 'unbelievers' as she called them – someone who refused to believe she had the gift of healing. While a lot of people didn't understand, at least they accepted it and were glad to benefit from her gift. Others, like Mick, were so suspicious of it that they actually disliked her for it.

Because of his intolerance, he didn't make her welcome in his home. Some instinct made her once ask Annie if Mick was ever unkind to her, but Annie had been so upset that she would think such a thing that she never asked her again. It didn't however keep her from always watching out for any sign of disharmony between them. Not wanting to cause trouble, Ellen only visited when she was sure he was out fishing and, of course, Annie often brought the children to see her. They also met up on market days or at gatherings like this one.

Having finished her piece of brack, Ellen made her way back over to her sister to make the most of their time together. The children were now back with Annie. The baby, Róisín, was on Annie's hip and their two-year-old, Michael, was by her side. Ellen sat beside them, placing her glass of porter on the ground by her feet, and put her arms out to the little boy. He happily climbed onto her lap and started playing with the fringe of her shawl.

Annie brought her up to date on the news of the village. Ellen didn't tell her about the stranger that had been washed up on her strand.

After a while Ellen put Michael down next to Annie and went to talk to some other women.

It was while she was sitting with one of the local fishermen's wives that she overheard a conversation near her.

"There's talk that the new landlord, Travers, is going to put up the rents," one man said.

Another cursed in response. "They say that fella was born with his hand sticking out ready to grab money that was never his!"

The others murmured in agreement.

"His main estate is near Bantry," the first man said, "and my cousin's a tenant there. He says his rent has gone up and that Travers is a bastard who would evict you as soon as look at you."

More angry comments followed.

Ellen bit her lip. She knew people could ill afford another rise in rents. It was hard enough to raise families on the small holdings or by selling fish. What kind of landlord didn't see how they struggled? The country still hadn't fully recovered from the effects of the famine forty years earlier and farmers were still working hard to make the land useful again. Some were lucky enough to have family sending them money from America now and then, but the farmers and fishermen were struggling to make a living. Angry spots coloured her cheeks. She knew it would affect Annie and Mick too. Mick was a fisherman and barely managed to make enough to feed the four of them and pay the rent each month.

Ellen was frowning into her porter when she became aware of

someone's sadness by an echo of it passing into her and resting around her heart. She looked around the room, expecting to see someone crying, but couldn't. Everyone seemed to be involved in some discussion or other. Her eyes were drawn to the window, through which she saw Johnny's sheepdog lying on the ground not far from the house. He had something on top of his paws and his head was resting on it.

Putting down her glass, she went out to him. As she got closer, she saw that what lay under his chin was his owner's cap. The dog was whining softly.

She hunkered down beside him and stroked the silky black head. He turned big sad eyes on her and whined again.

"You poor thing, your heart is breaking." She kept stroking him until the sadness around her heart melted into love for the young dog. After a while his whining stopped, he lifted his head and licked her hand once before settling back down on top of the cap. She gave a final stroke to his silky coat before going back inside.

Annie had been watching her through the window and beckoned her over.

"Poor Shep is missing Johnny, isn't he?" she asked.

Ellen nodded. "What will happen to him now?"

"Maybe Pádraig next door will take him."

Someone started to play the fiddle and someone else took up the bodhrán and so the serious business of sending Johnny off began in earnest. Ellen's foot tapped along to the rhythm. The talk and laughter became louder too. Fionn Doyle, the local stonemason, loomed up beside them as some people took to the floor to dance. He was strongly built from his work, but was well known for being light on his feet.

"Ah, here's our gentle giant," Annie greeted him warmly. "Are you going to give us a dance, Fionn?"

Fionn gave his deep chuckle. "I'd take both of you out onto the floor at once if I could get away with it. But since you have a babe in your arms, Annie, it'll have to be your sister first." His laughing eyes turned on Ellen. "C'mon, Ellen, let's see if we can do this music justice!"

Meeting the challenge with a smile, she stood. He took one of her hands and put the other around her waist, swinging her into a *casadh* along with the others already swirling at speed on the old flagstone floor.

Ellen was flushed and laughing when she sat down again. She took Róisín from Annie's lap so she could take her turn with Fionn.

Ellen smiled as she watched him tower over Annie while spinning her around and matching his steps with hers. Then she sighed, wondering how different things might have been if Annie had married Fionn instead of Mick. He was a good man. Perhaps it was the artist in him that had been totally accepting of Ellen's ability to heal. His mind and heart were so much more open and loving than Mick's.

After a few minutes they returned to her, Annie trying to catch her breath, while it hadn't taken a thing out of Fionn.

Ellen stood and passed Róisín back to Annie. "I'm away home now," she said. "I want to get back before dark."

"If you want to stay on, I can walk you home later," Fionn offered.

Just as he spoke, Nuala, another woman from the village came and stood beside him, slipping her arm into his. "I need a partner for the Walls of Limerick, Fionn," she said, smiling up into his big eyes.

"I –"

"It's all right, Fionn," Ellen said. "I'm happy to go now."

"If you're sure," he said over his shoulder as Nuala pulled him onto the floor.

Ellen laughingly waved him away.

"Will we see you tomorrow at the funeral Mass?" Annie asked her.

"You will. I'm curious to know what the new priest is like."

"Me too. I haven't seen him yet either."

Someone a little worse for drink swayed past them.

Annie laughed. "I'll be off too. It's late for the children."

Ellen hugged her tightly, remembering the talk of the rent increase. "Take care of yourself," she said.

Annie looked steadily at her. "Are you all right, Ellen?"

Ellen smiled brightly, not wanting her to know she worried about them. "Of course I am. Goodnight. See you tomorrow."

She left and walked away, up through the village with the noise of the wake fading behind her.

Leaving the road about a mile later she turned onto a lane. As she walked, she was facing directly west and the sun was a ball of fire in the sky ahead. Tugging the black shawl from her head, she let the breeze stir her hair. Hearing a cuckoo, she smiled. The peace of the evening wrapped itself around her as she crested a hill and the ocean spread out below her with a fiery path reaching across it to the sun. Leaving the lane, she went through a gap in the wall. Her cottage wasn't visible at that point, it was so neatly tucked in at the bottom of the hill. She crossed the sloping fields until it came into view, her heart swelling at the sight of it. She was never as grateful as now that she owned her cottage and never had dealings with a landlord.

It was a particularly warm night and, after the noise and crowd at the wake, Ellen decided to go to the spring pool. It was a twenty-minute walk from her house and a couple of hundred yards back from the sea. Beyond a particularly rocky piece of land, it was awkward to get at but that's what made it beautifully secluded and Ellen often bathed there by the light of the moon in the summer months. The purity of the water, fed from a nearby spring, left her skin soft and glowing. The pool itself lay beyond a copse of trees.

As she approached the trees she thought she heard a voice. She stopped and listened. A soft laugh reached her ears and she moved forward silently through the trees until she could see the pool but she herself remained hidden.

The beauty of the scene in front of her stole her breath away. Two young women stood facing each other, their naked bodies gleaming in the moonlight, the water rippling around their thighs. She knew she should have moved away but the sensuousness of the moment had her transfixed – besides, she was afraid that turning away would make some sound that would scare them.

One of the women dipped a cloth in the water and brought it up to wash the shoulder of the other in slow circles. Reaching up she lifted the other's hair and caressed her neck, drawing the cloth around to her throat. Little rivulets of water streamed down between her breasts. After dipping the cloth in the water again she raised it and circled first one breast and then the other.

The words 'I love you' were breathed into the night. But Ellen didn't need to hear the words to see what these women meant to each other – the very air around them vibrated with their love.

Tears rolled down Ellen's face as they embraced. She was deeply moved, knowing that their loving had to be kept secret as it would not be understood, or tolerated. It tore at her heart. She had been vaguely aware that some men loved other men and some women loved women but she had never witnessed it with her own eyes. The light around these two was so beautiful she knew that what was between them was true and real.

She watched as slowly they sank into the water and floated on their backs, holding hands.

As the moon lit their faces, she recognised them as the daughters of two local families. While water covered their ears, Ellen took the opportunity to move away unheard.

She was fearful for them. It might have been someone else who had found them there and that would mean serious trouble. She would have to talk to them soon and warn them to be more careful.

Arriving back at her cottage, she checked on Ned and then the henhouse, seeing that her neighbour Séamus had brought over the hen from his place, and it was now sleeping soundly with the others.

A while later she went to bed and dreamed of a fair-haired man lifting her from the sand and carrying her to the bathing pool where he lovingly caressed her in the moonlight.

Chapter 7

Blake had retired to bed after John's celebration dinner party quite optimistic about his future, and fell asleep feeling satisfied that Ellen, and her cottage by the sea, were no longer going to occupy his thoughts. It was the thought of Felicity Hannon and a large estate in Skibbereen that kept a smile on his face as he fell asleep.

But it was Ellen who appeared in his dreams, dreams in which he was tossed about by an angry sea and thrown again and again up on to the sand, where she gave him back his life.

He woke at dawn drenched in sweat, the fear and wonder of the dreams still pulling at him. He reasoned that it was natural that he had dreamed of her – she had saved his life. That moment when he looked up and saw her, her hair glowing in the sun, was enough to affect any man. And yet, he thought as he watched light creep across the sky, there was something more to it than that. Yes, she had rescued him, but something else had happened in that moment and he just couldn't grasp what it was. Remembering the way she had looked at him had his heart pounding again now and he was unable to go back to sleep.

He lay awake for a couple of hours, then throwing off the bedclothes he got up, cursing this new unsettled feeling. He would return to Bantry now instead of in the evening. He felt too restless to sit around for the day. Once home, he would lose himself in hard work and at the same time plan a visit to Miss Felicity Hannon in Skibbereen. Surely all that would be enough to put the blasted storm and his rescuer finally out of his mind.

Going to the desk, he sat and wrote a note to his hosts.

Dear Grace and John,

I'm sorry, but I have to cut my visit short and return home. I'm grateful for your hospitality these past few days. Dinner was superb last night, and my dinner partner well chosen, Grace! I hope to see both of you soon in Bantry or else I'll make a trip to Skibbereen when you are back there. Please say goodbye to Robert and David for me.

Having signed the note, he hurriedly packed his belongings in one saddlebag and the clothes Ellen had given him into the other, not wanting to leave them there in John's house. Without waiting for anyone else to come down for breakfast, he left the note on a table as he passed through the hall.

As he strode across the yard he startled the stable lad, who, since it was Sunday morning, was taking his time about his chores.

"It's all right, don't let me disturb your work," Blake reassured him, going over to his horse. "I'll saddle him myself."

The boy got on with his duties and within minutes Blake was leading the horse out into the yard. Mounting, he turned the animal and walked him down the avenue and onto the road for Durrus.

The village was still and quiet when he arrived there. Where he should have turned north for Bantry he reined the horse in. The animal pawed the ground while Blake looked along the road in the direction of Bantry and then looked south in the direction of Ellen's. Would a messenger be able to find her, if he sent one? Glancing down at his saddlebag, he suddenly felt an overwhelming urge to return the borrowed clothes to his rescuer himself, along with a reward. He told himself it was the polite thing to do, and would definitely help him to put it all behind him. Also, hadn't John said that to reward her was the wisest thing to do? He had plenty of time – Arthur wasn't expecting him back home until the evening.

He tugged on the reins and directed the horse onto the road he had travelled with Ellen the day before. He didn't attempt to examine the excitement he felt at the prospect of seeing her again.

He tried to picture again the angle from which he had seen Sheep's Head from her cottage. He guessed that she couldn't have been too far south of Durrus.

He rode on as far as Blair's Cove and took his bearings there at the water's edge. He felt he hadn't gone far enough south yet, but he stopped by a group of men smoking their pipes and leaning against a wall. He asked if they knew of a young woman, about twenty-five years old, with long red hair, called Ellen.

They looked at him curiously and shook their heads. Then one of them said, "Isn't O'Rourke's wife called Ellen?"

"That's right," said another with a cackle of a laugh, "but she's about sixty with very little hair and even less teeth." The three laughed heartily at the joke.

Blake smiled. "Eh no, that isn't who I'm looking for."

They shook their heads, still grinning.

Blake touched his hat in salute and moved on. Again, he felt sure Ellen wasn't married. There had been no sign that a man lived there with her – even the borrowed clothes had belonged to her father. Not that her marital situation was of any interest to him, he told himself. He was merely returning the clothes. As he rode on, he found he was humming a tune – he had no idea where he had heard it before.

To be sure of not missing her cove and riding on too far, he went down every lane to the sea he passed. Fields and ditches rolled away to his left and right and down each lane he passed a few smallholdings until he reached the rocky shore – but not her cottage or her sandy beach. Anyone he saw, he asked them if they knew Ellen, all the while feeling foolish that he didn't have her surname. But they all shook their heads. He was puzzled but thought that perhaps it was that they did know her, but weren't willing to tell him.

He meandered down another lane but it petered out by an old ruined cottage looking out to the sea. He figured he was too far south now. Yet how had he missed it? Frustrated, he dismounted by the ruin and led the horse to a stream that ran beside it, letting him graze for a bit on the grass nearby.

Blake sat on the ground with his back against the wall and stared out across the sea, studying the peninsula across the way again. Plucking a blade of grass, he put it between his teeth, wondering why he had felt compelled to come here. He knew the clothes and reward were only an excuse. If he was honest with himself he'd have to admit that he longed for a little more of the peace of mind and the sense of belonging he had felt with Ellen. Maybe it was nothing to do with her at all. It was some need within him. Where he lived in Bantry didn't feel like home to him since his father had died and Ellen's cottage had been very welcoming.

He threw away the blade of grass angrily and jumped up. Is that all he was, he wondered in disgust? A pathetic, lost soul, looking for comfort in the home of a perfect stranger, and only last night having met a woman he was planning to court?

He was beginning to question his sanity and regretted his impulsive decision to look for Ellen.

Mounting, he went back up the lane but, instead of continuing with his quest, he turned for Bantry.

It was around noon when he rode through the gates of the Travers estate. He was in foul humour and didn't feel like seeing Arthur.

Halfway up the drive, two farmhands were chopping up some fallen trees that lay next to the avenue. Blake stopped beside them.

"Mr. Blake," they both greeted in unison while doffing their caps.

"Shaughnessy, O'Brien," Blake said in return. "The storm?"

"Yes, sir. Three fell here, Friday night. The wind came up real sudden. There are others down too. Lots of firewood for you, sir."

Blake nodded. "But Sunday is your day off," he said, dismounting.

"Mr. Arthur wanted this cleared up straight away. We worked all day yesterday to move them off the avenue, but we didn't get time to chop them all up and store them."

Blake was rolling up his sleeves as the man spoke. "Right, O'Brien, you take my horse to the stables and get Aidan to look after it, then come back with an extra saw and we'll get through this as fast as we can so you can get back to your families for what's left of the day."

He didn't see the look of admiration both men gave him as he had turned to take his saddlebags off the horse before handing the reins to O'Brien.

Blake was only too pleased to delay his return to his brother's house and the physical labour was just what he needed after being in the saddle the last few hours.

The three of them worked steadily for over two hours and between them loaded the cart several times with chopped wood. Blake's good humour was restored while listening to Shaughnessy tell a few funny stories as they worked, and he forgot his own troubles for a while.

The men went home and he strode the rest of the way to the house with his jacket over one shoulder and his saddlebags over the other, his muscles aching sweetly from the exertion.

When the house came into view, he stopped and looked up at the vastness of it. It had a dull grey facade with no climbing plants to soften it. It boasted twelve bedrooms. The reception rooms were mostly large and pretentious. The only room he had liked when growing up was a small morning room that his mother had made her own. It had always been filled with flowers and her warm smiles. Stories had been read to him by her there, with the two of them tucked up together before the fire, and later when he was grown he would go and talk easily there with her. After her death, he had kept that room as his own private sitting room.

He shook his head now at the ridiculousness of himself and his brother rattling around in such a mansion. Going inside, he looked around the dreary foyer. It lacked a woman's touch and in his mind he saw the wild flowers on Ellen's dresser. His shoulders suddenly sagged with weariness as he went upstairs.

Going straight to his own quarters, he unpacked his clothes from one saddlebag and left the borrowed clothes in the other. He tossed it on a chair in the corner and went to his desk to review the work he had lined up around the estate for the following week. His task would be working closely with the men who looked after the stock, horses and crops and, like that afternoon, he was never afraid to get his hands dirty. In fact the more physically involved with the land he was, the happier it made him. He could never be like Arthur, whose greatest pleasure was to collect rents then sit behind his desk counting money. Blake believed him to be heartless, never seeing his tenants as people, but just as a source of income. Blake hoped there would be some news soon on contesting the will. One way or another he would get out from under Arthur's thumb, perhaps by marrying Felicity Hannon.

He stood and caught his reflection in the mirror, thinking that perhaps he was becoming mercenary, like his half-brother. He despised the idea. Suddenly Ellen came into his mind. There's a woman who would only marry for love, he thought. For some inexplicable reason the thought made him angry.

He whipped off his cravat. "Damn woman, get out of my head!" he muttered.

Arthur was already sitting at the head of the table when Blake arrived into the dining room. He took his seat at the opposite end.

"Well, how was your time with John and Grace?" Arthur asked. "Fine for you, gadding about while the rest of us had to deal with the damage that damn storm brought."

Blake glanced at his half-brother, ten years his senior with a similar build but with a more ample waist, and the same fair hair but thinner on top. His grey eyes were cold – like his heart, Blake thought. Arthur unfortunately hadn't inherited their father's good looks, and he had a rather menacing appearance which probably accounted for him still being a bachelor at forty.

"Well," he probed now when Blake didn't answer, "did you go hunting or shooting?"

Blake politely answered his questions but did not mention what had happened to him on Friday night. They discussed the repairs that needed to be made around the estate following the storm and some other estate business, Blake as always trying to get Arthur to invest more in the homes of the tenants, trying to improve their lot. As usual Arthur would change the subject as soon as he could. Eventually they fell silent.

As Blake ate, once again Ellen came into his mind. Fine, he thought, if you insist on being in my head then I'll just have to figure out why. What was it about you that has you so firmly planted there?

How could someone be so soft and caring, he pondered, and yet have such strength simmering just below the surface? And how did he even know she had this strength? Yet he did. He had sensed it, could see it in her eyes, and felt it when her hands were on his chest somehow restoring the heat to this body. She was a puzzle, and one he seemed drawn to solving. She had depths he wished he could investigate. His earlier disgust at seeking out the comfort of a stranger evaporated, because, he realised, Ellen wasn't a stranger. He couldn't find a word to describe her, but stranger was definitely not the right one. He realised she defied description, just as those moments with her defied description. With something like relief, he admitted to himself that he wanted to see her again and that fighting it was pointless. She was a mystery and if he could solve it then he would be able to forget her. Draining his wineglass, he silently called himself a fool for the second time that day, the first time when looking for her and now for having given up the search so easily. Pushing away from the table he resolved there and then to look for her again as soon as he could get away from the estate.

Distractedly he bade Arthur goodnight.

Chapter 8

Ellen joined the line of people filing into the church a few minutes before the start of Johnny's funeral Mass. It was another warm day and everyone was grateful for it but they were wondering if the good weather would hold. Ellen usually attended Mass every Sunday and on feast days and she had enjoyed going, as Father Goggin had given interesting and inspiring sermons. Ellen hoped the new priest would do the same.

Shep, Johnny's dog, was standing outside the door looking into the church, getting patted on the head by those who passed near him. He turned his big eyes up to Ellen when she stopped beside him. Bending down, she spoke softly, while stroking his head. Going inside she looked for Annie and the children and, seeing that Mick wasn't with them, she slipped in beside them. She was grateful they had chosen a seat near the back.

"Where's Mick?" she whispered.

"Still out on the water. He's making the most of this fine weather. If he brings home a good haul, I'll be taking the fish up to the salting rock tomorrow. Will you come up and give a hand?"

"Of course." She looked around then, noticing that all the fishermen were missing. Sorcha, one of the girls she'd seen at the bathing pool, was sitting in the seat in front of her. Ellen tapped her on the shoulder and smiled at her when she turned around. Leaning forward, she whispered: "Will you and Eve come over to visit me someday soon? There's something I'd like to talk to you about."

The girl nodded and Ellen could see the wariness in her eyes. She gave her what she hoped was a warm, reassuring smile before sitting back in her seat.

The new priest came out of the sacristy. He was a heavy man in his late thirties, with a dour expression. He began the prayers in a droning voice. The only change in tone came during his sermon when he became quite impassioned, hoping that Johnny Dunne was well on his way to heaven because as he, Father O'Riordan, could assure his parishioners, hell was one place Johnny would not want to go to and they all had to watch the way they lived their lives so that they too could avoid fiery damnation.

Ellen sighed. He was one of those priests who preferred to talk about the Devil than talk about God's love, kindness and mercy. If he kept feeding his parishioners a diet of bitterness, anger and revenge, how could he expect their day to be coloured with anything but that? She shook her head, wishing that Father Goggin was still their priest. He was a good man, who had shown nothing but kindness to his parishioners but unfortunately for them he had been moved to Bantry.

Eventually Father O'Riordan finished the Mass and said the prayers over the coffin where it stood before the altar. Six of Seamus's farming neighbours came forward to shoulder the coffin out of the church.

Ellen, Annie and the children joined the procession to the graveyard.

"Morning, Annie." Mrs. Scanlan came up beside them and spoke in lowered tones. "How are the children?"

"Good, thank you, Mrs. Scanlan. How are you?"

"Grand, thanks. How are you, Ellen?"

"I'm fine, thank you, Mrs. Scanlan."

"Any sign of settling down yet? You're not getting any younger – what is it – twenty-six now?"

"Twenty-seven." Ellen sighed inwardly, knowing where this was going, like many conversations before.

"You can't let it go much longer and your younger sister married long before you. It's not right you living out there on your own like that. The sooner you find a husband the better."

"There aren't that many eligible bachelors to choose from now, are there, Mrs. Scanlan?"

"Oh, I don't know about that." She sniffed. "Mrs. Hegarty's nephew, Eamon, is looking for a wife. That holding will soon be his." She lowered her voice. "His father's not well, you know."

Ellen had heard Annie's sharp intake of breath. Eamon Hegarty was a lazy man who hadn't done a day's work in his life. No one in their right mind would marry him even if he was the last man in West Cork.

Then, to Ellen's immense relief, Mrs. Scanlan was drawn into conversation with a woman on the other side of her and Annie and Ellen moved a little ahead of them.

"Even look at that man and I'll disown you," Annie whispered.

"Don't worry!"

"But she has a point, you know."

"Annie," Ellen warned, "you know she'd just like to see me married off to Eamon so that I wouldn't put my sights on her own son. She'd be scared out of her wits to have me as a daughter-in-law."

Annie snorted. "Still, I'd love to see you married, with someone to love you and take care of you. I worry about you living on your own."

"We've talked about this, Annie," Ellen chided gently. "I've been fine these last few years since you moved out, haven't I?" She glanced at Annie who just shook her head. "It would be hard enough to find someone to accept me and my ways," she added lightly, having accepted that a long time ago.

Annie looked at her sadly but said no more, as up ahead the coffin had arrived at the grave and silence fell as they gathered around it. The droning voice of the priest started up again.

Ellen stood a few rows back but between heads she could see Shep standing at the foot of the grave. After Father O'Riordan gave the final blessing, Shep moved away. She lost sight of him then until he pushed through the crowd and came to stand beside her. He sat and pressed his head against her thigh.

Annie gave a little laugh. "Looks like you're not going to be on your own in that cottage after all!"

Ellen grinned at her. "The abundance of blessings that come my way never ceases to amaze me." She laid her hand on Shep's head and he wagged his tail. She and Annie turned to leave the graveyard, Shep walking beside them.

Fionn caught up with them.

"Hello, you two! The music got even better after you left last night. You should have stayed on."

"I'd say you managed fine without us," Ellen teased. "Nuala is a great one to dance."

"And pretty," added Annie, winking mischievously at him.

The woman in question waved from across the church yard and Ellen saw Fionn blush.

"You're making a big impression on her, I think," Annie joked. "Well, if she breaks your heart, sure Ellen can heal it."

Just then the priest passed them by, his cold eye fixed on Ellen. Fionn immediately started to talk loudly about the weather, and she gave him a grateful smile. She didn't like the feeling she got from the new priest and knew she had to be careful. Their previous priest had been a kind soul and a friend of hers, who had known she was a healer and had respected her for it. She knew this new man would not be so tolerant.

"Sorry, Ellen," Annie whispered. "That was careless of me."

They bade goodbye to Fionn and Annie linked Ellen's arm, her eyes on Father O'Riordan as he strutted down the hill ahead of them.

"You'll have to watch yourself there, I think. He looks like a right cross one. It's a good job you attend Mass – at least that way, if he hears about you, he'll know you're Catholic."

"Hmm. It's important to me to belong to the community – that's one of the reasons I come – but I've told you before, Annie, I'm Christian first and Catholic second. Don't get me started on some of the mad ways of the Catholic Church and the *men* that have ruled it."

"Well, as you said, it matters to you to belong so don't go looking for trouble with Father O'Riordan. He looks like the type who wouldn't lose any sleep over asking you to leave." Frowning, she squeezed Ellen's arm to give emphasis to her words. "Stay well out of his way."

"Don't worry, I will." Ellen smiled at her sister, and didn't voice the rest of her thought – that she hoped the priest would stay out of her way too!

Annie sighed. "Fionn's a little darlin', though, isn't he?"

"'*Little*' is not a word I'd use for Fionn Doyle," Ellen laughed, "but yes, he is a pet."

"And that dark hair of his is like mahogany in the sunshine."

Ellen laughed. "You're very poetic this morning. Mahogany no less! What would we know of mahogany?"

Annie pretended indignation. "I've seen it in the parish house – that big sideboard in the parlour. But that aside, and speaking of eligible bachelors, why don't you walk out with him, Ellen?"

"He's never asked me."

Annie's eyes widened. "Would you? If he did ask, I mean?"

"No. I'm very fond of him – he's a wonderful man – but I'm happy to have him as a friend."

Annie lowered her voice. "If he'd moved here to Ballinmara before I saw Mick, I'd have set my cap at him, I can tell you."

Ellen felt the same sadness as she'd felt the previous evening, when she had wished Annie was with Fionn instead of that cold man she had inexplicably fallen in love with. But she smiled brightly and said: "And there's your husband and children now waiting for you by the wall. You'd best be off."

Tugging her shawl from her head on the way home, Ellen shook her hair free from its ribbon, enjoying the warmth of the sun on her head. She smiled indulgently at her sister's attempt at matchmaking, for she had come to terms with the fact that she would never marry.

She believed her life as a healer was to be a solitary one. She enjoyed her independence and guarded it fiercely. She thought of Fionn and how, since he had come to Ballinmara over a year ago, he had become a good friend to herself and Annie. He was a good man, Ellen knew it, but as for Annie's wish that she marry him, no, there had never been that kind of spark there for her.

She knew the power of being a healer. If she was ever to be with someone, she wanted to feel that same power as a woman. She knew she wouldn't settle for anything less all-consuming than that.

Blake immediately came into her mind. She had felt that pull of power, a vibrancy, when she was with him. Instinctively she had known they were equal in so many ways, except in the one thing she could not overcome – his place in society. Stoically, she told herself to stop wasting time thinking about him.

Chapter 9

It was two weeks later before Blake could get away. It was Sunday and little was happening on the estate so he knew he wouldn't be missed.

The compulsion to find Ellen hadn't gone away, and if anything it had grown along with his curiosity about her. He followed the same route he had taken before, carefully searching for a lane he might have missed. Clouds had rolled in and the landscape around him was a tapestry of changing shades. Again he followed a few lanes to the sea but still couldn't find the cottage.

He was farther south than on his previous trip.

Once again he turned the horse onto another lane towards the coast. There was a very gradual incline for a mile or more and eventually he ended up on a little promontory high over the sea. He looked at the land across the bay. The angle to him seemed very similar to his view that morning at her cottage.

The saddle creaked as he leant forward and looked at the waves surging against the rocks way down below. He swore. The sound of the waves reached his ears but did nothing to soothe his frustration. Feeling he must be close to her place, he felt sure that someone around here would know her, and this time might talk to him. He would ride back to the road and go on into the village of Ballinmara and ask about her there.

Pulling on the horse's reins, he turned the animal around to the right. As he did so, he got a glimpse of smoke rising up from a dip in the land. He frowned. He must have missed a smaller turning in that direction on the way out the promontory. But he was sure he hadn't.

He urged his horse on. The undulating landscape was quite rocky but fields were still marked out by stone walls and he examined any gap or entrance he came across.

Before long he saw a gap into a field which was wide enough to let a donkey and cart pass through. Getting closer he could see rutted tracks crossing the field, heading down towards sea level and going around the base of a small hill beyond.

Maybe at last, he thought, he could scratch this itch and get it over with.

With his heart beating faster, he urged the horse into the field. After going across it, he rounded the hill. The thin spiral of smoke came into view again beyond another hillock and the sea lay beyond it. The lie of the land looked familiar and with a surge of excitement he knew this was the place. He continued down the track, skirting the base of the hill. And all of a sudden there it was, her cottage, tucked away on a bit of land above the cove. He saw her garden and the donkey grazing in the next field, and his nostrils were filled with the comforting smell of burning turf.

Dismounting, he tied up his horse outside the wall and walked up to knock on her door, the top half of which was open.

"Ellen?" he called, looking in. The room was exactly as he had seen it in his mind every day since he'd been there. The fire burned in the hearth and a deliciously rich aroma of rosemary and meat came from a pot hanging over it.

There was no reply to his call. He was about to open the half door and step in when he heard a bark, followed by laughter, down on the beach.

Whirling around, he saw Ellen throw a stick for a dog. As she stood waiting for him to retrieve it, her hair danced free in the breeze and the same breeze moulded her skirts to her long legs. Blake stood transfixed. When the dog returned with the stick in his mouth, she tussled with him over it, her bare feet dancing on the sand. Her laughter rang out again, releasing something tight in Blake's stomach – his lips curved in a smile.

Ellen gained possession of the stick and with a lithe flick of her slender arm sent it sailing through the air once more. Blake watched for a further few moments, enjoying the scene and the pleasure he felt at finding her.

But, instead of bringing the stick back, Shep dropped it and walked over to her. He stood facing up the beach and barked once, making Ellen turn in the same direction. Blake raised his hand in greeting and started down towards her, his smile widening.

He stopped a few feet away. There was no answering smile from her. She stood before him, her beautiful green eyes wide with disbelief.

"Blake? How did you find me?" Her tone was cool, but also there was a touch of fear in it and he was confused at her lack of welcome. His smile slipped and he searched her face for any clues as to what she was thinking. Disappointment at her reaction warred with the unexpected pleasure he felt at seeing her again.

She remained silent. He knew it would sound foolish, or worse, desperate, if he told her he had searched for her on two occasions. He suddenly felt very unsure of himself. A feeling he wasn't used to. Her cool eyes held his. He cleared his throat.

"Just luck," he said nonchalantly. "I thought I should return your father's clothes, since you had been so kind to me that day." He had no intention of telling her that he couldn't stop thinking about her and that perversely he had come to see her in order to stop thinking about her! She would think him quite mad in the head.

She frowned. "You shouldn't have come back here," she said. "You need to leave now." Calling Shep to her, she started up the beach with the dog following obediently at her heels.

Blake turned and watched in puzzlement. His emotions were in turmoil. His confusion turned to annoyance. He had battled with himself about whether he should come here and she was making it very clear he wasn't welcome! He stormed after her.

"Ellen, wait!" He fell into step beside her. "Why are you in such a hurry to see me off? I've travelled a long way to see you – to return the clothes, that is, and I'd like to reward you for saving me that day."

"You weren't supposed to find me," she muttered, more to herself than to him, but he caught the words.

"Yes, and I have been wondering why you went to all that trouble to ensure that I wouldn't?"

She ignored his question. "It was very kind of you to want to return my father's things and I very much appreciate it. As for coming to see me – that really wasn't very wise and I need no reward, other than knowing you are safe and well."

"For goodness' sake, what's the harm in it? It's not forbidden for two people to pass the time of day, especially when one of them owes their life to the other!"

She kept walking.

"What the devil?" he muttered, forced to keep up with her. "Ellen!" He caught her arm, making her stop and look at him. He was surprised when she turned vulnerable eyes up to him. He thought he would drown in their green depths. "Ellen," he repeated, this time infinitely softer, drawn to her.

Quickly she lowered her gaze. Feeling her hesitate, Blake pushed his advantage and, loosening his grip, he let his fingers move down her arm to capture her hand in his.

"Please, I just want to talk with you for a small while. I'm here now, so don't send me away just yet." He willed her to change her mind.

He saw her chest rise on a deep inhalation and this time when she raised her eyes to his they were guarded.

"I've a stew cooking," she said, again in that reserved tone. "You're welcome to some before you return to Durrus."

His hand tightened briefly but she pulled hers away and pushed open the half door. Ducking his head, he followed in swiftly behind her before she could change her mind. Shep came in too and Blake went down on one knee, taking the dog's head in his hands and rubbing him behind the ears. Shep's tongue lolled out, his tail wagging.

"Hello, boy, you weren't here the last time," Blake said.

"No, he belonged to an old farmer who passed away since and he seemed to want to come and live with me."

Blake continued to croon to the dog while Ellen washed her hands before seeing to the pot over the fire.

Lifting the lid, she gave the stew a stir.

"If you'll excuse me for a moment," Blake said, "I need to see to my horse before we eat."

He went out, Shep prancing at his heels, and returned a few

minutes later with her father's clothes. He placed them on a stool and asked permission to wash his hands. She nodded her assent and poured some water into a large bowl for him. Shep meanwhile settled down on some old sacking near the open door and idly watched the seagulls strut around on the beach.

Putting a cloth around the handle of the pot, Ellen carried it to the table.

"Can I help?" Blake asked.

"Bring over two bowls, please," she replied, indicating a stack of wooden bowls on the dresser.

He placed them on the table and she invited him to sit, passing him a spoon. After serving, she sat opposite him.

For the first time since he had arrived, she smiled at him and his world felt all right again. He relaxed.

"How have you been?" she asked. "Did you have any ill effects from your night at sea?"

"I was perfectly well, thank you. Although I think it might be a while before I take out a boat again."

"If it gave you pleasure to be on the water before the storm, you should not let your fear stop you. I'm sure you're wiser to the dangers now and won't get caught out again."

"I suppose you're right."

"Do you live close to Durrus?"

"No, I was just visiting there."

"Oh." A small frown formed between her brows and he wanted to reach out and smooth it away.

"So where do you live then?" she asked.

He finished chewing his food before answering. "Bantry."

"Oh," she said again.

"Tell me a little about you," he urged. "You never told me your surname." He was trying to ignore the guilt he felt at having lied to her about his own, and yet was still glad she didn't know he was a Travers.

"Cassidy," she replied.

When she didn't say any more he prompted: "You live here alone?"

"Yes, but I grew up here with my grandmother, my parents and my younger sister."

Looking around he tried to imagine the two-roomed cottage holding so many of them.

"Granny died when I was thirteen. She was only sixty-one but had a weariness about her that made her seem much older. Her experiences had taken their toll on her, I suppose." She paused and seemed to drift away. Then, with a little shake of her head she continued: "Daddy died six years ago and Mam a year later. My sister and I lived here together for a further year, then she married Mick Leahy and moved to his cottage. She has two children now. I've lived on my own here since."

"Your parents must have been young." His voice was gentle.

She raised sad eyes to his and something twisted in his gut. "Too young. Da died in a fishing accident and Mam started having very bad pains in her chest soon afterwards and gradually became more sickly. The doctor said she had a disease of the heart. There was nothing I – anyone could do to make her well again." She pushed her bowl away although it wasn't empty.

Blake wanted to show sympathy by putting his hand over hers where it lay on the table, but he didn't want that wary look he'd seen on the beach to return to her eyes, so with effort he kept his hands on his side of the table. "I'm sorry, Ellen, I didn't mean to make you relive your sorrow."

To his relief a smile tugged at the corner of her lips. She lifted her chin and sat straighter, as if drawing on some inner strength. The smile lit her eyes. "She wanted to be with Daddy so I'm happy for her now."

"My own father passed away just over two months ago so I understand the pain of it," he said.

"Oh Blake, I'm sorry." Her hand shot out to rest on his for a moment before she hastily withdrew it again. "What happened to him?"

"Do you mind if we don't talk about it? It's still too painful for me."

"I understand."

"Thank you." He cleared his throat. "May I ask how you manage? I imagine it's unusual for a woman to live on her own around here?"

"Oh, I manage well enough. I grow some vegetables and herbs. I keep bees and hens, harvest seaweed and knit shawls, socks and ganseys which I sell at market."

His eyes had opened wide in appreciation of her self-sufficiency.

Laughing lightly, she said, "I'm well able to look after myself."

Casting his eye around the room, he commented: "You've made a good home here."

He realised he felt the same comfort and peace here that he used to know in his mother's sitting room. The two rooms couldn't have been more different, but it was the warmth and caring both women brought to each room that made them special.

With surprise, he acknowledged to himself that he liked who he was when he was here. The thought puzzled him. He suddenly remembered that he had come here to find a way to put her behind him and instead he knew he was creating new memories that would linger long after he left – memories he was enjoying making.

He glanced up at her bookshelf. "You like books?"

She smiled. "Yes. I only have a few, but our last parish priest, Father Goggin, was a great reader and encouraged me to read a lot too. He often lent me some of his and gave me some to keep. He sometimes borrowed books of mine if I found something of interest to him on market day. Do you like to read?"

"Yes. I only recently reread *Gulliver's Travels*, the Swift you have there." He pointed to a book at the end of the shelf.

"I liked that a lot. It made me laugh. My favourite, though," she continued, "is the one on beekeeping. Father Goggin brought that one back from a visit to a monastery in England a few years ago. Only for that, I wouldn't have started keeping bees or known how to care for them."

He nodded, his admiration for her ever increasing.

He finished his meal and looked up at her. "That was a very flavoursome stew, Ellen. You're good with herbs." He looked at her pointedly.

He saw her flush as, with flustered movements, she rose and went to hang the kettle over the fire.

"Would you like some tea?" she asked, turning.

"God, no! And find myself asleep in a ditch again! No, thank you," he joked.

A bubble of laugher rose from her throat. Her hand flew to her mouth to stifle it.

He cocked his head, waiting for a reply, amusement lighting his own eyes.

She managed to look charmingly guilty and totally unapologetic at the same time, her hands now clasped in front of her skirt, as she swung slightly from side to side.

"Well," he prompted, "are you going to tell me what you gave me that day and why?"

She moved back to the table and sat down again, meeting his eyes with her chin slightly raised.

"You had been through a lot that night, your body needed to heal. My grandmother taught me which plants and herbs to use to aid sleep. I mixed a little of this and that," she said with an enigmatic smile, "but mostly it was the root of the valerian plant that helped you sleep on the way to Durrus. The hot drink soothed your throat and your muscles. All completely harmless."

"And I thank you for all that. However, as I said before, I think you also drugged me because you didn't want me to know where you live."

"You're right," she admitted, looking at him without apology, "We come from different worlds, you and me. I thought it should stay that way."

He leaned forward a little. "I don't see what harm it could do to simply talk like this. I enjoyed being here before and I wondered what it would be like to be here again and to find out more about you. Is that such a terrible thing?"

To his disappointment, her eyes became clouded again. "No, it's not terrible at all – but friendship," she hesitated over the word before continuing, "between our classes just doesn't happen. As well as the fact that you are Protestant, aren't you?" At his curt nod, she continued. "And I'm Catholic. Some around here would not take kindly to me even talking to a Protestant, let alone sharing a meal with him!"

"Nonsense," he declared. "Who makes these ridiculous rules and who says they can't be broken? What's wrong with us having a civil conversation about the weather, the sea ..." he waved his hand in exasperation, "anything!"

She gave a sad smile at his retort. "It wouldn't be good for either of us, that's all." She stood. "Now I think it's time you went. Don't come back again, Blake. It's for the best. I wish you much happiness and a good life."

They both got up and he moved around the table to stand in front of her. She met his eyes without a flicker. Slowly he raised his hand to cup her face despite the voice in his head telling him to just go and put an end to all this.

Her skin was so soft beneath his palm that he almost groaned.

He heard himself say: "The thing is – I couldn't forget you, Ellen. I really tried but I couldn't. But I see that my going is what you want and I know myself it's for the best – you have been distracting me from other things." He thought guiltily about not having yet written to Felicity Hannon. "So I'll go, as you wish. Your welcome has been very gracious and I don't want to intrude any further."

"And you will *not* return!" Her voice rang with authority, telling of the power that lay inside her.

He brushed his thumb over her smooth cheek and he marvelled again at the contradiction of the softness and strength in her.

He removed his hand and stepped back. "I would like to leave you some money as a reward," he said.

"I told you no reward is necessary. It's enough to know you're safe."

Their eyes locked. Blake moved closer again. "I feel bound to you in some way, Ellen. I haven't been able to put you out of my mind."

"But you must! You shouldn't have come back. Just go, please."

Unable to resist her, he lowered his head and brushed his lips once over hers. Their softness made his head light. His arms went around her, slowly pulling her closer as he increased the pressure of his mouth on hers. He thrilled at feeling her tremble. For a moment she leaned into him, her lips moving against his. But then suddenly she wrenched away. Turning, she stood looking out the window, her back ramrod straight.

"Go now," she said quietly but firmly.

He watched her for a long moment, with a pain in his chest at the thought that this would be the last time he would see her. But there was no choice to be made. He had to go and she wanted him to go. Reluctantly he went outside where he saddled up and rode away from her.

Chapter 10

Blake was shaken. So much for unravelling the mystery of her and moving on! He shouldn't have kissed her, but he had, so now he also had the memory of those full, warm lips beneath his and her soft, slender body in his arms. She had trembled! He'd left when she asked him to, but for his own sake as well as hers.

Urging his horse on towards home, his mind was full of her. How she had looked while laughing on the beach, sitting at the table sharing her food with him, her scent when he had kissed her, her softness when he had held her. She was a mixture of strength and vulnerability – a contradiction, just like how he felt now – right and sensible to be riding away from her, and at the same time utterly wrong not to be staying. He wondered if perhaps she had slipped him some more herbs, this time ones to totally confuse his mind!

By the time he got back to the estate he was weary. On entering the house, he silently swore when his brother called him to join him in his study.

"Come in and sit down. I want to talk to you about something."

"Can't it wait until tomorrow, Arthur?" he asked, standing in the study doorway.

"It'll only take a minute."

Blake sat down in a chair at the other side of Arthur's desk.

"I've increased the rents recently for the tenants here, and there has been some resistance."

Blake frowned.

"I'm also increasing the rents for the new lands out on the Mizen peninsula. There's likely to be trouble there too, so I'll send more than one man out. They're unlikely to kick up a fuss if they're outnumbered. I've hired a couple of men for the job so you won't be shorthanded here."

Blake looked at his half-brother with disgust. "Why on earth do you need to increase the rents? You're doing well enough at present."

"Business is improving everywhere now, and goods are becoming more expensive, so outgoings are increasing."

"But if things are becoming expensive for you they're also becoming expensive for the tenants. They'll struggle to find the money to pay your rent."

"My rent! Might I remind you that that's what pays your wages, Blake?"

"I haven't asked for an increase in my wages, and besides you pay it out of the overall farm profits anyway!"

"It all comes out of the same pot." Arthur's voice was raised.

Blake's also rose. "You still don't need to increase rents. There are people out there barely managing to feed their families."

"My decision is made."

Blake stood up and left the study, slamming the door behind him, disgusted at his brother's greed. As he took the stairs two at a time, a roll of thunder sounded outside, matching his temper.

The thunder turned into another summer storm.

That night sleep eluded him and, as wind and rain whipped against the window, he wondered if Ellen was all right in the storm. In his mind her little cottage with its thatched roof was defenceless against such wind compared to the solid structure he lived in. He imagined the sea at full tide, raging not far from her front door. He wondered if she lay awake fearful of its angry sound, or if she was lulled by it.

But then he berated himself, acknowledging that she had lived by the sea all her life and in all kinds of weather and managed fine without his concern or protection. A cynical laugh escaped him: he had never come across any woman in less need of protection than Ellen. She had managed to get rid of him all right. Her fiery independence and self-sufficiency dared anyone to think she was weak or in need of a hero.

And yet, those mysterious green eyes had been unguarded for a moment that day and had pierced straight into his heart. When he had first approached her on the beach there had been a look of anxiety and fear. But he couldn't understand why. All had been serene between them the morning he had been washed up in the cove.

He knew he had his life to lead and an acquaintance with Felicity to pursue, but he still pondered over why Ellen had been so keen to push him away. That was a blow to his pride and just one more strand of mystery to her.

Blake thumped his pillow, trying to get comfortable. At last he fell into a dream-filled sleep only to awake in the morning with a severe headache and a mood to match it.

The wind had abated but the clouds seemed to press down on him and the day dragged on dark and wet. Blake worked relentlessly beside the other men in and out of sheds and fields, driven by the need to occupy his mind in an attempt to forget soft lips, red hair and green eyes. Despite the rain, summer temperatures stayed up and as he worked he sweated inside his coat.

By the time he got back to the house that night, he was wet from the outside in and the inside out. He peeled off his sodden leather boots and clothes and bathed with relief. Fortunately Arthur was out for the evening and Blake took supper in his own sitting room while making notes in a journal of the day's events out on the land. For an hour or two he was actually so preoccupied with the sale prices and purchase prices of cows and foals that he didn't think about Ellen at all.

Only when he put down his fountain pen and rubbed tired eyes did she float into his mind again. He gazed at the fire that was lighting in the grate more for company than heat, and saw the colour of her hair in the flames and the colour of her eyes in the sparks that flew when a log crumbled.

He stretched his stocking-clad feet to the fender and put his hands behind his head, picturing her sitting by her own fireside, knitting. She wouldn't fit in here, he thought. Not that he thought her inferior but he knew she would find this house soulless, like he did. He also believed that she belonged right there beside the sea, where the waves could sing lullabies to her.

That was probably why she sent him away and rightly so, so that she could get on with her life, and he'd get on with his. Watching the fire beginning to die, he decided to abide by Ellen's wishes and let her go. She was correct to say their worlds were different – she belonged where she was and he belonged here, for the moment. He liked the men he worked with and the land they worked together. He would do his best for the tenants, helping them where he could now that Arthur had increased their rent. As long as Arthur continued to let him get on with things without too much interference, life would be manageable until he eventually sorted things out. That reminded him that he should write to Felicity.

He stared at the glowing embers for another while before moving over to the writing desk to begin a note to her.

Dear Miss Hannon,

It was my great pleasure to meet you at John and Grace's home. Your father expressed a wish to see the estate here in Bantry and it would be my honour to entertain you and your parents here for tea at your convenience, if you should find yourselves in these parts any time soon.

Yours faithfully,
Blake Travers

If her father was as shrewd as Blake believed him to be, he felt sure he would already have found out that it was Arthur who owned the estate, and that Blake was the one who managed it. If Mr. Hannon still decided to visit, then Blake would know he was in with a chance of courting Felicity.

"There," he muttered, as he left the letter in the hall for posting, "the die is cast. I will move on, Ellen, just at you wish."

He fell asleep without difficulty. But, while in wakefulness he had let her go, in sleep his head was filled with dreams of her for the duration of the night.

Chapter 11

Sitting by the fire, Ellen listened to the wind and the roar of the waves. She couldn't remember a week like it in any June before and hadn't seen anyone for days because of it. She was very grateful to have Shep for company. At least the bad weather afforded her the opportunity to knit a lot, giving her a fine supply of items to take with her to the market. But it also gave her too much time to think about Blake.

His kiss still burned on her lips and often since she had caught herself staring into the air, just reliving the sensation of it. She told herself she was grateful that he had gone when she asked him to, because, being honest with herself, her resistance and good sense had been severely tested.

When she had seen him at the top of the beach her heart had pounded both with exhilaration and with fear. She couldn't believe he had found her despite her efforts and she was filled with dread that he would bring the trouble her grandmother had warned her of. But seeing him again and feeling that powerful attraction to him was in contradiction to the warning voice in her head about staying away from him.

For the hundredth time she tried to work out why her grandmother had the vision about him. How could someone as good and kind as Blake bring her harm? She hadn't sensed any danger in him. At her feet the dog twitched in his sleep. She smiled – even Shep had taken to him.

She had agreed to Blake staying for a short while because, she had reasoned to herself, he was already there anyway, and she planned to send him away again telling him not to return. That way she was letting Fate see she was doing her best to keep him away.

It had taken a lot of willpower to keep her guard up around him and keep him at a distance. She had liked having him back in her cottage, filling the room with life. His voice still echoed in her head and she remembered how his eyes had changed all the time, from thoughtful to mischievous, to concerned, to compassionate. There was depth to the man's soul, she could feel it, and it seemed to call out to her own.

She sighed and shook her head. Her wooden knitting needles clicked rhythmically against each other. She presumed the warning was in some way connected to her being a healer but perhaps it hadn't been about him personally having a problem with that. It might not bother him if he knew what she was capable of, but if he were to tell someone else, someone with authority, well, perhaps that was where the danger lay. Again she reminded herself that it was enough of a risk to make sending him away the right thing to do.

Putting down her knitting, she rubbed her tired eyes. Her hand drifted to her mouth again. The kiss had been warm, firm and devastating. It had shot sensation into every part of her, making her tingle. She recalled the tantalising male scent of his skin when he had pulled her close. He had made her want more. Laying her head back against the chair, she stared into the flames. She had been content before she'd met him, but not anymore.

With a puzzled frown she rose from the chair to fill the kettle, disturbing the dog where he lay at her feet. "I still believe he couldn't hurt anyone, Shep. It's all a mystery to me and a crying shame that I had to send him away again."

She went and stood at the window, looking out at the rain-soaked beach. If the weather had been fine and she had been busy with visitors she might have had some chance of putting him out of her mind. But the elements continued to conspire against her. They had washed him up on the beach and now they were giving her far too much time to think about him.

When she had said to Annie that she would never marry, she had meant it, and had reconciled herself to the fact that she would never have a husband. But she also knew she would take a lover if and when the time and the person was right for her. Her body had needs as well as her soul and she believed that loving and being loved was essential. She knew Blake could be that lover, equal to her intellectually, emotionally and physically, but unfortunately he was forbidden to her not only by class, but because of her grandmother's vision and warning. So she had sent him away again, though it had left an aching emptiness inside her.

Chapter 12

Annie was worried as she looked over at Mick. He paced up and down, every now and then stopping to peer out through the window as the panes were lashed by rain. His ruddy face was unshaven and he had dark circles under his eyes.

"Will this damn wind ever stop blowing?"

Annie didn't admonish him for swearing in front of the children, knowing that his temper was already pushed to breaking point.

"We've lost two market days already over the bloody weather! When will it let up?" He put his two hands on the windowsill, leaning forward with his shoulders hunched, shaking his head in despair. "We don't have enough money to pay the rent as it is, let alone the increase they all say is coming."

Picking up the baby, Annie ushered their two-year-old into the bedroom where she put them both down for their nap. Returning to the kitchen she began hanging damp clothes near the fire.

"Maybe the rent collector will take half," she suggested to Mick, who was still staring out the window. "He can explain to the new landlord about the bad weather stopping everyone from going out in the boats."

"Maybe, but I've heard this Travers is a mean one."

"I could ask Ellen for some money, just to tide us over this one time?" Annie offered tremulously, smoothing out a shirt.

Mick's hand hit the sill with a sharp smack. Annie jumped.

"*You will not!*" he roared. "I won't go cap in hand to that witch!"

"Mick!" Annie gasped, flicking a nervous look at the closed bedroom door. "You know she's no such a thing!" Her voice shook.

"She's a strange one and you know it!" he spat. "Making people think she can fix them and animals without being a doctor – there has to be witchcraft in there somewhere!"

"Witch? You've never used that word before," Annie said, staring at his back. "That kind of talk is very dangerous for her. You know she only does good. Please don't talk about her like that."

He whirled around and, taking a step towards her, raised his hand. She shrank back as he loomed over her, but he thought better of it and dropped his hand to his side again.

"With all her powers then, why doesn't she stop this damn wind?" he growled, taking a hold of her shoulders and shaking her hard.

Annie swallowed. "She doesn't have power over the weather, Mick – you know that."

He glared at her for a long moment before shoving her away and turning with a grunt. He went back to the window. "I still wouldn't take her charity," he said with disgust. "The wind will have to stop some time."

Hands shaking, Annie resumed her chores, relieved he hadn't hit her – this time.

Within the hour they heard horses approaching and a loud banging on the door followed a moment later. Mick went to answer it. Two burly men in wet coats stood outside, their hats pulled well down on their foreheads. They stepped inside and nodded in Annie's direction before addressing Mick.

"We're here to collect the rent for Mr. Travers. Bring me your rent book," one of the men ordered.

Mick took it down from its place on the dresser.

The man took it and wrote something on a new page, then held it out to Mick again. "This is your new rent."

Mick looked at it and threw a glance over at Annie. She saw him swallow.

"You see how the weather's been," he said, looking from one man to the other. "I'm a fisherman and we couldn't get out this past week.

I can give you half the rent now and the rest next week."

The same man spoke again. "I've instructions to give one chance only. We'll come back for the other half next week, but you'll have to have the full amount next month or Mr. Travers will have you evicted."

Annie felt the blood drain from her face. Evictions hadn't happened for many years around the area. She saw Mick's hands shake as he handed over the money. The man signed the book and returned it to him.

"Good day," they said and left.

Mick closed the door and sagged against it.

"It'll be all right, Mick. You'll get out fishing soon. Listen, the wind has eased a bit. The sea will be calm again by tomorrow or maybe the next day. We'll take every last fish to market. We can make do with potatoes and vegetables ourselves this week again and have the money by next week."

Mick turned to her with worried eyes. "Travers sounds like a tyrant. 'One chance', his man said. He must know there'll be other weeks like this. What'll we do in the winter if he isn't as understanding as the old landlord?"

"If the weather stays good, you can do some extra fishing over the summer months and we'll take the fish to the salting rocks, dry them, and sell them in the winter during the bad weather instead of fresh fish. But let's not worry about that now." She tried to sound cheerful. "Thank God paying half was enough for this week."

Mick sat and stared into the flames, hands hanging between his knees.

They were both subdued over supper later. Thankfully the children behaved and were quiet for the evening. Annie nearly cried with relief just before dark when the rain stopped and the wind slackened further.

She woke at dawn to a calmer sea. Mick was already gone, having left before first light. Blessing herself, she prayed for his safe return as she did every time he was out on the water.

Chapter 13

For the week, Blake had thrown himself into work and as soon as a thought of Ellen came into his head he forced it out immediately, reminding himself that Felicity might soon be visiting.

And indeed, a couple of days later a note arrived from her replying to his invitation and informing him that her mother was unwell but that she and her father would be happy to visit on Friday afternoon.

He was pleased. At least there was progress on some front. He had been frustrated the previous day upon receiving a letter from the solicitor in Cork saying that he was out sick for a few weeks and would be in touch in due course about contesting the will.

The way things were going, making a good match with Felicity seemed more likely to bring a positive outcome.

He advised the housekeeper and butler to expect two guests to afternoon tea on Friday. He did not invite Arthur to the planned tea party.

By Thursday morning, he tried to convince himself he was doing a good job of forgetting Ellen, but by the afternoon he realised he had only been building a dam of brittle twigs against a mighty river of thoughts that just flooded back in to swamp him when he wasn't looking.

It happened when he was riding out with some of the men to move cattle up to higher ground. Even though it was June it felt like he had been plunged straight into winter. Rain pelted down again and seeped inside the collar of his wet coat, making him shiver. He immediately remembered the warmth of the sun the previous Sunday on her beach and how happy he had been to see her. He was suddenly hit by a longing to see her that was like a physical blow to his stomach. He massaged the spot with a balled-up fist.

Now he thought he understood why she had tried to keep him from returning that first time. If she had succeeded, he wouldn't be thinking of that kiss and how she had felt in his arms, his feelings wouldn't be in turmoil, his stomach wouldn't be reeling with longing and his mind wouldn't be constantly battling against the need to return to her. And because of the huge social divide, he couldn't go back. He thanked God that Felicity and her father were coming the next day. It was very possible that that was where his future lay and he needed to think only of that.

With relief he realised they had reached the field which had the cattle in it and rounding them up and moving them to higher pastures needed all his concentration.

By Friday afternoon he was hungry for the distraction that the Hannons would bring. The carriage pulled up at three o'clock. Luckily the rain had cleared away that morning. The butler showed Felicity and her father into the drawing room. Blake stood waiting for them beside a roaring fire. He quickly took in the pretty sight Felicity made in a matching gown and summer coat of soft pink, beneath a little nonsense of a hat that was very fetching.

"Welcome to the Travers Estate," he said, then stepped forward to shake Mr. Hannon's hand. "How do you do, sir?"

"Jolly good, thank you."

"Miss Hannon?"

Blake took her hand and led her to a chair beside the fire, and indicated for her father to take one too. He took the third.

"I'm afraid my half-brother has gone to town, so you won't have the chance to meet him," he informed them, wholly relieved that Arthur was absent.

"From what I've glimpsed already you seem to have a fine estate here," Mr. Hannon commented, eyes slightly narrowed – testing him, Blake felt.

"Thank you, my father looked after it well. When he died two months ago it passed to my half-brother, and I manage it."

Mr. Hannon nodded in approval at Blake coming straight out with the truth.

"I look forward to showing you around it, sir, if you are interested?" Blake said.

"Absolutely. I've been looking forward to it."

Blake turned to Felicity. "I hope you have been well, Miss Hannon?"

"Yes, thank you. But please call me Felicity."

"If you will call me Blake?"

They smiled at each other.

"I hope this unseasonal rain hasn't been tempting you to leave for France to be with your grandmother?" Blake inquired.

"It has been rather appalling, but no, I'm quite content to remain in Ireland for the time being," she replied, a hint of a challenge in her words.

"That's very good to know," Blake responded, holding her look for a moment, before rising to pull the bell for tea.

Conversation was pleasant and Felicity's intelligence was obvious. She brought news of recent social events in Skibbereen and told him that they were going on to stay a couple of days at Grace and John's summer residence.

She then complimented the house.

"That's kind of you," Blake responded, "but I'm afraid it lacks my mother's touch now, especially in the gardens. She had such an eye for colour, but that part of things has been a bit neglected. I'm too taken up with the working of the estate and Arthur has no interest in the garden at all. It's kept neat but it could do with some new planting and colour. One of these days I'll turn my mind to it."

He turned to Mr. Hannon.

"Now, how about taking a drive around the estate? It has brightened up nicely outside now. Felicity, will you join us?"

"Yes, please. I'd love to see it."

"While you finish your tea I'll have the open carriage brought around."

They passed the next hour driving around the estate in conversation about tenants, crops, cattle, and horses. Once again

Felicity showed an intelligent interest and Blake couldn't but admire her, sitting there, with the sun glinting off her fair hair, her eyes smiling at him. Any man would have found her attractive and Blake was as human as the next man.

As she asked a question about the tenants, Blake pictured her arranging flowers for the hall and the dining room, or standing in the garden, shaded by a large summer hat, telling a gardener where she wanted her choice of flowers planted. He had no problem imagining her there. The role suited her genteel nature. She would indeed make the perfect wife, he thought.

The image of Ellen, standing on the beach with her long red hair loose and free, rose unbidden in his mind. He couldn't help thinking that where Felicity was genteel and pretty, Ellen was wild and magnificent in her beauty. Yet it was Felicity who looked at home here. It was Felicity who was more suited to him. It was Felicity that he needed to grow to love for his own sake. Surely it wouldn't be a difficult thing to do, he thought as Mr. Hannon said his name in attempt to regain his attention.

"Sorry, sir, what was that? I apologise – I was distracted there for a moment."

"I was saying that you are unusually hands-on – you were telling me at Grace's dinner party that you actually get out and work on the land yourself – you don't just give orders to get it done."

"That's correct, sir. I would be bored if I were to be in the house all day. You would quite often see me working beside the farm labourers here."

"Most unusual," Mr. Hannon repeated. "But that's why you have such a feel for it all, my boy. Your knowledge of crops and husbandry is most impressive as are the innovative ideas you are employing here."

Blake was pleased with the praise and relieved to be receiving Mr. Hannon's approval. It boded well.

Blake didn't allow his attention to wander again and, as he saw them into their carriage at the end of the afternoon, they both declared their enjoyment of their visit.

"You must come and see us soon in Skibbereen," Mr. Hannon said, taking his seat.

"I'd be delighted to," Blake replied. "And thank you both for coming. It was a pleasure to have your here."

"I will write soon and formally invite you to visit," Felicity said.

Blake smiled and bowed slightly before closing the carriage door. "Safe journey to you both."

He stepped back and, as the carriage rolled away, he felt a little bit more secure about his future.

Chapter 14

Early the following morning, the sunshine had Ellen's spirits lifting. Taking up a basket, she left the cottage. Her eyes quickly scanned the strand, which had become her new habit every morning, as though by some chance Blake would appear there again. But of course he wasn't to be seen and with a sigh she set to work.

First she gathered some driftwood and put it under a lean-to behind the cottage. The tide was out and she went down to the rocks just above the low-tide line looking for the purple dillisk. She tugged at the long fronds of seaweed and tossed them into her basket. Thanking the sea for its abundance, she hoisted the basket on her hip and took it up to a field beyond the cottage. There she rolled out some old netting and spread the dillisk out thinly to dry.

Shep gave a bark and wagged his tail.

"Hey, Ellen!"

The cheerful greeting had her straightening up. Shielding her eyes from the sun she was pleased to see Fionn, the stonemason, outside the wall, a big grin on his face.

"Good morning, Fionn!"

He hopped over the wall, his bag of tools clanking loudly. "I see you're drying the dillisk?" he commented.

She picked up the empty basket. "Yes, now that it's fine at last. I'll keep some for my own use and I'll sell the rest. What has you out this way this morning?"

He shook his head at her. "Didn't you tell me there was a hole in the shed that needed fixing?"

"Oh yes, of course. I forgot."

He held up the bag. "Well, I've brought the tools, so show me the problem."

"Thanks, Fionn, I appreciate it."

They walked down to the shed at the back of the cottage. The stones had crumbled in a corner near the eaves. They stood looking at it.

"It lets the rain in when the wind's from the north," Ellen said.

"I'll have it fixed in no time."

Ellen left him to it and went into the cottage to do some chores. She had just cleaned out the fire and was walking towards the door with the ashes when the dog started growling, the hairs standing up on the back of his neck.

"What is it, boy?' Ellen asked in a soothing tone, hoping he hadn't seen a rat in the house. The pulse in her left temple began to throb.

Shep growled deep in his throat again as a shadow fell across the open half-door.

Father O'Riordan appeared in the frame.

Ellen put her hand on the dog's silky head. "It's all right, Shep." The dog moved closer to her side, ears standing to attention, his eyes fixed on the priest.

"Good morning, Father."

"Good morning. May I come in?" he asked, already pushing open the half door before she could give her permission.

He walked in and stood with his back to the empty fireplace, his hands clasped behind him and his portly body rocking back and forth on the balls of his feet. His black soutane reached to the top of his shoes and must have been warm because he had a sheen of sweat on his forehead. His hair was either greasy or deliberately oiled, she couldn't tell which, but it gleamed unpleasantly, and his face creased into a smile that didn't reach his cold eyes.

Ellen lowered the bucket of ashes to the floor, all the while keeping her hand on Shep's head.

"Well, Miss Cassidy, I'm making my rounds of the parish, trying to get to know my new parishioners," Father O'Riordan said.

"I'd offer you some tea, but as you can see I don't have the fire going yet," she said politely.

"That's all right. I had some at the last house."

An awkward silence fell.

The priest broke it eventually. "So you live here alone?"

Ellen gave a quick nod.

"That's most unusual and you having a sister in the village. How is it that you're not living with her until you're married?"

Ellen could feel her temper rising. "Because I choose to live here in what has always been our family home."

"Hmm ..." He contemplated her for a moment. "I've seen you in the church. I hope you are a regular Mass-goer."

"Yes, Father."

"And Confession?"

"Yes. To Father Dempsey."

"And you contribute to the upkeep of the church by paying your dues?"

"Yes, Father."

His eyes narrowed. "And tell me, how do you manage that when you've no man bringing money into the house?"

Ellen breathed deeply, wanting to tell him to mind his own business, but knew she shouldn't make an enemy of him.

She looked him squarely in the eye. "I make enough money to get by. I knit items of clothing for selling at the markets in Schull and Bantry. And I sell some seaweed there too."

"Good. Make sure you keep doing that." He stepped away from the fire and nearer to her, causing Shep to growl again. "I don't like any strange things going on in my parish." He stared hard at her, standing much too close for her comfort.

She made no response.

From the doorway, Fionn's deep voice broke the silence.

"Everything all right here, Ellen?" he asked, the handle of a lump hammer in one hand and the head of it in the other. "Morning, Father."

"Everything's fine, thank you, Fionn. Father O'Riordan was just leaving."

The priest looked at Fionn and the hammer in his hand. "And what are you doing here?" he asked.

Fionn raised the head of the hammer then let it fall into his large palm before answering. "Repairs."

The priest nodded and looked back at Ellen, his eyes narrow. "Good day to you, then, Miss Cassidy," he said and with a swish of his black skirts he sailed out the door, giving Fionn a curt nod.

Fionn stood watching him make his way to the pony and trap which he had left a bit away from the cottage.

Ellen's legs were shaking from the effort of controlling her temper so she sank down onto a chair. Shep licked her hand and she rubbed his head. "Good boy. You don't like him either, do you?" He licked her hand again.

Fionn came in and looked at her strained face. "Are you all right, Ellen? What did he want?" he asked, pulling up a stool near her.

"I think someone has told him about me, or at least hinted at it. He was warning me, Fionn. Either that or he suspects I make my living in a very different way! Did you see the way he looked at you? The cheek of the man! And I can't tell him the truth about what I do to straighten him out. How dare he insult you and me like that!"

"You'll have to be extra careful, Ellen. I can't say that I like him at all."

"What am I supposed to do? Stop healing?"

He placed a rough, calloused hand gently on top of hers, his eyes intense with concern.

"Of course not, but work only with those you trust and keep a watchful eye out. You don't want him witnessing it with his own eyes. He wouldn't think twice before making an example of you, I'm sure."

"I know. I'm so glad you were here, Fionn. Thank you." Suddenly she smirked at him. "Mind you, the hammer was a bit much, don't you think?"

He laughed and, rising from the stool, patted her shoulder. "I was just pretending to be tough!"

"Let me get the fire started, "she said, "and we'll have a cup of tea when you're finished outside."

When he had gone back to the shed, Ellen put her hand on the mantelpiece which was at eye level and rested her head on her arm. It saddened her that her gift was not trusted by some in the church. Wasn't Jesus a healer himself? And didn't she know she was just an instrument of the Divine, nothing more – a vessel, as her grandmother had told her when she first discovered what she could do.

She let her mind go back ...

Chapter 15

Ellen had just turned ten when one morning in spring she and her mother, Kate, and younger sister, Annie, were returning home from the village.

Along the way, a rustling in the ditch drew Ellen's attention. Moving closer she saw that a rabbit was trying to push through the briars but was hampered by an injured leg, which it was dragging behind it.

A wave of compassion washed over Ellen, urging her towards the small animal.

Kneeling beside it, a great heat came into her hands and instinctively she reached out and laid them on the rabbit's leg. She didn't notice that Annie had come to kneel beside her or that her mother had said her name. After a minute the rabbit's leg twitched, Ellen removed her hands and the rabbit bounded off.

She sat back on her haunches, not sure what had just happened, but very much aware of a great contentment welling up inside her.

"Ellen!"

Her mother's voice eventually registered with her and she didn't sound very happy. Ellen looked over her shoulder at her.

"Why did you let it go? It would have made a lovely stew," she scolded.

Ellen got slowly to her feet and turned around to look up at her.

"It was hurt and I had to help it."

"What?" Kate frowned, looking intently at her.

"I – I think I fixed it. I mean, my hands got very warm and I put them on its leg and I just knew I was making it better. How did I do that, Mammy?"

"Jesus, Mary and Joseph," Kate whispered and crossed herself, looking a little frightened. She grabbed Ellen and pulled her into a hard embrace, rocking her from side to side.

"What is it, Mammy? What's wrong?"

"Nothing, my pet, nothing. We have to get home – Granny will be wondering what's keeping us. We'll talk there." Taking each child by the hand, she walked them briskly down the road.

Both Kate and Ellen were silent, each consumed with their own thoughts. Annie, only eight, chattered away, oblivious of the lack of response from the other two.

When they got to the cottage Ellen and Annie ran ahead and pushed open the half door. Their granny, Nora, was sitting by the fire and opened her arms.

They ran into them and were enveloped in her hug.

Kate watched while hanging her shawl on a hook inside the door and then taking down an apron to tie around her waist.

"Any news from the village?" Nora asked her, releasing the girls.

"Not a lot," Kate replied, before addressing Ellen. "Daddy's below on the strand, Ellen, cleaning his nets. Take Annie and go down to him for a while."

Ellen saw her granny's eyes dart towards her mother.

"What is it?" Granny asked her.

She didn't reply. "Off you go, Ellen."

Kate smiled at her, but Ellen could still see something strange in her eyes.

"There's a good girl. I'll call you back in when we're done."

She longed to listen in to the conversation outside the half door, but would have been murdered if she was caught, so she did as she was told. Annie raced off towards their father, while Ellen wandered down at a slower pace, trying to make sense of what had happened with the rabbit. Nothing like that had ever happened before and she didn't understand it.

Before long her mother came to the door and called her. Annie stayed with their father. When she got inside, her mother was sitting down opposite her granny at the fireplace and a stool was drawn up near them.

"Sit down, pet – we need to talk to you," Kate said.

She and Nora looked very serious.

Ellen sat down.

Nora cleared her throat and pulled her shawl tighter around her.

"Ellen, your mother told me what happened this morning with the rabbit. Do you know what this means?"

Ellen shook her head, looking up at her.

"I have a special gift," her granny said. "My mother had it and her mother before her. I had no daughters of my own so I thought it ended with me. Your father doesn't have it."

"What is it, Granny?" Ellen could feel her eyes widen as if to help her absorb more easily what her grandmother was saying.

"You come from a long line of healers, Ellen."

Ellen looked from one to the other, then back to her granny again. "Healers?"

"A healer is someone who can make other people, or animals, better,"

"So I did make the rabbit better?'

"Yes, child."

Ellen frowned. It all seemed very strange to her. She looked at her mother.

"Did you know Granny could make people better?"

Kate nodded. "Your father told me all about it when we first met. Your granny is a very special person, Ellen, as are you."

Granny spoke again. "You are the vessel, Ellen Cassidy. God does the healing, but it flows through you. That's what happened today. Usually you ask God to help but today your compassion for the rabbit was enough to invoke help without you needing to ask. But you will learn how to invoke the power of the Divine in time."

"So do you fix rabbits too, Granny?"

"Not anymore, child." She turned her wrinkled face towards the fire.

Ellen thought her grandmother looked very sad all of a sudden.

Nora gave a shuddering sigh before looking back at Ellen. "Like you, I have the gift –" She stopped and gave a bitter laugh. "Or curse

– it depends on how you look at it."

"Nora!" Kate warned her mother-in-law.

A look Ellen didn't understand passed between the two women. Her granny sighed again before continuing.

"Yes, the gift can be a wonderful thing. I'm fifty-eight years old now and I don't heal anyone any more. But I helped many sick people and animals from when I was about twelve years old until I was twenty-nine. It was wonderful but frightening too. People are afraid of things they don't understand, Ellen, and sometimes they don't treat people who are different very well."

"Nora!" Again Kate's warning voice cut across her.

"No, Kate!" the old woman said firmly. "If Ellen has the gift she needs to know that she has to use it carefully and wisely. People haven't changed all that much since I was young. She needs to protect herself."

She leant forward and took one of Ellen's hands in her own.

"Ellen, you must remember that your gift comes from God. Some people will understand this and appreciate it. Others, the closed-minded, will think you are dealing in the Devil's work."

Ellen, in fright, tried to pull her hands away.

But her grandmother held on tightly, forcing her to keep eye contact. "It is not the Devil's work and you must never think that. It's a beautiful gift and you are special because you were chosen to have it."

Ellen could feel their hands warming up and she looked down at them. They seemed to glow, but she wasn't sure if it was just a trick of the firelight.

She felt deeply connected to her grandmother and looked back up into her eyes.

The fear drifted away as heat passed up her arms and over her whole body until she felt strong and peaceful all at once.

"Granny, you still have the gift, haven't you?" Ellen said in awe.

"Yes, child."

"But you said you stopped using it. Why?"

Releasing her hands gently, Nora sat back in her chair and began to rock backwards and forwards, gazing into the fire.

"You can have the gift but decide not use it. That's our choice. I tried to use my gift as best I could. I liked to help people, even though it had to be done in secret. But then – the famine came in forty-five. The potatoes failed year after year. There wasn't enough food." Her fists clenched in her lap. "I tried to help people at the start, but children were dying everywhere and I couldn't stop it." Her voice cracked. "Then their parents were dying too."

"No healer could stop starvation," Kate said gently to her mother-in-law.

"I know that now, but then I was overwhelmed. The potato crop failed three years in a row. First it was starvation that took so many lives. Then the arrival of Indian corn from America helped a little as did the soup kitchens, but by then disease was everywhere – the yellow fever, black fever and many other sicknesses. I couldn't help anyone and your grandfather and I had to try to keep ourselves and our son, your father, alive with the few fish your granddad was able to catch. I know a lot of people from all over the country emigrated to America, but not many from around here – they couldn't afford the fare. Cousins of mine from Skibbereen and all their children were lost – whole families! They were all buried together in the famine pits in Abbeystrowry graveyard over there. They say thousands were buried in that one graveyard. Out here nearly every fisherman on the peninsula had to pawn their nets in an effort to pay their rents and sure then they weren't able to fish at all! Without fish, they had nothing. Some made it to the poorhouse but so many didn't. Oh, it was a terrible, terrible time."

"Did Granddad have to pawn his nets too?" Ellen asked.

"No."

"Why not?"

A light came into her granny's eyes. "A few years before the crops started to fail I had healed the son of our landlord. He was only two or three and his mother had brought him to the beach to look at the waves while her husband went around the nearby farms collecting rent. The child was playing near the rocks when suddenly he fell down onto the wet sand and had trouble breathing. His mother lifted him up and called out for help. I was collecting seaweed nearby and ran over to them. The little boy was turning blue when I got to them. I put my hands on his chest and it was as if I could see right into his lungs. I knew they were swollen and blocked up, and he was making a wheezing sound. I put him across my knees and moved my hands over his back. He began to cough and spit out a lot of stuff onto the sand. This went on for a while, until he was taking clear, healthy breaths again. The whole time his mother was kneeling on the sand beside us, crying quietly. I passed the little boy back to her and she cradled him, sobbing out her thanks. After a while she said: 'You're the healer that I've heard rumours about, aren't you?' I was terrified. She was married to a rich and powerful man, our landlord, and he could have thrown me into prison, or worse, if he wanted to. But she saw my fear. 'Your secret is safe with me,' she said. 'I will tell my husband how you helped Eugene to breathe again. And I will ask him to reward you. Although how I can put a price on the life of our son I cannot imagine.' She kissed the top of her child's head. 'Where do you live?' she asked. I pointed to this cottage. She nodded. 'I shall think of something to show you my gratitude. What's your name?' 'Nora Cassidy,' I replied. We walked to the top of the strand together and talked for a while, then I said goodbye and slipped away.

"A week later your granddad and I had just sat down to supper when we heard a horse approaching. Tom, your granddad, got to his feet but before he could reach the door there was a loud knock. He opened it. The landlord, Mr. Berkley, and one of his men were standing outside. I froze with fear. 'Good evening,' he said. 'I am James Berkley and I wonder if I could speak to you and your wife, Nora Cassidy, for a moment.' Tom and I were amazed at his courteous greeting and request. 'You're welcome. Please come in, Mr. Berkley,' Tom said. I remained standing behind the table.

"Mr. Berkley removed his hat, then came and extended his hand to me. 'My wife told me that you saved the life of our son. You have our eternal gratitude.' I shook his hand then withdrew it quickly, still nervous. He continued, 'We want to show our appreciation.' He beckoned his man forward and took a document he held out to him. He spread it on the table in front of us. 'This is the deed to your cottage. When you sign this you will cease to be my tenants and you will be the owners of this cottage and holding.'

"Well, I couldn't believe it. Tom and I looked at each other in amazement. We didn't know what to say and tripped over our tongues thanking him. I had been taught to read by my mother who was the daughter of a schoolteacher and I looked carefully at the document. Though I didn't understand some of the words, I saw that it said that I was to be the owner of the cottage and surrounding piece of land. But it was in my name not Tom's. 'Shouldn't it have the name of the man of the house on it?' I asked. 'It is you we are indebted to,' he said, 'so it is our wish that the cottage is in your name.' He handed me his fountain pen and asked me to sign it. Still amazed at our good fortune, I carefully wrote my name on it. He and his man then signed their names. 'Now the cottage is yours,' he said. Then bidding us goodnight, they left. I ran after him and asked him to thank his wife for us too. He touched his hat and climbed up on his horse. They rode away and I ran back into the house where Tom and I laughed and cried and danced a jig around the kitchen."

Ellen stared at her granny who was still smiling at the memory of that night. She cocked her head. "But what did that have to do with Granddad not pawning his nets?"

Nora eyes clouded again as her thoughts returned to the grimness of those years. "You see, we didn't have to come up with the money for rent every month like everyone else," she explained. "We were able to survive on the fish, and seaweed and some vegetables that I was able to grow." She sobered again. "We did what we could for our neighbours but it wasn't enough. Another thing was that we were out of the way down here and that meant that people from Ballinmara were too weak to come to us and we were spared from fever and sickness being brought to the house. One day I ventured to the top of the field and saw some poor souls leaving for Bantry." A shiver passed over her. "They were like walking ghosts. Some had only undergarments on – they'd had to pawn the shirts off their backs for some money for food. My heart broke for them. I heard after how so many of them had frozen to death while working on the relief roads for a few pennies." Nora stared into the fire again, her face creased with grief.

After a few moments she shook herself and startled Ellen when she sat forward suddenly.

"But that is all in the past and too painful to dwell on. Now you can heal others as the Cassidys were meant to. You can continue where I left off. I must teach you all I know so that you can do good where you can. You'll start to grow your own herbs and you'll harvest the riches of the sea by collecting the different seaweeds. The healing gift will live on in you, Ellen, my little one. You will bring blessings on so many people."

Ellen's head was full of the vivid images her grandmother had painted of those terrible famine years and sympathy for those suffering people made her heart hurt. Her desire to help and heal people and animals stirred strongly inside her and, meeting her granny's eyes steadily, she smiled her consent and willingness. The old woman nodded her head in approval.

Ellen brought her mind back to the present and, arranging some kindling in the grate, she set it alight, then built a pile of turf up around it. She took out the bucket of ashes and fetched some water from the stream. She promised herself that the next time she was in Skibbereen she would visit Abbeystrowry graveyard and pay her respects to her deceased ancestors. She hadn't been for a while. Her grandmother would have been pleased with the plaque the people of Skibbereen had erected in recent years to remember those who were buried there as a result of the famine. Now they would not be forgotten.

She hadn't thought about the famine very much because very few people spoke of it, despite it not even being quite fifty years earlier. The wound of it was still too raw. Her grandmother had certainly never mentioned it in her presence except that one time.

With her jobs done, Ellen took some dried sage and bound the stems together. She touched it to the fire and let it take light. Then, blowing out the flames, she let it smoulder. This was one of the first things her grandmother had taught her back then. She took the smouldering herb around to the corners of the each room and asked that the house be cleansed of any bad feelings or intentions that Father O'Riordan had left behind. When she was happy with the atmosphere in her home again she placed the rest of the sage to smoulder out in a bowl on the table. She suddenly thought that it would have made more sense if her grandmother had given her a warning about Father O'Riordan instead of Blake. The priest was the one she felt the danger from, not Blake.

A while later, when Fionn came back in, the fire was going strong and the kettle was steaming. Ellen made the tea and they took it outside, to sit on the low wall, looking out to sea, without talking.

Eventually Ellen spoke, her voice soft.

"I'm nervous, Fionn. For the first time in my life I understand why my grandmother said healing could be a curse as well as a gift. Up to now the healing has mostly brought me joy – I know there have been some sad times when things were beyond my control, and that some people are put off me, but I've always been good at accepting that. And I know I've had to be cautious, because people don't always understand it, but now it's different. This Father O'Riordan –" She paused. "I got a bad feeling the moment I saw him. I think we all did. I think he's threatened by me, and threatened people are sometimes fearful people and like a cornered rat can strike out and bite. Father Goggin was a gentle soul and I knew he meant me no harm, and he knew I was no threat to him or the church. I wish he was still our parish priest." She sighed. "How am I supposed to be content, if I'm constantly looking over my shoulder?"

Fionn's thumbnail worried a callous on the palm of his hand. "Keep going to Mass, give him no cause for concern. You can call on me any time if he gives you any more trouble."

"You're a good friend, Fionn."

For the first time since she lived alone, Ellen felt the remoteness of her little cottage and felt her sanctuary had been violated by the priest's presence.

Shep came up and sat beside her, putting his head in her lap.

"Lucky for you that you have the dog now," Fionn said with a reassuring smile.

Ellen bent and hugged Shep tightly. "I knew he was a blessing!"

"Come on!" Fionn tossed the dregs of his tea onto the grass. "I'll show you what I've done with the shed."

Ellen was pleased with the repairs and insisted he take, as payment, a pair of socks she had just finished knitting. After Fionn gathered his tools together, she walked as far as the village with him because she wanted to see Annie.

The day was equally fine in Bantry. Blake was attending a horse fair on the edge of the town in the hopes of procuring another work horse for the estate as they were heading into the busy harvesting months.

The fair was crowded and there was the usual current of excitement as deals were struck. Blake had brought O'Brien with him and together they assessed the animals on display.

Eventually they both agreed on a grey mare and Blake bid for it. He succeeded in acquiring the animal and asked O'Brien to take her back to the estate. He stayed on to view some foals.

The air was ripe with the smell of horseflesh and manure, so when a waft of roses drifted across his nose, Blake whipped his head around, his heart beating a little faster. He was sure for a moment that Ellen must be near him. But he could not see a flash of red hair or her radiant face among the crowd. Still he moved along looking out for her. Within moments a peasant woman ahead of him turned around and proffered a basket of roses, asking if he wanted to buy any.

The scent again filled his nostrils and his disappointment was acute at discovering its source.

Turning on his heel, he walked away, but the longing to see Ellen was overwhelming. He reasoned with himself that he had set things in motion with Felicity Hannon and he would accept the invitation to visit Skibbereen when it arrived, but for now he was still a free man and if he chose to spend some time in Ellen's company then what harm could there be in stealing a few more kisses?

She kissed me back before pushing me away, he reminded himself. Perhaps her resistance wouldn't remain as firm next time.

Chapter 16

Ellen went up to the salting rocks, up in the hills behind the village. She knew she would find Annie there as she was pretty sure the fishermen would have taken advantage of the calmer seas and have already been back in with one load of fish.

Sure enough Annie was there with a group of other women. On the back of a cart they had baskets of fish, which they had already gutted and cleaned down at the harbour. They were now salting them and arranging them on the large flat rocks for drying. Other baskets of fresh fish would already be on their way to the markets. As Ellen approached she could hear plenty of laughter. The women were in good spirits, relieved at the good weather and having their men able to fish again.

So Ellen was surprised to find Annie looking worried as she worked at a salting rock at the end of the line.

"Hello, Annie," Ellen said, looking closely at her.

"Hello," she replied with an attempt at a smile, which she didn't quite pull off.

Ellen frowned at her pale face. "Everything all right?"

Annie dragged a basket off the back of the cart. Ellen helped her tip the contents onto the rock and waited.

Annie brushed a stray hair from her forehead with the back of her wrist and grimaced at Ellen. "The new landlord has put up the rent.

We were only able to pay half yesterday but he wants the second half next week. Then all next month's in one payment again."

"Oh."

"I'm sure it'll be fine," she rushed on, giving Ellen a falsely bright smile. "The weather is settling again. Sure today is a grand day, isn't it?"

"Annie?" Ellen prompted her, knowing there was more.

Annie's hands stilled in the work. "This new landlord is tough, Ellen. His men said he's giving one chance only to miss the rent, and after that it's eviction." She whispered the last word, hating having to say it.

"What? I thought that was just a rumour. Is the man crazy? He must know that fishermen can't always pay on time. For goodness sake, it's the nature of their business!"

"This Mr. Travers lives near Bantry, but they say his estate is inland – that all his tenants there are farmers not fishermen. He knows nothing of our ways, I'd say." She resumed the task of spreading the salted fish evenly over the rock. "I told Mick that he should get in some extra fishing, not just the fish we sell and salt for ourselves, but extra catches that we could salt and sell during the times he can't get to sea. We should be able to manage week to week, but the threat will always be hanging over us."

Ellen laid a hand on her shoulder. "Listen, Annie, I have put some money by. I can help you."

Annie shook her head. "Mick wouldn't hear of it. He's fiercely independent."

Ellen looked knowingly at her, guessing correctly that Mick wouldn't take *her* money. She let it go for now.

They took another basket off the cart and moved to another rock.

"We've had two bad storms already this summer, Annie. Hopefully that will be the end of it and the fishing will be good from now on."

Annie nodded and changed the subject. "Have you any news? It must've been a long week for you in the rain?"

Ellen told her about Fionn's visit that morning but refrained from telling her about the priest as she knew it would only worry her.

Nor did she tell Annie about Blake, even though she had met him twice now. After all, the warning had been about her and her kin and she couldn't bear to be the one responsible for bringing trouble on Annie by associating with Blake. The sooner he was forgotten the better for all of them.

The sisters passed a pleasant hour together and Ellen left before Mick was due back.

As she was leaving the village, she heard someone calling her name. Stopping and turning, she saw Sorcha and Eve catching up with her.

"Hello, Ellen," Sorcha said when they drew level with her. "We were just coming over to see you, like you asked. We're sorry we weren't over before, but the rain kept us at home this week."

"Hello, Sorcha, hello, Eve," she said. "We can walk and talk now if that suits you?"

Eve gave her a shy smile.

"That's grand," Sorcha replied, obviously the spokeswoman for the two of them.

They fell into step beside her.

"What did you want to talk to us about?" Sorcha inquired.

Ellen lifted her face to the warm breeze and thought for a moment before answering.

"Love."

Eve gasped.

"Love?" Sorcha repeated with a nervous laugh.

"You see," Ellen said softly, "I believe that when two souls are meant to be together, then meet, and intertwine in love, then it doesn't matter what bodies they are encased in."

The two women walked beside her, stunned into silence at the unexpectedness of her words.

"But, unfortunately, as you well know, not many think like this, which means you have to be very careful when you're together."

"How did you know?" It was Eve who spoke, her quiet voice shaking slightly, her eyes lowered to the road ahead of her.

"I saw you together at the spring pool," Ellen said, her voice without censure.

Both girls gasped this time, whipping their heads around to stare at her as blushes seared their cheeks.

"I know it's very rocky over there and people rarely walk there but, still, it could have been someone other than me who saw you, so you have to be more careful. The community will not accept you being together like this."

Eve started to cry.

"You're not going to tell on us, are you?" Sorcha asked.

"Of course not," Ellen reassured them. "You must continue to love each other. But I also fear that our new priest is looking for people to find fault with, so you have to be doubly careful."

"But what are we to do?" Eve beseeched her. "All we want is to be together. My parents want me to marry Denis O'Reilly from next door, but I could never be with a man. I love Sorcha!"

Ellen stopped and turned to look from one to the other. Though they were both around twenty, they seemed much younger than that.

"I don't know, but you must be careful for your own sakes."

They nodded and dejectedly turned back towards the village. Feeling helpless, she watched them go.

Chapter 17

During the following weeks, Ellen's days followed their usual pattern, helping the people and animals that needed her, tending to her bees, hens and garden and going to market days to sell her knitting and honey. But she was cautious and therefore asked all the people who came not to tell the priest about the healing.

Though she was busy, Blake was always there on the edge of her thoughts and despite her better judgement she wished she could see him again. She reread *Gulliver's Travels* just because he had spoken of it.

It was when she was swimming in the sea that she thought of him most, knowing it had carried him to her that first day, and as she floated in its crystal-clear waters she imagined being cradled in his arms as the sea cradled her now. She thought his memory would fade with the passing of each day, but instead it grew stronger. She had felt the connection between them and, just as in the case of Sorcha and Eve, she felt that her soul and Blake's had somehow become entwined despite her sending him away twice.

She had fallen in love with him, but because it was not possible from them to be together, she would have to hold his memory in that secret part of her heart, trying not to yearn for him too much. As she went about her days she tried to accept her fate and give thanks for the short time they had had together.

The weather remained lovely and she swam every day when the

tide came in over the hot sand, making the water silky warm on her skin. She always had the beach to herself as everyone else tended to go to the long strand just beyond the village.

On the Wednesday of the second week after Blake's visit, Ellen was walking restlessly around the cottage early in the morning. She knew she should be knitting – she didn't even have enough to make it worth her while to go to the market in Schull that week – but still she couldn't settle to it. She pulled down her beekeeping book but even that couldn't hold her interest.

Closing it with a snap, she returned it to the shelf and her eyes fell on the play, *Hamlet* by Shakespeare, which she had bought at the market a few weeks earlier. She had struggled to read it but had not liked it at all. She smiled suddenly. Father Goggin would probably like to have it, if he didn't already have a copy, and she hadn't visited him since he moved from Ballinamara to Bantry over a month ago. This would be as good a time as any to make the trip to see him. It would take her nearly three hours with the donkey and cart but she would get there sooner if she borrowed the pony and trap from Andy Minehane in the pubic house.

And she told herself that if she happened to see Blake while she was in Bantry that wouldn't be her fault.

In the village she was delighted to find that Andy didn't need the pony and trap for the day and that she was welcome to it.

"Give Father Goggin my best!" he called after her as she drove the trap away.

As she drove through the square in Bantry a couple of hours later, she turned her head this way and that, looking at those on horseback or walking, in case Blake was among them. But she didn't see him. Even though she knew it was for the best a small sigh of disappointment slipped through her lips.

She continued on to the Parish House and, tethering the pony to the railings, she advanced to the door.

Father Goggin himself opened to her knock and his face lit up when he saw her standing there.

"Ellen Cassidy! What a lovely surprise! Come in, come in. How are all my flock down in Ballinmara?"

"Missing you," Ellen said, stepping in and following him as he led her to the kitchen. She smiled, pleased he hadn't shown her into a formal front parlour or dining room. She couldn't help comparing this lovely gentle man, in his late forties, with his taciturn replacement in Ballinmara.

A fire glowed in the hearth and he ushered her into a seat. "You timed it perfectly I'm just sitting down to an early lunch. It's only cold meats because it's my housekeeper's day off. But there's plenty there as you can see – so you'll join me, of course."

"Yes, thank you."

He set another place at the table and, taking the seat opposite her, put some cold ham and tongue on her plate. He told her to help herself to the soda bread.

"How are you getting on here?" she asked, loosening her shawl and picking up her fork.

"I'm finding my way, although there are so many new faces and names. But I'm managing." He smiled warmly at her as he poured her some tea.

"How are you?" he asked, returning the pot to the hearth to keep warm.

"I'm very well."

"And Annie, Mick and the children?"

"All doing fine."

"And eh, how are you getting on with Father O'Riordan?" He looked at her shrewdly over the rim of his cup.

"He's not as – eh – understanding as you."

"Oh."

"He has left me in no doubt that he's keeping an eye on me."

"It doesn't surprise me. Everything is very black and white with him. He strikes me as being a bit fervent in his doctrine. Your gift would not be an easy pill for him to swallow."

"I'll be careful. I've asked those who come to me not to talk to him about me and what I do. And if he asks me about it I'll try to explain it to him as best I can and hope he understands."

Father Goggin nodded. "If he gives you any trouble, you must tell me, Ellen, and I'll see what I can do to help. But just be careful."

"I will, thank you," she said, touched by his genuine concern.

"I know you're not that far away but I just haven't had the time to get down there yet. I'm kept busy here and I have to go to Skibbereen regularly as I'm one of the advisors to the Bishop. On my days off I go northwards beyond Ballylickey to visit my ageing aunt."

"I wanted to give you some time to settle in here before I visited."

He nodded his understanding. "Now tell me all the news of my old parishioners!"

Ellen filled him in on all she knew of the lives of those in Ballinmara, and he told her a little about his new life there in Bantry.

When she was finished eating, she reached into her basket and pulled out the book she had brought with her.

"Do you have a copy of this?" she asked.

"No, and I'd love to read it again." He turned it over in his hands. "Did you like it?" He sounded surprised at her choice.

She laughed. "No! It was too much for me. I couldn't get very far into it, I'm afraid."

"Well, I have something you might like to borrow. Let me get it."

He left and returned a few moments later. "It a book of poetry by William Wordsworth. Very beautiful."

"Thank you, Father. I'll return it on the next market day I'm in town."

"Oh, my dear, keep it for the rest of the summer. Dip in and out of it. Poetry is to be savoured, not rushed."

She beamed at him, so glad she had followed her impulse to visit him. She hadn't realised how much she had missed him and their conversations.

When their tea was finished, Father Goggin shook her hand warmly and showed her out. "Give my regards to all in Ballinmara," he said.

With a smile Ellen returned to the pony and trap and drove back through Bantry. Although she didn't see Blake this time either, nothing could dampen her warm mood after spending time with Father Goggin.

She was back in Ballinmara by late afternoon, and returned the pony and trap to Andy. As she strolled through the fields to her cottage she was glad she had gone out for the day as the break in routine had been good. She looked forward to reading the borrowed book that evening and reflected on the fact that not seeing Blake that day was the way it should be. But as she rounded the bottom of the hill and the beach came into view, the image of him lying there that first morning filled her head again. A fatalistic sigh escaped her, knowing that some madness in her longed to see him again despite fearing the danger it could bring.

She was glad of the distraction when Shep came bounding towards her to welcome her home.

Chapter 18

Blake had a lot of work to catch up on after the bad weather, but each day began and ended with thoughts of Ellen. It was another two weeks before he was able to find the time to leave the estate to go to see her. It was Friday morning of the second week and he got up with a light heart and a stomach churning with anticipation. He worked fast so that he could leave early in the afternoon.

This time he had no trouble finding his way and turned into the field above Ellen's at the end of the afternoon. There was no wind and it was warm. The sea sparkled silver and blue ahead of him, and wispy clouds barely tickled the sky.

Impatient now to see her, he urged his horse into a canter, only slowing as her cottage came into view.

Dismounting quickly, he remembered that she had been on the beach on his last visit so he looked there first this time.

Shep lay near the water's edge. In the sea beyond him, Blake saw the sun glint off red hair, as a sleek head and shoulders surfaced. Ellen doubled over and dived back in, her cloth-covered rear-end surfacing briefly before also disappearing under the water. Blake strode down the beach, squaring his shoulders determinedly as he remembered her cool reception and dismissal on his previous visit.

Shep got up and came to meet him, his tail wagging.

Oblivious to Blake's approach, Ellen dived under again and did several strokes before returning to the surface. Allowing the water to pull her hair back from her face, she stood up. Up to her waist in water, her eyes closed, she raised her arms and smoothed her hands back over her face. The movement made the white under-slip she was wearing cling to her. As she opened her eyes she saw Blake walking down the beach. Joy at seeing him rushed through her.

She stood motionless. "I can't fight him, or my own needs anymore," she murmured, the pent-up longing for him making her tremble. She wasn't sure if she was talking to herself, her grandmother or Fate, but all she knew was that she wanted to love him.

He stopped at the water's edge and their eyes locked. His beseeched hers to welcome him. Her lips parted and then curved into a smile that set his heart pounding.

She had been correct to dismiss his suggestion that simple conversation and friendship was possible between them. It wasn't, nor would it ever be, enough. He wanted more. He wanted her. He wanted to love her as a woman like her deserved to be loved – passionately, tenderly, and completely.

Pulling off his shirt he tossed it onto the sand, followed swiftly by his boots and trousers. The sun lit the muscles of his arms and shoulders. In just his undergarment, he took a few swift strides until the water was up to his thighs then he dived in and surfaced in front of her, water surging off his head and shoulders.

"I had to come back," he said, water sparking on his eyelashes.

She nodded.

It was all the permission he required. He reached out and put his hands on her sides, pulling her towards him. Lowering his head, he hungrily took her lips with his own, tasting her and the saltwater all at once. His hands slid around to her back and crushed her against his bare chest as she matched his heated kisses with a burning passion of her own.

Pulling away to catch her breath, she rested her wet cheek against his and whispered in his ear.

"I think I knew you would come back to me, Blake. And while I tried to put you out of my head, I ached with the wanting of you."

A shuddering breath escaped him at her honesty, as his fingers tangled in her hair. He tugged gently so that she was forced to tilt her head back to look up at him again.

"I couldn't stop thinking about you," he murmured, his eyes roving over her face, her hair, her neck. He kissed the tip of her nose.

The tenderness of it nearly had her weeping.

Lifting her into his arms he carried her out of the water. He nearly stumbled when he saw how the wet material clung to her. She laughed – a soft, husky sound.

Blake stood her on the sand, a question burning in his eyes. In answer, she took his hand and led him up the beach and into the cottage. Shep lay down outside the front door.

Ellen continued into the bedroom, where she stopped beside the bed. Slowly Blake worked the material of her slip upwards with his fingers, until the hem was in his grasp. He tugged it up her wet body and off over her head.

She stood before him like a magnificent work of art. His heart pounded and he felt weak with need.

"Ellen," he said, moving her closer to the bed, wanting to lie with her immediately.

But she stepped away and took a towel from the shelf near the bed. She started to dry his skin with slow deliberate movements, moving it in circles over his stomach, chest and shoulders. Walking around behind him she repeated the movements on his back. His need heightened all the more as she made him pause and savour each touch.

Everything about her was slow and sensual, he thought, so he should have known this was how it would be too when she made love with him. He gave himself over to her.

She pushed down his undergarment and he obligingly stepped out of it, his back still to her. Putting her arms around him, she pressed her breasts against his back and her stomach against his buttocks, wanting to explore every inch of him. He moaned. Still pressed to him she slid around his side and up against the front of him. The evidence of his arousal pressed against her stomach and made her gasp. She looked down, then quickly raised wide eyes to his. He kissed her lips softly. She kissed him back, her breath uneven and quickening.

Taking the towel from her, he dried her skin, copying her slow movements, enjoying the discovery of each curve and hollow. When he was done, he lowered her onto the bed and, lying beside her, brushed little kisses all over her face. Equally slowly, he moved his lips down over her neck and breasts.

Ellen sighed with pleasure. When his mouth captured a nipple, she arched up in need as new sensations rippled through her, making her ache even more for him. He moved to the other breast, tasting the sensitive skin with the tip of his tongue. She gasped at the delicious sensation, thrusting her hands into his hair, and all slowness now forgotten she spoke his name with a new urgency.

He lifted his head. "Are you sure that this is what you want, Ellen?" he asked, searching her eyes intently.

"Yes," she breathed.

He lay on top of her, holding her gaze, and she opened for him, tensing at the initial resistance and dart of pain, then arching again as he eased inside her. She saw his eyes drift closed with pleasure, before her own drifted shut in wonder, for nothing had ever felt so perfect, so complete.

"Ellen." Her name was like a prayer on his lips.

He began moving rhythmically inside her. The pleasure of it had her repeating his name over and over. The speed of their movements increased and she cried out his name as they soared together, exploding into a million sensations, before floating down in the safety of each other's arms.

"My beautiful, beautiful Ellen," he murmured over and over as he touched tiny kisses on her earlobe and neck.

She kissed his shoulder, inhaling his scent as she caressed his back slowly, feeling lazy and replete.

Blake rolled onto his side and gathered her close. "Are you all right?" he asked tenderly.

She looked up at him with shining eyes. "I've never felt so wonderful," she replied, watching a smile light his eyes.

Blake made a sound of satisfaction and hugged her close again as their hearts settled.

A few minutes later Ellen moved in his arms.

"Your clothes," she said. "They're still on the beach. They're safe from the tide, because it's on the way out, but I still think you should go and gather them up."

He laughed and nuzzled her neck. "I forgot all about them, and it's no wonder," he said, his fingers caressing the side of her breast.

Batting his hand away, she gave him a nudge. "Go on, Blake. What if someone comes by?"

Rising from the bed, he reached for his undergarment and hissed in a breath as the cold damp material came in contact with his skin.

Ellen laughed at him and stretched.

"Stretch like that again and the damn clothes can stay on the beach," Blake warned.

She pulled a blanket over herself. "Go," she ordered, grinning.

He laughed. "I'll be back, woman. Don't move!"

Chapter 19

While he was gone, Ellen lay with an arm thrown above her head, marvelling at what had just happened between them. She didn't regret what they'd done. She knew that he couldn't take her as his wife and, if she was to spend the rest of her life without him, at least she would have this to remember and treasure. He had somehow worked his way into her heart on that very first morning and she would not deny herself the loving he could give her for now. And, she would never think it wrong.

Thinking of her grandmother's warning though, she shivered, but she knew now that it was too late. If it did prove to be prophetic, then she would just have to see what happened. Or by some miracle, the vision might have been wrong. If she had to save him again that first day she would, and, she reasoned, she had tried to keep him away. But when she had seen him on the beach earlier she just knew that she could no longer fight the inevitable. It had been a relief to let her feelings show and to act on them, to take what she could of his affection before he came to his senses.

She could hear him outside talking to his horse as he removed the saddle. She heard him walking the horse away and presumed he was putting him into the field behind the cottage, where the donkey was. That meant he intended to stay another while. Relief washed over her and she realised she was longing for him to return to her so that they could make love again.

And that's how he found her, blushing slightly at the strength of her desire for him. As though reading her mind, his eyes danced with laughter as he dropped the clothes and boots he'd collected from the beach, stripped off and climbed in beside her.

They made love again, discovering and exploring each other at their leisure. When they reached the point where their passion could no longer be held in check, it was even more exquisite than the first time and, as Ellen gasped out Blake's name, she knew joy like never before.

Blake collapsed on her for a moment and then shifted his weight so she could breathe properly.

"Ellen, you are a wonder,' he said, his voice sleepy beside her ear.

She felt his body relax and his breathing settle. He fell asleep and, as she watched him, she traced her finger over his forehead and eyebrows, then down his nose and over his firm lips. Then resting her head on his shoulder, she laid her palm on the soft hairs of his chest, watching it rise and fall.

He woke again within minutes and tightened his arms around her.

"Can I stay with you tonight?"

Her lips curved against his skin. "Yes," she whispered, rising up on her elbow to look down into his eyes.

Her hair fell onto his chest and he lifted a hand to brush it back over her ear. The rays from the evening sun were coming through the window and turned the red strands to gold.

"God, you are lovely," he said.

Leaning forward she kissed him, trying to tell him without words how she felt. His hand moved to the back of her head and he pressed gently, keeping her lips against his for a long moment. Releasing her, he sighed and smiled. She searched his eyes which seemed full of words he wasn't saying.

After dropping one last kiss on his lips, she threw back the blanket and got up. Her skin seemed to glow and she was sorry she had to cover it up. She left her feet bare. "I'll make us some supper. Are you hungry?"

"Ravenous!"

"All right then – get up and fetch me some water from the stream, please. It's just beyond the shed."

"Yes, ma'am," he said but, instead of getting up, he reached for her hand and pulled her back so that she sat on the edge of the bed.

"And after we eat, we'll go for a walk, and we'll talk. I want to do so much with you, Ellen."

His earnest face and smouldering eyes filled her with joy.

She nodded. "I'd like that. Today is the summer solstice and I thought I would be celebrating it alone but now we can dance together at the setting of the sun and celebrate it together."

They were just dressed, albeit without undergarments for Blake, when Shep started barking. They heard a cart approaching.

"Wait here," Ellen instructed. "I'll go and see who it is and send them on their way."

A donkey and cart was outside with her neighbour Séamus driving it and beside him his wife, Síle. A child was bundled in her arms and Ellen could see she was very agitated. Séamus jumped down.

"Ellen, it's Úna. Please, can you help her?"

Ellen glanced back at the door.

Blake, hearing what Séamus had said, came out and stood beside her.

"Ellen, what's the matter?" he asked.

Síle and Séamus looked startled at his sudden appearance.

Heart racing, Ellen looked from him to the child, then back to him. If she helped the child he would know about her healing and she didn't know what outcome that would have. She could possibly lose him and bring danger to herself. It felt as though her heart was being torn in two.

But she didn't really have a choice. Without answering Blake, she turned to Séamus. "Bring her into the house, quickly."

Séamus took the girl from Síle's arms and carried her swiftly into the cottage, Ellen and Síle on his heels.

Ellen was aware of Blake coming in too, but he stood in the corner, out of the way.

"Put her on the table," she instructed, whipping off her shawl and putting it down as a pillow for the girl's head.

Úna's eyes darted about and she whimpered as her father held her hands down, trying to stop her from scratching the huge blisters that covered her arms. Her heels rapped loudly off the wooden table. Síle removed her shawl too and placed it under Úna's heels. The noise quietened to dull thudding.

"What's wrong with her?" her mother beseeched Ellen. "Is it the pox?" Her voice shook.

Ellen shook her head, her hand on Úna's forehead. "No, she doesn't have a fever."

She looked closely at the blisters.

"Did she eat anything out of the ordinary?"

Síle shook her head but then said, "She went picking wild strawberries with the older ones this afternoon. But she has eaten them lots of times before and nothing like this has happened to her. Do you think she might have eaten something poisonous?" Her eyes were wide with fear as she looked down on her child.

Ellen placed her hands on Úna's stomach, leaving them there for several moments. "No, her stomach is fine," she said with relief. She studied the blisters on Úna's arms. "This has come from the outside. It looks like a reaction to that plant – the giant hogweed. When she was picking the strawberries her arms must have rubbed off some of the leaves. It's nasty, but it's not serious."

"Oh thank God and his Merciful Mother!" Síle gasped.

"What's giant hogweed?" Séamus asked.

"It's a new plant that some of the big houses have brought in for their gardens. Fionn told me about it. He's seen it and how the seeds have blown into nearby fields where it then grows wild. It looks like our own cow parsley but much bigger. But there's something nasty in it that can do this to the skin. There must be some of it on your land, Séamus. You should root it out as soon as you can."

Séamus nodded. "Can you fix her arms, do you think?"

"I'll certainly do my best. They need to be soothed and covered up." She thought for a moment. "I'll need some watercress." She looked over at Blake.

He stepped forward from the shadows. To her relief his face didn't display disgust or anger.

Reaching for a bowl, she handed it to him. "There's some growing on the edge of the stream," she said. "Gather up enough to fill this, please. I'll get a cabbage from the garden."

Ellen noticed that Síle and Séamus looked after Blake wonderingly as he left, no doubt noting his fine clothing. But she had no time to worry now about what they might think. She went to get the cabbage.

A couple of minutes later she and Blake were both back in the kitchen. Glancing at the watercress, she nodded in approval. She handed him a large round stone.

"Press the cress until the juices are released," she said.

She peeled several leaves off the head of cabbage, then washed and dried them. Then, going to the basket by the rocking chair, she took out a ball of wool and cut several lengths off it.

First she bathed Úna's arms to remove any poison that might still be on the surface of the skin, then, when the cress was mashed up, she scooped up some of the soggy mess into a leaf of cabbage, and spooned more of the cress juice over it. Blake watched her closely. Going to the table, she wrapped the leaf around Úna's lower arm, asking Séamus to hold it in place while she bound it with layers of muslin from the dresser drawer, which she secured with strands of wool. She turned to fill another cabbage leaf, only to find that Blake had already done so and was holding it out to her. In that instant her love for him deepened. She gave him a grateful look before turning back to the child.

She repeated her actions with the upper arm and then the other arm, murmuring soothingly to Úna as she worked. "I know it's terribly itchy, pet, but this will take the itch away."

As she was applying the last leaf she spoke to Blake again. "Can you go out and pick four carrots, and wash them, please?"

He went out without a word, returning moments later to do as she had asked.

When all the leaves were in place and they began to soothe the skin, Úna's restlessness stilled.

"You're a great girl," Ellen said, smiling down at her. "Is that feeling better? I'm sure it was very itchy."

Úna nodded.

Ellen raised her eyes to Síle's. "Keep these on. I'll make up new ones and bring them over to you around noon and we'll change them then. Now, Úna, will you eat a raw carrot for me? The carrot will help your skin from the inside." She gave the little girl a big smile.

"Séamus, will you take Úna onto your lap?"

Séamus lifted the little girl from the table into his arms and sat down with her in the rocking chair. Ellen drew up a stool next to them and gave Úna a carrot to chew on. She obligingly ate it.

"You're the best little girl in all of West Cork," Ellen told her.

She smiled at Síle who was standing with her hand on Séamus's shoulder.

"Thank you so much, Ellen," Síle said, her voice cracked. "And I'm sorry for barging in here when you have company, but she was crying so hard and scratching. We got a fright, you see."

Ellen stood and put her hand on her arm. "I'm glad I could help. You know you can come here any time. Here, take the rest of the carrots with you and get her to eat them during the day."

The family got up to go and thanked Ellen again.

Síle looked over at Blake who had stepped back into the corner of the room. "Thank you too, sir," she said, giving him a shy smile.

Séamus gave him a polite nod before going out, Úna in his arms.

Ellen remained standing by the fireplace. Silence fell with the closing of the door. Outside they heard the cart rumble away.

She moved her eyes to his as he slowly crossed the room. Her heart began to thud hard, but she raised her chin defiantly as he stopped in front of her.

"You heal people? Why didn't you tell me?" he asked without anger. "You could tell by putting your hands on her stomach that she was all right, and you put your hands on my chest on the beach and somehow took away the cold and my aches too."

There wasn't awe or fear, just inquisitiveness, admiration and acceptance in his eyes. She sagged with relief and, reaching out, she took his hand in hers. She had been correct to think they could be equal.

"Not everyone approves of what I do. I didn't know how you would take it, but you aren't put off by it at all, are you?"

"Absolutely not. I don't see how anyone could disapprove of someone who helps others," he said with a puzzled frown.

"Sometimes it's a religious thing. Some think they can't even speak to me, as though I'm from a different world, while some people are threatened by it and see my gift as some kind of black art. But in fact I never work with anyone without first invoking God's help. Look!" With a smile, she pointed to the cross made of rushes over the door. "Have you seen one of those before? It's a St. Brigid's cross. Brigid is reputed to have been a healing woman too. I keep it there over the threshold to bless people as they come and go." She paused, then said his name. "Blake."

Her soft voice brought his eyes back to hers and he put his arms around her.

"I'm sorry I didn't tell you," she said, "but it was fear that kept me silent. I've had to be cautious all my life. I have to be careful about who knows about my gift."

"I understand."

"Thank you for the way you helped."

"It was my privilege," he said.

"You've earned your supper. Let's make a start."

Chapter 20

After hanging their wet garments by the fire, Blake brought in water from the stream and filled the kettle. As Ellen prepared the simple meal, she hummed a bright little tune, enjoying the simple pleasure of sharing the domestic chores with him.

"That song you're singing. It was from you I heard it before, wasn't it? It has been inside my head for weeks but I couldn't recall where I had heard it."

Ellen laughed softly. "I think I probably hummed it when I was taking you to Durrus. You must have heard it your sleep."

"I must have."

He came and stood behind her as she worked at the table, and slipped his arms around her waist, pressing his lips to the side of her neck. It caused tiny shivers to skim across her skin.

"I love the smell of you." He breathed in the scent of her hair. "Is it roses and lavender?"

Nodding, she leaned back against him, letting the back of her head rest on his shoulder, savouring the feel of his hard chest at her back and his arms around her.

Sitting opposite each other for the simple meal, they talked softly as the light changed outside. Ellen lit the candle on the table and she saw its flicker dance in his eyes. She learned that he managed an estate near Bantry and she told him about her healing work with people and animals and how she had discovered that she had the gift. He listened avidly.

Towards the end of the meal, he looked at her as he took a drink of ale.

"I'll bring some wine the next time," he said, putting it down.

Her eyes darted up to his and he held her gaze. Ellen swallowed what she had been chewing.

"I expect nothing of you, Blake. What you have given me here today has been wonderful, but it does not bind you to me in any way. You are free to do as you please."

His head tilted slightly and a frown drew his brows together as he considered her words.

"What I please is to come back to see you again very soon," he said, a hint of anger in his voice. "Don't tell me you thought you could send me on my merry way again, requesting that I don't return like the other two times, after today being so magnificent?"

She lowered her eyes, about to tell him how special the day had been for her too, but he rushed on.

"What kind of man do you think I am? Do you think that I came here for a bit of fun? Just to satisfy my curiosity, or my lust? I don't know if you are insulting me or yourself?" His temper rose because, if she did believe that, he knew she was correct. He had come here today to take what he could before moving on to a more 'suitable' future. He was disgusted at himself. How could he tell her all he had felt in the previous hours and still not be offering her anything?

She looked up into his angry eyes. "Blake, I want to see you again. All I meant was that I expect no commitment from you."

He continued to frown at her, the hurt her words caused surprising him. "That's all right then, because I cannot offer you any," he said harshly, trying to ignore the pain.

His eyes roved over her face, her green eyes and her soft smile, as she sat there with her air of independence and self-assurance. A wave of love for her washed over him, nearly overwhelming him.

He looked down at his plate to hide his confusion and tried to make sense of his feelings. Making love with her earlier had moved him deeply. He had felt totally at one with her – complete. What man wouldn't be grinning from ear to ear at what was being offered to him – the passionate love of a woman who asked for no commitment? And, he wondered angrily, how could she be happy with that?

He looked at her. How could she sit there, looking so sweet and calm and – he searched for the word and landed on 'un-needy' – yes, how could she be so un-needy when he suddenly felt that he needed her as much as he needed to breathe.

His heart was racing with the suddenness and strength of these feelings, leaving him light-headed. He pushed back from the table and got to his feet.

"I need a little air," he told her, walking to the door.

He strode outside and down onto the strand.

Ellen had watched his emotions play over his face as he sat at the table. When he had stormed out, she knew that his feelings were hurt and perhaps his pride too. She thought that a lot of men would be delighted to have a lover who made no demands, or didn't expect marriage after what had passed between them. But her words had really bothered him. She frowned. They both knew this could only be temporary.

She stared at the candle. Surely he didn't think there could be some commitment between them, something more permanent? He would need to marry someone of his own class and she would not continue to see him when the time came for that.

Perhaps this was the warning her granny had given. Were she and Blake heading for a lot of pain because they would only be able to love like this for a short while and then would have to give each other up? She chewed her lip. What had they let themselves in for by starting what they had? Yet deep down, she didn't regret that they had made love – she was glad she would have the memory of it, and if pain was inevitable anyway then shouldn't they continue to take their joy while they could? She would make him live in the moment and not think about the future for now.

Rising from the table, she extinguished the candle and went outside. The sun was setting over the peninsula across the way. Blake was standing down near the water's edge, looking across at it.

With the sand cool beneath her feet, Ellen walked down to him.

"Blake?"

He turned, his face impassive.

"I wasn't sending you away. I was simply inviting you to love me freely without any talk of the future."

"I don't know what I'm offering you, Ellen."

"Just let me have this time with you now, Blake, tonight. Tomorrow is a long way away."

He waited a heartbeat then reached out and pulled her into his embrace, rocking her from side to side, his face pressed to her hair. "I don't know what you do to me," he said, "but I give myself over to it willingly."

He put his hands on either side of her face and bent his head, drawing her into a sweet kiss.

"Let's go for that walk," she said, taking his hand. "I want to show you a little of my world.

Chapter 21

They wandered along the shore hand in hand, still in their bare feet.

"Do you know much about seaweed?" Ellen asked as they approached the rocks.

"Very little.""

"There," she pointed. "See the purple plant growing on the rocks? That's dillisk. And that brown one there is kelp. There are different types of seaweed that you can eat and it's all very good for you. See that one there? The reddish-purple one? That's carrageen moss."

"Now that one I do know. I've often had carrageen pudding."

"Well, it's some of that I put in your hot drink that day to soothe your throat. I already had some prepared in a jar."

He looked at the weed, half-submerged in the salty water. "How do you change it into a drink?"

"You wash it in fresh water first, then soak it for a few minutes, before boiling it up. The moss begins to break up then. When it's done you sieve it through some muslin and add honey to the liquid you get and then store it in a jar. Simple and curative!" She smiled at him.

"Wonderful," he said, looking down at the moss with a new respect and then looking at Ellen the same way.

"Of course seaweed is also good for the land," she said.

Blake nodded. "We often spread it on our fields. It makes the soil richer."

Ellen tugged on his hand. "Come on, let's go up the cliff path while we have the last bit of daylight." She looked up at the clear sky. "We'll have enough moonlight to guide us back through the fields later."

They crossed the rocks carefully in their bare feet, then Ellen went ahead of him up the narrow grassy path. It widened near the top and Blake took her hand again to walk beside her. They strolled near the edge of the cliff, looking out over the vastness of the sea as it stretched to the horizon, shimmering in the rays of the setting sun.

Blake loved the feel of the grass, realising he hadn't walked barefoot like that since he was a boy. Looking around him, he realised he'd been up there before when he was searching for her. He turned and pulled her into his arms. The reflection of the sun glowed in her eyes.

"This is where hope of finding you returned to me. I saw the smoke from your cottage coming from the hollow down there and I couldn't wait to lay eyes on you again. I fought this, Ellen, so hard, but I was so drawn to you. These green eyes of yours and your smile," he rubbed his thumb over her lips, "wove a web around me on the strand that first day – a web I don't want to break free of."

Her lips parted at his words and he lowered his head and kissed first her top lip and then the lower.

Sensation ripped through Ellen, and her arms tightened around him. They stood there for a long time, mouth to mouth, enjoying, giving and taking, as the sun set and the moon appeared in the sky behind them.

Ellen opened her eyes. There was a halo of early stars in the pale sky above Blake's head. She smiled softly at him.

He wanted to dive into those eyes and swim there for eternity. He couldn't hold back what he was feeling. "I love you," he said solemnly.

Emotion surged through her, and a part of her wondered if the earth beneath their feet would crumble, or thunder would shake the sky as a reminder of her grandmother's warning. But all was still. She placed her hand on his cheek, holding his gaze.

"I love you," she replied. "I wouldn't have taken you as a lover if I didn't." She spoke with quiet confidence.

Blake's heart swelled, loving her all the more for her honesty and self-knowledge. He had to clamp down on the desire to talk about how they could have a life together. He had promised not to talk of the future yet so he stayed quiet and instead drank in her bewitching beauty as she stood there, her eyes full of love for him. It was enough for now. And if he couldn't use words, he would show her how he was completely hers.

"Let's go back to the cottage," he said.

Fire jumped in her eyes at his suggestion and she nodded.

Totally familiar with the terrain, she led him back through the fields. Just as they got to the cottage she gasped and pointed out to sea. The moon glinted off three large, black curves that rose and fell way out in the water. They were enormous.

"My God! What are those?" Blake asked.

To his surprise, Ellen turned a face bright with excitement up to him. "Whales! Oh Blake, I've only seen them once before in my life! There have always been stories of how they pass up this way heading north for the summer months and pass back down in the winter. The only other time I saw them I was just a girl. I was out fishing with my father and it was November. Daddy said they were going south for the winter and were here, feeding, on their way. This time they must be going north. We must go and listen to them sing! Wait here!"

"What?" Blake asked incredulously, but she had run into the house.

She came back out with a large tin bowl in her hand. She grabbed his hand and, laughing, ran with him across the sand.

He was bewildered when she stopped at the water's edge, took off all her clothes, and urged him to do the same. Infected by her excitement, he did as he was told, admiring her body in the moonlight as she ran ahead of him into the calm sea, gasping as the cold water hit her. He questioned his own sanity as he followed her in.

When they were standing at waist level, she rested the bowl on the surface, the open side facing up, and then pressed it down a little, not allowing the water to flow in.

"What are you doing?" Blake asked, shivering, his arms folded over his chest.

"Wait," she said, smiling at him mischievously.

He looked nervously towards the horizon. They both stared when in the distance the massive creatures loomed out of the water, blowing loudly into the night air, before sweeping majestically under again.

"Incredible!" Blake exhaled.

Suddenly the air was filled with high-pitched sounds, followed by deeper groaning and grunting noises. The sounds seemed to come out of the bowl.

"What on earth?" he asked, his eyes huge.

"Oh, isn't it beautiful?" Ellen said, her eyes shining. "It's the whales calling to one another."

Blake shook his head in wonder as he looked at the bowl. "How did you know how to do this?"

"My father showed me that day in the boat. He used the bowl he had for bailing seawater out. Isn't it magical?"

Blake could only nod. What he thought was magical was the whole scene – this amazing woman standing naked in the water in front of him without inhibition and totally at one with the sea, the sight of those creatures, and their amazing sound filling the air. He felt he must be dreaming.

They listened for another while. He only realised his teeth had started to chatter when Ellen laughed, her own jaw trembling.

"We'd best go up before we catch our death of cold," she said.

She lifted the bowl from the water and they were plunged into silence. Blake stared at her as she stood bathed in moonlight and surrounded by shimmering water, her hair and body glowing like silver.

"My very own mermaid," he murmured.

She smiled, pressed a quick kiss to his lips then rushed out of the water to grab up her clothes, with Blake close behind. "Race you!" she challenged and ran, laughing, up the beach.

They arrived breathless into the cottage, bundled clothes clutched to their bodies. They washed quickly with hot water to warm themselves. Having towelled dry with swift movements, they fell into the bed laughing.

At six the next morning Blake was getting ready to leave. The hours of darkness had been short and dawn light streaked the sky as Ellen stood nearby, watching him saddle up his horse. The tide was in and swished tiny waves in and out. While holding her shawl tightly around her with folded arms, she was trying to suppress the ache of his leaving. To give him his due he had not spoken of the long-term future during the intimate hours of the night and she had wondered what he would say when it was time to go. She hoped with all her heart that he would talk of coming back soon.

He patted the horse on the neck before coming over to her, his eyes locking with hers. Putting his arms around her he drew her close, holding her tenderly against him.

"I have never known such a night, Ellen. The wonder of you, the whales, their song, you in the sea in the moonlight, your loving, your healing that child ..." His voice trailed away as he tightened his grip on her.

Ellen concentrated hard on the feel of his arms around her, his shoulder beneath her cheek, the rise and fall of his chest against hers. She felt like she was dragging the moment in through every pore, to make it linger. She stored it all away for remembering later.

After a few moments, she pulled back a little to look up into his face. "Thank you for coming back to me, Blake. Be safe on your journey."

Reaching up one hand, he pushed her hair back and traced a finger down one side of her face. Savouring the love she saw in his eyes, she smiled.

"Can I come and see you again soon?" he asked, his voice raw with emotion and feeling anxious about her reply.

"Yes," she whispered.

With relief, he rested his forehead against hers for a moment. Then, with a puzzled look, he asked: "What changed? Why did you let me stay this time?"

"My body needed you as much as my soul. I couldn't fight it any longer."

He took in her words, which found a resonance deep within himself. He nodded slowly then pressed a kiss to her forehead.

"I'm not sure when I can get back. It might be Saturday, a week from today."

This time she nodded, already looking forward to it.

His eyes roamed her face before he glanced out at the brightening sky. "I really have to go."

"Of course," she said.

She was about to move away, but he pulled her in and placed a kiss as soft as butterfly wings on her lips before releasing her and swinging himself up onto his horse. He gave her one long lingering look before touching his heels to the horse's sides.

He disappeared around the side of the house, the horse's hooves loud in the stillness. Ellen stared out to sea, listening to the sound receding as he rode away over the fields.

Wrapping the joy of each precious memory around her like a comforting blanket, she continued to watch the light get stronger. She hoped that when the time came to let him go for good, her heart would survive the pain.

Chapter 22

Shortly before noon the same day, Ellen went over to Síle and Séamus's farm.

Síle saw her coming and was waiting at the door, an anxious look on her face.

"Síle? Is Úna all right?" Ellen asked.

"Come in, Ellen. Yes, she's fine, hasn't been scratching at all."

"Then what is it?"

"Father O'Riordan was here. I'm sorry, Ellen, but he saw Úna's arms all wrapped up and asked what happened to her. Before I could stop her, Úna told him that it was you who put the leaves on her arms. He looked very cross when he heard that. I'm sorry."

A shiver ran down Ellen's spine, but she gave Síle a reassuring smile. "Don't worry. He can't have a problem with me putting a few cabbage leaves on an itchy arm! Now," she said brightly, putting the basket she was carrying down on the table, "let's put on some fresh ones."

Síle gave her a relieved smile and called Úna out of the bedroom.

"Hello, Úna. How do your arms feel?"

"They're not itchy anymore, but I don't like the smell," she said, wrinkling up her nose.

Ellen laughed. "No, it's not the nicest, is it? But I've brought a lovely lavender ointment you can put on them tonight and that smells so much better!"

123

On removing the leaves, the three of them were relieved to see the blisters had shrunk down and the skin was far less red than it had been earlier.

It didn't take Ellen long to put on fresh cress and cabbage leaves.

"Keep these on until tonight and take them off before she goes to bed. Her arms should be fine by then," she said, binding them all up with fresh muslin. "Wash and dry them and put some of the lavender ointment on them. Come and see me tomorrow, if there's any problem. And I think it would be a good idea if Séamus made sure Úna and the others knows which plant is the hogweed." She raised her eyes to Úna's. "Because you don't want this to happen again, do you, pet?"

Úna shook her head. "The strawberries were nice though."

Ellen laughed at the child's indomitable spirit as she took the jar of ointment from her bag and put it on the table.

"Thank you so much, Ellen," Síle said. "You'll have a cup of tea now before you go?"

"Yes, thank you."

Ellen stayed for a while with Síle, enjoying the chat between Úna and the other children as they came and went from the house, curious to see what Ellen had done.

After leaving the farm, Ellen walked to the village. The day was pleasantly warm, and she found herself smiling as she thought back on her evening and night with Blake. Her body felt alive in a new way, as if it had taken Blake to wake it from a long sleep. She gave thanks that he had appeared in her life and for all the new feelings she was experiencing. She would treasure the gift of him while she could.

Her steps were light as she entered the village and she thought she just might tell Annie about him.

Unusually for that time of the day, there was a large group of people gathered outside the pubic house. Voices were raised in angry discussion.

From across the street, Ellen saw Annie at the edge of the group. She quickly came over to her, the baby on her hip and Michael's small hand in hers. Her face was very serious.

"What's going on?" Ellen asked her.

124

"There's been an eviction! Late last night. The widow Gertie Coughlan and her four children tossed out of their home!" Annie's voice shook. "She tried to make a go of the farming herself since her husband died last year, but the children were too young to help and things went from bad to worse. She couldn't pay the rent this time or last. Travers' men came and it was over before anyone else could help. Neighbours took her in for the night and she's going to go to Skibbereen to see if she can get work there. If not, it might be the poorhouse for all of them."

"Lord bless us!" Ellen crossed herself.

"The men are very angry and scared. Some of them want to bring in the Land League. They're going to tell them what's going on with this new landlord. They think we need the League to fight for our rights. Others think it's a bad idea and that we should just keep our heads down. But they are the ones who can afford to pay the rent without too much difficulty. "

"But being involved with the Land League could bring terrible trouble on them from the authorities," Ellen said, looking at the men worriedly. She could see Mick's angry face among them.

"I'm going to take the children home," Annie said. "Tempers are too high here to stay around."

"Is the fishing going well?"

"Yes, thank God."

A voice was raised in the crowd and they heard clearly someone say: "Travers needs to be shown that we won't be walked on!"

A worried look passed between the two sisters.

"I'm just going to get some bones from the butcher's for Shep and I'll be away home too," Ellen said, knowing this was not the time to mention Blake, he being from the class these people were very angry with. Knowing that Blake was an estate manager, she hoped whoever he worked for was treating his tenants better than Mr. Travers was.

Just then a donkey and cart turned onto the street.

It was the Coughlan family with what belongings and bits of furniture they had piled in the cart with them. The widow was driving with the two smaller children sitting beside her and the other two were walking behind the cart, their heads hanging low.

Silence fell on the street as the cart moved towards them like a funeral procession.

Annie was the first to break the silence as she called out to the shattered-looking woman.

"Take care of yourself, Gertie! May the blessings of God go with you!"

A cacophony of sound broke out then as all the others added their wishes to hers. The butcher's wife ran out from the shop and passed a parcel up to Gertie. Father Dempsey was there and lifted a hand and made the Sign of the Cross.

Gertie, tears streaming down her face and unable to speak, could only nod her head.

As the last of the good wishes faded away, silence descended again except for the hollow clip-clop of the donkey's hooves as the cart continued on. Heads turned as one to watch them leave, heartbreak for the family etched onto each face.

The crowd dispersed, heartsick. Even Ellen and Annie couldn't find words. They hugged each other briefly and parted.

After leaving the butcher's, Ellen turned the corner to leave the main street and ran straight into Father O'Riordan. They both apologised at once and stepped back. But his heavy face darkened.

"Oh, it's you!" he sneered. "I hear you were tending the sick!"

Ellen, still caught up in the emotion of what she had just seen, was shocked by his tone and took a moment to realise he was talking about healing Úna. Taking a steadying breath she pulled herself up to her full height and looked down her nose at him, thinking his behaviour petty after what she had just witnessed.

His eyes narrowed.

"If you mean putting a few leaves on a child's arm," she said coolly, "yes, I did that."

"How did you know what to do?"

Ellen gave a short laugh. "Anyone growing up in the country knows how to use leaves to relieve itching. I'm sure you are no stranger yourself to putting a dock leaf on a nettle sting?" She stared at him, her eyes daring him to challenge her further.

He assessed her for a moment, not having an answer to that. Colour suffused his cheeks.

"I'm watching you!" he barked.

"And for some reason looking for something bad. Isn't it the Christian way to see the good in people, Father O'Riordan?" she asked mildly. "Now if you'll excuse me, I must be on my way."

As she went past him she heard him huffing out a breath like an angry bull. She kept walking up the hill, knowing she probably shouldn't have landed that parting shot as it would surely come back to bite her. The man wouldn't like being made a fool of, but she needed him to know that she wasn't one to be bullied.

Chapter 23

The rest of the day passed quickly. Though sad for the Coughlan family, Ellen's mind eventually returned to the events of the previous day and she began to hum as she went about her chores. She lifted the tub and washboard outside to start the washing. She kept an eye on the sea, hoping she might again see the great whales, but in vain – they must have fed their fill and moved on.

A sensual smile settled on her lips as she scrubbed the towel that she had used to dry Blake's body the evening before. She could see again the strong muscles of his shoulders and back. A pleasant shudder shook her as she remembered the weight of his body on hers and his whispered words of love.

Her hands had stilled and she laughed at her wandering mind. Setting to work again, she washed and rinsed until she had a large basketful done. Taking it around to the clothes line, she pegged the clothes out, where they billowed in the breeze. Glancing up at the clear blue sky, she knew she would get them all dry before evening.

Having thrown away the water, she stored the tub in the shed and returned to the cottage. Because the soap had been hard on her hands, she rubbed some ointment into them to keep them soft. Continuing with her chores, she swept and dusted. Wisps of hair had come loose and she tucked one behind her ear, thinking about the evening to come.

There was to be a céilí in the church hall that evening. Andy had organised for musicians who were visiting to play and told them all that they were in for a treat. What with the mood that had pervaded the village at the sight of the Coughlan family leaving, Ellen wasn't sure if anyone would turn up, or if they did what the atmosphere would be like. But she had promised Andy earlier in the week that she would go and she hoped for the sake of the musicians, who had to make their living too, that others would also go.

In the meantime, overcome by a series of yawns, she sat on the rocking chair to rest a while. She gently rocked back and forth, smiling, knowing that she was tired out from all their lovemaking and from the small amount of sleep they'd had during the night. Within moments she felt herself drift off and she gladly let go.

At eight, much refreshed after her nap, she set off with the sun sinking in the sky, to go to the céilí at the hall.

She paid her few pennies to Andy who was collecting the fee just inside the door.

"I was afraid no one would show up," she commented, glancing around and seeing it already quite full and the dance floor vibrating beneath the feet of the set dancers.

Andy nodded. "Nothing like a bit of music to brighten everyone's spirits. God knows we need it badly. And these boys are marvellous."

Ellen agreed. The fiddle music was lively and well played. She took herself off to get a glass of lemonade. Looking around, she saw Father O'Riordan walking up and down, watching for any impropriety on the dance floor. She sighed and moved away to take a seat.

She was admiring the energy of some of the older couples on the floor, as they went through the dance steps, when she was whisked onto the floor herself.

The evening was well advanced when she saw Eve and Sorcha go to the lemonade stand together. Sorcha whispered something to Eva, who nodded, and the two girls went outside. Ellen saw Father O'Riordan's eyes narrow as he watched them leave. He followed them, probably suspecting them of meeting some of the men.

Ellen, who was further away from the door, hurried after him. She was just in time to see the two women, in the shadows of a tree, jump away from each other as Father O'Riordan approached them.

Ellen's heart raced. What had he seen? Had they kissed or embraced? Even if they had, had it been too dark for him to see?

She called out: "Eve, there you are! Fionn has been looking for you for the next dance! And Sorcha, you and I were going to do the Cashel set together. Come on in!"

"Excuse us, Father," they mumbled as they hurried up to Ellen.

The priest didn't try to stop them so she hoped that he couldn't be sure of what he had or hadn't seen.

Inside, she led Sorcha and Eve across the hall and told them to wait there.

Ellen darted over to Fionn who was talking to someone nearby. She tugged on his sleeve and whispered urgently into his ear. "Go and take Eve onto the dance floor straight away, please, and tell her to look like she's really enjoying herself."

Fionn looked at her in puzzlement.

"Please, Fionn, just do it."

Seeing the seriousness in her eyes, he did as she asked. With a big smile he whisked Eve onto the floor. He said something to her and Ellen saw her arrange her pale face into a smile.

Father O'Riordan had come back in and was watching them. Ellen returned to Sorcha who was blushing furiously.

"Let's see if we can partner up with someone for the Cashel Set," said Ellen.

They went over to Sorcha's brother and his friends and asked if they needed their numbers made up for the next dance.

When they were lined up, Ellen whispered to Sorcha: "Do not leave together. You go home with your brother and I'll ask Fionn to walk Eve home."

"I'm sorry, Ellen! You warned us to be careful. It was stupid of us. Do you think he saw? We – we were embracing ..."

"I'm not sure. But he suspects something."

Sorcha groaned.

"You must pretend nothing happened and if possible flirt with one of your brother's friends for the rest of the evening. It might be enough to throw him off the scent."

Fionn stayed on the floor for the next dance with Eve but, when it was over, he returned to Ellen. She asked him to dance with Eve several more times and, when he raised his eyebrows, she promised she would explain later.

"I'll do it," he said, "but only if you let me walk you home after so that you can tell me what's going on."

She agreed.

The evening went on and Ellen didn't enjoy a moment of it. Her eyes kept returning to the priest who was keeping a very close eye on the girls. Fionn kept his word and both girls gave a great performance of thoroughly enjoying the male company they were in. They avoided each other completely.

Eventually Father O'Riordan was distracted by a couple dancing too close together and went over to put some distance between them, giving them the usual line about leaving room for the Holy Spirit.

To Ellen's relief the céilí finished at eleven, after which Fionn came and stood beside her. "I hope you have a good explanation for this, because my feet are killing me."

Ellen didn't reply as she watched Sorcha leave the hall with her brother. Then her heart started to pound again when she saw Father O'Riordan talking to Eve's mother. She watched as the woman blushed then blanched at what she was hearing. She then shook her head violently, obviously denying what he might be suggesting. She looked both shocked and disgusted. The priest held up his finger and wagged it in warning. Ellen felt sick as she watched Eve's mother go over to the girl, take her roughly by the arm and march her out of the hall without a word.

Oblivious, Fionn asked, "Are you ready to go?"

"Yes, thanks."

They walked through the village, discussing the quality of the musicians and their choice of tunes, but as soon as they were alone on the road Fionn asked his question.

"Well, what on earth was all that about? I hope you're not trying to match-make, Ellen Cassidy? I would not take kindly to that."

"You know I was doing nothing of the sort or you wouldn't have played along."

"True. Tell me so."

Ellen thought for a second. "Out of loyalty to Eve, I can't tell you exactly. I can only say that she might me in some trouble with Father O'Riordan and I needed you to provide a distraction, which you did magnificently. I'm very grateful to you and I know Eve is too."

"But will she think I'm sweet on her now? I wouldn't like to lead the poor girl on."

Ellen smiled. "No, you don't need to worry about that."

"Good."

Ellen pulled her shawl a little tighter against the chill of the night air. Fionn removed his coat and put it around her shoulders.

"Thank you, Fionn, but you'll get cold now."

He gave a bellow of a laugh. "I spend my days out working in all weather – a little night dew won't harm me."

Silence fell until they turned off the road to cross the fields to Ellen's.

Fionn broke it.

"Would you think of walking out with me, Ellen?"

Her heart jumped. She was very fond of him, but had to turn him down. She couldn't tell him about Blake because she didn't want to see hurt and disapproval in his eyes, nor could she have anyone around here knowing she was spending time with landed gentry.

"That's nice of you to ask, Fionn, and you are a wonderful man. But you and I have a great friendship and I think that's how it should stay."

"I'm very fond of you, Ellen, and I'd like it to be more than that. Will you think about it?"

"No, Fionn, it wouldn't be fair to keep you dangling like that. The life of a healer is going to be a solitary one for me. It's bad enough that people look funny at me sometimes, so I would hate it if they looked at you that way too, if things got serious between us."

"I wouldn't care about that, Ellen. It would be water off a duck's back to me."

"I'd care about it. Let's just go on as we are. I like my independence."

They had reached the cottage. Shep gave a welcoming bark from inside.

She slipped the coat from her shoulders and handed it back to Fionn. "Thank you and thanks again for your help tonight and for walking me home."

"Good night, Ellen. Sweet dreams."

Ellen was saddened that she had disappointed him and selfishly hoped that it wouldn't cause strangeness now to settle between them.

Chapter 24

The next morning Ellen went to the early Mass, expecting that Father Dempsey would be saying it. Father O'Riordan usually preferred to stay in his bed longer on Sunday mornings and say the later Mass instead. But, to her dismay, it was Father O'Riordan who strode out onto the altar. If she had known she would have sat in the last seat, as far from the priest as possible.

The experience was every bit as bad as she could have expected. Considering what Father O'Riordan had heard about Úna's arm, she thought it was no coincidence that the sermon contained a dire warning against worshipping false gods. Now she was sure that he suspected she was involved in some way with the Devil. Of course it also had dire warnings about the wages of sin and the pleasures of the flesh, saying dances were all very well but that everyone had to be on guard against the Devil's work. She could imagine his wrath if he found out about Blake and her and also wondered what he had said to Eve's mother.

The church suddenly felt very warm and she wished the end of the Mass would come soon. But Father O'Riordan moved on to the importance of everyone paying their dues, and spoke at length about the upkeep of the church being expensive and how it was no joke trying to look after the needs of such a far-flung parish.

"I know times are hard," he said, "but looking after your clergy is as important as looking after your own children, because we in turn take care of your souls."

Ellen just stopped herself from snorting in disgust. The man didn't seem to need much taking care of, if his girth was anything to go by. It looked like he ate much better than any of his parishioners. He didn't even mention the poor Coughlan family and their plight. He was a self-absorbed man and she didn't like him one bit.

She noticed that Eve and Sorcha were sitting in different parts of the church, carefully avoiding looking at each other. Both looked very pale indeed. She also saw that Eve's mother was stony-faced.

Ellen went up to Communion. Father O'Riordan glared at her but he couldn't refuse to serve her as, for all he knew, she had been to Confession with Father Dempsey. She hadn't.

Coming back to her seat, she lost herself in her prayers and sighed with relief when Mass eventually ended.

Ellen knew it would be unwise to seek out the girls outside afterwards and she would have to wait and see what the priest had said to Eve's mother.

As was usual, the women gathered together in groups to catch up on news and the men did the same. Children ran about, glad to be free to make noise again. The banter of the evening before was missing though as the men were huddled in groups discussing yesterday's eviction and their own fears. Dejection seemed to have settled again. There were no guffaws of laughter as they stood closely together, speaking in lowered tones. The women too were uneasy, nervous of what the men were plotting in order to protect their families.

Ellen didn't stay around for long and after a brief talk with Annie she returned to her cottage.

Just after lunch Sorcha arrived at her door in tears. Ellen brought her in and sat her down.

"Father O'Riordan told Eve's mam at the dance last night that he thought Eve and I were getting too familiar with each other and that she should make us end our friendship. He said there shouldn't be 'particular friendships' between girls. Eve's mam didn't know what to say to him and couldn't really understand what he was saying. But she dragged Eve home in anger anyway because she was so ashamed to have the priest give out about one of her children. She asked Eve to explain what the priest was talking about." Sorcha wiped her eyes before continuing.

"Eve said she didn't know. Her mother said that there was no smoke without fire and that if 'that Sorcha girl was up to any mischief' she didn't want her daughter to be dragged into any of it. She's forbidden her from being friends with me. Oh Ellen, what are we going to do?"

"Well, look at it this way. They still have no proof you are together, so you're lucky that the whole village hasn't got wind of it. I'm pretty sure Eva's mother won't be spreading it about that the priest spoke to her. Look, Sorcha, you two are adults, twenty years of age! I think you need to get away from here. Live your lives for yourselves, not through your family or the priest. I've been thinking about it and wondered if you could go to Cork City to look for jobs. You'd be able to live together there – sisters or cousins live together all the time in the city. Let people up there think that's what you are to each other. You'd be out from under the eye of Father O'Riordan. Maybe you could go first and, when things have settled down here, then Eve could go too."

Sorcha stared at her for a moment, not daring to believe that a future with Eve might still be possible.

Ellen continued: "And if that's still too close to home, try Dublin or London. There are choices, Sorcha."

Sorcha gave a laugh that was half sob. "You're right and they'll be glad to see us go after the eviction yesterday. Sure they'd be happy for us to find work in Cork where we could send home a few bob, maybe."

"Andy Minehane's sister lives there. She's lovely. I'm sure she could help you with finding work and a boarding house for now."

"Thank you so much, Ellen."

"You're welcome, but in the meantime be very careful. You don't want to leave your family behind in the midst of a scandal."

After Sorcha left, Ellen took a long walk with Shep which took her across the cliffs for miles. At one point she stopped and turned to look out to sea, slowly lifting her arms and letting the sea breeze caress her skin. She felt wonderful. Every moment she had spent with Blake was vivid in her mind and she was grateful for each remembered feeling and sensation.

By the time she was crossing the beach to go back to the cottage, she was pleasantly tired and was planning to bring a stool outside so she could eat her supper in the warmth of the evening sun.

But when she walked up to the door, she stopped and looked

curiously at it. She was sure she had latched it properly but the top half was slightly ajar. Shep was still down by the water and she called him. He ran up to her, his paws covered in sand.

Putting her hand on his head she stilled him and waited. Nothing happened – he didn't start growling – so taking that as a sign that there wasn't anyone in the house she moved forward, taking him with her while pushing the door fully open. Shep suddenly sniffed the air, but still didn't growl. He moved away and lowered his nose to the ground, sniffing as he went. Knowing he was picking up a strange scent, Ellen continued in cautiously. Shep sniffed all around the floor of the kitchen and on into the bedroom. Whoever had come in had gone around every inch of her home.

Ellen eyes darted around. She could see for herself that they had searched the place. They hadn't left a mess or damaged anything, but she knew her things were slightly out of place. Her herb jars had been lifted and replaced not quite correctly. One drawer was not completely closed. She continued to look around, examining everything. Even her knitting basket had been disturbed. The wool she had used for Úna's arms was now half hidden under a different ball.

In the bedroom she saw that the contents of the chest had also been disturbed as had the things in the drawers.

She shivered. Who had been in her house and what had they been looking for?

Back in the kitchen she sank onto a stool, her eyes continuing to rove over the room. Shep came and sat beside her. He put his head in her lap and whined softly.

No one had ever intruded like this before and she had never felt the need to lock her door. Nothing had been taken, so the only conclusion she could come to was that Father O'Riordan had been there looking for evidence against her. Her eyes flew to the herb jars. Did he think there was anything harmful in them? Would he imagine she conjured spells with some of them?

Rising, she went to the door and shot home the bolt, thoughts of sitting outside with her supper vanishing. The key to the door hung on a hook beside it, not having been used for years. She inserted it into the lock but it wouldn't turn. In the morning she would grease the lock and try to make it work then. The bolt would have to do for the moment.

Once again, she set about burning her sage and taking it to all corners of the house. She lit the fire and, aware that her heart was pounding, she rubbed some lavender ointment into her temples and sat in the rocking chair until she became calm again.

That night she let Shep sleep in the bedroom but, despite his company and her tiredness, she had a very restless night.

Chapter 25

Blake bent, picked a stalk of grass and chewed on it as he and Shaughnessy walked through a field on the Bantry estate. Their eyes scanned the grasses carefully as they moved along, shirtsleeves rolled up to their elbows.

"Just about to flower, I'd say," Shaughnessy commented, a stalk also protruding from his mouth. Lifting his cap, he scratched his head.

Blake nodded, eyes still roving over the field. "Yes, it'll be ready by the weekend I should think. Let's hope the weather holds. That gives us a few more days to get the scythes sharpened and ready." As he spoke they passed into another field and continued their survey.

"I received a letter last week," Blake continued, "from a friend of mine who has just acquired something called a fingerbar mower, which he tells me is a new machine drawn by a horse for cutting the hay."

"Go on with ya!" Shaughnessy exclaimed.

"Apparently it has two wheels and a seat, and two blades which stick out the side. As the wheels turn they move one blade over and back over the other, cutting the hay. Now, what do you think of that?"

"It would certainly save a few sore backs and blistered hands around here!"

"He's going to write to me again and let me know how he gets on with it. If it's successful for him I would certainly consider getting one for next year."

"Wouldn't that be grand?" Shaughnessy said, squinting at the field and trying to imagine what the machine would look like and him sitting on top of it.

They stopped walking and continued to look around.

"Pass the word that we're likely to start saving the hay this Saturday and put O'Brien in charge of getting all the tools ready. The tenant farmers will need help with their hay too. Get them helping out here and we'll help them in turn."

The two men returned to the yard in companionable silence. Blake was lost in his own thoughts. He had promised Ellen he would return on Saturday but that wasn't going to be possible now. The hay didn't wait for anyone – when the grasses flowered and the weather was good, the job had to be done there and then. His mind raced over all the preparations required before the weekend and decided that he would be able to get away to see her on Thursday before the work on the hay began. He trusted Shaughnessy to oversee things in his absence.

Blake was still smiling over their time together. When he had set out for her cottage he could never have dreamed things would have turned out the way they had. He was intoxicated by her, remembering every word she had said, every sound she had made, the way she had felt in his arms, the way she had loved him so generously, so passionately and yet with such a sweet innocence, and her joy at every newly discovered sensation and emotion.

He turned his attention back to work when they arrived at the yard where O'Brien was cleaning out the milking parlour and two of the younger farmhands were herding the cows out to pasture.

O'Brien came out to join Blake and Shaughnessy and the three of them went off to the equipment shed, deep in discussion about what needed to be done.

An hour later, Blake left them to return to his office in the house, rolling down his sleeves as he went. Only minutes into some paperwork, he found his mind wandering. Through the open window the scent from a rose bush that his mother had planted years before drifted his way. He was immediately reminded of Ellen. A smile lifted the corners of his mouth and not for the first time he shook his head in wonder at the extraordinary skill he had witnessed in her house the day before. He was in awe of her healing and only now understood that sense of power and strength in her that he had been aware of from the start. From the first moment he had known there was something different about her, something that had drawn him to her.

His smile slipped into a frown when he remembered her saying that some people didn't trust her healing powers. He wondered if she was safe from people like that. The isolation of her cottage didn't reassure him either. A desire to protect her rose up in him and a moment later he chided himself. He had only just been admiring her strength and power and now he arrogantly assumed she needed protection from him all of a sudden, having managed fine without him up to now.

He returned his attention to the papers on his desk, but still couldn't shake this new feeling. He wanted to know if she was all right and the days until Thursday seemed to stretch endlessly before him.

The butler brought in the post. With a sinking feeling, Blake took the three envelopes, very much afraid that one might contain the invitation to visit the Hannons in Skibbereen. If it was there, it would force him to face reality and make decisions and he was not ready for that. How he felt for Ellen had his head in the clouds and he wanted to remain that way for now. Being in love was such a delicious feeling, and one he did not want to have to relinquish just yet. With relief, he saw that all three were business letters.

After attending to some more paperwork, he pushed back from the desk and returned to the yard. Rolling up his sleeves again he went to the equipment shed to lend a hand in sharpening the scythes.

Ellen was busy. Saving the hay had already started on the farm holdings around her and in the afternoons she went to help out when she could, wielding a pitch fork, turning the swaths to dry. People still came to her, mostly in the mornings, with their ailments and she dealt with them and sent them on their way. They were all people she knew and trusted, and her unease faded. She did, however, warn all of them not to mention the healing to the new priest.

She had greased the lock on her front door and any time she had to go away from the cottage she made sure she locked it up first. She hated having to do it but she hated more the idea of Father O'Riordan snooping around in it again – if it had been him that day.

On Wednesday of that week, Annie stopped by with the children. Ellen went down onto the strand with them.

"You look happier," Ellen said, taking the baby from Annie's arms, so she could hold Michael's hand as he splashed about at the water's edge.

"The fishing has been good so Mick is in great form and we'll make the extra rent this week."

Ellen heard the relief in her voice. Her unease about Mick's temper rose again. "That's great that he's busy, Annie, and the weather is looking fairly settled – all the farmers are saying it too. They think it'll be no problem saving the hay this year."

Michael pulled free of Annie and ran back a little from the water's edge to start digging in the sand with his hands. Ellen and Annie continued to walk back and forth, while keeping an eye on him.

"Everything all right between you two?" Ellen asked lightly.

"Yes, of course. Did you know Sorcha McGinty is moving up to Cork?"

The sudden change of topic made Ellen even more anxious but she knew Annie could be both stubborn and very defensive where Mick was concerned. She was sure that if Annie felt she had made a mistake in marrying him she would never admit it. She also knew that if she ever saw even the hint of a bruise on Annie she wouldn't hesitate about interfering. Though her instincts screamed at her to probe, she answered the question and moved on.

"I knew she was thinking about it. I didn't think she would get it organised so quickly."

"Andy told me she'd written to his sister to see if she could stay with her for a while until she can find a boarding house. Andy was all for the idea and was pretty sure his sister would love to have her. She misses the crowd here at home. I'd hate to live in the city," Annie continued dreamily, looking out over the water. "I'd miss the sea too much."

"Me too. I couldn't imagine a life without its moods, its smell, its sounds."

Annie laughed. "Sure it's in our bones since the day we were born. We'd shrivel up and die if we lived inland, let alone in the city."

"We have so much to be grateful for, Annie."

Annie reached out and squeezed her hand affectionately before relieving her of the baby so she could dangle the infant's toes in the water. Róisín squealed in delight and Michael came to join in the fun, splashing them all as he ran around. Soon they were all laughing and were wetter than they had planned.

Later over a cup of tea Ellen asked Annie about the talk in the village. "Are they still thinking of bringing in the Land League to negotiate the rents?"

"Things have quietened down a little since the weather has been good these past few days. They are all too busy fishing or tending the land. I hope they let it all drop. It's bad enough having the landlord breathing down our necks without the authorities doing the same."

"We'll keep praying for fine weather and that this landlord will come to his senses before too long."

Soon after, Annie and the children left to return to Ballinmara, and Ellen returned to salting and storing some dillisk.

After a simple supper of eggs and potatoes, she did some knitting. Before bed she went outside to watch the setting sun change the colours in the sky. Near the horizon, wisps of clouds changed from white to yellow, to deep crimson. Only two more sunsets and she would see Blake again, she thought with a smile.

The tide was in and it was as though the waves whispered goodnight to her as she turned to go back inside.

Chapter 26

The next morning, Ellen had a visit from Maureen, a woman from the village who suffered from her nerves. She liked to come to talk to her now and then. Ellen made tea and listened without interruption. When Maureen had said all she wanted to say about how depressed she had been feeling, Ellen gently asked her some questions.

"Even though you didn't feel great these past few days, Maureen, did anything make you smile, can you remember?"

Maureen cradled her cup in her hand and thought for a moment, frowning into her tea. A smile began to tug at her lips and she raised her eyes to Ellen's, who saw the light returning to them.

"Yes," she said. "The cat had a new litter of kittens recently and yesterday morning I couldn't help smiling at the antics of them as each tried to be the first to get the milk from their mother."

Ellen nodded. "Anything else?"

Again Maureen paused before answering. "Well, I had to go to the butcher's and his wife is such a lovely woman, she always has time to talk even if they're busy. I think I smiled at her when we finished our conversation."

"It's these little things you must think of if you are feeling low, Maureen. And if nothing is making you smile, go out and find things that give you pleasure. Listen to the cuckoo in the evening, or marvel at how well your vegetables are growing. Enjoy the smell of the wild

143

flowers in the ditches. You have such a lovely smile, Maureen. Pick up those kittens, give them a cuddle and feel their warmth when you want to feel better. If we are aware of what gives us pleasure and are thankful for it, not only does it make us feel better, but I believe it brings us more things to be grateful for."

"Thank you, Ellen. Talking with you is better than any doctor's tonic." Maureen stood up to go, visibly brighter than when she had arrived.

Ellen gave her some herbs to take away with her to make a drink that would calm her each night for a better sleep, and bid her good day.

She was washing up the cups when she heard a horse approaching. Her heart jumped at the hope of it being Blake, even though it was only Thursday.

Grabbing a cloth, she dashed out the door while drying her hands. Within seconds the horse and rider appeared, drawing to a stop outside the cottage wall.

"Blake!" she laughed a little breathlessly.

A grin split his face as, jumping down, he strode over to her.

"Hello, Ellen. I hope you don't mind but I had to come today instead of Saturday. We start on the hay that day."

"Of course I don't mind."

His eyes searched hers for a long moment then he pulled her into his arms and held her tightly against him.

Ellen's lids drifted closed and she rested her head against his shoulder.

Blake drew back and her hands slipped up around his neck, the cloth still held in one of them, as Blake lowered his lips to hers. The memory of his kisses and the reality of them merged into one exquisite sensation.

"I'm glad the hay gave you an excuse to come back early. I've been wishing for you."

"How have you been?" he asked, once more looking into her eyes, thrilled at the welcome that shone in them.

"I'm well. Happy," she stated simply.

He hugged her close. "Good. That's all that's important to me."

Ellen breathed in his now familiar scent. "How long can you stay? I like to know how much time we'll have together."

"I'll have to leave around six this evening. It's very busy at the estate and I'll have to catch up tomorrow on all I'm not getting done today."

His smile let her know that he didn't mind in the least the extra work.

"Well, let's make the most of it! You tend to your horse and I'll finish in the kitchen."

The day passed too quickly for Ellen. But every moment was precious. They walked again and swam. They talked and laughed and Ellen marvelled at the lightness of her spirit when she was in his company.

They made love in the afternoon.

As six o'clock drew near, they lay on their sides in Ellen's bed, facing each other. Blake tucked a strand of her hair behind her ear. She could see in his eyes the beginning of the goodbye. Sadness passed over her own heart.

"Why does the time go so fast when we're together and crawl when we're apart?" he asked, echoing the thoughts in her head. "And I'm not sure what day I'll get back to you again. It's such a busy time of the year. It might be two weeks or more."

"I'll live for the surprise of it," she said before kissing him tenderly. "Now it must be nearly six so you had best be on your way."

Blake pulled her in against him and held her there, his lips pressed against her hair.

"I'll be back as soon as I can."

When they were dressed, Ellen walked him outside and watched him saddle up his horse. When he was done, he reached into a saddle bag and pulled out a book and handed it to her.

"I saw that you had some of Jane Austen's novels but not this one, I think."

"*Sense and Sensibility*! I have been looking out for that in the markets."

"It was my mother's and one of her favourites. I'd like you to have it."

"Oh thank you, Blake!"

"When you're reading it, you might think of me while I'm away from you."

"I need no reminder, nor gifts," Ellen murmured, her fingertips caressing the cover.

"Keep it, Ellen, as a small token of my love," he said, pulling her into his arms and kissing her.

Releasing her, he turned and climbed into the saddle. Looking down at her, he saw her cheeks were still flushed from loving and her eyes sparkled. The urge to reach down and pull her up beside him was huge.

But she was already lifting a hand to wave goodbye. He nudged the horse on. "See you soon," he called back over his shoulder, burning the image of her into his mind.

Ellen went back inside.

She missed him the moment he had ridden away. She wondered how long it would be before the pain of knowing that he would always leave would start to outweigh the joy of his visits. When that happened she would say goodbye to him for good.

Sitting in the chair by the fire, she opened the book with reverence, and with a little sigh of pleasure began reading.

Chapter 27

Ellen put a basket over her arm, locked the cottage and left for the village. It was nearly two weeks since Blake's visit and she was reluctant to leave in case he arrived, thinking it would surely be any day now, but she needed some supplies. She strolled, watching out for any sign of a horse and rider. But the road was quiet until she got nearer to the village, and then it was only filled with local people going about their business.

Half an hour later, with her basket full, she went down by the harbour to make her way to Annie's house. She presumed Mick would be fishing as the sea was calm enough that morning. A boat pulled up on the shore as she was passing and she heard shouting but couldn't make out the words. Stopping, she rested her basket on the wall.

A young fisherman ran up over the stony beach with the other men from the boat shouting something after him. As he got closer she recognised him.

"What's the matter, Seán?" she asked as he approached.

He looked up without slowing his pace.

"There's been an accident out on the water."

Ellen felt chilled.

Seán rushed on. "I have to fetch your sister. It's Mick. His arm is badly broken. They'll be bringing him in soon."

"I'll go for Annie," Ellen said, knowing the sight of his pale face would scare the wits out of her sister.

Leaving her basket on the wall, Ellen ran back up the road and made for Annie's cottage.

Sweat broke out on her forehead as she got near and her stomach seemed to somersault. She slowed to a walk and pressed a hand to it.

Seeing Annie at the door of the house, talking to a neighbour, she ignored her own discomfort and walked up to the cottage.

"Hello, Annie,' she said calmly. "Hello, Mary," she greeted the neighbour. Before either could reply she continued, "Mary, is there any chance you could mind Annie's children for a bit? I need to talk to her."

Annie was puzzled but not alarmed by Ellen's gentle request.

"Sure, of course," Mary replied.

Ellen gave her a grateful smile and, linking arms with Annie, walked her back towards the harbour.

"Mick broke his arm out on the boat. They're bringing him in to shore shortly."

"What? Oh my God! How did it happen?" Annie asked, increasing her pace and pulling Ellen along with her.

"I don't know."

They arrived at the shore and saw Seán standing at the water's edge, staring out to sea. He turned when he heard the women approaching.

"The others have gone for a horse and cart to get him to the doctor."

Annie gripped Ellen's arm, her scared eyes huge in her face. "Surely it's not that bad? You might be able to fix him, Ellen."

"I'll certainly try, but you know how he is, Annie," she warned, before turning to Seán. "Do you know what happened?"

"No, they sent us ahead to get help."

"Here they come now," Ellen said, as three rowing boats came around the headland.

The three on the beach were silent and the minutes dragged as the boats slowly got closer. The news had spread and some other villagers came down and gathered round.

Ellen massaged her stomach which still hadn't settled down after the run up to Annie's.

At last the three boats made land. The able men jumped out and dragged them up onto the shale. The others ran over.

Mick sat in the bow of the middle boat, pale and mumbling. The left arm of his shirt was soaked in blood and the jagged tips of two bones stuck out through it below the elbow. Sea water, stained red, sloshed around his feet.

"Jesus, Mary and Joseph!" Annie exclaimed, crossing herself. "What happened?"

"All was grand," Will Brady, owner of the boat, said crossly, "then these two eejits started arguing with each other over something stupid." He pointed at Mick and at his own son, a man a couple of years younger than Mick. "In the middle of hauling in the nets, Mick took a swing at Eoghan – Eoghan ducked, Mick lost his balance and fell out of the boat. But a rope was around his wrist so his arm hit the gunwale of the boat hard as he went over. I heard the crack." The man shuddered. "Mick was in the water, hanging by his arm from the rope. We got him back in quickly but the arm was badly broken."

While he was talking they were helping Mick to stand up in the boat. His face was grey with pain and shock. Up on the road the horse and cart pulled up. Someone had brought some blankets. They laid one on the shale.

"Help him out as carefully as you can," Ellen instructed as the men gathered around. "We don't want the skin to tear any more than it has already."

As gingerly as they could, they supported him as he climbed out. A scream pierced the air as the injured arm was jolted.

Annie started to cry.

Mick's legs gave way and they lowered him down to lie on the blanket. His eyes drifted shut. A piece of wood was slipped under his injured arm.

Ellen went to look at the injury. Carefully she ripped the material of the shirt sleeve, pushing it up and away from the break. The flesh was badly torn where the bones protruded. She knew she wouldn't be able to fix it. The bones would have to be reset and the skin stitched back together.

Mick lifted his head and fixed his eyes on her. "Get her away from me!" he spat, glaring at her with open hatred.

"There's nothing I can do for you anyway, Mick. You'll have to go to a doctor in Schull."

"I'd go all the way to Donegal before I'd let you touch me!" he growled.

Audible gasps ran around the assembled group.

Ellen stood and moved away, taken aback by his venom. She let some of the other women move forward to bind the arm as best they could before he could be moved onto the cart.

She went and stood beside Annie, who was shaking. She leant close and whispered, "I'm sorry I can't help him, Annie. All I can hope is that he passes out and stays unconscious until they get him to Schull. I could give him something to make him sleep but I don't think he'd take it."

"I'm sorry he spoke to you like that." Annie said, unable to look at her.

But Ellen hugged her tight. "I've got a thick skin. You go on with him and I'll go and stay with the children until you get back."

"No!" Annie said fiercely. "I don't want you to get into any more trouble with him. He wouldn't want you at the house when we get back. They'll be fine with Mary. Just tell her we mightn't be back until tomorrow, will you, Ellen?"

"Of course." Ellen hugged her again, hating that her sister was torn between the two people she loved.

Annie knelt as two of the men sat Mick up and removed his wet shirt. One of the men gave him the dry one off his own back to wear for the journey. Annie slipped it over the good arm and tied the lower buttons across his stomach. She wrapped a blanket around his shoulders.

Mick moaned as they helped him to his feet and then up into the back of the cart. Annie and a couple of the men got up beside them.

Ellen stood watching as the horse and cart rattled away and she puzzled, not for the first time, over why Mick hated and feared her so much.

The crowd gradually dispersed, some bidding her good day and some not meeting her eyes, embarrassed at Mick's words. Ellen felt relief that Father O'Riordan hadn't been around to hear it.

Ellen could hear Will Brady nearby giving out to his son. "If you ever behave like that in my boat again, it'll be the last time you come fishing with me, do you hear me? We could all have ended up in the water, along with that bad-tempered eejit!" He walked away but then turned back. "And stay away from him on land too – he's trouble."

Ellen hurried away to Mary's cottage to check on Annie's children. They were quite content in Mary's care. She thanked her and went in to Annie's to make sure a kettle or a pot hadn't been left over the fire. Satisfied that all was in order, she pulled the door shut behind her and went back down to the harbour wall in search of her basket. It wasn't there, but she found it had been handed into the shop for her. Putting it over her arm, she went home.

Chapter 28

Ellen felt drained by the time she got back to her cottage. Placing the basket on the table, she sank into the rocking chair with relief. She put the chair in motion but quickly found that it made her feel sick again. She stopped rocking abruptly and put a shaking hand to her stomach.

She couldn't remember being sick a day in her life. A sheen of perspiration broke out on her forehead and she wiped it away with the back of her hand. Getting up, she went to the table, unwrapped a loaf of bread she had made earlier and broke off a piece. Having put some honey on it, she took it outside where she sat on the wall to eat it, the sea breeze refreshing on her face. To her relief the food seemed to settle her stomach.

Looking out on the water, she wondered how Annie and Mick were getting on. The journey to Schull would seem endless to poor Annie. Ellen couldn't help but worry about what they would do now that Mick wouldn't be able to work for the foreseeable future. Maybe someone could go and talk to Travers, the new landlord, get him to give Mick some sort of reprieve until his arm healed. She tut-tutted over the fact that Mick wouldn't let her give them some of her money.

Frustrated, she stood up quickly and suddenly the scene in front of her blurred and wavered. She sat down again, lowering her head until her vision cleared. She had never felt faint before but she'd been told about it often enough by the women who had come to her when they were first expecting. Ellen raised her head as realisation dawned.

Once again she laid a hand on her stomach, this time not to quell the sick feeling but as though to protect what she guessed had begun to grow inside her. Time seemed to stand still as she tried to take it in. As she counted the weeks now she realised that it was almost four since she and Blake had first lain together and that she should have had her monthly bleed a week ago but it hadn't come. She must have fallen pregnant on their very first day as lovers. She had not protected against it when she had been with him that first time, it had all happened so fast. She had protected against it the times after that . . . but it had been too late.

Fear shook her. Her situation was already delicate because of the new priest and his attitude. Now she was pregnant and unmarried! What would he make of that? No one knew about Blake. Wouldn't this confirm one of Father O'Riordan's suspicions – that she slept with men for money? But what would he do about it?

She had heard of women being banished from their communities because of being pregnant outside of wedlock. Again she was grateful she wasn't living in the village, that her home was somewhat removed from the community. And it was her home, she owned it, she reminded herself. She couldn't be cast out of it. But would the priest tell everyone to shun her? Stop the shopkeepers from serving her, stop her from visiting her own sister. Did he have that power? She might like her solitude at times but she also needed to be a part of the community of Ballinmara.

Maybe, she thought, she could keep it a secret. She began to count on her fingers. It was nearly July and she wouldn't begin to show until the autumn. Then it would be cold enough to go everywhere in her cloak which would surely conceal her growing stomach from prying eyes.

But then, in less than nine months, early March, there would be a baby that she could not keep hidden. She moaned.

She would think of something – she would have to. She would not be driven out of the place she loved. She would tell Annie when the time was right, and she might help her work things out.

Getting up slowly to prevent getting dizzy again, Ellen moved down onto the strand, thinking of Blake and how he would he react. Would he be very angry to have an illegitimate child growing up here on the peninsula? Would he think she was trying to bind him to her in some way? He surely wouldn't think she would expect him to marry her, a fisherman's daughter? Perhaps he might think that she wanted money from him.

For goodness' sake, this is Blake you are talking of, she reminded herself. Deep down she knew he wouldn't think any of those things of her. If anything, he was so caring he might actually offer to marry her, but the absurdity of it made her laugh.

"He dines off fine china, and I serve stew in wooden bowls!" she told the sky.

He couldn't be lowered and she could not be elevated. She didn't know where they could go from here. Sorrow squeezed her heart. She pictured Blake here on the beach, holding their child in his arms and she, Ellen, by his side, and she yearned for it to be possible.

But it wasn't. However, she would have his child to love and nurture. Perhaps he would come and visit sometimes. She took consolation from this, knowing she loved him more than she ever thought it possible to love anyone.

She wrapped her arms around her stomach. A life was growing inside her – a life made from the love she and Blake shared.

Stopping at the edge of the water, she watched the power in the waves. She felt that elemental power course through her veins. Closing her eyes she opened her palms towards the sea. The salty spray drifted her way, touching her face with the delicacy of a spider's web. Strength seeped into her, moving from her feet to the top of her head, giving her courage. She smiled, confident that she was fully capable of raising their baby by herself, even though she would always wish for the presence of its father.

Opening her eyes she looked into the endless depth of the blue sky.

"Thank you for the gift of this new life," she said. "May it grow well inside me. Bless me so that I may be a worthy mother to it, and that I may love and protect it all my days."

Lowering her hands to her stomach, Ellen breathed deeply and felt a new and powerful love.

Chapter 29

There was no word from Annie that night or the next morning. Not wanting to wait any longer for news of Mick, Ellen struck off for the village in the afternoon. She had felt queasy again for a while that morning, but luckily it had passed off by mid-morning. What she felt in her stomach now was anxiety at the thought of telling Blake, and part of her wished he wouldn't visit for another few days so she could get used to the idea herself first.

Knowing she couldn't go to Mick and Annie's house, she hoped someone in the village would know if they were back from Schull. More than likely the butcher's wife would be the best person to talk to, but as she walked onto the main street she saw Annie coming out of the shop, with the baby on her hip, a basket in her hand and Michael walking beside her, holding onto her skirts.

"Annie?" she called.

Annie turned a pale, tired face towards her. Ellen rushed over and took the baby into her own arms.

"Come and sit by the harbour and tell me how things are," Ellen said.

"I only have a few minutes," Annie replied wearily.

"You look dead on your feet," Ellen said, leading them to a low wall where they could sit down.

Michael played near some fishing nets that were laid out on the ground, and Ellen settled Róisín on her lap, dropping a kiss on the top of her head, thinking of her own secret which she would keep from Annie until a more appropriate time.

"Don't touch those nets, Michael," Annie called, seeing that the nets were glistening. "They're still wet after being cured in the barking pot."

He nodded and started throwing pebbles in a pool of water instead.

"We only got back an hour ago," Annie told Ellen. "I left Mick sleeping, he was exhausted. I had to come down to get some meat. He bled a lot and needs to build up his strength, the doctor said. Mary is watching him for me."

"Was it awful?" Ellen asked.

Annie, who had tried to be strong in front of Mick, let the tears come. "I was so afraid because it kept bleeding," she said, swiping the tears away with her hand. "Luckily, like you said, he passed out so didn't suffer too much on the way there. The men carried him into the doctor's house and he put something on a cloth and pressed it over Mick's nose and mouth which knocked him out entirely. Then he pushed the bones back into place." A shudder shook Annie's body. "He spent a long time stitching the wound up, having to put that cloth over Mick's nose twice more before he was finished. Then he bandaged up the arm and made a splint for it. He let us stay there for the rest of the night. Mick was in a lot of pain on the journey back this morning – every bump in the road had him breaking out in a sweat and cursing until the air was blue." Annie gave a weak smile but then started sobbing in earnest. "Oh Ellen, what are we going to do? The doctor said it could take a couple of months for the arm to heal. How are we going to pay the rent? We could be evicted next week!" Her voice rose in terror. "And all because of some stupid fight. Eoghan and Mick are always sparking off each other over one thing or another."

Ellen put her free arm around her and drew her against her shoulder, where Annie sobbed out her fear. Ellen rested her chin on her hair and stared out to sea.

Michael ran over, upset to see his mother crying. Annie straightened up and quickly rubbed the tears from her face. "It's all right, Michael, Mammy is fine." She smiled at him though her voice was still shaky, and pulled him in for a hug.

"We'll think of something, Annie," Ellen murmured. A plan began to form in her mind but she had no intention of sharing it with her in case it didn't work.

"I'd best be getting back," Annie said, picking up her basket. "I need to get this food into Mick."

"You concentrate on making him well for now, all right?" Ellen said, passing Róisín back to her and bending down to give Michael a hug.

She watched them walking away then turned for home herself. She took her time and for once did not take in the scene around her as she walked. Her mind was totally preoccupied with how she might help Annie and Mick.

She had already decided that it should be herself that would go to Bantry and talk to this Travers person and see if he would give Mick a reprieve from paying rent until he could go back fishing. Around here they all said he was cold and hard-hearted, and judging by the way he had callously sent out his men to evict the Coughlan family, it would seem to be true. And, though she tried to see the good in everyone, she was not so naive that she didn't know there were people out there who just did not feel compassion for their fellow men. Perhaps this Travers was one of them, like they were all saying, but all she could do was try to talk to him and let him see that Annie and Mick and the children were real people with a real problem, and also were people who would work hard to make up the rent as soon as they could.

Her temper rose at the thought of the worry this man was putting on Annie and her family, and how arrogant he must be up there in his big house in Bantry making cruel decisions and ruining people's lives – a man who didn't think twice before throwing people out of their homes.

Flushed with her emotions, she turned around and went back into the village. Passing by the butcher's and the post office, she pushed open the door of the pub. It was too early in the day for anyone to be in drinking, but the owner, Andy Minehane, was in there sweeping the floor, an apron tied around his waist.

"Good afternoon, Andy."

Andy looked up in surprise. "Well, good afternoon yourself, Ellen.

A bit early in the day to be calling in for a drop of the hard stuff?" He leant the broom against the wall, and crossed his arms over this chest. "What can I do for you?"

"I was wondering if I could borrow your pony and trap to go to Bantry tomorrow? I have a bit of important business there."

Curiosity lit his eyes but to give him his due he didn't pry. "That would be no bother at all. What time do you want him ready for?"

"Ten, please."

"Grand. I'll see you in the morning then," he said, reaching for his broom.

"Thanks, Andy. Good day to you."

Ellen left, planning that once she got to Bantry she would ask the whereabouts of Mr. Travers' estate. She hoped that after going all the way, Travers would be at home when she got there.

Chapter 30

Ellen was up in plenty of time the next morning. She moved slowly about the cottage doing her chores, not wanting to bring on a fainting spell. She was very nervous that the journey would make her sick and she had too much to accomplish as it was. Of course if Annie and Mick were evicted they were welcome to move in with her, but she knew Mick wouldn't hear of it.

She had already discovered that if she ate often it stopped her from feeling sick, so she had a good breakfast and wrapped up a large amount of buttered bread and cheese to take with her for the journey. She also brought an earthenware jar of water.

To help with her confidence at having to face this landlord, she dressed in her best dress and tied her hair back with ribbon. Her black boots she had polished the night before until they shone. She laced them up and straightened her skirt. Gathering up her parcel of food and water, she put on her straw hat and walked into Ballinmara and straight to the public house.

It was ten on the dot and Andy, having kept to his word, had the pony and trap ready outside.

"Morning, Ellen," he greeted her.

"Good morning, Andy. Thanks again. Here – I brought you a pot of honey and some dried carrageen."

He took them from her. "There's no need for that. You're

welcome to borrow the trap any time, you know that. Still, you know I love the honey." Smiling, he reached out and gave her a hand up.

"Thanks, Andy. Pleasant enough day for the trip anyway," she commented, glancing up at the light cloud cover which she felt sure would burn off as the day went on.

"You'll get there and back without being rained on, I think – the sun will be out soon," Andy predicted. He reached into his pocket. "Sorcha asked me to give you this. She left for Cork yesterday to stay with my sister."

Ellen opened the envelope and read the note.

Dear Ellen,

I'm leaving for Cork today. Thank you so much for suggesting this to us. Andy's sister has two interviews arranged for me – one at the Imperial Hotel and the other at the railway offices on Penrose Quay. I'll be staying with Andy Minehane's sister but will starting looking for a boarding house soon. Eve will come up then and I'll help her look for a job too.

When we're both settled, we plan to go to school by night because some day I want to work in an office, maybe in the bank or the Opera House even!

Thank you again and if ever there is anything we can do for you, just ask.

Sorcha

Ellen smiled wistfully down at the letter in her hand. She hoped that what she had feared for them, the community turning on them, might not now be her own fate. She was pleased Sorcha had got away and hoped it wouldn't be too long before Eve could leave too.

"Your sister is very good to help her get a start in Cork," she said as she folded the letter and put it in her pocket.

"She's a good soul. She likes it in the city. Me, I could never leave here. I think I'd be miserable if I didn't have sea air to breathe," he chuckled.

"I know exactly how you feel."

"Go on now. I'm delaying you."

Ellen clicked at the pony and they took off at a trot.

The road wasn't very busy. Market day in Schull wasn't until the following day. She hoped she wouldn't be too tired to go after making this trip today. She had her knitting to sell but if she was too tired she'd have to wait until the following week. This trip to Bantry was more important.

The countryside looked well as she drove on. In most fields the swaths of hay had been gathered up into stacks seven or eight feet high, drying in the sun before they could be drawn into the haggards.

Halfway to Bantry, Ellen began to feel sick. Stopping the trap, she took up her parcel, opened it and ate.

When her stomach had settled she moved on again. It was with relief that she reached the outskirts of Bantry.

In the town she pulled to the side of the road by the shoemaker's and went in. The smell of leather was strong. A man was bent over his work, but looked up as she approached.

"Excuse me, but could you tell me where the Travers estate is?" she asked him.

"It's inland a bit," he answered, a small tack hanging from the side of his mouth and an unfinished shoe on the wooden last in front of him. "Go up through the town on this road until you come to the fork and take the right. Go along there for about a mile and take a left – there's an old tree stump on the corner. It's along there about a half a mile."

"Thank you," Ellen said. "You've been very helpful."

The shoemaker nodded before taking the tack from his mouth and tapping it into the sole of the shoe with his hammer.

Ellen returned to the trap

She followed his directions, her stomach now jittery with nerves. When she saw the tree stump her palms began to sweat but determinedly she pulled on the reins and turned down the lane. On the small country road the air was full of birdsong and the scent of cut hay drifted her way. She rounded a bend and saw two huge gateposts at the entrance to an avenue. Her grip tightened on the reins, forcing the pony to stop. Taking a determined breath, she urged him on again through the gates. The avenue was lined with trees, their leaves whispering softly in the breeze. The same breeze touched a welcome coolness to her warm cheeks.

The avenue curved and a massive three-storey house came into view. Ellen gasped. It was huge and austere. The avenue split in two, to circle around a fountain, to meet again in front of a set of stone steps which led up to an imposing front door.

Ellen hesitated, unsure how to proceed. Surely it would be an affront to Mr. Travers to knock at his front door without an appointment and she not even of his kind? The wisest choice would be to go to the servants' entrance and ask to see him. Trying not to be intimidated by the grandeur of her surroundings, she stopped the trap beside an arch to the right of the house, presuming it would lead her to the back entrance. She could hear voices and activity coming from that direction.

Having tethered the pony to a nearby branch, she walked over to the arch and paused. In front of her was a courtyard, with the house to its left, stables to the right and on the side opposite her an opening to another yard which gave way to other sheds and open fields. Servants were going about their chores. A maid was carrying two buckets towards the house and there were sounds of activity from the stables, while a stable lad was leading a couple of horses out into the yard. Three men were standing talking at the far side.

Ellen was wondering who she should approach when one of the men turned and made to go towards the house.

The breath was stolen from Ellen when she saw who it was.

Blake!

Though puzzled at seeing him there, her heart soared with relief at seeing the familiar in such a foreign place, and she was just about to call out his name when one of the men he had been talking to called after him.

"Mr. Travers, sir! Was it the east field you said?"

Blake stopped and turned back. "That's right." He turned again and disappeared into the house.

Ellen stared for a moment in shock at what she had just heard, then swiftly stepped back under the arch out of sight of the courtyard. Feeling ill, she leant back against the wall.

Travers! He had said his name was Stephens. He had lied to her about his name. No, no, no, her mind repeated over and over. Blake cannot be Mr. Travers – he could not be the cruel landlord they were all so frightened of! But hadn't her own eyes and ears just told her it was so?

Maybe she hadn't heard correctly. She would follow him in and they would be laughing in a few moments about what she thought she'd heard! She walked quickly across the yard and in through the same door Blake had used. Before she could change her mind, she ran up a flight of stairs and found herself in the main hall. Blake wasn't there. She looked around at the many doors leading from it, unsure what to do next.

Then she heard a voice from behind a closed door near her. She moved close to it. The voice was muffled but, listening intently, she was sure it was Blake's. She had raised her hand to knock when the words he was speaking registered with her.

"I want you and Pearse to keep up the pressure on my tenants on the Mizen. And they'll pay up if they know what's good for them."

He was Travers all right!

Jerking away from the door, she moved rapidly across the hall. She opened the heavy door as quietly as she could and, having pulled it to behind her, she hurried to the pony, untied him and climbed into the trap. Flicking the reins she sent him racing down the avenue, wishing to get as far away as she could, her reason for coming completely forgotten.

How could she, of all people, with her intuition and instincts, have been so wrong about his character? To think he had it in him to threaten to throw families out of their homes without a care! Why hadn't she sensed some evil in him?

And she was carrying his child. She prayed she wasn't going to be sick as she was jostled about in the trap.

She reached the gates and had to slow to take the turn onto the road, but then she flicked the reins again for the pony to pick up the pace, as her whole body trembled. "Granny's vision is coming true," she said aloud. "'He and his kin will bring trouble to you and yours!' He will evict Annie and Mick and it will be all my fault for not paying heed to the warning, making these bad things happen."

A bird, startled by the pony's hooves, rose squawking from the ditch.

Leaving the lane by the tree stump and turning onto the wider road, she slowed the pony and tried to steady her breath. She could scarcely take it in. Travers the landlord was a monster. How could Blake, the gentle kind man she knew, and he be one and the same?

The sound of a cart approaching from the opposite direction

roused her from her dark thoughts. She wiped the sweat from her brow with the corner of her shawl, and pulled the trap over to let it pass.

Back in the town square, she let the pony drink from a water trough there, while she ate some bread and drank some water from her jar, still feeling sick with Blake's betrayal.

She returned to Ballinmara weary and troubled. When Andy saw her pull up outside the public house, he came out.

He reached out a hand to help her down and stared into her face. "You unwell, Ellen? You look a bit flushed?"

"I'm fine. It's very hot today."

"Did you manage to get your business done?" he asked cheerily.

His question brought on the desire to cry and, not trusting herself to speak, Ellen just nodded.

She made to lead the pony round the back but he said, "That's all right – I'll take her round and unhitch her."

Ellen cleared her throat. "Thanks, Andy. Goodbye."

She walked home, burning with the pain of Blake's deception.

Chapter 31

Blake was frustrated at not being able to get away from the estate. They'd had some sick cattle and fearing that whatever ailed them would spread to the rest of the herd, they had been trying to keep the sick animals apart from the healthy ones, and watch every animal daily for symptoms. He longed to return to Ellen but he knew he just couldn't leave for another few days at least. He trusted the men who worked for him but he had to be on hand.

It was mid-July already, nearly two months since he had first met her and he often thanked God for the storm that washed him up on her beach.

She was the joy in his days, days which otherwise were often fraught with tension especially since his relationship with his half-brother had deteriorated further of late. They continued to disagree on Arthur's treatment of his tenants.

Blake tried to make up for Arthur's greed by gifting food to the workers on the farm and by visiting the tenants' holdings and paying for repairs if they were required.

When Shaughnessy's widowed sister was ill a couple of weeks back and he saw how worried Shaughnessy was, he insisted on bringing in the doctor and paying for the visits himself.

Shaughnessy was extremely grateful and, when she was well again, he thanked Blake profusely and pledged his continued loyalty.

Blake brushed off his thanks, saying that Shaughnessy was a valued worker and he joked about needing him to be able to concentrate on his work rather than on any of the family being sick. But Shaughnessy knew that Blake cared deeply about the people who worked for him and they in turn were grateful to have him as a buffer between them and his brother.

One evening, at dinner with Arthur, Blake raised the issue of their father's will. He had not told Arthur that he was going to contest the will because he wanted to keep things peaceful until it was necessary to tell him. But he felt he had to prepare the ground a little first – make Arthur aware of the unfairness of it. He chose his words carefully, keen to see what reaction he would get from him.

"Father knew I loved this estate and he praised the way I did things. You know the effort I have put into it over the last number of years. So do you not think it unfair that you got the whole estate? I wonder what you think about the possibility of splitting the estate evenly with me? Of course you would keep the house."

Arthur was pouring wine into his glass and replaced the bottle on the table none too gently. He looked at Blake aghast and then burst out laughing.

"Have you lost your senses? I was his firstborn from his first marriage. The entire estate is rightfully mine. You earn enough from managing, to supplement the money he left you. I give you a damn fine salary." He snorted then drank half the glass of wine in one go. "Being the son of his second marriage," he continued scornfully, "you ought to be grateful you have a good living from the estate."

Blake bristled at the insult to his mother but knew from experience that it was pointless trying to make Arthur see things differently.

"I am still his son," he said quietly, trying to suppress his temper.

"Yes, but I have no intention of going against Father's wishes, so you might as well drop the subject." He waved his knife at him. "If you're getting restless here and are unhappy with the circumstances of it, you could always move on, you know. But you'll never have it as good as you do here – what with your free bed and board and the salary I pay you," he finished with a smug gleam in his eye.

"And you'll never have it so good with an estate manager who works like I do, and you know it."

Arthur shrugged and refilled his glass, but a steely look had come into his eyes. "Just be warned, Blake. I won't keep having this conversation with you. The matter is closed. Father made his choice and that is the end of it."

Blake clenched his jaw at the finality of Arthur's tone, swallowing hard on the words that rose in his throat. He forced himself to continue eating, knowing he would have to bide his time.

He would have to get away in the next few days to see Ellen and bring some sanity back to his life. The simplicity of her life was a balm to his agitation.

Thinking now that the silence over the meal was going to burst his eardrums, Blake spoke again. "What about your new holdings on the peninsula? How are things going out there?"

Arthur coughed, almost choking on a piece of food. Blake had to stand and hit him on the back. Eventually he recovered his breath, wiping at his watering eyes with his napkin.

Blake resumed his seat.

"Excuse me," said Arthur.

Blake persisted. "I was asking – how are things going out on Mizen?"

"It's all fine."

"You don't talk about it. Do you have anyone managing it?"

"The land is all given over to holdings. All that is to be done is to collect the rents when they are due."

"I could have a look around out there for you if you like, check that everything is all right with the tenants."

"No!" Arthur replied sharply. "There's no need for you to involve yourself with it. Just concentrate on here – surely that keeps you busy enough? If not, then perhaps I'm paying you too much."

Blake didn't dignify that nasty remark with a response.

But after a moment he said, "Where are your new lands exactly?"

"They are my business. Leave it alone."

"Just make sure you are doing things correctly in your pet project, Arthur. At least honour Father's good name." Blake threw his napkin on the table and left the room.

Chapter 32

Annie was waiting at the cottage when Ellen got back from Bantry. Sitting on the low wall she had to shield her eyes against the sun to look up at Ellen, who Shep was welcoming home with furious tail-wagging.

"Where have you been?" Annie asked. "I didn't see you in the village on my way through and I've been waiting here for half an hour."

Ellen didn't answer but asked a question of her own, as she took a key from her pocket and unlocked the door. "Where are the children?"

"Mary took them to give me a little rest and I took the opportunity to come here," Annie replied but her voice sounded distracted and she didn't follow Ellen in.

Ellen turned to see her standing outside with her hands on her hips.

"And since when did you start locking your door?"

Ellen wearily brushed a hair back off her face and went to hang up her shawl.

"A couple of weeks ago."

"Why?"

Ellen thought quickly. "Well, I keep a lot of herbs here and I just thought if someone ever strolled in they might help themselves and

168

do themselves more harm than good. I thought it the wise thing to do – I should always have been doing it."

"Oh." The puzzlement left Annie's face and she followed her in. "I wondered if you had something you could give me that I could put into Mick's tea to help with the pain. He's very crotchety."

Ellen had bent down to light the fire and when she turned around Annie saw her face properly.

"Ellen? You look exhausted. What's the matter?" she asked, going over and gently pushing Ellen down onto the chair.

The tenderness in Annie's voice was Ellen's undoing and the tears she had held in all day started to fall.

"Annie, I've let you down."

Her words were only a whisper, but Annie could hear the anguish.

"What is it, Ellen? What's happened?"

"It's a long story, I'm afraid," she said.

"I've got time," Annie encouraged, pulling up the other chair near her.

Ellen looked across at her sister, wondering if she should tell her everything. Ellen had always been the strong one and had always looked out for Annie, but today she desperately needed to lean on someone.

Taking a steadying breath she wiped her eyes and began her story. "I met a stranger back in May. He was washed up on the shore after a storm and I helped him and then sent him on his way. He was strong but gentle in nature, with fine blue eyes and fair hair. And though he was gentry he looked well in my cottage, sitting by my fireside." She sighed wistfully at the memory. "I know I should have forgotten him straight away but I couldn't stop thinking about him." She looked into Annie's eyes, willing her to understand. "It was as if he was still here with me even though I had sent him away! I could hear his voice, see his smile, all inside my head. I missed him! Missed someone I had only spent a few hours with." She shook her head in bafflement.

But Annie nodded.

"The moment I helped him, something changed in here." Ellen pressed a fist to her chest.

"But why did you send him away?"

"I had no choice. He was gentry. He didn't belong in a place like this," she replied, withholding some of the story.

"But I'm guessing that's not the end of it?" Annie encouraged softly.

Ellen gave a small shake to her head. "He came back to thank me and I sent him away again but I already knew that doing that was pointless. I had lost my heart to him."

Annie waited.

"He came back a third time and declared his love for me! Me, a fisherman's daughter! The man had no sense." A faint smile lit Ellen's eyes. "I was so happy, Annie. I knew we didn't have a future and that we were both fooling ourselves but I felt complete when I was with him and I wanted love just for a while. Was that so wrong?" Her eyes pleaded with Annie for some unspoken absolution for her own weakness.

Annie reached out and gave Ellen's fisted hands a quick squeeze, then waited for her to continue, quite amazed at the secret life her sister had been leading.

Ellen continued. "He was gentle and kind and interested in my life here. When he discovered I was a healer it didn't bother him at all!" She shook her head in wonder at the memory.

Annie still remained quiet, knowing the story was about to take a turn.

Predictably, Ellen's face clouded over again. "He wasn't from here and I never knew his real surname – until today." She lifted huge sad eyes to Annie's. "I went to Bantry to see if I could get the landlord to give you and Mick a reprieve of some sort until Mick was able to fish again."

Annie gasped. "By yourself! Are you mad in the head? What happened?"

"It was him – Blake! Blake Travers, your landlord, is the man I helped and fell in love with."

"Oh Ellen!" Annie breathed.

"How could it have been, Annie? If you had met Blake, you couldn't believe he could be so cruel to his tenants. Even Shep liked him." She gave a weak laugh that turned into a sob. "How could I have been wrong about him?"

"What did he have to say for himself?" Annie asked, indignant on her sister's behalf. At the same time, while her heart was breaking for

Ellen, she wondered if there was any hope that Travers' feelings for Ellen would make him look more kindly on Mick's situation.

Ellen hung her head. "I didn't speak to him. I went into the house after him, sure that I must have heard wrong, but then I heard him behind a closed door talking about his tenants here and that he'd make them pay their rent. I couldn't face him after I heard that. I was scared and I ran out as fast as I could." She raised eyes full of shame. "I ran away, Annie, before putting your case to him. I'm so sorry."

Annie swallowed her disappointment while at the same time she felt huge love for Ellen. "I'm so sorry he lied to you, Ellen. What will you do now?"

"He and I had no future anyway. At least my first instincts were correct there. But I thought I would know his love for a while yet. I can have nothing more to do with a man who treats his tenants like that and who wilfully deceived me."

Annie leant forward and took her in her arms, rocking her as she would have one of her children. They pulled apart and Ellen sat back, defeated.

"You understand that I can't go back to Bantry to see him again, Annie, to plead your case? I'm sorry."

"Of course I understand, but maybe I could go and tell him I'm your sister. If he loves you, maybe he will show me some kindness?"

Ellen hated to shatter the hope she saw in Annie's eyes but she had to say what she felt. "I thought I knew him, but obviously I don't – so your guess is as good as mine as to what he would do. But I wouldn't hold out any hope. If he could do what he did to the widow Coughlan, well ..."

A minute passed before Annie spoke. "Fishing is all Mick knows. And who would give him work anyway with a broken arm? The fish we salted for the winter I'm going to have to sell now to pay next month's rent, but then after that I don't what will happen."

Ellen looked sadly at her, knowing she still hadn't told her everything. But she just couldn't tell her about the baby yet because she felt so confused and upset herself.

"Is there any work at all you could get yourself? Does Andy need help in the pub maybe? I could mind the children for you."

Annie was chewing her bottom lip. "It's worth a try, but I doubt it. There are so few jobs for women here."

Ellen didn't comment. Wearily she rose from the chair. "I'd best get you those herbs for Mick. He'll be screaming the place down by the time you get back."

Annie stood. "Yes, I've stayed longer than I meant to. But what about you, what are you going to do about Travers?"

"I don't know, but I want nothing to do with him, that's one thing certain, now that I know the truth about him."

She quickly wrapped the dried herbs in a cloth and gave them to Annie.

"One spoon in his tea should be enough to help the pain. Be sure to hide them where neither he nor the children can find them.

"Thanks, Ellen. Will you be all right?"

"Yes," Ellen replied, not believing her own words. "Off you go and look after your man."

Annie gave her an attempt at a reassuring smile and left.

Chapter 33

A sliver of waxing moon was framed in Ellen's window later that night. It had been a long and emotional day and, though exhausted, she wasn't able to sleep. She tossed and turned, tormented by something else her grandmother had once told her.

They had been tying up some herbs together when she said something that had shocked Ellen. She had told her that a certain concoction of herbs could make a woman lose the baby she was carrying.

Horrified at the thought, Ellen had asked her grandmother if she had ever had cause to use it.

The old woman had looked her straight in the eye and answered her.

"Yes," she had said. "Not for myself but for my own sister, who was set upon by a drunken man one night, who forced himself on her. He was a cruel man even when sober and she was young and unable to cope with the thought that she might be carrying his baby. No one knew what had happened, except me – she didn't want the shame of it. She came to me straight away, the morning after the attack, and I gave her the herbs. She bled the next day and shortly after moved to Galway so she would never have to see that man again. She married a nice young man there. He had big dreams for them and luckily for them they emigrated to America before the famine came. They made a good life together over there."

Ellen had stared at her. "But wasn't it wrong, Granny?"

"I won't know that until I meet my Maker, child, but my sister knew peace and love for the rest of her life and was a loving wife and mother. Who can say what's right and wrong for different people? I said I would teach you all I know. It will always be your choice as to what you do with that knowledge."

Now, remembering that, Ellen rose, threw a shawl over her nightgown and left the bedroom. For several minutes she stood as still as a statue in the middle of the kitchen, facing the dresser.

Her grandmother had told her that day exactly what herbs could be used to make a woman bleed, and though she had been asked for them a few times before by mothers who felt they couldn't cope with another baby, she had always talked them out of the desire to use the herbs, teaching them instead how to prevent further pregnancies She believed her gift was to sustain life, not end it. As a result, she had never given out that combination of herbs before.

Ellen's feet grew cold on the hard flagstones as she stared at her assortment of jars for a very long time. In the flickering light of a candle, her hand looked pale as it seemed to move of its own volition towards the jars. With stilted movements she transferred some of them from the dresser to the table before pouring out neat little piles onto a board there. Heartsick, she moved to the hearth, stirred up the embers of the fire and placed a kettle of water above the renewed flames. Straightening, she absently rubbed her hands to stop their trembling.

While standing there, staring, she suddenly felt like she couldn't breathe. Backing away she turned, flung open the door and fled from the cottage down to the beach. Her feet slapped out a rhythm on the hard sand which couldn't drown out the sound of her pounding heart.

Stopping at the water's edge she let the water lap over her feet. Shaking and feeling sick, she gulped in the cool night air. She gazed for a long time at the black peninsula across the water and eventually her heart beat and her breathing slowed to a more natural rhythm.

After a while she became aware that her feet were becoming numb. She stepped back out of the water and spoke out loud into the clear night air.

"Maybe Blake Travers was greedy but does that mean I shouldn't have his child?"

174

No, it doesn't mean that!

She felt as though her head asked the question and her heart gave the answer. She rested her hands on her stomach and continued the conversation, her eyes searching the stars.

"Because Blake couldn't be in my life or this baby's life, is that a reason not to have it?" Again the question came from her head.

Definitely not, her heart replied again.

"Just because the child might have his blue eyes ..."

The question remained unfinished as Ellen moaned. The image of Blake rose before her, those same blue eyes full of tenderness – tenderness for her as they had made love.

She hugged her stomach, rocking back and forth in turmoil. When her grandmother had given those herbs to her sister it had been in very different circumstances. She couldn't equate that situation with her own. It was Blake's wonderful loving of her that brought this baby into being. Also her grandmother and grandaunt didn't know for definite if she had fallen pregnant. This life had been growing inside Ellen for nearly a month.

With sudden clarity she knew she couldn't do it, wouldn't do it. She already loved this baby with all that was in her.

With a cry that was wrenched from her very soul she turned and raced back up the beach and into the cottage. Stopping inside the door, she looked at the assortment of herbs she had laid out on the table, her heart pounding once more. Taking a sure step forward, she swept her arm across the table and knocked everything onto the floor, totally ashamed of herself for having laid them out in the first place, for even contemplating it.

With a surge of energy she rushed back out in the darkness and ran back down on to the beach where she stripped off her nightgown and dived into the sea. She dived and surfaced several times, letting the cool water stream over her body, cleansing her mind and her spirit.

After a while she floated on her back to catch her breath. She knew there would always be an ache in her heart for the loss of Blake, but now she was confident of moving forward as the only parent to her child. Who knew, she thought, maybe he or she would be a healer too?

She woke the next morning, totally calm. Her decision not to rid herself of the baby had also been her decision to move forward without regret. Her strength had returned and she felt peaceful.

The first thing she did was to clean up the mess that was scattered across the floor. When she had the fire lighting she threw the herbs onto it and with relief watched their smoke disappear up the chimney.

She put her hand on her stomach and spoke to her child.

"Forgive me. You are mine and I love you. It's because I wanted you that I couldn't do it and, from this moment on, I promise to do all in my power not to let you down."

Putting on some water to boil, Ellen set about making some porridge for her breakfast before getting on with her chores.

About an hour later a woman from the village arrived with her three-month-old baby who had a small burn on its arm.

"How did it happen, Aoife?" Ellen asked, examining the burn.

"I was just finished feeding him, sitting in the rocking chair by the fire like I always do, and a log hissed and spat out one single spark that landed right there on his arm. I couldn't believe it. I've fed three other children in that chair and never saw the likes of it. I brushed it off immediately so I don't think it's too bad, but it certainly made him roar. I'm telling you, I won't be sitting that close to the fire again." She crossed herself. "It could have been his face!"

"Thank God it wasn't," Ellen said, bringing over a jar of ointment. After putting some on the burn, she wrapped a piece of clean muslin around it. "It's not a bad burn at all. Keep the air off it for a few days and it should be fine. Come back again if you think it isn't healing up."

Aoife cuddled her baby close and Ellen longed to reach out and take the baby in her own arms.

Smiling tenderly at the two of them, she showed them out.

Not ten minutes later a second woman arrived, also with a baby. This one was going on eight months. Ellen wondered at the coincidence. Was Fate giving her a chance to heal babies this morning, to in some way make up for her thoughts the previous night?

"She's such a bad sleeper, Ellen, we are all exhausted from her. And even during the day she seems agitated."

"Does she feed all right, Treasa?"

"Yes, there doesn't seem to be any problem there."

"Let's take a look at her then."

The mother stripped the baby down and laid her on the cloth which Ellen had spread on the table.

Ellen felt all around the baby's body, then laid her hands on her stomach. She shook her head. "There doesn't seem to be any problem there," she said. "Sometimes, some babies need more soothing than others. I'm going to show you how you can rub her feet and then the rest of the body in a way that will relax her. You should do this a couple of times a day and especially before you put her down for the night. Try it for one week and let me know if there's any improvement."

Ellen showed the mother what to do, always working the movements towards the baby's heart. She was cooing softly by the time they were done and the mother laughed at the change in her. Ellen prayed for a blessing on both of them.

After they left Ellen went up onto the cliffs and sat there for a long time, preparing herself for Blake's visit, knowing he would surely come that day, which was Saturday, or if not, then the next.

In Annie's cottage, Mick had been quiet all morning. Annie was making him some tea, pleased that the herbs she had slipped into it the day before and that morning seemed to have eased his pain. With her back turned to him now as he sat by the fire, she stirred in some more. Then Róisín started crying and, afraid that this might attract Mick's attention, she rushed what she was doing, spilling some herbs on the table.

"What have you got there?" Mick said, jumping up and shoving her out of the way. "What are you putting in my tea, woman?"

"It – it's just something to take away the pain in your arm," Annie said, backing away from him. "I gave it to you yesterday too and it's been much better, hasn't it?"

"Is it from her?" he roared.

Anne said nothing.

With lighting speed, his good arm shot out and punched her in the stomach. She dropped to her knees, winded, her two arms wrapped around the pain.

Mick swiped the cup off the table where it smashed on the floor, spraying Annie's skirt with tea.

"Don't you ever bring anything from her into this house again," he snarled and, leaving her there fighting for breath, he stormed out.

Annie gasped in air and sank further onto the floor. Her gasps turned to sobs.

Chapter 34

Saturday passed and Blake didn't arrive. The following morning, Ellen had just returned from Mass and was removing her shawl when she heard a horse approaching. Her eyes closed as she took a deep but shaky breath, preparing herself for what she had to do. The day was blustery and threatened rain so she stayed inside, moving over to the fireplace to wait for him to knock.

There was one quick rap on the door and he called her name as he opened it.

His handsome face was smiling and his eyes were full of warmth when he saw her standing there.

"Hello, Ellen," he said, crossing the floor in two strides and pulling her into his arms. "How I've missed you!" he murmured, his lips pressed to her hair. "I'm so sorry I've been gone so long."

Ellen allowed herself to be held, while her heart ached at the fact that it would be for the last time. Her hands however, remained by her sides, a fact that soon registered with Blake.

He drew back.

"Ellen?" he queried, searching her eyes.

"Will you take a seat, Blake?" she said softly, her heart still so disbelieving that this wonderfully warm, tender man could be cruel to anyone. She forced herself to remember the Coughlan family leaving the village with no home of their own anymore and that he had lied to her about his surname that very first day.

"What's the matter?" he asked, waiting for her to sit, before taking a seat himself.

Up on the cliff the day before, she had worked out what she was going to say, knowing that he would not tolerate being sent away like the first times. She also felt sure that he would not believe that she had stopped loving him. The only way was to appeal to his love for her.

"We've been discovered," she lied, though the anguish in her voice was very real. "And it has brought trouble for me."

Blake moved to the edge of his seat, towards her, his face darkening with concern.

"Someone saw us on the beach and told the parish priest. He has threatened to make an example of me, saying he would ask everyone in the parish to have nothing to do with me if I continued to be a loose woman."

"It's none of his business!" Blake exploded.

"Unfortunately he thinks everyone and everything that goes on in his parish is his business. I don't want to be treated like that by everyone if he carries out his threat, so I'm going to ask that you don't visit me for the rest of the summer."

"What!"

"It's just so that things will quieten down for a while. He probably has his spies watching me, and this place."

"This is ridiculous. We'll marry and that'll show him. Loose woman – how dare the man!"

Pain and confusion shot through Ellen. How could he be so willing to cast all convention aside in an attempt to protect her reputation? These were the impetuous actions of the man she had thought him to be. Reminding herself of who he really was, she clenched her fists, and went on, battling to keep her voice even.

"No, Blake, thank you for the generous offer. But it is a ridiculous suggestion. You and I are worlds apart. You would be the laughing stock of your class if you brought a fisherman's daughter home as your wife. And even if that was not the case, I would not marry you. It would be for the wrong reasons and much too soon." A look passed between them and she knew he was thinking about how soon they had become lovers. She blushed but lifted her chin and continued as she saw him about to protest. "I've already told you that I believe a marriage between two people from different classes, and in our case religions, won't work. You have your life there in Bantry," her voice faltered as she remembered him standing in his own yard, "and I have my life here, one I don't want to leave. We'll appease Father O'Riordan for now, by making sure we are not seen together, and in the autumn we can see how things are." And by then, when he had been away from her all that time, he might be more able to believe that she didn't want him.

"But how will anything have changed by the autumn? Your priest is hardly going to be any more tolerant by then?"

Ellen thought quickly. "It'll give us time to think of something and might remove his preoccupation with me."

Seeing he was going to continue arguing with her, she reached out and put her hand in his. His fingers quickly closed over hers.

"Please, Blake, you wouldn't see me shamed in front of my own people, would you? If you really love me, you'll do this for me." She dropped her eyes from his, hating herself for the deception, and forcing herself to think of who he really was out there in the world beyond her home.

Blake shook his head in disbelief. "I would do anything for you, but this is madness. Are you sure the priest has that kind of power?"

Ellen sighed inwardly with relief, knowing he was believing her lies. "Oh, he has that kind of power all right," she said, this time speaking the truth. She withdrew her hand, warmed by his touch, and placed it on her lap. She looked up at him and saw love for her all over his face and felt as though Blake was one person and Blake Travers another. If only it were true, she thought.

"I can't believe you are asking this of me, Ellen." His eyes searched her face. "You could move to Bantry," he suggested, grasping at a solution.

"I could never leave here. It's not just where I live, Blake. It's my spiritual home. All that I am is interwoven into this place – the sea, the land, the sky, the generations of my family who have lived, loved and toiled here before me." Rising, she went to the door and opened it, letting him hear the rush of the waves. "That sound is as familiar to me as my own heartbeat. I go to sleep to the sound of it and I wake to the sound of it."

He came and stood beside her, listening, before pulling her into his arms. "If you think this is what has to be done, then of course, for your sake, I'll do it. I want to keep seeing you but your safety and happiness are the most important things to me." He lifted her chin so she was forced to look into his eyes. "I will use the time to think, to figure out how to change your mind, and find a way of seeing each other again."

Ellen wanted to scream: I can never be with you, when you treat people the way you do – why did you have to be Travers? I loved Blake, just Blake, the person you are when you're with me!

"Perhaps it would be wise for you to spend the time thinking of your own future, Blake. You're under no obligation to come back to me in the autumn. We always knew this was temporary anyway. I would never keep on seeing you once you marry someone more suitable."

Blake swore beneath his breath, not wanting to think of anything beyond these four walls and the woman in his arms at that moment.

Ellen lowered her eyes and pushed back from him, afraid that she would break down if he didn't leave right away.

"You have to go. That way if you were seen arriving they can report that you only stayed a very short while."

"You think someone is watching the cottage now?" he asked, concern for her pushing out all other thoughts for the moment.

She shrugged. "Perhaps the lane to here, watching who is coming and going."

He pulled her close again, crushing his lips against hers. Her traitorous mouth kissed him back – kissing Blake – the man she had saved on the beach.

Then he was gone – leaving her shaking with a need that she shouldn't be feeling, now that she knew what he was.

But before he left there was something else she had to do. So, pulling herself together, she ran outside. He was already in the saddle.

"Wait!" she called, going over and catching hold of the reins, placing her hand on the horse's neck to calm him. "I need to ask a favour of you." Her heart pounded and she had to take a steadying breath before continuing but still her voice shook. "My sister Annie and her husband Mick Leahy are tenants of a landlord near Bantry, who now owns land around here. He has already evicted a widow and her children who couldn't pay the rent two months in a row." Ellen saw Blake's jaw muscles flex and his eyes harden. She swallowed and ploughed on, her grip on the reins tightening. "Mick is a fisherman and he's broken his arm. He won't be able to work for the next couple of months. They have two children. If you know this landlord, can you appeal to his good nature and ask for leniency for them? The landlord's name is Travers."

A look of disgust passed over Blake's face and Ellen felt sick. She waited, her heart thundering, praying he wasn't going to admit it was him. She didn't want that confrontation – the pretence was easier to deal with.

"I'll see what I can do," he said, his words clipped and his eyes clouded with anger. "Take care of yourself, Ellen."

She stepped back. He pulled on the reins, turned the horse and set off at a gallop.

Ellen stumbled onto the beach and threw up, again and again, her body heaving with the effort.

With her eyes still watering, she returned to the cottage, trembling and weak. After washing her face, she crawled under the blankets fully clothed. She closed her eyes but Blake's angry face was there beneath her lids. Bereft, she curled into a ball and wept.

Chapter 35

Furious, Blake galloped along the road away from Ellen's. Disgust at his brother seeped from his every pore, making his skin crawl. To see the woman he loved having to plead with him to speak to a stranger on behalf of her sister made him seethe. He was so ashamed of Arthur's behaviour that he hadn't been able to bring himself to tell her that he was his half-brother. Whether that was to spare his feelings or hers he wasn't sure, but there had been enough pain in her eyes without him adding more. He was glad now that he had given her a false surname at the beginning and had never told her since what his real name was.

The heartlessness of Arthur's actions sickened him and he couldn't get back to Bantry fast enough to talk to him and do all in his power to take this burden of worry from Ellen. He knew his anger was masking deeper feelings of loss at her decision to once again send him away from her so soon after they had become lovers. He buried those feelings deep for now, the anger being easier to cope with.

He could understand now why she was pale today. She was under so much strain, worrying about whether her sister and her family might be heading for the poorhouse, and she herself dealing with the fear of being ostracised by her community because of her association with him. He was angry at himself for bringing such trouble to her. He should have heeded John and Grace when they warned him to stay away from her.

Blake was still in the grip of a temper when he arrived back at the estate. Handing his sweating horse over to the stable lad, he strode into the house and straight to Arthur's study, bursting in without knocking.

Arthur's head snapped up. "What the devil?"

"You greedy bastard! You evicted a widow and her children out on the Mizen!"

Arthur leaned back in his chair, folding his hands carefully over his ample belly. "I've warned you stay out of my business, Blake!" His voice was low and cold.

"No, I will not. We share the Travers name but, by God, we will not share your reputation!" Blake put his hands on the desk and leant over it, his eyes level with Arthur's. "No more evictions, Arthur! Tenants are people – people doing their best to make a living to feed and house their families!"

Arthur was growing red in the face. But Blake held up a hand to stop him from speaking.

"You're a businessman, Arthur. The promise of rent further down the road is better than an empty holding. Where do you think you are going to get new tenants to fill the cottages you have evicted families from? You must have been out of your mind buying holdings on the peninsula when you didn't have a clue about the way of life there. It's only a couple of hours away but it's very different. All your tenants here are farmers. There they are farmers and fishermen. When the sea is rough, the men cannot fish. No fish, no income – no income, no rent until the sea calms again. A man gets injured then he cannot fish – again no income, no rent, until he gets better. But then they pay again when they can, and make up the difference – if – they – can!" Breathing heavily he glared at Arthur. "A landlord has to be flexible!"

He straightened and tried to rein in his temper before continuing.

"The lands around here are good – your tenants here rarely miss a payment. But out there it's different. The weather is harder on them. The land is rocky for the farmers and the sea unpredictable for the fishermen. You should have got to know all this before you took them on as your tenants or better again you shouldn't have taken them on at all! I want you to withdraw your threats of eviction and I want you to show flexibility. I am talking particularly about Mick Leahy and his family in Ballinmara. He's injured his arm and won't be able to fish for two months or more, and therefore won't be able to pay rent. You can well afford to show him leniency." He waved his arm at the opulence of the study.

"How dare you give me orders!" Arthur raged.

"I dare for the sake of those people but also because, if you don't start taking proper care of them, I'll start dropping words into the ears of your society friends and let them know what kind of man you really are. Then let's see how your business dealings slide and how your invitations to shooting parties start to dwindle. No one admires cruelty, Arthur."

"So you are threatening me, you little upstart!"

"That's exactly what I'm doing," Blake said coldly, "and you'd be wise to heed it!" Leaving Arthur fumbling for a reply he turned on his heel and left, not bothering to close the door after him.

Going straight out to the yard, he went looking for Shaughnessy. The only one he saw was the same stable lad who was still brushing down Blake's stallion.

"Eh, it's Sunday, Mr. Travers, sir. He'll be at home with his family."

"Oh yes, of course," Blake said, knowing he badly needed to cool down since he had even forgotten which day of the week it was. "Thank you," he said absently to the boy.

On foot, he made his way across the fields to Shaughnessy's cottage. Passing a cock of hay, he ripped out a stalk and stuck it in his mouth. Shaughnessy was a good man and he knew him to be loyal to him and not to Arthur. Blake needed to speak with him.

As he walked, he promised himself that he would write to the solicitor in Cork to try to get things moving. If the man was still sick, then he would take the business elsewhere. If the estate could become his, it would sort so many things out.

The walk took the edge off his temper. At the cottage he tossed away the stalk of hay and knocked. Shaughnessy's sister opened the door and gave him a shy smile. "Mr. Travers, nice to see you, sir. Won't you come in?" She opened the door wide.

Blake smiled his thanks, bent his head and entered the cottage. "How have you been, May?"

"Much better, thank you, sir, and thanks to you for getting the doctor to visit me."

"That's good news. I apologise for disturbing your Sunday afternoon but I wanted a word with your brother."

"It's no trouble at all, Mr. Travers," she said warmly. "He's out the back, by the stream, showing my Donal how to catch minnows."

Thanking her, he went back outside and around to the stream that ran behind the cottage. He could hear voices and laughter, and soon saw Shaughnessy and his nephew standing in the water with their boots on the bank beside them and their trousers rolled up to their knees. The sight of them made Blake pause.

Their heads were close together as they examined the contents of a jar. It was an affectionate and intimate moment and a stab of longing shot through Blake for the warmth of a proper family. Shaking off the feeling, he moved forward but was already regretting his intrusion.

Shaughnessy caught the movement, lifted his head and greeted him warmly.

"Ah Mr. Blake, sir. We've been catching some minnows."

"Good afternoon, Shaughnessy. Hello, Donal." The young boy nodded at him. "I was wrong to come down here and interrupt your leisure time. What I wanted to talk about will keep." He smiled and looked at the jar with the tiny fish swimming around inside. "Enjoy your fishing. I'll talk to you tomorrow, Shaughnessy." He started to turn away but Shaughnessy stopped him.

"Not at all, sir – we can have a word now. My feet are shrivelling up we've been standing in the water so long!" Shaughnessy ruffled his nephew's hair. "Go on in with you and show your mother what you caught, but put them back in the stream before too long."

The young lad trotted off with his jar while Shaughnessy stepped up out of the stream and sat on the grass, shaking his feet free of water.

"Don't bother trying to get your boots on," said Blake, lowering himself onto the grass. "We can sit here for a while, and let your feet dry."

The ride to and from Ellen's and the fight with Arthur had left him weary. Sitting with his knees drawn up and his forearms resting on them, he gazed at the clear stream. Shaughnessy stretched his legs out. Trees lined the bank, and the sun's rays streamed through them, causing a dance of light and shadow on the lazily moving water. Only a few birds were singing in the warmth of the afternoon. Blake felt the peace begin to seep into his soul. He sighed, wishing he didn't have to turn his mind back to Arthur, but it had to be done. His gut twisted at the thought of not being able to fix this for Ellen.

"Shaughnessy, did you know that my brother evicted a woman and her children from her home down on the Mizen and that he has threatened to evict a fisherman and his family next?"

Shaughnessy nodded his head. "I did. I overheard Pearse and Nolan talking about it in the pub."

"That was my next question. Are they the men that Arthur sends down there to collect the rent?"

"Yes, sir. Begging your pardon, but I don't think he would use any of the men from this estate in case it would get back to you."

"I'm sickened by Arthur's behaviour."

"I thought you might be," he looked apologetically at him, "but it wasn't my place to tell you about it, sir."

"I know that, Shaughnessy. What are those two men like?"

"They're hard – will do any job for money, I'd say. Mr. Travers pays them to go down there once a month to collect for him and to let it be known he's not for bending. What I overheard was that some widow couldn't pay them the last time they were there and that Mr. Travers sent them back down to throw her out. That was their words, not mine." Shaughnessy also drew up his knees and lowered his voice. "None of us here would do such a thing, sir."

"I know it. It cannot go on and I just told him so." Blake heard the other man's sharp intake of breath. Turning his head, he smiled at him. "Foolish of me, you probably think, but it's about time I stood up to him. The people need to be helped to improve their lives, not be constantly knocked back by another man's greed."

"Well said, sir. But how will you get him to change his ways?"

"I just threatened to ruin his standing with his social circle by telling them of his uncharitable deeds!"

Shaughnessy burst out laughing. "You really did stick your neck out the whole way today, didn't you, sir?"

Blake smile ruefully. "The question is whether Arthur thinks I would have the ear of any of them and whether it's enough to scare him. You know how he loves to go to all those hunting parties. I couldn't think of any other way in the heat of the moment, or in the temper I was in!"

"Well, good for you for trying."

"If only he would let me manage the holdings down there too. But he seems to have a particular attachment to his new project, and is very secretive about it."

Both men stared at the stream for a moment in silence.

"So ..." Blake plucked a blade of grass, thinking. "So," he repeated, "I would appreciate it if you could keep an ear out for any information about the tenants down there."

"Certainly I will."

"That fisherman he is threatening to evict?"

"Yes?"

"His wife's sister is a friend of mine. It is important to me that they are treated well. I've told Arthur not to evict them, and to give them grace on their rent as the man has broken his arm."

"He won't be in the best of humour with you for that!"

"I know, but it had to be done." Blake jumped to his feet and offered his hand to the other man, pulling him up. "I appreciate your support in this, Shaughnessy."

"My pleasure, sir." Shaughnessy bent to pick up his boots and socks and walked beside him barefoot.

"May is looking well," Blake remarked.

"Yes, thanks to you. Also we got good news yesterday. Her other son, Timmy, got a job as an apprentice in an office in town. He's a bright boy. I always knew he'd go places. We're very pleased for him. He was never one for the farming, but a great one for the learning. It was tough on him when their father died. But he'll make his way now all right. And his earnings will help May too."

"That's great news. I wish him the best of luck." He looked speculatively at Shaughnessy. "I suppose you might start thinking about marriage yourself now," he teased. "An old man of thirty like yourself, aren't you leaving it a bit late?"

Shaughnessy laughed. "Ha – I'm a year younger than yourself, sir. I haven't met the girl for me yet, but can't say as I'd mind settling down with her when I do."

Blake clapped a hand on his shoulder. "That's one wedding I'd like to dance at. I'll see you tomorrow. Thank you again, Shaughnessy"

Blake left, pleased he had another piece of the plan in place. He would send Shaughnessy down there in a few weeks to make sure that Arthur was treating Ellen's sister well. And when next he, Blake, got to see her and tell her that he was Arthur's half-brother, she would know by his actions that he was nothing like him. Shaughnessy might also be able to get some news of Ellen for him.

Stopping, he leant on a fence, and looked out over a field of what was as yet a sea of green barley. Looking harder he could see that a few stalks here and there were beginning to change colour.

He missed Ellen and knew he was going to find it hard to abide by her request to stay away. All the joy he had felt at going to see her that morning had been dashed by her words and he longed to go back and take her away from there. But he knew she didn't want that, and fear for her and what the priest might say about her would have to be the thing that would restrain him for now.

Back in the main house, Arthur was seething. Getting up, he went to a side table and poured a generous glass of port. He had resented his father trying to replace his mother with a second wife and it was the last straw when she gave his father a second son. He had hated Blake from the moment he'd set eyes on his bawling red face and never once considered him a real brother.

And now to think that Blake was telling him how to manage his affairs and daring to threaten him! He didn't want Blake to get any more involved in the Mizen holdings. He would have to appease him for now by showing some leniency to this fisherman he spoke of – Mick Leahy – if only to stop Blake's further interference. If Blake wasn't so good at keeping the estate so profitable, he would have got rid of him before now.

With a grunt he sat back at his desk and pulled open the drawer containing the papers for the lands on the peninsula. Withdrawing a logbook and a map, he placed them before him on the desk. He unrolled the map which had the various holdings marked on it, while hoping that the whole darn thing wasn't going to be more trouble than it was worth. He found Mick Leahy's name in the logbook and the number allocated to his holding. Then he found that holding on the map, cursing the fact that he wouldn't earn a penny from it for several weeks at least. "Bloody fishermen," he muttered as he glared down at it.

Blake had been correct that he hadn't once considered the unpredictability of a fisherman's income. He decided to make a list of the various occupations of the tenants of all his holdings on the peninsula, just to see what he was up against. As he did so, he checked the list against the map, getting a sense of where the farmers lived and where the fishermen lived. He was halfway down the list when he came across a number and a name that he had not noticed before. The holding was on the western side of the peninsula, right on the edge of the sea and the name was Tom Cassidy. He checked the rent books himself every month and it was a name he had not come across before. But the holding was clearly marked as number fifteen on what was now Travers land. He pulled out his rent books and searched for the name. There was no Cassidy listed.

A conniving smile slowly lifted the corners of Arthur's mouth and he rubbed his hands together in glee. He drew a circle around the holding. If someone was living there all this while and had not been paying rent, they would owe him a fortune. If they could not pay, he would definitely evict them. Even Blake could not object to him kicking out people who had cheated their landlord of rent for a long time. And though he would show leniency to that damn fisherman, this other eviction would stop other tenants from thinking he was soft – it would keep them on their toes.

Giving a self-satisfied laugh, Arthur continued to study the map. He would let the dust settle for a couple of weeks around the Leahy business then he would send his two rent collectors out to this Cassidy holding and find out exactly how long they had been in arrears and how much they owed him.

Chapter 36

Ellen was sitting on the grass on the cliff the next morning. The sea whispered soothingly to her from a distance. Knowing she had no one to blame but herself for the situation she was in, she knew she had to put thoughts of Blake behind her and get in touch with her own strength and power again. The heady scent of gorse wafted her way.

Closing her eyes, she breathed deeply, a warm breeze caressing her face.

Acknowledging the sadness of losing Blake, and that it was a sadness she would always carry hidden in her heart, she gave thanks for the love she'd shared with him for a brief time.

"Please bless him and change his heart in his working life to mirror the heart of the man I knew."

She raised her open palms slowly towards the sky.

"I let him go and I release my fears and my weakness. I pray for the strength to continue my work and to nurture this life inside me. I call on the spirits of my ancestors to wrap their light of protection around me so that I can move through each day and do my best for my child. Please help me to ensure its safety and that we can continue to live here when it comes into the world."

Ellen sat there until her arms grew tired. Slowly she lowered them, bringing her hands to rest in her lap. Peace settled over her. Opening her eyes, she looked at the great expanse of blue sea and sky, and then the land across the way, loving every inch of it.

Getting up, she bowed and turned inland. She had to go and see Annie and tell her about her petition to Blake.

Near Annie's cottage she hovered for a while, knowing she couldn't go and knock on the door with Mick at home. When Annie didn't appear, she had to ask one of the neighbour's children to go in and call her out.

Annie opened the door and bent down to hear what the child had to say, then quickly looked over in Ellen's direction. Saying something over her shoulder, she closed the door behind her and hurried over to her while wiping her hands on her apron. She bustled Ellen around the side of the neighbour's house, out of sight of her own cottage.

Annie looked exhausted.

"How is Mick today?" Ellen asked

"A bit better. One of the men suggested he go down to the harbour and help with the catch with his good arm later today if he feels up to it. That would be a relief for all of us if that happens. It doesn't suit him to be in the house." She smiled tiredly at her sister.

"You need to take care of yourself too, Annie. It's taking its toll on you."

Annie shrugged.

"Is he taking his bad temper out on you in any way?"

"He shouts a bit, but sure I'm used to that and I know he's in pain. But we're grand."

Ellen studied her for a moment, not quite believing her and feeling uneasy, but deciding to let it go for now. "Did you have any luck getting a job?" she asked.

She shook her head. "No, Andy isn't taking anyone on, and anyway Mick couldn't manage on his own all day with the children. Why are you here, Ellen? I have to get back."

Ellen glanced around before speaking again. "I spoke to Blake Travers yesterday," she said, lowering her voice, not wanting anyone to hear her utter that name.

Annie's eyes widened. "He came to see you?"

"Yes, but I didn't let on that I knew he was Travers. I asked him to put in a good word for you, if he knew the new landlord for here."

"What did he say?" Annie whispered, gripping her arm.

"He didn't acknowledge that it was him. He just said that he would see what he could do, and though he didn't say anything else I could see he wasn't pleased."

"Oh Ellen, thank you so much for trying!"

"When are you expecting them to come again for the rent?"

"In a couple of days." Annie's eyes were huge with a mixture of fear and hope.

"We'll have to pray that Blake will do us this favour, Annie."

Annie searched her eyes. "And did you tell him that you couldn't see him again?"

Ellen nodded.

"What excuse did you give him?"

Ellen told her what she had said.

"Do you think he'll stay away?"

"If not for my sake, then now surely for his own. He must know that I'll discover his surname sometime in the future. It's all very strange. I still cannot believe he can be this wonderful person with me and this cruel landlord to everyone else."

"I know, and I'm sorry for you that things have turned out this way."

"I brought this pain on myself by giving in to my feelings."

"I'm so sorry, Ellen! And thank you!" Annie glanced back at the house. "Sorry, but I have to go back in now."

Ellen held her arm. "When the rent collectors come, see if Blake has told them to offer any compromise. If not, then you must use this." She held a purse out to her. "It will get you one more month's grace anyway."

Annie looked down at the purse, then up at Ellen with frightened eyes. "But Mick –"

"Surely Mick will relent this one time rather than allowing you all to be evicted?"

Annie pushed the purse away. "No. If the time comes, I'll ask for it, but best not to take it now."

"I just wish Mick didn't hate me and that you all could come to live with me if anything happens, until you get back on your feet."

"Me too," Annie said sadly before turning and dashing back to the house.

Ellen walked by the schoolhouse, closed now for the summer holiday.

That didn't stop a group of children from playing a game with a ball made from a cow's bladder in the front yard. She smiled as she heard their laughter. Wondering if her child would be a boy or a girl, she went home in a daydream.

Ellen fell into a routine for the next week or so, doing her chores and her healing, pushing any sad thoughts away and daydreaming about her baby. She regularly checked on Annie, waiting to hear if the rent collectors had returned. But, as yet, no one had come.

Towards the end of the second week, she heard a knock on her door mid-morning. A man and child she had never seen before were outside.

"Excuse me," he said, removing his cap. "I've travelled over from Schull with my son here because I heard you might be able to help us."

Ellen looked from the man to the boy, who gave her a shy smile, displaying a gap from a missing tooth. She smiled back at him while remembering Fionn's words of caution about treating strangers.

Looking back at the man, she noticed that he wasn't very good at keeping eye contact with her. He spoke again, putting his hand on the boy's shoulder.

"He has pains in his head nearly every day. The doctor doesn't know what it is."

"Who told you to come here?" Ellen asked.

"My wife's friend has an in-law down this way who said you can fix people. I don't know the in-law's name, I'm afraid."

Ellen was sorely tempted to turn them away, feeling an unease at the man's furtiveness, but looking down at the little boy she knew she couldn't refuse him her help.

"I'm in the right place, aren't I?" the man queried. "You are the healer woman?"

Nodding, she stepped back and invited them in. Pulling out two chairs from the table for them, she sat down on a stool in front of the boy and looked into his eyes.

"What's your name?" she asked.

"Colm," he replied.

"Can you tell me about your head, Colm?"

He looked up at the man who nodded at him. "When I wake up

every morning I have a pain here." He pointed to the middle of his forehead.

"And is it a little pain or a really bad pain?"

"Very bad," he said, frowning.

"Is it there all the time?"

The boy was silent and the man answered for him. "He says it fades away by supper time."

The boy nodded vigorously.

"So is it there now?" Ellen asked, watching him closely.

"Yes," he said, again pointing to his forehead before glancing up at the man, then back at her.

"I'm just going to put my hands on your head for a minute, Colm."

Again he nodded.

She placed one palm on his forehead and one on the back of his head, channelling energy between the two. The flow moved unhindered. Ellen frowned.

"Are you sure it's hurting you now," she asked.

"Ye-es." The boy's voice faltered.

Ellen felt her unease return.

"I'm afraid I can't help you," she said, standing up. She caught the narrowing of the man's eyes before he assumed a blank expression. "I think perhaps you should take him back to the doctor."

Moving to the door, she held it open for them. The man put on his cap, thanked her for her time but didn't offer to pay her anything.

Ellen closed the door behind them, her palms sweating.

There had been nothing at all wrong with the boy and she was absolutely sure the answers he had given had been learnt off.

It had been a trap, she was sure of it. She shot the bolt home on the door, wondering if Father O'Riordan had sent them. She hadn't performed a healing, so that could not be reported, but with sinking heart she remembered that the man had asked if she was the healer woman and she had said yes.

With a groan, she ran to the window to watch them leave. They were just walking out of sight around the hill behind the cottage. Dismay was warring with outrage that a child would be used in such a way. If this was Father O'Riordan's doing she disliked him even more than before.

"Dear God, what will he do now if that man goes back to tell him of the visit?" she wondered aloud.

Annoyed at her stupidity, she knew she should have sent them away without letting them in. After the warning Fionn had given her the day the priest had come by, he would be very cross with her for letting her guard down.

It was the middle of the day and she couldn't stay locked inside for the remainder of it.

Standing in the middle of the room, she tried to think what to do. If Father O'Riordan came again, would there be any point in denying what she'd said? It would be that man's word against hers, but she still felt he would believe what he wanted to believe. Would he denounce her from the altar, tell people not to visit her? How would she feel if she were not permitted to help people anymore? It was part of who she was. She knew she would be very frustrated and unhappy if she couldn't continue to use her gift. And on a more practical level, she needed the gifts and money they gave her for treatment in order to get by.

She had told Blake that the priest was causing trouble for her – well, now it looked like that was the truth.

Chapter 37

Two hours passed while Ellen waited, expecting every minute that Father O'Riordan would turn up at the door to give her another lecture. She alternated between being indignant at his interference and being afraid of him.

Just after supper, unable to settle to her knitting, she went out and stood watching the sea. To her relief and pleasure, Fionn Doyle came whistling through the fields. Shep bounded to meet him.

"I was in need of company," Ellen said as he walked up to her, "so this is a real pleasure, Fionn."

He gave her his gentle smile as he crossed his strong arms over his chest.

"I didn't want you thinking I was gone off with my tail between my legs, and not wanting to talk to you again, rejected and heartbroken," he teased lightly.

Ellen laughed. "Oh thank goodness, because I don't know what I'd do without you, Fionn. Would you like a cup of tea or some ale maybe?"

"Ale would be great. I've worked up a thirst on the way over here."

They went in and sat at the table.

"How have you been?" he asked.

She sighed. "You're going to be cross when I tell you what happened today."

He frowned at her serious tone and listened intently as she shared her suspicions about the strangers who had come to see her.

He leant his arms on the table, continuing to frown. "It certainly sounds like they were trying to catch you out."

She nodded. "The boy's answers were well practised, I'm sure of it, and there was nothing at all wrong with him."

Fionn scratched his beard. "If it was the priest who put them up to it, then he's one devious bas–" He stopped himself. "Sorry, Ellen."

She dismissed it with a shake of her head.

"Well, he's certainly up to no good," he finished lamely.

"I kept expecting him to call, but he'll hardly come at this time of the evening."

"I'll watch out for him on my way back and, if he's heading this way, I'll keep him company."

Ellen smiled. "You're so good to me, Fionn." She put her hand on his arm. "And you know I'm sorry that ..."

"It's all right, Ellen – you can't force these things, but let me know if you ever change your mind. I'm a great catch, you know!"

She smiled fondly at him, wishing that she was in love with him instead of Blake – it would make so much more sense.

Fionn changed the subject and told her about his work and the pathway he was crafting at a big house beyond Durrus.

After a while, he got up to go. The sun was low in the west but there were still a few hours before it would set. Shep darted about, following the scent of rabbits.

"Be safe, Ellen," Fionn urged, his look intense.

She went up on her toes and placed a light kiss on his check.

"Thank you, Fionn, for everything."

He nodded and she saw the trace of sadness in his eyes. But he bid her goodbye and strolled off, whistling softly.

Ellen was more relaxed after his visit and very happy that there was no awkwardness between them.

Calling Shep in, she locked the door behind them. She took her time pottering around before bed, but gratefully got into it eventually, falling asleep within minutes.

A short time after, she was awoken from a deep sleep by Shep barking and a moment later heard knocking at the cottage door. Disoriented, she threw a shawl over her nightgown and stumbled in the dark from the bedroom, while shushing Shep whose barking had become louder. The knocking came again. Lighting a candle, she moved towards the door and heard a man call her name.

"Ellen. Open up quickly, we need your help."

Still groggy, Ellen pulled back the bolt and opened the door, while lifting the candle to see who was there.

She only got a brief glimpse of a man with a handkerchief covering his mouth and nose, before the candle was knocked out of her hand.

In the dark she felt Shep leap past her at the man. She heard a dull thud and a whimper, then nothing. She didn't even have time to cry out before she was pulled forward and turned around. A rag was tied around her mouth, preventing her from screaming and her flailing arms were dragged painfully behind her back and tied. Again from behind, a bag made of sacking was pulled roughly over her head and tied around her neck.

She was terrified, and in an effort to breathe her nostrils flared like a horse at a gallop. She was made to walk by being dragged by each arm, someone on either side of her. She heard them grunting as she was lifted and thrown on her stomach across the back of a horse, the animal's withers hitting her stomach and making her groan. With her legs hanging down one side, her head down the other and her hands tied behind her back, her weight pressed down on her chest. She couldn't breathe properly.

Fortunately, within seconds, her hands were untied and pulled down below her head, where they were tied again, the rope burning against her wrists. With her elbows she was able to lever her weight up a little to help her breathing. Then she felt her knees being bound and a tugging on her wrists and she guessed that the rope had been strung under the horse's belly to secure her to the animal. The blood throbbed in her temples when the horse was jerked into walking forward. Her mouth ached from the tight rag and the rhythm of the horse was making her feel ill. The men seemed to be on foot. Her mind raced with fearful questions. Where were they taking her? What were they going to do with her? A vivid image of a woman burning at the stake entered her mind and she imagined her own screams. Terrified, she wriggled against her binding and grunted.

"Not another sound out of you or you'll regret it!" a gruff voice sounded near her ear.

Ellen instantly recognised it as that of the man who had come to the cottage that morning, confirming her suspicions.

They walked on for another while and the man spoke again. "Don't make a sound now."

The horse's pace slowed, and Ellen guessed they were moving through the village. After a few minutes the horse stopped and she felt the ropes being untied. She was pulled down into a standing position and the suddenness of the movement had the blood draining swiftly from her head. She fainted.

Chapter 38

When Ellen came round she was kneeling on cold hard ground, with someone supporting her. Someone else was untying the rope at her neck. Briefly she saw lights flickering through the sacking before it was ripped from her head. Her hair tumbled down around her face and she shook it out of her eyes, frantically trying to take in the scene around her.

She was in the church and Father O'Riordan's portly shape loomed over her, draped in a white surplice and purple stole, his face a hard mask of cold superiority. A ring of candles surrounded her on the floor.

Looking behind her, Ellen saw her abductors standing outside the circle of light, half their faces covered by handkerchiefs, and caps pulled down on their foreheads. Their clothes were the plain work clothes of any man from around there. With a sick feeling, she noticed one man had one of his arms tucked inside his coat, the empty sleeve dangling. Her eyes darted to what she could see of a very pale face. The eyes were hidden in the shade of his cap, but she knew it had to be Mick. Her own brother-in-law! How could he be a part of this? Her head spun with the question. Didn't he know that limp sleeve would give him away? Or, she wondered, was his hatred of her so immense that he didn't care if she knew he was there?

She whipped her head back to stare at the priest, her heart

drumming rapidly. If her own brother-in-law was crazed enough to be helping Father O'Riordan with this, then what was the priest himself – to whom she was nothing – thinking or feeling? Although relieved that she wasn't in some field, tied to a stake, she was still terrified that something like that was yet possible because she felt this man was insane enough to think it justifiable.

Her stomach and back ached and she longed to curl up into a ball, but she straightened her spine and fixed her eyes on the priest's forehead, while silently calling on God to give her strength and to give this man a sense of mercy.

He raised a book that Ellen hadn't even noticed in his hand, and opened it.

"Ellen Cassidy, you are brought here charged of being possessed by the Devil. And with God's help I will drive him from you this night!"

Ellen's gasp was stifled by the rag – the man was going to perform an exorcism! Then she thought: better than burning at least!

Despite her resolve she sank back down onto her heels.

"Kneel up!" he commanded.

She jerked her spine straight again. Despite the ring of candles being part of his ceremony, she called on the light of each one to fill her and keep her strong.

Father O'Riordan made the Sign of the Cross on himself then on Ellen's forehead with oil, making her shudder. He then blessed the two men behind her. Picking up a bowl, he sprinkled them all with holy water.

Resuming his position in front of Ellen, he began the Litany of the Saints. After each saint's name the men responded with "Pray for us!".

His voice droned on and on until he had listed them all, then he moved onto the next prayer.

The stone flagging was unforgiving beneath Ellen's knees.

"From all evil deliver us, O Lord."

The men replied: "Deliver us, O Lord!"

"From all sin –"

"Deliver us, O Lord!"

And on and on it went, his eyes rolling toward heaven in piety. Waves of sickness washed over Ellen again. The prayers led on to gospel readings, then more prayers and Ellen's eyes drifted shut. She stopped listening to the words, but the rhythm of them had her almost in a trance. But then the priest's tone changed, becoming deeper and angrier. Her eyes flew open to behold his flushed face leaning closer and his arm raised above her.

"I cast you out, unclean spirit!" he boomed, "along with every satanic power of the enemy!"

The 's' in 'satanic' sent spittle shooting from his lips to land on her cheek. But she dared not rub it clean against her shoulder for fear of bringing that arm down to strike her in all his rage.

He ranted on and Ellen heard him say "Satan, the corrupter of justice, root of all evil and vice," and she thought of the day her grandmother explained about her gift, and how it was from God and was for the benefit of his children. And now this priest was saying it was all from the Devil. She would have laughed at his ignorance if she wasn't so exhausted and frightened. Instead she stopped listening and prayed to her gentle, loving god, while the self-righteous priest prayed to his vengeful one.

After what seemed like hours, he stopped and took a step closer. Making the Sign of the Cross on her forehead three times with oil, he asked Satan to be gone and God and the Holy Spirit to come in his place.

Ellen's spirit rebelled. Drawing on all her strength she straightened up as best she could, the ache in her knees almost unbearable. She kept her eyes lowered, not wanting him to see the defiance in them. In her head she said: I am already full of the Divine. I always have been and I always will be. I am his child and I am loved.

But knowing that he needed to think Satan had left her and that she would be contrite, Ellen sagged back down as though her spirit was broken. But he still wasn't finished. He continued with more prayers. Ellen began to sway with tiredness and thought she would faint again when eventually he gave a final blessing and told the men to take her home.

She looked up at him.

He gave her one more piercing look. "You have been rid of the Devil, Ellen Cassidy. Be sure to lead a life of God from now on. I'll be telling everyone on Sunday not to come asking you for healing again, so you won't be tempted."

Ellen heard the warning in his words and the threat of further consequences if she didn't comply. She had a fleeting moment of compassion for him, realising that the man actually believed he was doing God's work.

"Hurry now," he said to her abductors. "It'll be getting light soon." He turned back to Ellen. "You'll be permitted to sit on the horse going back but the rag must stay in place to ensure your silence."

Outside in the dark she was lifted onto the bare back of what she now saw was a large workhorse. She was given the reins to hold onto while the man who wasn't Mick, led the horse by the bridle. Mick walked behind. She shivered in the thin covering of her nightgown.

Mick spoke to his accomplice. "I didn't think it would take so long – he's right – it'll be bright soon."

"We'll leave her at the top of the fields. She can make her own way home from there. I don't want to be seen."

Mick just grunted in reply.

Sure enough when they got to the gap in the road that opened into the field near her home, they took her down from the horse without a word being said by either man. But for a brief moment Ellen's eyes met Mick's above the handkerchief, letting him know that she knew it was him. His eyes didn't flicker, just coldly stared back at her. His helpmate nudged him and they both got on the horse and rode away into what was left of the night.

Ellen pulled the rag from her mouth and stood watching them go. She turned to move across the grass on her bare feet, but after only a few steps her legs gave from under her and she slumped to the ground in exhaustion.

She wasn't sure if she had fainted again, but next thing she knew she heard Fionn calling her name and him running towards her. She opened her eyes to see that the dawn had arrived. Fionn's bag of tools were thrown to the ground as he fell to his knees beside her.

"In God's name? What's happened? Why are you out in only your night clothes?" He pushed her hair off her face. "You're as pale as a sea fog!" He helped her up.

She licked her dry lips. "Fionn, can you help me home?"

With a smothered oath he carefully lifted her into his arms.

"I'll have you there in no time," he murmured. "I'll build you a nice fire and get you grand and warm again."

Ellen pressed her face against his chest and sank into his strength as he kept murmuring words of comfort.

On arriving at the cottage, he pushed the door open with his foot and carried her inside. Ellen lifted her head, looking for Shep in the dim light. He was lying by the hearth. With a whimper he got up and walked on unsteady legs towards them.

Fionn set Ellen down in the rocking chair and lit a candle. He pulled her shawl from the hook by the door and put it around her shoulders.

Ellen pulled Shep towards her. Her cheek rubbed against a damp patch on his head. She angled it towards the candlelight and saw that he had bled from the blow he had received.

"Shep's been hurt. Can you bring a bowl of water?"

Fionn did as she asked and began building up the fire while she cleaned the dog's wound. For the first time since the ordeal began, she let her tears fall.

"Oh Shep, I'm sorry," she crooned as she carefully wiped the small gash on the side of his head. "This wasn't your battle, but thank you for trying to help me. They shouldn't have done this to you." She swiped at her tears, and Shep licked the saltiness from her fingers, his eyes dull and subdued. When she had cleaned him up, he laid his head in her lap and they stayed there for a while, drawing comfort from each other.

Fionn looked on in anguish. "For the love of God, Ellen, please tell me what happened?"

Ellen raised a tearstained face and her heart twisted to see such loving concern etched on his.

Her stomach was still aching. "Can you give me a few minutes, Fionn? I want to change out of this nightgown and into something warmer."

"Of course," he said. "I'll make you some tea."

"Thank you."

In her bedroom, she stripped off her nightgown, feeling humiliated and grubby after her mistreatment.

Tossing it on the bed she saw spots of blood on the back of it. She thought for a second that it was from Shep, but his blood was on the front of the nightgown.

Her hand flew to her stomach and a new kind of fear ripped through her at the thought that she might be losing her baby. She bathed and put on her clothes, praying for herself and for her child, praying that her body, despite all it had been through over the last miserable hours, would be able to hold onto it.

Ellen had never felt so vulnerable. She returned to the kitchen, where Fionn was now sitting in the other chair next to the fire. He took one look at her large, frightened eyes and held out his arms to her.

Tired of carrying everything alone, she sank down onto his lap and curled up like a child, her head resting beneath his chin and his comforting arms around her.

"Father O'Riordan performed an exorcism on me," she said.

She felt Fionn's muscles tense.

"Holy Mary, Mother of God!"

She nodded against his shirt. "He believes I was evil but that the demons are gone now."

"Is the man insane? How did he even know what to do! I thought they were a thing of the past."

"He read it all out of a book."

His arms tightened protectively around her. "Did he hurt you?"

"No, but it was exhausting. I had to kneel on the floor of the church for what seemed like hours. He didn't lay a finger on me, except to put oil on my forehead. I just had to kneel there for a very long time while he talked on and on, and sprinkled holy water over me every now and then."

"But how did he get you to go there?"

Ellen told him exactly what had happened but omitted that she had recognised one of the men.

"I can't believe someone from our own parish would be a party to that."

"I think Father O'Riordan actually thinks he was doing me a huge service. Perhaps those men think the same thing. And now that they think I'm cleansed, hopefully that will be the end of it."

A weary sigh escaped her, and Fionn kissed the top of her head.

She watched the flames flicker and dance and thought how easy it would be to let this become her life: Fionn here, taking care of her, loving her. But she had loved Blake and now she was carrying his child. That changed everything.

There in the quiet of the cottage and in the warm haven of Fionn's arms she told him everything, from Blake appearing on the beach to her grandmother's warning, to their falling in love, to Blake's deception, and lastly that she was now carrying his child. When she was done, she pressed her hand to his chest to lever herself away, but he didn't release her, moving one hand to gently press her head back down on his chest.

Several minutes of silence passed. "So you say Travers isn't going to be part of your future?"

"Of course, not. It's impossible." Her voice trembled a little with the reply.

"Then, Ellen, let me take care of both of you. You don't need to be alone."

Hearing the love and sincerity in his words made tears once again escape and roll down Ellen's cheeks. If only she could accept his offer.

She clung to him for a moment until she felt able to speak. "I'm not worthy of such love, Fionn, and you're being impulsive." She wiped away the tears with the back of her hand. "You can't possibly know that this is what you want after what you've just heard. You haven't had time to think about what you would be taking on. Please, let's not talk about it now. Too much has happened. I'm too tired to think straight and you were on your way to work and I'm keeping you from it."

This time when she moved, he let her get up, but once standing he took her hands in his, holding her gaze. "I'll let it lie for the moment, but please think about it, Ellen. Can I come back to check on you this evening?"

She could only nod, as tears once more clogged her throat at his tenderness. She was so very fond of him. And as she watched him go, she wondered for the first time if it might be enough.

Thoroughly exhausted, she went to bed, where she curled up under the blankets fully clothed and once again prayed for her baby. Shep came in and lay down beside the bed. She was glad of his company.

Chapter 39

Ellen's slept until the afternoon sun shone through the bedroom window. The ache in her stomach had eased. To her relief the bleeding, which had been slight, had stopped during the morning and she had whispered words of encouragement and love to her unborn baby.

Now, moving gingerly, she sat up on the edge of the bed, her eyes falling on the burn marks on her wrists where the ropes had chaffed them. She then examined her knees, which were badly bruised.

Cautiously she stood and, with every muscle aching, she moved into the other room where she spread ointment on the burns and bruises.

To her relief, Shep's eyes were brighter. He went and stood by the door and she let him out.

Even though she had very little appetite, she ate some bread before returning to bed. She had often heard from the midwife that women who bleed before their time had to rest as much as possible so they could hold onto the baby.

She forced herself to lie still, willing her body to heal and become strong. Instead of feeling anger at the priest, she pitied him for his ignorance and closed-mindedness and again prayed for him. As regards Mick, her thoughts were for her sister, fearing for her that she was married to someone so full of hate. She prayed hard that his feelings toward her didn't affect his love for Annie.

She was grateful that no one had come to her door that day.

When thoughts of Blake began to whisper at the edge of her mind, she let them in. The memory of that first evening and night they'd had together was the comfort she needed at that moment. She wouldn't destroy those memories by becoming bitter over what couldn't be. For the sake of their child she would always treasure that time together, keep it separate in her mind from all that had happened since, and honour it, because it was what had given their baby life. The passion she had known with him was something she would never forget.

The warmth of the dawn hours in Fionn's arms was also with her. There was a lot to be said for feeling safe too, she thought.

In the early evening, she got up to prepare some food and check on the donkey and the hens. Shep was a bit more energetic and was back barking at the seagulls down on the beach. She had only just sat down in the rocking chair when she heard Fionn outside calling out a greeting to her.

He tapped on the door and came in.

She remained seated and invited him to take the other chair.

"How are you now?" he asked.

She smiled. "I'm fine. Still a bit tired. Thank you so much for helping me, Fionn. I could have perished from the cold, if you hadn't come along."

"Father O'Riordan hasn't been here, has he?" he asked gruffly.

"I don't think he'll be bothering me anymore now. I'm sure he feels his work is done. "

They sat in silence for a moment.

Then Ellen spoke her thoughts. "I believe I'm lucky that he thought I was possessed by the Devil."

Fionn snorted in disbelief, but she held up her hand, stopping him from speaking, and continued: "At least he felt he could rid me of that. What I feared was that he might think I was a witch and he might resort to another obsolete practice to sort that particular problem."

What she was implying slowly registered with Fionn and his eyes widened in horror.

"You don't really think he would be capable of that, do you?"

"I honestly don't know."

"And what now?"

"I think he'll continue to check on me and he'll tell his parishioners not to come to me for healing."

"And you won't be healing any strangers again!" Fionn warned.

"Indeed I won't – I've learnt my lesson."

"I'm not going to stay since you're still tired." He glanced around the room. "Are you going to be all right? Is there anything you need?"

"I'll be fine, but would you mind drawing a bucket of water for me from the stream before you go."

"Of course. Anything else? Turf, firewood?"

She shook her head.

When he had brought in the water she gave him a reassuring smile, and stood to see him out.

"Thanks, Fionn. And oh, please don't tell Annie. She has enough to worry about."

"Don't worry, I won't tell a soul. Goodnight, Ellen," he said softly.

"Goodnight."

Ellen looked down at the sea. She had always prided herself on her independence but she was forced to admit that she felt vulnerable and lonely. The wind was off the land and the sound of the waves was carried off over the water, making all quiet where she stood. Even the lonesome gee-uck, gee-uck cries of the seagulls seemed far away as they dipped and dived near the edge.

Calling Shep to come up to her, they went inside. Locking the door behind them, she settled in for the evening with some knitting in her lap, and she allowed the memory of the tender look in Fionn's eyes to give her comfort.

Chapter 40

Three days after Ellen's ordeal and oblivious to it, Annie was going about her usual morning routine of dressing the children and getting breakfast for Mick. One of the children was crying and they weren't aware someone had approached the cottage on horseback. A sudden pounding on the door startled them.

Annie's face blanched as a look passed between her and Mick. Swallowing, she went to open the door. The same two rent collectors were outside – one stood at the door and the other remained astride his horse.

"Mrs. Leahy, is your husband at home?"

Annie stepped back to let him see Mick rising from his chair, his splinted arm held up by an old torn shirt which was tied around his neck. He winced as pain shot through it. It had been aching horribly since the night at the church and he had been exhausted in the days afterwards. It had been too soon after the accident to be so active but when Billy, the other man there that night, approached him, knowing how he felt about Ellen's healing, he agreed readily to help as he relished the thought of being involved in 'fixing her'. The pain he was feeling now he believed was worth it, to put a stop to Ellen's deeds.

But Ellen and her healing were insignificant now when he had the matter of these rent collectors to deal with. The man at the door moved inside and removed his cap.

"I've been told to inform you that you don't have to pay rent for the next two months. It's presumed that your arm will be mended by then and that you'll be back fishing. If you're not better, then at that point Mr. Travers will require a letter from the doctor telling him how much longer he thinks it will take."

Mick stared at him, hardly able to take in what he was hearing. "Th-thank you," he stammered.

Annie had twisted her apron into a knot and was also staring at the man, who then turned on his heel and strode out, leaving the door ajar.

A speechless Annie closed it after him. Relief radiated from her face as she turned back towards Mick. He smiled, the first time in ages, and held out his good arm. She went to him, hugging him hard, hoping things could improve.

"How can this be?" Mick muttered.

Annie lifted her head and laughed. "Who cares, as long as it's not a dream! Tell me I'm not dreaming, Mick!"

"You're not, love," he said, planting a solid kiss on her lips. "If it wasn't for this arm, I'd pick you up and dance a jig with you around the floor this very minute," he said, now laughing along with her.

Moving away, she picked up the baby and took Michael by the hand. "We'll dance for Daddy," she said, dancing them around the floor, while Mick hummed a jig, tapping his foot and watching them with laughter in his eyes.

Later that morning, feeling energetic again, Ellen was getting through her chores. Her morning sickness persisted, which only made her smile, confirming her baby's existence. The marks had faded on her wrists, but the bruises on her knees had turned into all the colours of the rainbow.

She was making bread when she heard Annie calling her name excitedly. She burst through the door as Ellen was rinsing her hands. Ellen saw the change in her immediately, the careworn look replaced by a huge smile.

Throwing her arms around Ellen, she laughed and babbled all at once. "Thank you, thank you! It worked! Travers says we don't have to pay rent for the next two months!"

Ellen pulled back and held her by the shoulders, incredulity spreading across her face. "Really?" she gasped.

"Yes, the same rent collectors came but they said that we didn't have to pay for two months and even then only if Mick can fish again!"

Relief flooded through Ellen, not just for Annie's situation but because of the good Blake had found within himself in dealing with it.

"Oh Annie, this is wonderful news!" She hugged her again.

Annie took Ellen's hands. "He did this because of his feelings for you, Ellen. You must let that give you comfort."

"It does, it does. Oh, thank the good Lord, Annie!"

They moved outside. Sitting in the sunshine on the old stone wall, Annie recounted what had happened. Then looking at Ellen she said: "Maybe your Blake Travers is redeemable. Maybe all it takes is the love of a good woman like yourself to make him kinder?"

Ellen smiled. "Maybe," she murmured, a part of her wishing she had the opportunity to influence him further. But she had sent him away and she still believed that that was for the best and, besides, it had been only one gesture of kindness to one tenant. She wondered if his attitude to all the others would remain hard.

Afraid Annie would press the issue further, she asked after the children and Mick, working hard at keeping her voice neutral as she said his name.

"I've never seen him in such high spirits! I think he'll mend quicker now, knowing there's hope for the future."

"It really is wonderful, Annie," Ellen said and, remembering how awful Annie looked the other day, she longed to ask her if Mick was treating her well, knowing how roughly he had treated her the night of the exorcism. But she didn't want to raise Annie's suspicions, so she didn't ask. Instead, she decided to give her a version of the truth about Father O'Riordan's wishes.

"I've something to tell you too. Father O'Riordan has spoken to me. He knows about the healing and he doesn't approve of it. He has told me to stop."

"No!"

"He's going make some kind of announcement from the altar on Sunday, telling people not to come to see me with their ailments. I've already turned away two people yesterday and it nearly broke my heart to do it."

"But what if you just ignore him?"

"He'll make trouble for me, Annie. I have to do as he says. So don't send anyone to me."

"But how are you going to manage?"

Ellen smiled brightly. "I'll just have to knit more!"

"Well, I'll make sure you always have plenty of fish. We owe you that at least for your help. But besides making a living, how will you feel, not being able to do your healing?"

"Maybe I can still treat animals without upsetting him. That might have to be enough for now. We'll see. But I'll have to lie low for a while." She sighed and went on. "But I know you're right – being a healer is a huge part of who I am, so to keep doing it I'd have to sell this cottage and move somewhere else, but the problem is that living here is also a huge part of me and I don't think I could ever leave." A lump formed in her throat at the thought of it.

"No, you can't go," Annie said, looking desolate at the thought.

Ellen still couldn't bring herself to tell Annie about the baby. She had given her enough to worry about for one day and, besides, this was a good day for Annie and she wanted her to leave as happy as she arrived.

"But no more thinking just now. Your news is wonderful. Come on, let's go down to the water – it looks lovely today, doesn't it?" Giving a light laugh, she rose and they walked onto the sand and across the beach with Shep dancing around them.

When Annie was leaving, Ellen gave her a letter to post on her way back through the village. The letter was to Father Goggin. He had asked her to let him know if Father O'Riordan caused her any trouble, so she wrote about the exorcism and how unhappy she was at not being able to help people.

She didn't know if there was anything he could do to help, but writing to him reminded her of his kindness and understanding and that had brought her some comfort.

At the same time, in Bantry, Blake sat at his desk reading a letter, the first of two that had been delivered that day. It was from Felicity Hannon.

Dear Blake,
It has been several weeks since our pleasant afternoon in Bantry.

I trust you are well and I apologise for the delay in writing, but Mother was unwell for a while and not disposed to having visitors.

However, she is well again now and my father is holding a hunt here in two weeks' time and we would be delighted to have you as our house guest for the weekend.

Yours,

Felicity Hannon

This was the invitation he had put so much hope in receiving back in June. The idea of marriage to Felicity suited him fine back then because he thought it was what he needed.

Tossing down the letter, he stared out the window.

What had Ellen said just before he left the last time? That she wouldn't keep on seeing him once he was married. For a moment he tried to imagine what it would be like to be married to Felicity and to have Ellen as his mistress. The thought twisted his gut. It would be a loveless marriage and a lie. And, though married to Felicity, he felt the betrayal would be against Ellen. And he knew he could never leave her arms and go falsely into the arms of his wife, feigning affection for her. The whole idea was abhorrent to him but so was the thought of a marriage to Felicity and never seeing Ellen again.

Ellen had said more than once that she would not fit into his world and he had to admit the truth of it.

He thumped his fist on the desk.

But what if he was to move into hers? He was deeply in love with her, and believed it vital for him to have her in his life.

He had thought gaining Felicity's hand in marriage and gaining an estate of his own was the best thing for him. But he had come to realise that working the land was what gave him satisfaction and that socialising in rarefied circles had never held much appeal for him. It would not cost him a thought to give it up. If the solicitor in Cork could not do anything about their father's will, he might just leave the Bantry estate. With his savings perhaps he could buy a decent enough amount of land closer to Ellen. Maybe he could even persuade Arthur to sell him his land out there, now that he was having difficulty with the tenants. What with working his own land and receiving income from the holdings, he could carve out a simple living for himself and Ellen. He knew he could be happy there – the difficult part would be convincing her of that. Yes, he thought, working his own land, with the woman he loved by his side – now that was a satisfying thought. If Ellen could be happy in her cottage with her garden and herbs, then he couldn't see any reason why he couldn't be too.

Pulling a sheet of paper towards him, he wrote a reply to Felicity, expressing his regret that he would not be able to attend the hunting weekend. He didn't attempt to explain anything in the note, for there was no easy way to describe the situation he was in. And if he tried, he would be laughed at, he felt sure. He hoped that someday soon he would get a chance to explain his position to her and ask her forgiveness for allowing her to think that something might develop between them.

He could almost smell the smoke from the bridge he was burning, and it was with a certain amount of regret that he sealed the envelope, knowing he had chosen the more difficult course. But he also knew that if he could make things work out the greatest reward would be his.

With that task completed, he reached for the second letter, which had a London postmark on it.

The letter inside was from his aunt Violet, his father's sister. It read:

My Dear Blake,

Once again I apologise for not being able to attend your dear father's funeral. I still cannot believe Jeremiah is gone and that I will never see him again. I hope you received my letter of condolence. Since Henry's tour of duty in India was near its end, it was impossible for us to leave at that time.

But we are now back in London for good. However, on my arrival I went to see my solicitor who had written to me before my return from India. I made a discovery there that requires a visit to you immediately.

The only detail you need to know of my journey is that your Uncle Henry and I will be taking your South Coast Railway from Cork to Bantry, arriving on the evening of Friday 10th August. I would be obliged if you could arrange to have us collected from the station.

Blake, it is imperative that you be there to receive us – I have something very important to disclose to you. Do not discuss the contents of this letter with Arthur, except to tell him that we intend to visit.

Best Wishes,
Aunt Violet

Blake reread the letter, wondering what 'discovery' could prompt such a letter and indeed have her make this visit so soon after her long journey from India.

He destroyed the letter and put the date in his diary – it was just over a week away. Having informed Arthur and the housekeeper of the proposed visit, he pushed it to the back of his mind as he had his future to plan out.

Chapter 41

Sunday morning came and, as Ellen left for Mass, her thoughts were on what Father O'Riordan might say about her. She had considered going to Father Dempsey's Mass instead but decided that would be cowardly. While walking to the village, she thought about the fact that all her grandmother's healing had to be done in secret because she was afraid of reprisal. For the sake of the baby and the commotion that it would bring, Ellen felt that she couldn't risk healing even in secret for the immediate future, but she promised herself that she would return to it eventually. She firmly believed that she couldn't deny her gift indefinitely. This particular priest, she consoled herself, hopefully wouldn't be in the parish forever.

She sat near the back of the church, and was relieved when Fionn came and sat beside her. He smiled reassuringly and Ellen gave thanks for the blessing of good friends. Annie and the children were in the back row with Mick. As Mass began, she braced herself. She couldn't believe the irony of the situation when Father O'Riordan read the gospel story of the talents. And she further couldn't believe that the man couldn't see the irony himself about reading a gospel story that told everyone that if God gave them a talent they should use it, when only days before he had taken upon himself the attempt to remove that talent from her in his inability to see it as God's gift.

Her head sank down and she stared at her clenched fists. As he began his sermon, Fionn covered one of her fists with his hand and gave it a squeeze.

"It has come to my attention," Father O'Riordan's voice boomed from the lectern, "that some people with ailments in this parish are not going to the doctor with them, but rather are seeking help in other quarters." A few people shifted uncomfortably in their seats. "I am telling you now that Jesus Christ is the only healer. No one else has that power. It's flying in the face of God to believe otherwise and if in the past you have gone to see – a healer – then you must come to Confession and seek God's forgiveness. You must then promise to never seek out this person again. It is forbidden!" He thumped the lectern for good measure.

Ellen kept her head lowered, knowing her cheeks were flaming. But it was not from embarrassment. It was anger – anger that he was making these people believe they had committed a sin by benefitting from her God-given gift. It took all her willpower to sit through the rest of the sermon which was, again, mostly about parishioners paying their dues.

When Communion time came she straightened her shoulders and took her turn at the altar rail. Closing her eyes as the altar boy placed the paten under her chin, she opened her mouth to receive the host, concentrating with all her might on her belief that she was receiving the Body of Christ, so as to not think negatively of the person who was distributing it.

When Mass was over she went outside with the others. Some of those she had helped in the past looked sadly at her and smiled, and she knew they didn't agree with the priest's words. Others couldn't bring themselves to make eye contact with her, now that their priest had told them to stay away from her. Some of those who never believed in her gift looked smugly at her.

Annie came over. Ellen held her head high and talked to her about the weather as they moved away from the church door out of earshot of anyone else. They stopped and stood talking for a moment, Annie telling her to be brave. Ellen had her back to the church but she felt her temple begin to throb a moment before Father O'Riordan appeared beside them.

"I spared your feelings in there by not using your name." He looked at her as though expecting her gratitude.

All she could do was look at him in amazement – everyone knew exactly who he'd been talking about!

He continued: "Now that the parishioners have been told to stay away from you, there shouldn't be any temptation for you to return to your, eh, old ways. If you find yourself weakening you must come and talk to me. I will give you all the support I can." He gave a thoroughly self-satisfied smile, nodded at them both and moved away.

Both women stared at his retreating back.

"The arrogance of the man!" Annie fumed.

Ellen could only shake her head at his stupidity.

Mick passed them and, without looking at them or stopping, he spoke to Annie.

"Annie, dinnertime!"

Ellen saw Annie's embarrassment at his rudeness and kissed her on the cheek and whispered, "It doesn't bother me, so don't let it bother you. Go on, and enjoy your Sunday."

Ellen waved goodbye to Fionn who was chatting with some men, relieved he wasn't putting pressure on her by offering to walk her home. She was glad to leave the village behind and return to the solitude of her own place by the sea. Having changed into her everyday dress, she left her feet bare to walk across the sand, enjoying its familiar firmness beneath her. As she strolled she couldn't help wondering what Blake was doing and what he was feeling.

Chapter 42

Shaughnessy rode into Ballinmara on Monday afternoon. Stopping at the public house, he ordered some bread, cheese and ale. Blake had advised him not to say who he worked for as he knew of the ill feeling there was for Arthur in these parts. His instructions were to find Annie Leahy's family and see if Arthur had done as Mr. Blake asked. So when the barman made a friendly enquiry about what brought him to Ballinmara, Shaughnessy just said he was passing through.

On leaving the pub he went to the butcher's and enquired as to the whereabouts of the Leahy family's cottage.

"Up that road there," the butcher said, pointing from where he stood in the doorway. "It's the last cottage at the top."

Shaughnessy thanked him, untethered his horse and made his way up the hill. Children played outside the cottages he passed and women chatted to each other as they went about their chores. They all looked at him suspiciously and he figured that Mr. Arthur had struck fear into the hearts of all his tenants here, causing them to be wary of any stranger. He touched his cap politely in their direction, hoping they wouldn't think he was another of Arthur's hired thugs. As he moved on they turned back to what they had been doing.

Approaching the last cottage in that row, he observed that it wasn't in the best condition. The thatched roof looked neglected and the door and window frames could have done with painting. The evidence was there before him that the Leahys didn't have much money.

Dismounting, he went and knocked at the open door.

A pretty, fair-haired woman came towards him from within, with a baby on her hip. Her look was open and warm.

Shaughnessy pulled off his cap.

"I'm sorry to disturb you, Mrs. Leahy, but I was sent here by Mr. Blake Travers to see if the rent collectors have been here to explain that you do not have to pay rent while your husband is injured."

The woman's eyes opened wide at his words. "Yes, thank you, Mr. ... ?"

"Shaughnessy."

"Thank you, Mr. Shaughnessy. It's very nice of Mr. Travers to do this for us. My husband isn't here right now. He's gone down to the harbour to see today's catch. He's not used to being in the house all day." She smiled. "He would thank you himself otherwise. But I'm sure you could go to see him there yourself, if you like."

"No, there's no need for that as long as I can return with your assurance that all is well with you and your family."

The woman looked quite amazed at the courtesy being paid to her.

"Yes, thank you. Mr. Travers' kindness has been a blessing for us and you can tell him that Mick, that's my husband, will be back out in that boat as soon as he can. As I said, it doesn't suit him to be sitting around doing nothing." Again the smile returned to her face.

"Grand, grand," he said, trying not to notice the attractive little dimple that formed in her right cheek. He cleared his throat and turned his cap around and around in his hands. If this woman's sister was anything like her he could understand why Mr. Blake was interested in her welfare. This reminded him of his other reason for being here.

"Eh, I was also told to enquire if your sister, Ellen, is well."

"Oh." Her eyebrows lifted. "Yes, she's grand, and she's very grateful too for Mr. Travers' kindness to us. I know she'd want you to thank him again for us."

"I'll certainly do that, Mrs. Leahy, and I'm glad to do it. I'll bid you good day then."

Replacing his cap, he nodded and made to leave.

"Wait, would you like a cup of tea or some ale before you go?" she said.

"That's kind of you, but I've just had something at the public house." He smiled to soften the rejection of her offer.

"All right, then – well, thank you again for coming," she said as she walked him out.

As he turned his horse he looked back to see the woman still standing in the door, looking a little bemused. His heart was saddened that someone like Arthur Travers could cause a situation where a bit of kindness was something to cause surprise. But he was very relieved that he would be taking good news back to Mr. Blake that this nice woman had got the reprieve from Arthur.

Shaughnessy regretted the passing of old Mr. Travers, who had been a good man. Rumour had it that it was old Mr. Travers' first wife that Mr. Arthur took after. She had been a cold and very strange woman by all accounts. Luckily for Shaughnessy and the other men, Mr. Blake took after both his father and mother who was a very gentle soul.

As he passed by the harbour, he saw a group of men bringing their boats ashore. A man stood watching them, sharing some banter with them, with his arm in a splint, and Shaughnessy guessed that it was Mick Leahy. He rode on, back towards Bantry.

Blake kept glancing up from the fence he was mending near the house, thinking that Shaughnessy should have been back by now. Eventually he heard a horse approach and to his relief he saw him ride towards him. Tossing down his tools, he waited with his fists on his hips.

"Well?" Blake asked as Shaughnessy dismounted.

"All's good. Mr. Arthur did as you asked and Mrs. Leahy seemed very content and was very grateful for your help. She's a very nice woman."

Blake nodded curtly, impatient for news of Ellen. "And what of her sister?"

"She said her sister is well and is also grateful for Mr. Travers' kindness."

"Ha! Arthur kind! That's a laugh! But I'm glad she's well – that they are all well, of course," he qualified when he saw a gleam in

Shaughnessy's eyes. He knew Shaughnessy had been curious about being sent to check on those two women but, to give him his due, Blake knew he could rely on his discretion.

"I'm grateful to you for making the journey for me, Shaughnessy. It would only have caused trouble with Arthur if I'd taken it upon myself to go. He'd see it as more interference. I hope you don't mind if I ask you to go again in another few weeks."

"No trouble at all, sir," he said, feeling an unfamiliar thrill at the thought of returning to Ballinmara. Another few words of chat with a pleasant person like Mrs. Leahy would lift anyone's spirits, he reasoned to himself.

Shaughnessy went off to stable his horse and Blake resumed his work on the fence. But it was Ellen's face he was seeing, remembering how worried she'd looked the morning he left her, and now imagining that worry replaced with her relaxed smile in the knowledge that her sister was all right. He was gratified that Arthur had heeded his warning.

Chapter 43

Ellen wore some very thin muslin over an old straw hat for protection when she was working around the beehives. When she was done, she sat on the grass close by, watching the bees coming and going with different colour pollen stuck to the pollen sacks on their hind legs. She was always pleased to see dark orange or red pollen as that would result in a rich golden colour to the honey.

She had four hives. Each year she got a carpenter in Bantry to make her a new one, which he would do by copying the design of the very first one she had bought from a monastery in Killarney the summer Annie moved out. In May of each year she had searched for a new Queen cell in one of the older hives. She had lifted out the frame, complete with new cell and worker bees, and placed it in the new hive, where they had established a new colony.

Now, sitting here on this warm August day, and completely mesmerised by the constant drone of the bees coming from within the hive, she was in a world of her own and didn't see that Annie had arrived and was watching her over the wall.

"Ellen!" she called.

"Oh, hello, Annie," she replied, getting up. "How long have you been there?"

"A few minutes. You never even noticed me, you were so fascinated with your bees. I still expect them to sting you, even after all this time."

"I've told you before that as long as I'm totally relaxed and move very slowly and carefully when I'm moving the wooden frames in and out, there isn't a problem"

"You'll never change my mind, I'm afraid. They make me shiver just to look at them from here." But she was grinning as she spoke.

Ellen took a second look at her. "You look very pleased with yourself! What's going on and where are the children?"

"Mick is minding the children and he's promised to ask Mary next door for help if he needs it."

Ellen removed her hat and the two of them strolled to the beach, where they sat on a rock watching the waves.

"All right, spit it out," Ellen said, smiling at her sister. "You're jittery with excitement!"

Annie grinned at her for a moment. "I think your Blake Travers loves you a fierce amount!"

Ellen sobered. "Why do you say that?"

"Well, first he lets us off the rent, then this morning he sends one of his men all the way down here to check that we are all right and that the debt collectors had done as he'd instructed. And this man he sent, a Mr. Shaughnessy, was nothing like them. He had lovely manners and a gentle way about him."

"Oh," was all Ellen could say. Thinking of how angry Blake had looked that day, she was surprised at this show of thoughtfulness.

"That's not all," Annie continued.

Ellen saw a gleam in her eye. When Annie didn't go on, she prompted her: "Well, what else has you all worked up?"

"Mr. Shaughnessy was also told by Mr. Travers to enquire as to how you were!"

Ellen could only stare at her as the heat rose into her cheeks. She couldn't believe how much it meant to her to hear Annie say those words, despite what she knew about him now.

"Well," Annie said, "what have you to say about that?"

Ellen frowned at her, trying to calm the traitorous leaping of her heart. "Don't tell me you approve of the man now? He would have thrown you out of your house if I hadn't spoken to him? Have you forgotten already?"

The smile slipped from Annie's face. "Of course I haven't forgotten, but hasn't this shown him to be kinder than we thought?

Maybe he just needed the guidance of a woman with a loving heart. Maybe you were wrong to send him away. I'm thinking, if you could make him do this, maybe you could get him to change his ways altogether, so that he would become a better landlord to everyone?"

"You're being naive," Ellen said, looking at her sister sadly. "One act of kindness does not mean the man has changed. And, as far as my relationship with him is concerned, he was deceitful in not telling me that he was Travers."

"I don't know what 'naïve' means but if you're calling me stupid, it's you're the stupid one. You were deceitful in not telling him that you knew him to be Travers!" Annie glared at her. "Why are you unwilling to believe you could change him?"

"The risks are too great. I can't let myself hope. Because what if I can't change him and he remains two kinds of people – one with me and another in all his dealing with others? My love for him would slowly die if that were to happen and where would that leave us then?" She looked into Annie's eyes and took a deep breath before revealing her secret: "I'm carrying his child."

Annie's mouth fell open.

"I loved him, Annie, and I believed he loved me too. I knew we were worlds apart but I wanted memories if I was going to be living alone here for the future. But it seems I was fooled by his character, and I cannot let one act of kindness now fool me again. If he has the capacity to be cruel and unfeeling to his tenants, I won't risk him knowing that this is his child." She put her hand on her stomach.

"Oh Ellen," Annie whispered. "But what'll you do? Everyone will want to know whose it is – and they'll call you horrible names, like fallen woman and – and worse!"

"I know. Father O'Riordan especially will have something to say! But I've been thinking about it and I think I'll be able to conceal the pregnancy until well into the autumn. Then I might go to Cork for the last three months – Sorcha or Andy's sister might be able to help me find some place to stay. I'll have the baby there and bring it back, saying it's our cousin's child, and that she's unable to mind it herself." She looked at Annie's troubled face. "I know I'll have to tell lies but, if it means I can keep my own baby, then I think God will forgive me."

To her relief, Annie reached out and put her arms around her. "I'll do all I can for you, Ellen." Pulling back, she looked at her face more closely and at her still flat stomach.

"How far along are you?"

"Not far – just over a month."

"Sick?"

"A little."

"Now that I really look at you – you are a bit washy. I've been so caught up in my own troubles I didn't notice – I'm sorry. All this time you must have been worried sick, and then to find out Blake was Travers!"

Ellen smiled, albeit sadly. "I'm going to be fine, Annie. You know I've always been fiercely independent. I can, and will, raise this baby myself. I've thought long and hard about it. I love it already and I will love the memory of its father as he was when he was here with me."

"But when he or she starts asking questions about its father, what will you say?"

"That, I haven't thought about yet. Plenty of time before that happens." She smiled reassuringly at her, hiding her sadness. "We have to keep it a secret for now. Don't trust anyone! You mustn't even tell Mick."

"I won't, I promise."

After a while, and after giving her lots of advice about taking care of herself, Annie left. With a sigh Ellen went inside and picked up her knitting. She was devoting a lot more hours to it each day as she had to increase her income from market days now that the healing had stopped. No one had come to the house that day and she was sure all her usual visitors were so scared of Father O'Riordan that they would heed his words and stay away.

It made her heart break thinking that there was pain and suffering out there that she could remove but was now forbidden to. It went against her nature, making her restless and dissatisfied. But she continued to grow her herbs and make her remedies for when they might be needed.

A whole week passed without anyone asking her for help. On Friday she joined other villagers on the way to Schull for market day. Luckily she had an upturned crate to sit on for the day as the pregnancy was making her feel very tired. She liked to watch the folk

228

stroll up and down, stopping here and there to barter a good price. On these days some of the gentry came too and mingled with the ordinary folk. They never came to her stall. Looking at the fine dresses they wore, she smiled to herself at the thought of them wearing one of her woollen ganseys. Of course that thought immediately took her back to the morning Blake had worn her father's gansey. Her heart was squeezed at the memory of how wonderful he looked and her longing for him almost overwhelmed her, despite all she now knew about him. Looking now at the men and women who passed by her in their lace and tweeds, she reminded herself of the gulf between her world and his.

Her attention returned to her stall as a man and his wife, dressed in the same plain clothes as herself, came to look at her wares.

The woman held a gansey up against his chest. "This looks very warm. It'll be perfect for you when the cold of autumn comes and the draught starts whistling through that workshop of yours." She turned to Ellen. "It's very well made – did you knit it yourself?"

Ellen smiled. "Thank you – yes, I did. I use the traditional stitches for fishermen's ganseys. It's closely woven to keep the wind out."

"My husband builds boats," the woman remarked, "down there by the harbour. It's exactly what he needs." She addressed her husband again: "You need a new one. The one you have is worn thin and wouldn't keep a kettle warm over a fire!" She laughed at her own joke. "We'll take it."

The whole time, the husband didn't say a word, only rolled his eyes before smiling at Ellen, indicating he was well used to his wife making such decisions without any input from him. The woman handed over the money.

By mid-afternoon Ellen had sold three ganseys and all of the socks she had brought with her. And in between she had read a few of the poems from the book Father Goggin had given her. When the market was closing up and she was just about to climb back up into her cart to head for home, one of her neighbours who had been selling sheepskins further along the street came up to her.

Looking around furtively, he stood close to her, his voice very low when he spoke. "Ellen, there's something bothering the goat. Father O'Riordan didn't say anything about you not helping the animals, did he?" He gave her a conspiratorial wink.

Ellen liked him and knew she could trust him. "No, he didn't, now that you come to mention it," she said with a smile.

"Will you look in on him on your way home?"

"Of course I will. I'll follow behind you now 'til we get there."

A little while later Ellen was standing on a patch of ground behind the man's house where the goat was tethered. There was a gash on its leg that had become infected. She went to her own house and collected some ointment, returning a little while later to clean the wound before applying it. When she had wrapped it well, she prayed and laid her hands over the wound for several minutes, feeling the familiar heat flow through her and out through her palms. The satisfaction Ellen felt was immense and she was so grateful to be doing what she loved.

When she was done the farmer spoke. "I had cleaned it myself," he said, "but I didn't do the job right. Thanks, Ellen. Here, take this." He put some coins in her hand. "I did well at the market today, so I can pay you with money this time instead of goat's milk!"

"Thank you and blessings on you! Your asking me to do this means a lot to me."

He nodded his understanding.

Ellen returned home, knowing that if Father O'Riordan questioned her after Mass the following day she could honestly say she hadn't healed any person. But she missed it and didn't like him having this power over her. She wished there was some way to get around him.

Chapter 44

It was just gone midday on Monday when Ellen heard horses. She saw two riders appear around from behind the hill. Her heart thudded, fearing the priest had sent someone again, but these two didn't have their faces covered and she didn't know them. They eased their pace as they got closer to the cottage. They were on fine horses and were dressed well enough.

But it was still with some caution that she waited with Shep beside her. The men were large and strongly built, with hard features. They dismounted and came to stand in front of her, holding the reins of their horses.

Shep growled. Placing her hand on his head, she quietened him. All the same, the men didn't come any closer.

"Good day, missus," one said gruffly, touching his cap but not removing it. "Would you be Mrs. Cassidy?"

"Miss Cassidy," she corrected.

"We need to speak to Mr. Cassidy."

Not knowing who the men were, Ellen didn't want them to know she lived alone.

"And who is looking for him?" she asked politely.

"We've been sent by Mr. Travers."

Ellen's breath caught.

When she didn't say anything, the man continued: "We're here to collect rent owed on this property."

Ellen couldn't believe what she was hearing. Her mind raced. Was Blake excusing Annie of her rent only to recoup it through her? How could he be that despicable? How could he be that changeable? Appearing kind and lenient one moment and then doing this the next? Trying to control the hurt and her temper, she missed what the man said next, simply staring at him until he spoke again.

"Ma'am?"

"Sorry, what did you say?"

"I said can we speak to the man of the house then?"

Ellen inhaled a long slow breath and lifted her head proudly, allowing her fury to fuel her.

Sensing it, the horses jerked their heads and moved back restlessly. The men had to steady them. Both men looked at her warily, sensing something too and knowing that, whatever it was, it had spooked their horses.

Ellen spoke: "There is no Mr. Cassidy. I am Miss Cassidy and this is my cottage. I own it and I do not owe rent to Mr. Travers or anyone else."

"But the land on this part of the peninsula is all Travers land and Mr Travers wants what is owed to him."

"This house and property has been owned by the Cassidy family for three generations, so you can tell Mr. Travers there is nothing for him here."

Emphasising the last four words, she knew her double meaning was lost on them, but she knew they would not be lost on Blake. It was time to end all pretence.

"Good day to you both," she said firmly.

The men didn't argue further but hastily got on their horses, seeming relieved to leave.

Ellen stood watching them out of sight, continuing to feel her fury and relishing the power of it. She gave a bitter laugh. To think she had almost been persuaded by Annie that Blake was capable of changing! This move of his was low and it hurt ... badly. She had believed that love for her had him showing kindness to Annie, but doing this now to her made her think him incapable of love after all.

Her fury continued to invigorate her and she poured it into her chores. She was careful to stay well away from the bees, fearing that her mood would cause them to swarm.

Eventually even chores weren't enough and she walked to the village to tell Annie what had happened. The exercise helped to calm her. Seeing Mick down at the harbour, she was able to go to Annie's house and talk to her there.

"I can't believe it!" Annie exclaimed. "But that's shocking. How could he do such a thing?"

"He wasn't being kind to you, at all. He thought he could get his money from me instead – through years of rent owed!"

Annie looked crushed. The romantic part of her soul had painted a wonderful picture of Blake being changed by Ellen's love.

"So did they just leave?"

"Yes."

"Do you think that will be the end of it?"

"Well, Granny told me she signed the deeds herself."

"But where are they? What if Travers looks for proof? Surely that will be his next move."

They stared at each other for a moment.

"They have to be somewhere in the cottage, don't they?" Ellen said. "But I don't ever remember seeing them, do you?"

Annie shook her head. "Why didn't Da tell us where they were?"

"Maybe he thought he had plenty of time and meant to tell but then the accident happened, and then Mam went so quickly after too."

Shortly afterwards Ellen left, not feeling as confident as when she had arrived. Judging by the way Blake did things, there was no way he was going to take her word for it that the cottage was hers.

She couldn't get home fast enough to begin the search.

There weren't many places to look. It took only a short while to go through the drawers and cupboards. She knew she would have remembered if she had come across a box or envelope of documents before, so she searched while believing it to be futile. She even checked the old chest at the foot of the bed, which held bed linen, for a secret hiding place but there was nothing there. Checking behind the picture of the Sacred Heart revealed nothing either.

Defeated, she sat in the rocking chair to rest. Then sat bolt upright. Maybe they were hidden up in the attic. The old Brigid's crosses were put up there every year after the new one was woven, so maybe there was other stuff stored up there too – she had always just opened the hatch and pushed in the old cross.

She wouldn't risk climbing on the table and trying to get up there in her condition, in case she fell. She'd have to get someone else to do it, perhaps Fionn. Relieved that finding the deeds might still be possible, she breathed a little more easily. Suddenly feeling very tired, she decided that the next day was time enough to get Fionn's help.

The following day didn't start out well. Father O'Riordan came to check on her, not having spoken to her after Mass the day before as she had expected. Pretending meekness, she told him honestly that no one had come to her home for healing and that she had healed no one since. He appeared satisfied, totally believing in his own contribution to ridding her of her demons.

After drinking the tea she had forced herself to offer him, he left.

She was just reaching for her shawl when she heard horses again. Taking a moment to tie it, she stepped outside, Shep once again by her side.

The same two men were there. The dog growled at them and this time the men stayed in their saddles. One of them addressed her.

"Miss Casssidy, Mr. Travers has sent us again to inform you that this is his property unless you have some way of proving it to be otherwise. Are you able to show us the deeds?"

"I cannot show you today. You must come back another time."

A smirk passed between the two men, making Ellen grit her teeth.

"Mr. Travers thought that might be the case. However, he is prepared to give you the rest of the week to produce the document." Again a smirk. "We'll return on Friday."

Ellen's temper rose at their smugness and Blake's treatment of her, and she did something she rarely did – she spoke without thinking: "Tell Mr. Travers to come and do his own dirty work instead of hiding behind his hired help."

She got some satisfaction in seeing the smirks wiped from their faces. Without another word, they left. Although regretting her impulsive words, she thought perhaps it might be best to have it out with Blake face to face, so that he would know that she knew who he was and what he was doing.

Her resolve to find the deeds strengthened and she set off to Fionn's house, where she pushed a note under his door saying she needed his help with something and could he come visit her after work that evening.

On leaving, instead of turning for home she went to the village to get some meat from the butcher's. She saw Mick leaving the harbour and heading up the hill towards home. He saw her too and changed direction to come towards her.

Ellen quickly turned and walked in the opposite direction, but he caught up with her and fell into step beside her.

"What do you want, Mick?" she asked, without looking at him or breaking the rhythm of her stride.

"I know you know it was me there that night." His voice was low and threatening. "If you tell anyone, especially Annie, I'll make trouble for you, Ellen, I swear it."

Ellen stopped abruptly, not wanting to put any more distance between them and the village for the sake of her own safety. So, in sight of the shops but out of earshot of anyone going about their business, she turned and looked him in the eye.

"Why do you hate me so much, Mick? At least tell me that, so I can understand."

Narrowing his eyes, he stared hard at her for a moment.

"You healers are all tricksters and liars, who just go about playing with other people's lives!"

The venom dripping from his words had her taking a step back from him, but his eyes were those of a fierce but very wounded man, so she continued to hold his gaze.

"What makes you say that? What happened to you, to make you feel this way?"

"Hah! What difference does it make to talk about the past?" he spat.

"Every difference when it is very obviously part of you and how you feel now, Mick."

He seemed to debate with himself for a moment, moving restlessly from foot to foot. Then, making up his mind, he blurted out, "All right, I'll tell you, though I owe you no explanation! You and your kind are a joke and don't deserve my breath, but I want you to know how much I hate you."

A trembling had started somewhere deep inside Ellen as his rage increased, but she dampened it down, needing to hear where all his hate was coming from.

"My mother got very sick when I was only seven years old. I overheard some of the old women who came to look after her, saying that it was a great shame that old Nora Cassidy wasn't still doing her healing. They said she'd had the gift once and had worked miracles."

Ellen listened as scorn and scepticism contorted his features, and the man in front of her was transported back in his own mind to being that seven-year-old again.

"I thought they were talking about someone who was already dead but I found out that this Nora Cassidy was still living down there by that little cove. I ran all the way there, full of hope that I would find this powerful healing woman who could make my mother better. Instead I found a small, shrunken woman who told me that she didn't do healing anymore and hadn't for many a year. I begged her, but she just shook her head and said she couldn't do it. I cried all the way home, hope gone. My mother died a month later."

Ellen saw the agonised grief in his eyes before it was replaced with rage.

His words slowed as he continued. "Nora Cassidy came and paid her respects at the wake and as she left I heard someone say that they believed Nora Cassidy was still able to heal, but that it was her own choice to stop years before. As I looked at my mother's lifeless face, I hated Nora Cassidy with every inch of me."

The rage shook his whole body as he leaned closer to her, oblivious of the fact that tears were streaming down his face. Ellen's heart went out to the grieving little boy that still lived inside him.

"I'm so sorry, Mick, I didn't know."

He shrugged off her sympathy with a look of distaste. "And to think I fell in love with one of her granddaughters. But I couldn't help it, and though I married into the Cassidy family I hated myself for it. All I could do was try to keep you and your wicked ways away from us."

"Mick," Ellen said gently, "please try to understand. Yes, my grandmother chose to stop healing, but in a way she had no choice. She was broken by the devastation caused by the famine. A healer has to believe in her healing as well as having the gift, and after all the death and sickness she saw she couldn't believe in herself any more. I believe she told you the truth when she said she couldn't help your mother."

"Who was she to play with other people's lives like that?" He took a step closer to Ellen, panting heavily, trying to control the emotions ripping through him. "And here you are doing the same thing – playing God – with Nora Cassidy's ugly blood running through your veins." Mick wiped his face with his sleeve, before lifting flint-hard eyes to Ellen's. "I will never forgive that woman."

He spat on the ground, turned and walked away, his empty coat sleeve slapping in the wind.

Chilled and deeply sorry for him, Ellen watched his retreating figure, knowing that no words of hers would ever change his heart. But, at least, now she knew where his anger came from and she believed that he helped in the exorcism as a means to somehow deal with his own demons and to have revenge on her grandmother.

Chapter 45

Later that evening, Fionn grunted as he heaved himself up into the attic through the small hatch door. Kneeling on the rafters he put his arm back down to take the candle Ellen held up to him.

"For God's sake, don't set fire to the thatch, Fionn!" she cautioned, craning her neck to look up at him, "and don't crush the old crosses."

He winked down at her, then held the candle aloft to light the cramped space. There was a thud and an "Ouff" sound. "This place was not made for a man my size, Ellen Cassidy!"

"I'll owe you a big favour after this, Fionn, really I will."

Ellen watched him move out of sight, away from the hatch.

"There's nothing at all up here."

His muffled words had her shoulders sagging in disappointment.

"Are you sure? A box? Any old piece of clothing with something wrapped in it? Anything?"

Awkwardly moving his bulk, he shuffled slowly along the rafters to see as far he could into the recesses of the roof space with dim light of the candle.

"Nothing, Ellen, sorry."

"All right – then you'd better come down before you do yourself an injury."

His arm appeared again to pass her the candle. With more

grunting he squeezed out through the hatch, lowering his feet to the table below. Ellen was grateful for its sturdiness as it creaked under his weight.

He jumped down to the floor, rubbing the dust off his hands and onto the seat of his britches.

Ellen stood there, chewing her bottom lip.

"Sorry," he said again. "What now? Are you sure you tried everywhere in here?"

They both glanced around the small cottage. "There aren't many places it could be and I've searched them all."

Idly she pulled open a drawer in the dresser as she spoke, hoping that by some miracle the deeds would be just lying there. But all she could see were her sewing materials and some utensils.

Shep nudged in beside her and started sniffing at the side of the drawer and then the underneath of it. He barked and wagged his tail, looking up at Ellen before sticking his nose under the drawer again.

Ellen looked up at Fionn with wide eyes, not daring to hope, but Shep barked again and she bent down to look at the underside of the drawer. There was a folded piece of paper held there by a piece of wood stretched along the bottom of the drawer.

"There's something here, Fionn," she said in amazement, removing it very carefully. "Well done, Shep!" She scratched the dog behind the ears before taking the document to the table.

There she unfolded it.

"Is it the deeds?" Fionn asked, peering down as two sheets of parchment were revealed.

Ellen grinned at him. "No, but I think it's something just as good! Listen. *'This is the last will and testament of Nora Cassidy,'* and this one," she said, looking at the second page, "is the last will and testament of Thomas Cassidy.' She looked up at Fionn. "This is my father's will and my grandmother's. Look, there it says that Granny left the holding to Daddy and here," she pointed to the second will, "it says Daddy left it to me! I always knew it but I didn't think they had made wills."

"Maybe it's time you made a will yourself."

"Yes, you're right, but let's check the rest of the dresser and see if we can find the actual deeds."

A while later, having pulled out all the drawers, even emptying the dresser of all its contents, and having checked the back and the underneath, there was still no sign of them.

"The wills should be enough of proof for Mr. Travers, surely?" Ellen said.

Fionn nodded, pleased for her. "At least I don't have to go back in that attic again."

Ellen laughed and kissed his cheek. "I'm grateful to you, Fionn."

"I'll put all this back together," he said, beginning to put the dresser in order again. "You sit down and rest."

"I'm fine, Fionn."

He gave her a look that said he'd take no nonsense, so she sat in the rocking chair and watched as he tidied the mess they had created, enjoying the feeling of being taken care of.

Over a cup of tea, he asked when the men were coming back.

"On Friday."

"If it's all right with you, I'd like to be here when they come. You shouldn't have to face them alone."

Ellen's first reaction was to say no, to remain independent as usual, but that feeling of being taken care of was so nice that she instead said: "Thank you, Fionn, I'd appreciate it."

When he was gone, she studied the wills for another while, giving thanks for the shrewdness of her father and his mother. Returning the documents to their hiding place, she went around every stick of furniture in the cottage, examining every inch of them, but to no avail. The deeds still eluded her.

But now that she had the wills, and knowing Fionn would be there, she did not fear the return of the rent collectors. Hugging Shep close to her, she promised him an extra big bone from the butcher's the next time she went to the village. Shep barked as if he understood her words. Ellen laughed and hugged him again.

The next morning Ellen was sweeping the floor when Annie burst in.

"Father O'Riordan stopped me in the village and asked me to bring you this and said I was to bring you back with me to the church hall."

She handed Ellen a letter, her voice anxious.

"What is it?"

"Just open it."

"It says there's to be a meeting in the church hall at eleven and I have to attend. Do you know what this is about, Annie?"

Annie looked like she was about to burst into tears. She bit her lip.

"What is it?" Ellen urged.

"Oh Ellen, the whole village is buzzing with it. Father O'Riordan put up a notice in the window of the butcher's first thing this morning telling everyone who has ever asked you for help for themselves or their animals to come to the church hall during the morning and tell their story. Then there is to be a parish meeting at four this afternoon and everyone has to be there. This has never happened before, Ellen!"

"Oh Sacred Mother!" Ellen's voice was faint. "He's discovered that I haven't stopped the healing of animals."

"You what?"

"Just a few, Annie. They needed my help."

"But he told you to stop. He'll be really angry now, Ellen."

They stared at each other for a moment.

"Maybe when he hears people's stories, he'll see all the good you do," Annie said.

Ellen gave a mirthless laugh. "He's not looking to see the good in me – he only wants proof in order to condemn me."

"And all the fisherman will be there," Annie cried. "The sea is rough this morning so they haven't gone out. The word is spreading to the farmers too because I saw some of the wives rushing home from the village on my way here."

Ellen reached out and grasped Annie's arm. "You have to help me, Annie, and I'm sorry to ask this of you. Will you go to Bantry straight away and tell Father Goggin what's going on? He said I was to ask him for help if I needed it and by God I need it now."

Annie nodded. "The children are with Mary and she'll keep them for me."

"Don't tell Mick where you're going. He might try to stop you," Ellen warned.

Again Annie nodded.

"I'd ask Fionn to go, but he'll be already gone off to work today somewhere beyond Durrus. We'll leave a note at his house for when he gets back." She took Annie by the shoulders. "Go to the public house and ask Andy Minehane if you can borrow the pony and trap.

Don't let anyone else hear you asking and swear Andy to secrecy."

"Why can't I take you to Bantry with me and we can bring Father Goggin back with us?"

The thought was so appealing Ellen almost agreed.

"No, Annie. I'll do as Father O'Riordan says. It will prevent him doing anything rash until you manage to get Father Goggin here. If I don't go to the hall it could make things worse for me."

Annie looked doubtful. Ellen wrote a brief explanation for Fionn, she told Shep to stay at the cottage and then she and Annie hurried across the fields, dropping the note off on their way to the village.

All heads turned in their direction when they turned onto the street. Ellen moved ahead and all eyes followed her up the hill to the church hall.

While they were watching Ellen, Annie slipped into the pub and asked Andy for the pony and trap. He promised he'd have it ready for her after she ran up to ask Mary to keep the children for the rest of the day.

Stomach churning, Ellen walked into the church hall, looking much braver than she felt.

Father O'Riordan was already seated behind a table at the top of the hall, his face dark as thunder.

Father Dempsey and Mrs. Moran, their housekeeper, were there too. Ellen took some comfort from their presence.

Father Dempsey stood and, blushing furiously, came to meet her. He walked her to a chair in front of the table, so she was facing the three of them. He resumed his own seat near Father O'Riordan, eyes downcast.

Ellen looked straight at Father O'Riordan, trying not to let her fear show.

"You have defied me!" he said icily. "So I have decided to put an end to this matter once and for all. No more lies, no more guessing games. Your fellow parishioners will come here today and condemn you themselves with their own words."

Mrs. Moran gasped and turned it into a cough. Ellen met her eyes and knew she was remembering the numerous times Ellen had helped her gain relief for the gnarled fingers of her left hand. Ellen could see the battle that was going on inside her. She knew it would be the same for a lot of the others too – torn between loyalty to her and loyalty to, and fear of, their priest.

"When everyone has seen the extent of your deception – yes, your deception," he repeated as he saw her eyebrow rise, "pretending you are curing them, when it is the answer to their own prayers that cured them – then they will be of one mind that things cannot be allowed to go on like this."

Ellen opened her mouth to protest but no words came as the door opened and Mick Leahy strode up through the room.

Brazenly he stood to the side of the table. "I'd like to be the first to speak out against Ellen Cassidy."

Sadness had some of Ellen's spirit slipping away. Sadness because he was Annie's husband and yet couldn't wait to hurt her again.

"This woman is a liar and deceiver. And she comes from a long line of liars. Her grandmother was known around these parts for taking credit for people getting better when it was nothing but coincidence."

There was silence.

Father Dempsey was staring at him, sensing the fury in him.

"Well, you heard the man," Father O'Riordan said to him. "Write it all down and get him to sign it."

Father Dempsey made some notes and Mick signed his name.

Father O'Riordan addressed Mick before he left.

"I'd appreciate if you could remind everyone you see that they will have to deal with me if they do not come forth today. There will be no punishment for having been taken in by this woman. But there will be penance for not coming here to tell the truth."

Mick left and soon afterwards a steady trickle of people were coming in and out of the hall one by one.

Father O'Riordan asked them to tell their stories honestly and assured them that nothing bad would happen them.

Síle arrived, Úna with her.

"Ellen has helped Una twice. She's a very good and caring person. I came here today because I wanted you to know that, Father."

Father O'Riordan didn't make any comment, other than to remind her to be back in the hall with everyone else at four.

Síle gave Ellen an encouraging smile as she left with her daughter in tow.

And so the pattern was set. Everyone came and listed their

ailments and those of their animals and what Ellen had done for them. A lot of them were unable to say what herbs or ointments Ellen had used, but they felt sure it cured them all the same.

Others came and said that they never believed Ellen had the gift of healing and they would never let her near their family or animals. Some said that there had always been something strange about the Cassidy family and that Ellen spoke better than the rest of them even though she was only a fisherman's daughter, which had to mean there was something strange about her too.

None of it surprised Ellen. She knew the different ways folk thought about her, but it still hurt and scared her now under the circumstances.

Shortly after one o'clock, just as one person left the room, Mrs. Moran cleared her throat. "Father, don't you think we should break for the dinner? You must be very hungry?" But her eyes darted to Ellen, who she could see was sagging from tiredness in the chair.

"What?" he said, checking his pocket-watch. "Is that the time already? Very well, we'll resume in an hour. Father Dempsey, you please stay here with Ellen and Mrs. Moran can bring down your dinner."

Mrs. Moran ushered him out and returned shortly after with two plates of food, one for Ellen and one for Father Dempsey.

She stayed and made sure Ellen ate. Then she suggested that she take Ellen to the outside toilet. Father Dempsey blushed again but nodded.

Outside Ellen thanked her for her kindness and her thoughtfulness.

"What is happening to you is a disgrace, child. The man's mind will surely be changed by all the wonderful things he is hearing about you."

Wearily Ellen just smiled at her. She had no doubt that Father O'Riordan's mind was unchanged by the stories, and that for him every one of them confirmed that she was involved in the Devil's work. Those who were trying to help her were only succeeding in condemning her further.

But she was hopeful that Annie would have made it to Bantry by now and that she was on her way back with Father Goggin. What he would be able to do she didn't know, but she hoped for a little miracle of her own now.

The afternoon followed the same pattern as the morning. But each person's turn seemed to take longer as Father Dempsey was getting tired too and had become slower at writing everything down.

At three thirty, Mrs. Moran slipped out and returned with a tray of tea, making them take a rest. Bless her heart, Ellen thought, when she saw four cups. Father O'Riordan looked on disapprovingly as she served Ellen some too. Ellen smiled her thanks and touched her left hand briefly. Gentle heat radiated into Mrs. Moran's sore joints, giving them some ease. Her eyes filled with tears at the injustice being done to the poor girl.

Ellen handed the cup back to Mrs. Moran a while later. Anxiety was a twisted knot in her stomach. Annie and Father Goggin should have been here by now.

The door opened and she looked up hopefully, but it wasn't Annie, it was Fionn. His eyes searched Ellen's face as he walked up the hall. She gave him the ghost of a smile. He came and stood beside her.

Father O'Riordan waited for him to speak. Fionn said nothing.

"Well," the priest prompted, "what's your story?"

"I'm here to keep Ellen company," he said simply before reaching for a chair and putting it beside Ellen's. He sat down and gave her a reassuring look.

"This is an official parish affair and you have no business being here until the public meeting in an hour," Father O'Riordan said testily.

"I see three of you there. I believe Ellen is entitled to have someone by her side too." Fionn spoke softly, but firmly.

"We're almost done here anyway so I don't see that it matters. You can stay. Father Dempsey, go and see if there are many more outside."

"Thank you," Ellen managed to whisper to Fionn as Father Dempsey pushed back his chair and left the hall.

He returned, his eyes wide. "Eh, Father, there's no one else to tell their story, but there's about a hundred people outside."

A hundred! Ellen wondered how many were there to support her, how many were just plain curious and how many already supported Father O'Riordan's view.

"It's ten minutes to four now so you might as well let them in."

Ellen took a shaky breath as Father Dempsey opened the door and what looked like the whole population of Ballinmara and its surrounds flowed into the hall.

Under cover of the noise they were making, Ellen leant closer to Fionn and whispered to him. "Annie is gone to get Father Goggin and they should have been here by now. But I don't know what Father O'Riordan is planning and how Father Goggin could stop him anyway."

Fionn reached out and gave her hand a quick squeeze but Ellen saw fear in his eyes and she wanted to weep. Even Fionn wasn't going to be able to help this time.

The crowd was in and they stood muttering to each other while trying to get a look at Ellen, some with kindness, some without.

"Silence everyone, please!" Father O'Riordan shouted.

They stilled.

"Firstly I would like to thank you all for coming here throughout the day to help with this examination of Ellen Cassidy's deeds." He held up a thick sheaf of papers. "We now have overwhelming evidence of the amount of times Ellen Cassidy has portrayed herself as a healer, believing herself to have some sort of magic power. I know she has fooled a lot of you into thinking that she is doing God's work. But God does not work this way. I believe it is the Devil who controls her mind, making her think she is as powerful as God."

There were gasps and murmurs amongst the crowd.

"I hold nothing against any of you for being taken in – you or your care were sick or injured. At times like that your judgement can be weak. But I believe Ellen Cassidy knew exactly what she was doing and that was flying in the face of God!"

Oh God, Ellen thought, what is he going to do with me?

"So," Father O'Riordan continued, his chest puffed out with authority, "we have no choice but to banish Ellen Cassidy from Ballinmara, never to return."

Everyone seemed to shout at once.

There were some voices of dissent:

"*No!*"

"*We can't do that!*"

"*That's not right!*"

But there were also voices of assent:

"Yes!"

"It's what she deserves!"

"Out with her!"

But Ellen saw the faces of some of the women change from shock to fear. And she understood it. She knew that their ignorance and blind faith in their priest was not their fault. And she knew they would do what he told them. She didn't blame them. She blamed the so-called educated, pompous man sitting behind the desk who should know better.

Bravely, Síle pushed her way to the front. There were tears in her eyes. "Excuse me, Father. But this isn't right. Ellen is a good person, kind and loving. I wouldn't have spoken this morning if I thought my words were going to be twisted against her." Her voice shook. "You tricked us!"

"Be quiet!" a man in the crowd shouted. "She'll get what she deserves now, the witch!"

Again some of crowd clamoured in protest.

Ellen started to shake. Were they going to make her leave her home and her family?

"You can't do this!" she exclaimed, jumping up, thoughts of Annie and the children wrenching at her heart. "I have family here! The Cassidys have lived here for generations. Father, this is not right!"

Father O'Riordan held up his hands for silence.

"Ellen Cassidy is a danger to Ballinmara and therefore must leave. She will have one week to do this. And may God have mercy on her. This meeting is over."

"Not quite," a voice said from the back of the hall.

The crowd all turned, then those at the back shuffled out of the way to allow Father Goggin and Annie to move up to the front.

When Annie saw Ellen, she ran over and put her arms around her as she sat in the chair. She whispered into her ear. "Sorry for taking so long, Father Goggin was saying a funeral Mass when I got there. We've been here, at the back, for the last few minutes."

Ellen clung to her. "Thanks for getting him, Annie."

After a moment Annie straightened up but left her hand protectively on Ellen's shoulder.

Father Goggin stood in front of Father O'Riordan. The crowd

was quiet, not wanting to miss a word.

Father O'Riordan spoke first. "With all due respect, Father Goggin, this is no longer your parish and I must ask you to leave. We are in the middle of some very important business."

Father Goggin looked at him for another moment before turning to face the crowd. Some looked at him hopefully, while some dropped their eyes in shame.

"In the Bible we are told, *'Let he who is without sin cast the first stone.'* Father O'Riordan is not in a position to cast any stones and is not in a position to pass judgement on Ellen Cassidy. I have a letter here from the Bishop to Father O'Riordan, which I was intending to deliver tomorrow, but it seems that it is to be today instead." He handed it to Father O'Riordan. "The Bishop has summoned you to a meeting in Skibbereen. Father Dempsey is to run things here for the moment and you are relieved of your duties until you have met with the Bishop."

Father O'Riordan gaped at the letter in his hand, then back up at Father Goggin. "But ..."

"You need to leave this meeting now, Father O'Riordan. You have no authority here at present."

With his face flushed red, Father O'Riordan stormed out.

Father Dempsey's eyes were out on stalks.

"I will explain later," Father Goggin murmured to him.

He turned to the crowd.

"Father O'Riordan has done a grave injustice to Ellen Cassidy. Most of you know this, and some of you will never understand her gift. That's how it has been and how it will continue, no doubt. But Ellen is a good, Christian woman, who has only ever done good with her healing gift – a gift I firmly believe comes from God. She is very special and a wonderful part of this community – treasure her. Now it's time for you all to go home and to leave this woman in peace."

Someone started to clap in the crowd and many more took it up. Some of the women went to Ellen to hug her in their relief.

Eventually, only Ellen, Annie and Fionn were left with Father Goggin. He asked Annie and Fionn to wait outside while he had a word alone with Ellen.

When the door closed behind them. Ellen burst out with her thanks.

"Father Goggin, thank you so much! But the letter from the Bishop, what was that all about?"

"It was very fortunate timing for you, my dear. What I'm telling you now is in confidence."

"Of course."

"Father O'Riordan was moved here from Cork City because he was gambling on the horses. He was always attending the flat racing. The problem was that he bet a lot of money and not all of it his own – he started to use some of the parish funds. The Bishop was made aware of it and moved him down here, away from the city. He told him he'd bring him back to Cork after two years if he stayed out of trouble. Father O'Riordan is a city man and is not happy here, you see. But, while here, he was still finding the time to get to the races outside Skibbereen mid-week and again he was betting a lot of money. At a meeting I attended, the Bishop decided to summon Father O'Riordan to him and talk to him again before determining his future. He asked me to deliver the letter personally. As one of the Bishop's advisors, of course I will advise that he does not put him back here in Ballinmara."

"Thank you, Father, and thanks for what you said in here to everyone."

"I got your letter about the exorcism. What he did to you was shameful and came from a very closed mind indeed. It's just as well the Bishop has called him away. If this other matter hadn't worked to your advantage, I would have acted on your letter to find another solution for you."

She nodded and smiled.

"Go on home with you now, Ellen. It was a hard day for you, and should never have happened."

They walked outside where he handed her into the care of her friend and sister. "God bless you, child."

"What's going to happen now?" Annie asked as they walked her home.

"All I can say is that Father Goggin thinks Father O'Riordan will be leaving us for good. But do not say anything to anyone until it happens."

When they got to the cottage, the two of them fussed around her like a pair of old hens, preparing something to eat and making her tea, while Ellen told Annie about finding the wills the night before.

Shortly after they'd eaten, Ellen sent them home. Annie needed to get back to the children and Ellen was too tired for company.

She walked them out.

"The sea has calmed and there's a fog rolling in," commented Fionn.

Hugging them both, Ellen thanked them for all they had done for her that day.

She walked down onto the beach to watch the sea fog drift in from the south. Her fear of Father O'Riordan was gone and she felt lighter. She covered her stomach with her hand and spoke to her baby: "You and I are going to be just fine, my little darling. It seems everyone has their secrets. We mustn't judge but help where we can."

The sun became a faint white halo in the sky and Ellen was soon enveloped in the fog's pearly whiteness, enjoying its embrace and the silence it brought. There was something about it that always made her feel like she was being accompanied by her ancestors and all their good wishes for her.

She hoped her grandmother had forgiven her for not heeding her warning. The consequences of it had become obvious now but, though Travers was still causing problems for her, at least she had remedied things for Annie. What was done was done.

Every five minutes she barely heard the muffled blast explosions in the far distance from the Fastnet lighthouse, warning the seafarers of hazardous rocks.

Breathing deeply of the salty, damp air, she continued standing there, more content than she had been in recent weeks.

Chapter 46

"She said what!" Arthur Travers boomed at the two rent collectors.

"Come and do your own dirty –" one of them started.

"I heard you, dammit!" Arthur cut across him. "The effrontery of her and I having given her a week's grace to produce this 'non-existent' deed!"

The men looked bored, longing for some ale and something to eat. Neither of them were interested or bothered by Arthur's tantrum. They just wanted to get paid and go to the nearest public house.

"I'll go there all right!" he fumed. "And I'll have what's rightfully mine! Come back here in two days and this time I'll ride out with you."

"We said we'd be back on Friday."

"Well, I'm saying we're going back on Thursday. Be here at nine o'clock sharp!" He opened a leather purse and paid the two men. "Now off with you both. I have work to do."

The men left out without a word – like Arthur, all they wanted was their money and they were happy.

Arthur's frown turned into a wicked smile as he pictured confronting the woman himself and telling her that she had to start paying him rent, as well as rent in arrears, or get out.

Two days later Ellen was happily back healing. Some of those who had been loyal to her in the church hall dropped by to wish her well even though they were in no need of treatment. She loved being true to herself again by doing what she was born to do.

Though saddened by Mick's feelings, she knew she would have to accept his hostility and be even more careful about her contact with Annie and the children.

All her visitors that morning had arrived on foot or by donkey and cart, so when she was collecting seaweed from the rocks just before noon and saw horses approaching the cottage, she knew it was Travers' men again. Only this time there were three horses. And they were a day early, so Fionn wasn't with her.

With her heart lurching, she picked up her basket and placed it on her hip. On bare feet, she moved up the beach, eyes fixed on the riders, trying to make out Blake among them. Two were dark-haired and one fair, with a similar build to Blake. She braced herself for the confrontation, thinking he had accepted her taunt.

As she got closer she identified the same two rent collectors – but the fair-haired man was a stranger to her. Relief and puzzlement warred within her.

The man's clothes were of a fine quality and he had an air of superiority as he pulled his horse up, all the while watching her with cold grey eyes.

Shep ran over to her side. The riders didn't dismount.

"Good day," she said courteously, laying her basket down on the wall.

"Good day, Miss Cassidy." The refined voice of the fair-haired one had something very familiar in it.

At her lack of response he looked irritated.

"I'm Arthur Travers, your landlord," he announced haughtily.

Ellen could only stare at his unsmiling face, trying to take in what she was hearing. "Arthur Travers?" she repeated eventually.

"That's what I said, woman," he replied impatiently.

In a split second her racing mind leapt from improbabilities to possibilities, to a happy conclusion. "There are two Travers," she muttered, everything now beginning to make sense – this was the voice she had heard behind the door, so like Blake's but not his! Allowing the wealth of her love for Blake, which she'd had to deny, free from its traps, she was almost overwhelmed with joy.

"What's that? Speak up." His look clearly implied that he thought her simple.

And indeed she felt she might as well have been, considering the mistake she had made. She shook her head at her own stupidity. Relief brought a smile to her face and he looked quite startled.

"What can I do for you, Mr. Travers?" she asked.

"I'm here to see the deeds you claim to have to this holding, of course," he snapped.

"Oh, oh yes, of course," she said, returning her mind to the fact that she was still in a very dangerous situation. This man, Arthur, was not Blake, and therefore she could not appeal to him as she had to Blake. But she held her head up proudly. "Just a moment."

Hurrying into the cottage she returned with the wills in her hand.

"I don't have the deeds," she told him, "but here is my grandmother's will leaving the holding and cottage to my father and here is his will, leaving them to me." She held up the two documents for his perusal.

He gave them both a cursory glance.

"Doesn't mean a thing!" he declared. "I could write a will leaving you Dublin Castle but it wouldn't be worth the paper it was written on without the deeds, my good woman." His cold grey eyes were now lit with glee and he looked down his nose at her. "You are on my property and unless you can show me the deeds I will expect you to vacate this holding."

Lowering her eyes, Ellen tried to stop her hand from trembling as she refolded the wills slowly, giving herself time to think.

She raised her eyes to his again. "You need to give me more time to locate them. If there hadn't been deeds, I know these wills would never have been written. And I think you do too, Mr Travers," she challenged, her gaze unflinching.

Considering her for a moment, his eyes narrowed, like a cat with a mouse, and she instinctively knew he was enjoying the chase because he believed he would ultimately win.

"One day," he said, then lowering his voice ominously he continued, "I will give you one day." He turned a disparaging look on her cottage. "It's so small in there, it shouldn't take you that long to search for them. Have the deeds by two o'clock tomorrow afternoon or I will personally oversee your eviction if you do not produce them, Miss Cassidy." The last was a sneer rather than a civility.

Shep growled at him.

With a dismissive look, Travers turned his horse, dug his heels into the animal's sides and struck off, the other two close behind.

Ellen stood still, quite shocked at the difference between the temperaments of the two men who bore the same surname. They were obviously related, which explained the vague familiarity to Blake, but she hadn't dared to mention Blake's name to him.

Feeling guilty at how she had wronged Blake, she sank down onto the wall and hugged Shep to her. He whined and licked her hand. How stupid she had been, she berated herself. But then Blake had not said anything either when she had mentioned the Travers surname and she was now equally puzzled as to why he had not set her straight then. So the misunderstanding was not entirely her fault.

But for now she had a more urgent worry. She knew another search of the cottage would not reveal anything. She didn't know what to do. Her hand trembled as she stroked Shep's head.

Deciding that talking this through with Annie might help, she set out for the village with her thoughts and emotions in a chaotic whirl.

With luck, she spotted Mick going into the public house as she came around the corner and she hurried up the hill to Annie's house.

Without stopping to knock she called Annie's name and rushed in.

"What's happened?" Annie asked her.

Ellen caught her two hands in her own. "Arthur Travers is your landlord! Not Blake Travers!"

"What?"

"Arthur Travers came to see me today about the deeds," she told her. "He is your landlord, not Blake! I think they must be brothers or cousins perhaps." Tears slipped from her eyes but she impatiently wiped them away. "Blake's a good man, Annie. I knew it when I first met him and now I know it to be still true. But how I have wronged him! I so easily accepted that he was the landlord even though I found it so hard to reconcile that with the man I loved. Shame on me!"

"It's not your fault," Annie consoled her. "You had the same facts as everyone else – Travers was the name of the landlord who was evicting his tenants. You saw Blake at the Travers estate, and heard him reply to that name. What else were you to think?"

Annie moved them over to the table and sat Ellen down.

"You look very shaken, Ellen. I've a stew made. You need to keep up your strength. I won't eat yet and Mick won't be back for well over an hour."

She put a plate of food and a spoon in front of Ellen and sat down opposite her.

"Yes, but knowing him as I had," Ellen went on, ignoring the food, "I should have questioned it and confronted him. Even when he showed kindness to you, I kept my heart hard against him."

Annie, her faith in love restored, smiled mischievously at Ellen. "So he appealed to this Arthur Travers on my behalf because you asked him to, and he stayed away because he believed it was best for you because of Father O'Riordan, and he sent that lovely Mr Shaughnessy to see if we were all right here. It seems to me that he's a wonderful man and you should try to get him back."

"I'm not worthy of him, Annie, for mistrusting him so much. And besides he's gentry. But the thing is, I might need his help again. But how can I ask him now?"

"Why do you need his help?"

"Oh God, Annie, Arthur Travers won't accept the wills as proof of ownership. I've searched every inch of the cottage and I can't find them. I don't even know what Blake could do for me. I don't know how he got Arthur Travers to show you leniency. Do you think Blake could intervene again?" She worried her bottom lip, waiting for Annie's reply.

"I think you don't have a choice but to ask him. If anything, he might be able to give you advice. How did the landlord leave it with you?"

"He's given me one day. He comes back tomorrow afternoon and I'll have to show him the deeds then. I'll have to go to Bantry this afternoon and try to speak to Blake. I'll explain the whole misunderstanding to him."

"He loves you, Ellen. I don't think this will be as hard as you think. But you can't go there alone, and I can't go with you – Mick is in bad form today."

Ellen got up and paced.

"Ask Fionn. He'd take you."

"That's complicated. I can't. He knows about me and Blake and the baby."

Annie's eyes opened wide.

"I can't talk about all that now," Ellen said, blocking further questions from her. "Fionn will be working anyway. I'll have to go alone. I'll be careful."

"Eat your stew. I'm not letting you go anywhere until you've had a square meal."

Ellen sighed, but sat and under Annie's watchful eye tried to eat some of it.

After leaving Annie's, Ellen headed for home to feed Shep and gather a few things to take with her to Bantry. She needed to borrow Andy's horse and trap again but hadn't gone in when she passed because Mick had still been in there. The more she thought of going to the Travers estate, the more nervous she became. She wondered if perhaps Andy Minehane would go with her to Bantry – she didn't want to go alone in case she ran into Arthur Travers at the house. She hoped her going there to ask Blake for help wouldn't cause trouble between the two men.

Chapter 47

That same morning, Blake had arrived down to the dining room to find Arthur closeted in his study, having already had an early breakfast. Relieved not see him there, he ate breakfast in peace then instead of going straight to work went into the town on some errands.

Returning to the stable, he noticed Arthur's horse was gone, but thought nothing of it. Going to his study, he collected paperwork he had finished the night before and took it to Arthur's study to leave on his desk.

As he set the papers down, his eye was caught by an old map of the Mizen which was stretched out on the table. Blake leaned over it and saw that a holding marked number fifteen had a ring around it. Studying it, he realised that it was the location of Ellen's cottage. He swore. "The bastard is going after Ellen!" She had assured him that she was self-sufficient, so surely she was able to pay rent each month? So what could Arthur want with her, he wondered, clenching his jaw. Was he going to increase her rent beyond what she could pay?

Wasting no time, he burst out into the yard moments later, yelling out for Shaughnessy, who appeared from a nearby barn.

"Follow me!" he ordered, striding to the stables, while thrusting his arms into his coat. "I think Arthur has gone to Ellen's. You know? Annie Leahy's sister?"

"Yes, sir."

They entered the stables.

"Do you know where Mr Arthur is gone?" Blake asked the stable lad, while saddling his horse. Shaughnessy worked beside him silently, preparing another horse.

"No, sir."

"When did he leave?"

"About two hours ago now."

"Thank you," Blake said, tossing the reins over the horse's head.

The boy looked like he had something else to say and Shaughnessy nodded at him to speak.

"He was with the two men who go and collect the rent for him out at the new holdings."

A look passed between the two men over the backs of the horses and their movements became urgent.

They left at a gallop but had to slow to a canter for the horses' sake after a while.

Blake spoke his thoughts out loud. "If he hurts her in any way ...!" He glanced over at Shaughnessy. "Thank you for coming with me. This is personal and not part of your job."

"It's my pleasure, sir. Perhaps we should check on Annie Leahy too while we're there."

Preoccupied, Blake nodded. Now more than ever he was ashamed to be related to such a conniving man as Arthur. He regretted not warning Ellen about him that day she'd asked for his help.

"What are you going to do when you see him?" Shaughnessy's question broke into his thoughts.

"Intervene on her behalf – remind him of his reputation and the reputation of the Travers name. Appeal to his good sense. Hah! If he has any!"

Passing through Durrus, Blake saw Arthur and two others approaching in the distance.

"Quick, Shaughnessy!" he ordered, following an impulse that had them turning their horses in by the side of a house, out of sight.

When the riders had passed, Blake peered out to watch them riding off towards Bantry.

"It's best that we find out what he's been up to before I challenge him," he said, leading his horse out again so they could continue on.

When they came to the crossroads near Ellen's, Blake reined his horse in. "Now that I know Arthur has gone, I won't need you with me. Why don't you go and check on Ellen's sister, in case Arthur called on them. I'll meet you in the public house in a couple of hours. Get yourself some lunch." He passed some money to him.

Shaughnessy touched his cap and rode on, well pleased with that arrangement.

Annie Leahy's words of greeting were sweet in Shaughnessy's ears.

"Oh, Mr Shaughnessy, you've come back to see us again and I'm so happy to see you!" she said, opening the door wide. "Come on in."

"Thank you," he replied, stepping inside.

"I need to ask you something," she said abruptly, pulling out a stool for him and one for herself.

"Of course, ask away."

"Do you work for Mr Arthur Travers or Mr Blake Travers?"

He studied the frown that drew her neat eyebrows together with the earnestness of her question.

"For Mr Blake."

He saw a smile like dawn sunshine break over her face.

"It was Blake that sent you the last time, wasn't it, to see if the other Mr Travers had let us off our rent?"

He nodded, still puzzled as she beamed at him.

"Is Blake this Arthur's brother?"

"Half-brother."

She nodded, then forgetting herself she rested her hand on his sleeve and gave his arm a slight squeeze, while leaning closer in a conspiratorial fashion. "You see, we thought that Mr Blake was the landlord who was trying to evict us."

Shaughnessy's eyes widened in surprise. He shook his head slightly and laughed. "They couldn't be more different. Mr Blake is totally against eviction, and would never do such a thing. He's a very good man, Mrs. Leahy."

"He was certainly very good to us by speaking to his brother about us living here without paying rent until Mick's arm is better," Annie said.

"Yes, it was brave of him to stand up to Mr Arthur, who could very well have ignored his request."

"My sister, Ellen, has just left here and she has to go and see Blake in Bantry this afternoon. Do you think you could go back with her and take her to see him?"

"Mrs. Leahy, he rode out with me. He's gone to see your sister now."

"Oh, that's just grand!" she exclaimed, jumping up. "They have a lot to talk about so will you stay awhile and have some stew? I was just going to have some myself."

"Sure, if it's no bother, Mrs. Leahy," Shaughnessy said, trying to keep up.

"Please call me Annie, Mr Shaughnessy," she said in her friendly tone.

Shaughnessy could feel a blush colour his cheeks. He cleared his throat. "Only if you'll drop the Mister and call me Shaughnessy, like everyone does."

"Don't you have a first name?" she teased gently.

"It's Daniel – Dan."

"Daniel it is then," she decided matter of factly, going to the pot over the fire.

"Was Mr Arthur here today?"

"No. I've never seen him, just his men."

As she pottered about he glanced around, seeing some damp patches in the worn thatch.

"Looks like the roof could do with a bit of mending. I could mention it to Mr Blake if you like – maybe he could get it done for you."

Annie turned slowly from the fire and he thought for a moment she was going to cry, but to his relief she smiled instead.

"That's very good of you. You've shown me nothing but kindness and in your lovely gentle way too," she said softly.

He felt a little explosion of happiness in his chest at her compliment.

The baby started to cry and Annie picked her up, stroking a very red cheek.

"Poor thing is getting a new tooth, I think."

"Here," he said, "let me hold her for you."

Annie handed him the baby and watched as his cooing and smiles soothed her little girl. With a sigh that came from a sudden strange ache in her heart, she turned back to the pot.

"Just one thing, Daniel – if my husband comes in, don't talk about my sister, or Mr Blake."

He nodded his agreement though silently wondered what that was all about.

Serving up a tasty stew and joining him at the table, she asked him if he had always lived in Bantry and if he liked it there. He told her that it was where he had grown up in a cottage on the Travers estate and that he lived there still with his sister and her two sons. Then they talked about her life in Ballinmara and about his work back on the estate. He was glad of the opportunity to praise Mr Blake and told her what a good man he was to work for.

They had just finished eating when Mick came in from the pub. Annie was embarrassed by the smell of drink from him. She introduced the two men, explaining that Mr Shaughnessy was there to check that all was well.

Mick grunted and mumbled 'Thank you' before saying his arm was sore and he was going for a lie-down.

Shaughnessy saw the worried look Annie gave her husband's retreating back, but her face cleared as she turned back to him, offering him some tea.

Thinking he had already outstayed his welcome, he reached for his cap, though reluctantly. He thanked her for her hospitality and left.

The thought of a sweet woman like her living with a gruff man like that caused him to frown as he walked his horse back into the village.

Chapter 48

After Blake had sent Shaughnessy off to Annie's he turned his horse towards Ellen's place, anxious to know what Arthur had been up to. He desperately hoped that he had worried needlessly and that his visiting her now would not get back to the priest.

Leaving the road, he turned into the fields that led to her place. He saw her at the bottom of the field, walking away from him towards the cottage.

Ellen turned when she heard the horse. She couldn't believe it when she saw who it was. Her heart jumped then began thudding hard in her chest. Joy, excitement and relief filled her.

"Blake!" His name exploded from her lips.

He urged his horse on, drawing up near her and jumping down.

Pulling her into his arms, he held her against him. "Thank God you're well," he said, relieved to feel the strength in her arms as they circled his back and held on tightly.

Leaning back, he cupped her face in his two hands and scrutinised every inch of it. He caressed her cheekbones with his thumbs.

"Has Arthur been here?"

"Yes."

"He hasn't harmed you in any way, has he?" His voice was harsh with anguish.

"No, Blake, I'm fine." A smile lit her eyes and his relief was immense. "Is he your brother?"

"Half-brother. Why was he here?"

"It's a long story. Let's go back to the cottage so we can talk."

With Blake circling her waist with one arm and holding the reins with the other, they walked down to the cottage. Ellen went inside to put the kettle over the fire while he secured the horse. When he went in she was already sitting at the table. He pulled his chair close to hers and took her hands in his, but before he spoke she raised sad eyes to his.

"Blake, I owe you an apology."

"You! My darling, it is I who needs to apologise to you. I was so ashamed to tell you that Arthur Travers was my half-brother that day you mentioned his name. I didn't want you knowing that I was related to a brute like him. I don't condone any of his actions. How he treats people enrages me."

Realisation dawned in Ellen's eyes. "That's why you were so angry when I said his name! You see," she hesitated and gripped his hands tightly, "I thought it was because you were the landlord named Travers that everyone was afraid of and that you were angry because I had asked you to be lenient towards my sister."

Blake was puzzled. "You mean that the last time I was here you knew my name was Travers and you mistook me for Arthur."

"Yes, and I'm sorry."

"But how did you learn that I was Travers?"

Again she raised eyes full of regret to his. "When Annie needed help I went to Bantry to find this Travers fellow. I went to the Travers estate and I heard someone call you 'Mr Travers'. I followed you into the house but couldn't see you, but then I heard you speaking crossly from behind a closed door about the tenants here. Only I know now that it must have been your brother's voice I heard. What was I to think?"

Blake was shocked. "So you left? You didn't think to talk to me so I could confirm or deny it?"

"I didn't think at all, I just felt the pain of what I thought was your betrayal and I ran. I couldn't understand why you lied about your name that very first day!"

Now Blake nodded, affirming his guilt.

She continued: "As I left the estate, I tried to make sense of how you could be this wonderful, loving person with me and this heartless landlord too. Of course I couldn't and I was devastated, confused and hurt. You must understand that I thought I was suddenly looking at the man who had just evicted a widow and her children and was threatening to do the same to my own sister, and he was the man I had given my heart to. So, in panic, I ran away."

Blake groaned. "This is all my fault. I foolishly gave a false name on the spur of the moment when we first met. I didn't put you straight because I didn't want you to know that I was associated with someone as cold and uncaring as Arthur, but also I suppose I was weary of the battle that had been going on between me and my half-brother over my father's will and in that moment I just wanted to be somebody else, just for a day."

She shook her head. "I should have trusted what I already knew of you, instead of what my eyes and ears told me that day in Bantry. I regret it and I apologise."

"So is that why you asked me to stay away from you again?"

"Yes, partly, but it was true about Father O'Riordan watching me."

Blake considered her for a moment, his eyes troubled.

"I am the one who is sorry for causing you so much grief, through my own actions and those of my brother."

A tentative smile tugged at her lips and he leaned forward to brush them with his own.

Forcing his mind back to his main concern, he asked: "Now tell me why Arthur was here."

Watching her closely he saw the light that came into her eyes and the proud way she held her head.

"This cottage, and the land around it, is mine but he believes I am a tenant of his. I have my father's will and my grandmother's to prove it's mine but that's not enough for him. He says if I don't show him the deeds tomorrow afternoon he'll evict me."

A muscle worked in Blake's jaw.

Some of Ellen's defiance faded. "But the thing is, I can't find the deeds." She looked around the cottage as if some other hiding place might suddenly reveal itself. She shook her head in annoyance. "It's mine, Blake," she asserted again.

He listened intently while she told him the story of how the cottage was gifted to her grandmother, Nora Cassidy, by the then landlord.

"She said that Mr Berkley put the deeds in her name because she was the one who saved his son's life."

"May I see the wills?"

Ellen rose and fetched them from underneath the drawer.

Blake studied them.

"Your father's will was witnessed by a Henry Jacobs, Solicitor, in Jacobs Solicitors, Skibbereen." He looked up at Ellen. "It's more than likely that he has the deeds in safe keeping since he drew up the will."

"Oh! I'm so stupid! I never thought of that! Oh Blake, it would be an answer to prayer!" She sat down again, her eyes on the wills.

"I'd offer to take these there for you and to ask for the deeds, but I think you would have to be there yourself. Do you have a birth certificate to prove you are Ellen Cassidy?"

She shook her head. "No, but I could get a baptismal certificate from Father Dempsey."

"Good. Then we'll go to Skibbereen but it will take us four or five hours to get there and the office will be closed by that time. So this is what I suggest. We go to Skibbereen now and spend the night with John and Grace and that way we can be at the solicitor's first thing in the morning. We can be back here by two and I will only be too delighted to see Arthur's face when you produce those deeds. But is there a horse you could ride?"

She vigorously shook her head, feeling panic at the thought of riding in her condition. "We can borrow a pony and trap from Andy Minehane at the public house," she suggested hastily.

"All right, that will have to do. I hope it will get us back fast enough tomorrow."

"Who are John and Grace?"

"They are the friends I was staying with in their summer residence the day of the storm, remember? They returned to their estate in Skibbereen last week. We'll fix this, Ellen."

"Thank you, Blake, and I'm sorry that you have to rescue one of the Cassidys again. Actually, I was going to go to Bantry this afternoon to ask for your help, even though I felt I didn't deserve it."

He felt his shoulders relax as all his protective instincts came into play.

"Don't you know that I would do anything for you?" he said softly, thrilling at the light of love in her eyes at his words. He changed the subject, concern for her his priority. "And what about that priest fellow? Is he still keeping a watch on you? Will my being here today cause trouble? What if he knows it's me you are going to Skibbereen with?"

He saw a glint of fire in her eyes as she smiled at him. "We don't need to worry about him. He isn't here anymore. The Bishop called him away a couple of days ago. We'll be getting a new Parish Priest, I'm told."

Hope surged inside Blake. "Are you saying I don't have to stay away?"

She didn't answer. Instead she said: "Blake, there was another reason why I thought I had to send you away. My grandmother had the sight and she warned me that a stranger would be washed up on the beach, one who would bring trouble for me and my family, so I was to stay away from him. I believe you are the stranger she spoke of. But I had to help you, so the next best thing to honouring her warning was to try to keep you away."

Blake frowned as his thumbs moved over the backs of her hands. "Being washed up here was the best thing that could have happened to me, but to know that it has caused you so much distress grieves me. I'm so sorry, Ellen."

Pulling one hand away, she placed it on his cheek. "No, Blake, no apologies," she said tenderly. "I know now that the trouble has come from your brother and not from you."

His look was intense. "So when this business is sorted with the deeds, can we talk about the future, Ellen?"

"Yes. But for now there's a lot to be done." She walked towards the bedroom, but turned. "I can't stay in your friends' house. Not only would they not want the likes of me there, but I don't have clothes fancy enough for it. You can stay with them and I'll stay at an inn."

"They will love you and I won't take you unless you agree to it."

"Blake?" she entreated.

"No argument, Ellen – now go gather what you need. Shaughnessy will be waiting for me at the crossroads."

"Shaughnessy? That's the man you sent before to check on Annie and me, isn't it?" she asked from the bedroom. "Annie said he was very kind."

"He's a good man and he's been a good friend to me."

Ellen wrote a note for Fionn, telling briefly what had happened and where she was going. She put a nightdress and spare undergarments into a bag and put on her Sunday hat.

A short while later, after leaving extra water and food outside for Shep, they crossed the field. Ellen was on the back of Blake's horse as Blake led it by the reins.

Shaughnessy was at the crossroads before them. Blake introduced them. Ellen liked him straight away and thanked him for his kindness to her sister.

Blake explained what Arthur was up to and he told him of their plan, asking if Shaughnessy minded returning to Bantry without him.

"And will you tell the butler that I've gone to Cork on business, just in case Arthur is wondering where I've got to?"

"Certainly, Mr Blake. Best of luck to both of you."

Shaughnessy rode off.

"I'll have to stop by Fionn's cottage," Ellen said, "and leave him the note." Her heart ached at the thought of Fionn and his love for her. She knew it would hurt him that she had now turned to Blake for help. But this was too urgent.

She pushed it under the door like before, and they went into the village to borrow the trap from Andy again.

"I need to keep it until tomorrow, Andy – I have to stay overnight in Skibbereen. I'm sorry but it's for something really important."

"You're welcome to it. I won't be using it."

He shook hands with Blake as Ellen introduced them. She didn't give his surname as she didn't want to waste time on explanations. Andy agreed to stable Blake's horse behind the public house for the night. The two men hitched the pony to the trap, while Ellen went to the Parish House.

She gave a very quick explanation to Father Dempsey and asked if he could write out the certificate for her. He agreed readily, asking for her date of birth. As he turned to go to his study, a thought struck her.

"I might also need proof of my father's death. Can you write that down too from the church records?"

"Certainly."

She gave him her father's name and date of death, and he went to his study to look up the registers. He returned moments later with her baptismal certificate and a letter giving the date of her father's death. He had put the parish stamp on both, next to his signature.

"Thank you, Father. I'm very grateful."

He just nodded, then met her eyes very briefly before looking away. "I'm sorry about what happened the other day," he said, eyes downcast and a blush creeping up his face, "and I want you to know that I was there against my will."

"That's all right, Father. I knew that to be the case."

He saw her to the door. "Safe journey to you now and God bless you and your work."

Ellen smiled. "Thank you very much, Father Dempsey. That means a lot to me."

With a light step she returned to the pub, where she found the trap ready and waiting. She thanked Andy again. "Can I ask you one more favour? Will you please tell my sister that Blake is helping me and that I will be back tomorrow? She'll understand."

"Of course," he said, scratching his head, unsure what to make of it all.

She gave him a reassuring smile and a jaunty wave as they set off.

Blake handled the reins surely and she relaxed into her seat, praying there would be a good outcome from their journey.

Within minutes they were looking out over Dunmanus Bay, which was calm and clear blue.

Blake gave her a sideways glance. "It's nice to be awake on this trip to Durrus," he said.

She laughed, despite the seriousness of her situation, and smiled across into his mischievous eyes.

She promised herself that as soon as this business was settled she would tell him about the baby and decide about their future one way or another.

Chapter 49

Less than four hours later, as they approached Skibbereen, Ellen felt her stomach tighten with nerves and once more she attempted to persuade Blake to let her stay at an inn.

"It's nearly seven o'clock already – that's too late to call on anyone, asking for a bed for the night, and they'll probably be at dinner, which it would be rude to interrupt."

"They are more likely to dine at seven thirty or eight. They are very good friends of mine, Ellen, I know it will not be a problem."

"Not for you perhaps," Ellen said. "You'll know how to act and behave and I'll come across as a fool."

"Nonsense," he said softly.

Still Ellen could not help but gasp at the beauty of the two-storey house at the end of the long drive. It was surrounded by gardens full of colour and trees, with a terrace running all around the front and sides. As they pulled up at the main door she could see long glass doors standing open to the evening sun on one of the terraces.

A butler in smart clothes opened the door and came to assist them from the trap. He offered to take the cloth bag, into which Ellen had put a few items of clothing. Blake nodded and she let the butler take it. A bag containing the wills, her certificate and letter, she did not relinquish.

She scarcely had time to take in the loveliness of the foyer, with its

269

scent of fresh flowers coming from an exquisite arrangement of roses on a round table in its centre, before a petite woman came out through a door. She was wearing an elegant evening gown in what Ellen guessed was silk.

"Blake!" she cried in delight, her eyes warm with welcome. "We were not expecting you. What a lovely surprise!" They embraced affectionately, the top of her head barely reaching Blake's shoulder. "And who is this?" she asked.

Ellen fully expected her to look up and down at her plain dress, but the woman held Ellen's eyes steadily, while smiling warmly at her.

"Grace, let me introduce Miss Ellen Cassidy. Ellen, this is my dear friend Grace Newman."

"How do you do, Mrs. Newman?"

"Please call me Grace. It's very nice to meet you, Ellen."

Blake noticed the moment Grace remembered where she had heard the name before. Curiosity lit her eyes as she turned back to Blake. "Come on into the drawing room. John will be down in a moment. We'll be having dinner shortly and you must join us."

She turned to the butler.

"Please set the table for two more and inform Cook. Thank you."

The butler was about to move away when she asked him to wait. She turned back to her guests. "But you would probably like to freshen up first. Evans, please take Mr. Blake to the Green room and Miss Cassidy to the Rose room.

The butler whisked them upstairs.

Before Blake went into the Green room he told her he would meet her at the top of the stairs in ten minutes.

Unable to say a word, she just nodded. The butler held open a door for her and Ellen went in. He placed her bag on the bed and left, closing the door behind him, leaving her alone. For a moment she could only stand and stare. The room was bigger than her whole cottage. A huge bed stood to one side with a pretty covering and lots of pillows on it. There was a wardrobe with mirrors and a table and stool beside a large window. A washstand with a decorated bowl stood in one corner and a large comfortable looking armchair in another. Heavy crimson curtains, reaching down to the floor, hung open.

Ellen walked over and watched the sun slip down the sky. A soft breeze came through the open window and cooled her cheeks which were warm with embarrassment as she thought of Blake being in her humble cottage. How different, dull and small, he must find it compared to all this space, beauty and shine. And yet he had never let on, or looked down his nose at it or her.

She put her hand over her stomach and felt sad. Now more than ever she knew how different their worlds were, how odd she must look in all this grandeur.

She thought of Fionn, and smiled as she pictured him that day he had happily repaired her shed. He and she were so much more suited to each other. Their worlds were the same and if she had any sense she should accept his offer. If they couldn't find the deeds tomorrow and she was evicted she knew Fionn's home would become hers as soon as she gave him his answer. But while the thought should have brought a feeling of security and happiness, it left her with an almost unbearable ache because it would mean giving up Blake and all she felt for him.

A knock came on the door and a maid brought in a pitcher of hot water, poured it into a basin for her and left.

After removing her hat, Ellen washed her face and hands and tidied her hair. Straightening her shawl, she went out to Blake, who was waiting for her at the top of the stairs and they went down to the drawing room together. Grace was waiting for them there.

Once again Ellen was struck by the elegance. When Grace invited her to sit, she sat on the edge of a very fancy armchair, hoping her dress had no stains from the trap on it.

A man burst into the room. "Blake, my friend, this is a wonderful surprise."

The two men embraced and Blake turned him towards Ellen, who quickly stood up.

"John, this is my friend Miss Ellen Cassidy."

He bowed formally, his curious eyes studying her features, his smile as welcoming as that of his wife.

"Please call me Ellen," she said quietly, very surprised at the Newmans' friendliness.

"Let me get everyone a glass of sherry and then you can tell us what has brought you so suddenly to our door."

As he poured the drinks, Grace took the seat opposite Ellen, and Blake sat on the settee. After handing around tiny glasses of a dark liquid, John pulled up another chair.

Blake took a sip of his drink and began. "I know you both recognise Ellen's name. She is the person who saved my life back in May."

"Well, my dear," Grace said, "we must thank you most sincerely. He would have been a great loss indeed."

Ellen blushed.

Blake continued. "I renewed my acquaintance with Ellen and we have met on several occasions since."

Ellen flicked her eyes to his. He gave her a reassuring smile.

"It is a long and complicated story and I will not bore you with the details but my darling brother is now making life very difficult for Ellen. He is threatening to evict her from her home at two o'clock tomorrow if she cannot produce the deeds of her cottage by then. The cottage is, in fact, legally hers."

Grace gasped. "But that is dreadful!"

"We are hoping the deeds are here in Jacobs' Solicitors as they are the ones who witnessed her father's will. We need to get there first thing in the morning and return to Ellen's cottage before two."

"But surely the will was enough proof?" Grace asked.

"Not for someone like Arthur. Now more than ever I know he is led by greed. He is the most insensitive man I know."

"I hope you will stay with us tonight. John can take you to the solicitors in the morning."

"Thank you, Grace, we would appreciate that."

"I hope it doesn't put you out," Ellen said. "As I told Blake, I could stay at an inn."

"I wouldn't hear of it," Grace assured her.

"Thank you."

Ellen took a sip of her sherry and was surprised at its delicious warm flavour.

The butler came and announced dinner. When they all stood, Grace took Ellen's arm and walked with her into the dining room with the men following behind.

Ellen's eyes flew to the table which gleamed with glass and silverware. She swallowed hard. It was set for four on a white linen tablecloth. A silver candelabra stood tall in a centrepiece of purple flowers.

"Your house is beautiful," she told Grace.

"Thank you. I love flowers and spend ages on my knees in the flowerbeds. I might as well while I can." She laid her hand on the gentle curve of her stomach which Ellen had noticed the moment she walked into the house.

"Congratulations. That's wonderful for you," Ellen said, thinking about a child growing up amongst all these beautiful things, and the secret child within her own body, whose future at this moment was so uncertain.

The butler held out a chair for Ellen. She found she was facing a set of glass doors looking out over the gardens. "The gardens are lovely," she said.

Blake, taking the seat opposite her, told his hosts that Ellen lived in the most beautiful spot in West Cork. "Her house is right at the top of the shore, with a beach all to herself."

Ellen smiled gratefully at him. Being reminded of her own wealth of sea and sky made her feel more confident in the strangeness of these surroundings.

She was in awe of all the different implements for eating. She raised accusing eyes to Blake, a blatant message saying she knew she wouldn't fit into his world.

When soup was ladled into his bowl by the butler, he caught her eye and slowly lifted the spoon on his right, lying beside three knives, and dipped it into the soup.

She followed his lead. The soup was delicious. Every dish was exquisite – the fish that followed and the chicken that followed that, in a sauce she had never tasted the likes of before. The potatoes, brought around by the butler in a silver dish were without their skins, drizzled with melted butter and sprinkled with parsley. Carrots and parsnips were cut in small thin stick shapes and had a subtle flavour of oranges. Ellen was fascinated. The food was dainty but filling and by the time the butler came around offering her some fancy pudding she had to refuse. She had also refused the offer of wine, choosing water instead.

Neither of her hosts said anything to make her feel uncomfortable or unwelcome, but she believed they were an exception. She doubted very much that there were many other fine tables like this where she would be allowed, let alone welcomed.

Blake gave Grace and John more detail of what had been going on with Arthur and his tenants over the past weeks.

By the end of the meal Ellen was very tired, and couldn't suppress a yawn.

"You've had a long journey and by all accounts a long day. Would you like to retire to your room?" Grace asked.

"Yes, thank you."

"I'll take you up then," Grace offered, rising from her chair.

The men stood as the ladies left the room, both of them bidding Ellen goodnight.

As they walked up the stairs together, Ellen thanked Grace. "You have been very kind. I see that you and Blake are very close and you're probably wondering why he's doing this for me. But I want you to know that I'm fully aware that I do not belong in his world and I believe that someday soon he will realise this. I don't want you to worry about him."

They had reached the door of the room Ellen was in earlier. Grace stopped and turned to her.

"You might not have rank, my dear, but do not doubt for a moment that you are a true lady. I agree that you could complicate his life, but I am passionately in love with my husband and I would not wish for anything less for Blake. I see how he looks at you, my dear, and I do not think his feelings are something that will disappear like a puff of smoke. I do not know where you go from here but I wish you both well. And, might I say," she continued with laughter in her eyes, "that if I were not a lady myself, I might tell you how dreadfully jealous I am of that magnificent red hair of yours."

Delighted with her hostess, Ellen laughed. The warm rich sound made Grace beam back at her.

"Breakfast will be at eight in the morning. For now get a good night's sleep and hopefully all will go well tomorrow."

"Thank you, Grace. Goodnight."

Wearily Ellen pulled her plain cotton nightgown from her bag and, after putting it on, she released her hair from its ribbon and brushed it before climbing into a bed softer than anything she could ever have imagined.

She lay there missing the sound of the sea and wishing that she and Blake could have said goodnight in private. No sooner had she thought it when there was a tap on her door and Blake came in, closing it behind him.

"You shouldn't be here," she said, sitting up. "What will Grace and John think?"

"I had to check on you. This has been a difficult day for you and, now, to be in a strange place too."

He sat on the edge of the bed and took her hand in his.

"Are you all right, my love?"

His tenderness moved her deeply and all she could do was nod. He pulled her gently into his arms and kissed her, softly at first and then more deeply. She let herself fall into the kiss, to drift away from thoughts and worry for just a few moments, before sense rose up.

Her body ached for more of his touch, but gently she pressed her hands against his chest until her released her. "You'd best leave now. I don't want Grace and John's disapproval. "They've been so kind to me."

He ran his fingers through the thick silkiness of her hair, and brought her face close to his for one last light but exquisite kiss that left both of them trembling.

"I wish I could stay," he murmured, his voice ragged, but dutifully he stood and walked to the door. "Goodnight, Ellen. Sweet dreams."

Lying there, longing for him, Ellen wondered if she could tolerate being his mistress. At least that way she would see him now and then. Would it be better than not seeing him at all, she wondered, or would sharing him slowly kill her?

Chapter 50

The same maid woke Ellen the next morning. After knocking on the door she brought in a pitcher and placed it on the washstand.

"Good morning, miss. Here's your hot water. Breakfast will be served in half an hour. Do you need help with anything?"

"No, thank you."

The maid closed the door behind her and Ellen had the impulse to laugh out loud because she had just imagined Annie's face if she were to see her now. Getting out of bed the smile was wiped off her face as a wave of nausea swept over her. She sat down again and put her head between her knees. Despite having slept all night, the events of yesterday had tired her more than she realised. After a few moments, and feeling slightly better, she got up gingerly, and took her time washing and dressing. Her stomach was crying out for a bit of plain bread but she would have to wait until eight before going downstairs. She sat in the armchair and took deep breaths as another wave of nausea passed over her.

At last she heard voices in the corridor as they headed for the stairs. She waited another minute and then went down too.

The moment she walked into the dining room the smell of cooked food had her swallowing hard against another wave of sickness and she stood at the door, gripping the doorknob fiercely.

Grace looked over and smiled, then hurriedly rose and came to stand next to her.

"Ellen, are you unwell? You are deathly pale."

Ellen attempted a smile as Blake also hurried over. They took an arm each and led her to a chair at the table.

"I'm just a little tired."

"You sit right here and I'll prepare a plate for you," Grace said, moving towards an array of sliver-covered dishes on a sideboard. "A good breakfast will restore you."

"No!" Ellen said quickly, knowing that if a plate of hot food was put in front of her she was likely to vomit and she would die of embarrassment. "Please, may I just have some bread and tea for now?"

Blake stood beside her, looking very concerned. "Of course," he said, reaching for a basket of bread and putting a slice on her plate for her. He also reached for the butter but Ellen was already breaking off a piece of the bread and ate it dry.

Grace had resumed her seat and was studying her. Ellen looked up and saw that knowing look in her eye. Grace, probably having gone through something similar herself so recently, had guessed what was wrong. With her eyes, Ellen pleaded with her not to say anything.

"Blake, come and eat your own breakfast and let Ellen catch her breath. She's worried sick about losing her home and doesn't need us fussing over her. Ellen, you eat at your own pace, my dear, and if there is anything in particular you want, you just ask for it."

Ellen nearly wept with relief at her collusion and kindness. The dry bread settled her stomach and she felt able to ask for a bowl of porridge. Blake jumped up and got it for her from another dish on the sideboard.

Halfway through it she felt much better. Her colour must have improved too, because Blake looked a little less worried as he smiled at her.

"I'll take you down and introduce you to Finbarr Jacobs," John suggested. "I've met him once or twice socially. It was probably his father who witnessed the will."

"Thanks, John." Blake said. "Will you be up to it, Ellen?"

"Yes. I'm fine now. Thank you."

After breakfast, Ellen returned to her room and gathered her few bits and pieces into the larger of her two bags.

Blake knocked on her door and offered to take the bag and escort her down.

"Are you sure you're well?" he asked quietly.

"Yes, I'm fine, but very nervous about whether we'll get the deeds."

Down in the hall Grace embraced Blake and he thanked her for her hospitality before he walked out with John.

Grace then embraced Ellen.

"Thank you," Ellen whispered into her ear, "He doesn't know and I will not use it to keep him, I promise."

They pulled apart and Grace nodded, her eyes sad because she did not know how these two lovers were going to find a happy solution. But she gave Ellen an encouraging smile. "It was our pleasure to meet you, Ellen. I wish you the best of luck today in securing your home."

The housekeeper came bustling out from the back of the hall and handed Ellen a basket.

"Oh, I'd forgotten," said Grace. "Thank you, Mrs. Dillon."

The housekeeper bustled away again.

"I asked that Cook should prepare some food for your journey back. You mustn't allow yourself to get too hungry – it's then you begin to feel unwell."

Ellen was moved by her thoughtfulness. "Thank you for everything, Grace."

Ellen stepped out into the morning sun, glad of its warmth. Blake was waiting to help her into the trap and John was sitting astride a large black stallion.

The offices of Jacobs Solicitors were just opening when they arrived at nine. John introduced himself and asked to speak to Mr. Jacobs. They were asked to take a seat while the clerk went to speak to the solicitor. Ellen's palms began to sweat. She wiped them on her skirt.

A few moments later the clerk returned and showed them into Mr. Jacob's office. A slim man, with thinning while hair, came out from behind a cluttered desk and greeted John.

"Mr. Newman."

"Good morning, Mr. Jacobs. May I introduce my friends, Mr. Blake Travers and Miss Ellen Cassidy."

They shook hands and Mr. Jacobs invited them to sit down.

"What can I do for you today?" he enquired.

Blake drew a breath to speak but Ellen lay a hand on his arm, and spoke herself. "Mr. Jacobs, I would like you to take a look at my father's will, please." She unfolded it and handed it to him. "I believe it was witnessed by someone from this office."

Mr. Jacobs read the document. "Yes, this is my father's signature and the other witness is a clerk who worked for him at the time. I had only begun my own apprenticeship here the year this was drawn up."

"As you can see my father left the cottage to me. He passed away six years ago."

"My condolences."

"Thank you. The reason we are here is because I need to know if you hold the deeds of the cottage."

"It's very likely. Let me write down the details." He copied information from the will on to a piece of paper and Ellen's heart beat faster in anticipation.

Mr. Jacobs called in his clerk and gave him the piece of paper. He then linked his fingers and laid them on the desk. He offered them tea while they waited for the clerk to do his search. They declined.

"May I enquire as to why you want to see the deeds? Are you selling the property?"

"No. Someone is saying I don't own it and I need to prove that I do."

"I see. These are important legal documents and they remain here with us. What needs to happen is that your name has to be added to them and I then prepare a document stating that you are the present owner. It's that document that you can take away with you. However, before I can do that I will need proof that you are who you say you are and proof of your father's death, which proves your rightful inheritance."

Ellen heard Blake's sharp intake of breath because he thought she only had the baptismal cert, but she pulled the certificate and the letter from her bag and passed them to him. "I brought both," she said.

Blake looked at her with admiration.

Mr. Jacobs surveyed the documents and nodded in approval. "Excellent. You have come well prepared. Once the deeds are found we can proceed."

A few minutes later the clerk returned and placed a document on the desk.

Ellen held her breath while the solicitor read it.

He looked up and smiled. "Yes, this is what you are looking for."

Ellen's relief was immense as she heard her father's name being read out.

The solicitor added her name to the document and had it witnessed by one of his clerks.

"I would advise," said Mr. Jacobs, "that you make a will yourself, Miss Cassidy. We would be willing to assist you in that matter."

"Yes, of course. Thank you. I'll return another day."

He called his clerk to show them out.

"I'll pay you back," Ellen murmured as they left the solicitor's office, Blake having paid the fee for the job just done.

"You'll do no such thing," he declared.

Back out on the pavement, they hurriedly thanked John, said their goodbyes and got on the road back to Ballinmara. On leaving Skibbereen they passed Abbeystrowry graveyard. Ellen blessed herself and asked her ancestors who were buried there to intercede for her that all would turn out well.

"We should get back in time and I for one can't wait to see Arthur's face," Blake said with relish.

Ellen shivered. "He'll surely resent your helping me. Perhaps you should leave as soon as we get there. I'll show Arthur the deeds myself – that way he needn't know of your involvement."

"I have no intention of leaving you at the mercy of that man. I will stand beside you and that's that. You're only claiming what's rightfully yours. No one is cheating him of anything – he'll have to realise that."

"In a way he has done me a favour. I didn't know that I was supposed to add my name to the deeds in that office, and hadn't thought about making a will."

Ellen remained anxious for the rest of the journey because, despite having all the right documents, she was not looking forward to a confrontation with Arthur Travers.

Chapter 51

It was approaching half past one on Blake's pocket-watch when they turned off the road and into the field above Ellen's. Blake said he would return the horse and trap to the public house later.

As they drew near the cottage, Ellen heard Shep barking from inside the shed. Three horses were tethered to a post. As Blake pulled the trap to a stop they heard a crash. Before Blake could stop her, Ellen got out and ran around the side of the cottage. Some of her furniture was outside. There was a second crash as a stool flew out the door and landed on the ground next to her rocking chair.

Rushing in, she saw Arthur leaning against the dresser, smiling smugly, with his arms crossed over his chest, as he watched his henchmen lifting up Ellen's kitchen table. Blake stood behind her but was blocked from Arthur's view by the door

"Put that down right now and leave my property," she said coldly.

The men, unsure, lowered the table to the floor.

"Well, if it isn't Miss Cassidy! You weren't here to show me the deeds as we agreed so I'm carrying out my threat."

"And you said you would not arrive until two."

"A few minutes don't make a difference. Please move out of the way and let my men do their job."

They lifted the table again and Ellen stepped forward to put her hand on the arm of the nearest man. The look in her eye and the peculiar sensation he felt in his arm made him release the table and step back from her.

Arthur grabbed her shoulders from behind and swung her roughly away. She cried out as her hip struck the corner of the dresser.

"Take your hands off her!" Blake's words snapped out like a whiplash.

Arthur released Ellen abruptly, causing her to stumble forward, where she had to use the table to keep upright. Turning quickly, she watched the two brothers squaring up to one another.

"Ah, the hero of the natives tries to intervene in my business again!" Arthur's grey eyes were like shards of ice. "What are you doing here, Blake? I warned you to stay out of my affairs."

"A bit heavy-handed against one woman, aren't you, Arthur? But then you never play fair, do you? But before you set your thugs on us, maybe you should consider how many years in jail a man gets for theft."

Arthur snorted. "Theft?"

"Oh yes, Arthur, theft – to take property belonging to someone else is most definitely theft and most definitely punishable." He held out the new document, allowing Arthur to read it, but still keeping a firm grip on it. He knew better than to leave it out of his hands. "Yes, Arthur, here's your proof that Miss Cassidy owns this property."

Ellen stepped forward. "And you and your men are trespassing."

Arthur's face flushed with anger and his chest heaved.

"You'll be sorry!" he spat at Blake as he pushed past him to get outside. His two men followed him out.

Blake closed the distance between him and Ellen in a heartbeat, and took her into his arms. "Are you hurt?"

"Just a bruised hip. But I fear you've made an enemy of Arthur."

"Don't worry about him. It's not like we were on good terms anyway. I'll deal with all that in due course." But, as he pulled her close again, he did indeed wonder what was ahead of him on his return home and in his heart he knew that the time had come for him and Arthur to part ways. His plan to move out might happen sooner rather than later, but it would break his heart to have to leave the tenants and workers to the mercy of Arthur.

Ellen pulled away. "I have to let Shep out. The brutes locked him in. I hope they haven't hurt him."

Shep was fine and danced around them in delight, licking their hands, while his tail wagged furiously.

Ellen looked around at the scattered furniture. "Luckily we got here before they did too much damage."

"I'll take it back in," Blake said, "and then perhaps we can have the food Grace gave us."

Ellen examined her rocking chair. There were scratches on the back but other than that it was intact. However, a leg had broken off the three-legged stool that she had seen flying through the air.

She was so glad that they hadn't time to move the dresser or her store of herbs. As she straightened up a candle, she couldn't help but remember the splendour of Grace's house. But she smiled.

"Grace's house is beautiful, but this is my home and I love it."

Blake came and put his arms around her. "I love it too. I meant it when I said this is a beautiful place. It has captured my heart."

She laughed. "Then you are fooling yourself. You would tire of its cramped conditions very quickly I think, now that I have seen inside a grand house."

"But your house has a charm that cannot be matched." He released her. "Let's eat because I have to return to Bantry straight after."

"So soon?"

"Yes, I'm afraid. When I heard the solicitor mention today's date I suddenly remembered that this is the day my aunt and her husband are arriving from London. I have to be there to meet them off the train this evening." He told her about the letter he had received the previous week.

"That's all very mysterious," Ellen said.

"It certainly is. Right – let's eat – I must go. But I'll be back soon to settle things with you. I'll take the trap back to the publican and pay him for the use of it. Do you want me to find your sister and send her to you?"

"No, thank you. I'm exhausted after all the travelling and excitement and need some quiet after the madness of it all."

Half an hour later he got up to go. Holding her close, he promised to return as soon as he could.

"Thank you for all you've done for me, Blake," Ellen said, pressing her cheek to his.

He gave her one last passionate kiss.

"One for the road," he murmured.

Her breathless laugh followed him as he slapped the reins on the horse's rump and drove away.

Chapter 52

"Aggh! This blasted arm is never going to get better," Mick said, fumbling with his coat.

Annie cringed as she heard the familiar edge in his voice that meant his temper was close to breaking.

She went to untangle the sleeve, but he shoved her roughly away. "I can do it myself – for God's sake, stop treating me like a child!" he roared.

"Please, Mick," she entreated, "you'll wake the children."

"*I'll speak as I want in my own house!*" he bellowed at her.

Moving back until the table was digging into the back of her thighs, she willed him to leave without hitting her.

He was going out to the public house again. Two nights ago he said he was going there and Annie had been foolish enough to question the spending of money on drink when they needed it so badly.

Fury had leapt from his eyes and he had grabbed her by her upper arm with his good hand, shoving her roughly against the wall, badly bruising her shoulder.

"Don't you question me!" he had growled at her before slapping her across the face and going out, slamming the door behind him.

Annie had been humiliated and sore, but she had been grateful that he hadn't blackened her eye. The slap had left a redness which was gone by morning and her clothes covered the bruises on her arm and shoulder.

Now she held her breath as he glowered at her. Turning away suddenly, he grabbed up his cap and swept out.

Annie let the tears fall – the tears she had almost cried when Daniel Shaughnessy had shown her such kindness a few days earlier. His gentle manner had been in such stark contrast to Mick's lack of attention or softness that she had almost wept at the beauty of it. Daniel noticed things too, like seeing that the roof needed fixing. She had liked him looking out for her.

With a sigh that sounded like it had come right up from her toes, she finished her tidying and took herself off to bed. That way, she hoped to get some sleep before Mick staggered in the worse for the drink. Drunk or sober, he had become more and more dour, and more and more likely to hurt her again.

Ellen sat in her rocking chair with a smile on her face, and the document in her hands stating that the cottage was hers. She had taken them out to look at several times already, still amazed at how things had turned out, and glad she was a lot wiser about these legal matters than she had been.

She marvelled at the events of the past week and all that had changed. She was free to do her healing again, her home was secure from Arthur and she was even more in love with Blake than she had been. But thinking of him made her worry.

Arthur had been very angry when he left and Ellen was anxious about what was happening at that moment in Bantry. She prayed for Blake's safety.

Even though it was early evening and still bright outside, she rose and lit a candle in the window.

"Please bring him back safely to me," she prayed. She shook her head at the irony of it. Over two months ago she had been praying that he would stay away. "Shep," she said to the dog, "the unpredictability of life is a constant wonder to me."

Shep gave a soft bark and wagged his tail at her, making her laugh as she went to open the door.

"Go on out with you before we settle down for the evening. I think we'll have an early night tonight – I'm too tired to think another thought."

Around midnight, Ellen was woken by Shep's barking. She was afraid Arthur Travers had returned and her heart began thundering. She threw a shawl around her shoulders. A gentle knock sounded at the door, but images from the night of the exorcism had her calling cautiously through the door.

"Who's there?" she asked.

But it was a woman's voice that replied. "It's Mrs. Moran, dear."

Startled and much relieved, Ellen opened the door for the priest's housekeeper, holding her candle aloft. The woman was standing there with her shawl held firmly around her, looking half-frightened to death in the moonlight.

"Come in, Mrs. Moran, please," Ellen invited.

Mrs. Moran stepped in.

"Father Dempsey sent me to fetch you, dear. I have the pony and trap outside. There's been an accident and he knew your sister would need you."

"Annie? Is she all right?" Ellen's voice rose in alarm.

"Oh sorry, dear, it's not her, it's her husband."

"What's happened?"

"I'm afraid he has just been pulled out of the harbour."

"What?" Ellen gasped.

Mrs. Moran nodded sadly.

"Drowned?" Ellen whispered.

"Yes, I'm afraid so, dear."

"How did it happen?"

"I don't know."

Ellen rushed into the bedroom to change. Within minutes she emerged dressed and they hurried out while Ellen haphazardly threw on her shawl and told Shep to stay.

Arriving at the harbour, they saw that a crowd had gathered. Ellen could hear Annie's sobs cut through the still night air.

At the centre of the crowd, Mick's lifeless body was lying in Annie's arms and Father Dempsey was praying quietly over him.

Ellen pushed through and knelt beside her sister, putting her arms around her shoulders.

When Father Dempsey finished his prayers, Ellen helped Annie up and caught the curate's eye. "Thank you for sending for me. It was very kind."

He nodded. Some of the men came forward and lifted Mick onto a cart.

"God, Annie, how did it happen?" Ellen asked.

"No one seems to know. Some of the men saw him in the water when they were on their way home from the pub."

Andy Minehane was standing near and came closer. "I'm so sorry for your trouble, Annie. Mick was drinking in the pub up to an hour ago but he left saying he was going home. It's hard to believe he's gone. At least the tide hadn't turned or he mightn't have been found at all."

Annie could only nod at him, but she turned to thank the men who had brought Mick ashore. Then she stood back as the cart moved to take the body home. Ellen admired Annie's strength and dignity as she walked behind it.

Everyone else fell in behind them. In the moonlight and silence, it was a ghostly procession that walked up the road out of the village.

On reaching the cottage the men lifted Mick down. Mary had already taken the children to her house. Annie rushed in, lit a candle and led the way into the bedroom. She pulled the blankets off the bed with Ellen's help and the men laid him on it.

Without looking at his lifeless body, Annie thanked them and followed them outside to speak to those gathered there.

"Thank you all very much for your help tonight. I hope you'll all come back tomorrow to wake Mick here in our home." Her voice broke but she kept her spine straight as she accepted offers of help for the following few days.

Cáit, one of Annie's neighbours, offered to stay and prepare the body, but Annie said she wanted to do it herself.

"Are you sure?" Ellen asked.

"Yes. You'll help me, won't you?"

"Of course."

"But, Cáit, I'd be grateful if you could come back in a while and keep vigil with us until morning."

Cáit hugged her. "Certainly I will."

Annie went back inside.

Ellen knew it would be a long night for some of the men, those who would stay up making a coffin for Mick. She walked over to Andy before he could leave.

"Andy, do you really not know what happened?" she asked in a whisper.

"All I know is that earlier Mick and Eoghan Brady started up a row in the pub. Eoghan said that his father was unlikely to take Mick back on his fishing boat once his arm was better. They started hurling insults at each other. I told them to pipe down or they'd have to leave. They stopped and Eoghan left shortly after. Mick left an hour or so after that. Some of the men were on their way home later and saw something in the water. When they saw it was a body they raised the alarm and a boat went out for him. "

Ellen felt a chill. "Do you think he and Eoghan continued their fight later?"

"I don't know. Eoghan and his wife were here just now and I heard someone asking him the same question. He got very angry and told them that he went straight home after leaving the pub. His wife agreed that he had." Andy shrugged. "Mick was drunk when he left, Ellen. He probably just missed his footing. The constabulary will be asked to look into it, I'm sure, but I suspect they'll quickly find it was just a tragic accident."

"Thanks, Andy."

She went back inside to Annie. She found her standing in the middle of the bedroom, looking like she didn't know where to start.

Ellen took charge. "I'll revive the fire and get some water on. Can you gather some bowls and cloths?"

Annie nodded, relieved to follow instructions.

When the water was warm enough they returned to the bedroom.

Moving to the bed, Ellen looked down on Mick. The animosity he had shown her didn't matter now. She had already forgiven him for his actions and lack of understanding because she knew it had come from a place of fear and grief.

Annie squeezed out a cloth and gently began to wipe his face. Her tears fell on the back of her hand as she worked.

"He was a good man when I met him. I know you never approved of me marrying him but ..."

"That doesn't matter now, Annie," Ellen said softly.

Annie continued as if she didn't hear her. "I loved him. He took good care of me and I was so lonely after Mammy and Daddy died. And he was so happy when first Michael and then Róisín were born. He loved them very much." The movement of the cloth over his face became a repeated caress. "It wasn't his fault that times became hard for us. At least he won't hurt me any more now." She paused to rinse out the cloth.

The candle flickered and the muscles in Ellen's stomach tightened at her words. She watched a trickle of water run down Mick's cheek, to disappear below his ear.

"What did he do to you, Annie?"

Annie continued to wipe his face. "He slapped me a couple of times and punched me once."

"Oh God, Annie, why didn't you tell me? You shouldn't have tried to deal with that alone." Ellen felt both anger and sadness. "The children?"

"No! He would never hurt them!"

"He should never have hurt you either!"

Annie's body was suddenly racked with sobs. "I had stopped loving him, Ellen! And now he's gone and I can't make things right!"

Ellen came around the bed and held her.

"You can't blame yourself for that, Annie. He damaged that love by mistreating you, and you have no way of knowing if he would've got better or worse. You loved him once, that's what you need to think of when you remember him."

She held her sister until she cried herself out, remembering her own fear of Mick that night in the church, and she wondered if perhaps his death was a blessing in disguise for them all.

"Let's get this finished," Annie said, pulling away and drying her face.

Without any more talk, the sisters worked together to get the wet clothes off Mick. Ellen removed the splint from his arm and, after washing him, they dressed him in his Sunday clothes. They placed candles at his head and feet.

Cáit and some other neighbours returned shortly after to sit with them.

Chapter 53

Blake heard the whistle as the Cork train approached, and rubbed a weary hand over his face as he waited on the small platform. All the travelling he had done over the past two days was taking its toll.

He spotted his aunt and uncle easily among the few passengers who alighted. Violet was tall like Blake's father and very finely dressed beneath a large hat. She carried a parasol. Her husband wore a white suit and had a curling handlebar moustache. His face was tanned from the Indian sunshine.

Waving, he caught their eye and moved forward with a porter, who took care of their luggage.

"Aunt Violet, Uncle Henry! Welcome to West Cork!" He shook his uncle's hand and kissed his aunt on the cheek.

"Blake, my dear boy," Violet said. "How lovely to see you! How are you holding up?" Tears filled her eyes and she dabbed at them with a handkerchief and gave a shaky laugh. "I promised myself that I wouldn't cry the moment I saw you, but I still cannot believe your father is no longer with us."

Blake offered her his arm and walked them out to the waiting carriage. "I'm sure you must both be tired and hungry after your journey. Dinner will be at eight. I'm afraid Arthur had a prior, longstanding arrangement to have dinner with friends in Ballylickey tonight so you won't see him until tomorrow. He sends his apologies."

Blake thought he heard his uncle snort.

When they were settled in the carriage Blake questioned his aunt about the urgency in her letter.

"I would prefer to wait and discuss it at the house. It's quite complicated. But, tell me, are you managing the estate now for Arthur?"

"Yes, that's right."

"Hmm. As I thought."

Blake's curiosity was even more spiked by the considering way she was looking at him, but he bit back any further questions about the reason for her visit. He would find out soon enough.

The conversation over dinner that evening centred around India and descriptions of the journey home. It was only when the three of them had settled in the drawing room and the butler had been dismissed after serving brandy to the men and port to Violet, that she began her explanation for her visit.

"Blake, my dear boy, you have been grievously wronged regarding your inheritance."

"Thank you, Aunt Violet. I also feel that things should have been different."

"But that's just it, dear! They are different and you have been lied to!"

Blake frowned. "What do you mean?"

"Your father wanted you to inherit the estate and not Arthur."

"I know that, Aunt Violet, but he obviously didn't change his will in time and it's now Arthur's," he said wearily.

"That's where you're mistaken. He did change his will – a full four months before his death."

"But –"

She held up her hand and pointed to a sapphire ring on her finger. "Do you see this?"

"Yes, it's the ring father left you in his will along with a diamond necklace and bracelet. I don't see –"

"Your father wrote to me and told me that if I received this ring in my bequest then the incorrect will had been brought to bear. The ring was waiting for me in our solicitor's office when I returned from India."

Blake's frustration was rising. "Please, Aunt Violet, what is going on?"

Instead of answering, she pulled a letter from her bag. "Your father wrote to me after he remade his will, four months before his death. Read it. It will explain it all."

Blake took the letter and swallowed the lump that rose in his throat at the sight of his father's handwriting.

My dear Violet,

I hope all is well with you and Henry in India.

I'm afraid that with this letter I am charging you with a very important task.

Allow me to explain.

As you know Arthur is my firstborn, and should inherit my estate. However, though it grieves me to write it, he is a useless and greedy man, concerned only with his own pleasure and comfort. He has shown no interest in the land or compassion for our tenants.

Blake, however, has a natural gift when it comes to running the estate and an instinct for it. It is to him I wish to entrust my life's work.

Blake had to clear his throat before continuing to read.

I have made a new will stating that Blake is to inherit the estate and that Arthur has the right to live in the house and the option of helping out on the estate if he wishes. I will leave him comfortably enough off if he wishes to pursue a different career.

I do not believe Arthur will accept these terms and might legally contest this new will.

But here is the shameful thing. I do not think it will come to that because I believe Arthur will not wait for legal means to take their course. I regret to say I do not trust my firstborn son one iota.

When I went to our solicitor, one Richard Williams of Bantry, to draw up a new will, I got the distinct impression that he was not impressed with my decision and I remembered that he and Arthur were friends. I asked that he should treat the matter confidentially, but I still felt unsure of him. The new will was signed by him and another clerk in the office and I took it away with me. I planned to destroy my old will when I got home, but I had to go directly to Cork on business and was gone for two days.

This is where it gets complicated, my dear sister, but please bear with me.

When I returned to the estate, the old will was missing. I believe Arthur took it, preventing me from destroying it. At that point I absolutely knew that the solicitor had told Arthur about the new will and my intention to leave the estate to Blake.

But I had no proof. I thought long and hard about it and this is the only solution I could come up with to ensure my wishes are carried out.

I again travelled to Cork and, calling in some favours, I was given the name of a man who did forgeries. I got him to make a copy of my new will which I then brought back and filed in my study.

The authentic, new will I have sent to your solicitor in London to be kept for you, with a copy of this letter. Please keep your letter safe.

In this new will I am leaving my mother's diamonds to you. In the old will, I also left you my wife's sapphire ring.

I do not wish to be proved right about my firstborn's deviousness, but I suspect that on my death Arthur will destroy the forged will in my study, clearing the way for them to produce the old will.

So, if your solicitor receives the sapphire ring on your behalf as a bequest from me you will know that this is exactly what has happened and my true wishes will not have been carried out. And Blake will be cheated out of what I want him to have.

I do hope that you are following this, my dear, and that you don't suspect me of being fanciful and paranoid. For all our sakes, I hope my suspicions are not proved correct.

Please keep this letter safe, for please God I have many a good year left in me yet.

However, at my eventual passing, if you receive the sapphire ring, please take it and the will from your solicitor to Blake in West Cork, so justice can be done.

As I said, this is a precaution, and I will explain all this again on your return from India when I get an opportunity to visit you in London.

Your loving brother always,
Jeremiah Travers

Blake's hands were shaking as he lowered the letter. Anger and sadness were ripping him apart.

"Alas, poor Jeremiah died sooner than any of us could have

thought," said Violet gently, "and when we returned to London the bequest was waiting for me. And there was the sapphire ring. I knew then that your father had been correct about Arthur's intention of producing the old will."

She passed the will to Blake and he saw for himself that his father had, after all, left the estate to him, just as he had said he would.

It was several moments before he could get his emotions under control, allowing him to speak.

"So with my father still warm in his grave, Arthur took what he believed to be an authentic copy of father's most recent will and destroyed it, then produced the old will for the solicitor to read from." Blake's temper was rising. "A solicitor who had the audacity to sit in this very house and read out a will he knew to be obsolete! Good God Almighty!" he exploded. Then apologised. "Sorry, Aunt Violet."

She brushed it aside. "I believe I said something similar myself when I saw the ring."

"My father was extremely astute and was not as foolishly trusting as I have been."

Henry spoke up. "It was extremely fortunate that your father's suspicions were aroused when the old will went missing. And I think he was very wise not to challenge Arthur at the point because the boy would more than likely have come up with some other scheme to get his way. Now he won't have a leg to stand on. Both he and that solicitor are both guilty of fraud, Blake."

Blake nodded. "I'll go to the authorities first thing in the morning. Arthur is due back around noon. Aunt Violet, Father chose you well. I can't thank you enough for what you have given me by coming here tonight with these." He held up the will and the letter, looking at them as if half expecting them to vanish.

"I am only too delighted to play my part as I know Jeremiah has made the right choice."

Blake smiled at her. "In that case, I insist you keep the sapphire ring!"

She laughed and Blake laughed too, utterly amazed that the estate was going to be his after all.

Blake spent a rough night. The letter and will were under his pillow and his door was locked but he slept little and the words of the letter went around and around in his head. He knew Arthur was hard and cold, but he had never suspected this level of deviousness. He felt enormously proud of his father's cleverness and his determination to see him as the owner of the estate.

Chapter 54

Blake was at the police barracks by eight in the morning. To his relief the Chief Constable was already there and Blake explained how he had been cheated out of his inheritance. He showed him the letter and the will.

The Chief needed a couple of hours to organise a warrant to arrest the solicitor and Arthur, but promised he would have them in custody by lunchtime. Blake told him that Arthur would be at home soon after noon.

All Blake could do was return to the house and wait. To pass the hours he took his aunt and uncle for a drive around the estate. But they were back by noon, with Blake pacing up and down the drawing room, and stopping to check the avenue every few moments.

"You'll have a path worn in the rug, Blake dear," Violet commented.

Before he could reply they heard the sound of a horse approaching. He shot to the window.

"It's him!" His voice shook with rage, as his anger at his half-brother's lack of respect for their father's wishes and the injustice done to him because of it, boiled near the surface.

The groom had run from the stables to take the horse from Arthur.

Henry put a hand on Blake's shoulder. "Don't give the game away at this stage, boy. Keep a grip on your temper for now."

Blake gave him a grateful look and took a few calming breaths. Moving away from the window, he went to stand by the hearth.

When Arthur came in, Blake held back while his aunt and uncle stood to greet him. Blake admired their acting skills, knowing full well that they both would love to give him a lash of their respective tongues. He didn't say a word as Arthur quizzed them about their two years in India, showing an interest that Blake was pretty sure was not genuine.

Within a quarter of an hour, they heard more horses outside. Arthur rose and looked through the window.

"What the devil ... ?" he said when he saw a half a dozen constabulary dismount.

He went out into the hall. Violet made to follow.

"Perhaps you should wait in here, Aunt?" Blake suggested.

She turned with a gleam in her eye. "I wouldn't miss this for the world."

All three went out to the hall where the butler was opening the door.

The policemen came in, led by the Chief Constable himself. He stood in front of Arthur.

"Arthur Travers?"

"Yes, I'm Arthur Travers. What's this all about?"

"You are under arrest, sir, for fraud. You will be tried at a court of law for cheating your brother out of his inheritance."

"What the devil are you talking about?" Arthur argued as one of the constabulary pulled his hands behind his back. "Blake, tell them you were here when Father's will was read – you saw it with your own eyes."

"I saw it all right. But I've also seen Father's most recent will – the one leaving the estate to me."

"But –" Arthur spluttered.

"Father sent the most recent will to Aunt Violet's solicitor in London for safe keeping. What you found in his study, and presumably destroyed, was a copy!"

Blake had never seen Arthur so stunned. With his mouth open he stared at Violet as though unable to believe what he was hearing.

"Your father knew you well, Arthur," she said drily.

"Come along, sir," the Chief Constable said. "We have a nice cell waiting for you and some fine company too. Your friend Richard Williams, Solicitor, was also arrested this morning!"

Arthur sent Blake a look of pure hatred. "I'm the firstborn!" he spat. "It should have been mine. I was entitled to it, not you. Father should never have changed his will."

"That's enough. Take him outside," the Chief ordered.

Two officers marched Arthur out.

The Chief Constable turned to Blake. "There will have to be a court case where all the evidence is presented but it will only be a formality, especially as all my men just witnessed him admitting his guilt."

Blake shook his hand. "I'm extremely grateful to you for acting so swiftly."

"And I'm sure the people of Bantry are grateful to you. You can be sure that a crooked solicitor has committed more offences than just this one. His offices will be thoroughly investigated. I bid you good day."

They left and Blake stood in the doorway as Arthur was helped into a prison cart and driven away.

"Any champagne in your cellar, boy?" Henry asked from behind him. "I think this calls for a celebration, don't you?"

The three of them had a celebratory lunch in the dining room, all of them jubilant over the successful outcome.

While the others left to take a rest in their room, Blake swirled the last of his coffee around his cup. He couldn't wait to tell Ellen. He wondered now what would happen about the land on the Mizen – if Arthur was to be in jail, then perhaps Blake could buy it from him. But so much had happened in the past few days that he couldn't think straight. There was so much that would have to be worked out. He laughed aloud and let himself feel the elation of owning the estate. It made him happy to think the tenants need not fear Arthur anymore and that he, Blake, could improve the estate now with a free hand.

He went into Arthur's study and sat in his chair. He put his hands behind his head. His eyes fell on a portrait of his father on the opposite wall. "I'll prove worthy of your trust, Father. I give you my word."

Idly he pulled open a drawer in the desk, knowing that all this was now his to sort out. At least Arthur was neat, he thought with relief as he looked as the tidiness of the first drawer. The other drawers were similarly kept, full of account and record books.

The third drawer on the left-hand side was locked. Blake searched around for keys but couldn't find any.

"No more secrets, Arthur," he murmured as he forced the drawer open with a letter knife.

Inside lay an envelope marked 'Mizen Lands'. Blake pulled out the contents and found himself holding the sales agreement for the lands on the Mizen.

Blake eyes widened as he read the date of sale and his father's signature beneath it. "Arthur didn't buy them! Father did! Two days before he died!"

Blake thought back, remembering that his father had told him that he was thinking of buying more land. Blake had been away visiting John and Grace in Skibbereen the few days before his father's death. The land on the Mizen must have become available at a good price while he was away and his father had gone ahead and purchased it without ever getting the chance to tell him. He had died within hours of his returning from Skibbereen. They had only exchanged a quick greeting in the courtyard as Blake had wanted to ride out and check with Shaughnessy on the new calves that had arrived during his absence. His father had said he had something to tell him over dinner. It must have been about the Mizen lands, but the heart attack had taken his life during the afternoon.

Once again disbelief and anger at the depths to which Arthur had sunk had Blake shaking with rage, because this meant that, though not mentioned in the will, the Mizen lands had been Blake's all along too, because they had been part of his father's estate.

Anger turned to incredulity. He was now the landlord that Ellen once mistakenly thought him to be. He shook his head at the bizarre turn of events.

Thinking the day could surely not hold any more surprises, he left the study to seek out Shaughnessy and tell him all that had transpired.

With a lightness of step he left the house. He had only gone a few yards when a horse and cart rattled into the yard. Andy Minehane from the public house was sitting on top. He jumped down, and removed his cap.

"Nice to meet you again, sir," he said.

Blake frowned. "Hello, Andy. What brings you here? Is it Ellen?"

"I have a letter from her for you, sir."

Blake's heart skipped a beat. "Is she all right?" he asked, grasping the letter that was proffered to him.

"Yes, sir, but there's been a tragedy in Ballinmara."

Blake went cold at his words and quickly started reading.

"Dear Blake,

Mick Leahy, my sister's husband, has died in an accident. Being a widow now with no means, I presume your brother will evict her and the children. Is this ever going to end? But, if and when eviction happens, at least I still have a cottage they can share, thanks to your help.

The funeral is on Monday at eleven. Can you come?

Ellen

"Thank you for delivering this, Andy. I'm sorry to hear of Mr. Leahy's death. Are you returning there this evening?"

"Yes, sir, once I've collected some supplies. There'll be a wake tonight."

"Can you please tell Ellen that I'll be there on Monday for the funeral? And not to worry, everything will be all right."

"Of course, sir."

"Now, please go on into the kitchens and get some refreshment before your return journey."

"Thank you, sir. You're very kind."

Andy went off and Blake continued to the sheds. Finding Shaughnessy there, he told him about the death.

"Poor Annie," Shaughnessy murmured, shaking his head sadly.

Blake heard the concern in his voice. "I'm going to the funeral on Monday. Would you like to come with me?"

Shaughnessy's eyes lit up. "Oh yes, sir, I would. Mrs. Leahy is a good woman and I'd like to pay my respects."

Blake was amused, knowing Shaughnessy was completely unaware that he had called her Annie moments earlier.

"I have other news too – and a damn sight more cheerful!" he said.

Shaughnessy cocked an eyebrow.

"You work for me!"

Blake, enjoying the moment immensely, smiled at Shaughnessy's puzzled look.

"Haven't I always, sir?"

"You've always taken your orders from me, it's true, but now I'm your employer. The estate is mine – my father left it to me! Arthur tried to cheat me out of it by using an obsolete will."

"Well, I'll be damned!"

The look on Shaughnessy's face made Blake laugh. "And there's more – it was my father who bought the lands on the Mizen peninsula, not Arthur, so they are mine now too!"

Shaughnessy grinned. "How did all this come about?"

"It's a long story, and one I'll share with you on the ride to Ballinmara on Monday if you want to hear it."

"I certainly do. And if you don't mind me saying, sir, you'll make an excellent employer and landlord."

Blake laughed again, clapping him on the shoulder. "Well, let's get on with our work then. Enough time has been wasted over all this cloak and dagger stuff. And we'll be away again on Monday at the funeral, where I can reassure Annie Leahy that she isn't going to be evicted!"

Chapter 55

Ellen and Annie sat side by side in the front row of the empty church. The plain wooden coffin was just a few feet away from them. They had come early so they could put some wild flowers on the altar and to have a few minutes of quiet before anyone else arrived. Annie's children were too small to attend and were being minded by a neighbour's daughter.

Dressed in black, they sat in silence for a while before Annie spoke.

"There was a good turnout for the wake, wasn't there?"

"He got a good send-off all right."

Annie nodded and silence fell again.

Annie whispered her next words but Ellen still heard the raw fear and despair.

"I'm a widow now without any income. Arthur Travers will definitely evict me this time."

"You know Blake will do what he can. I've already written to him and he sent word that he'll be here today."

"He can't keep asking his brother for favours. And I don't think Arthur Travers is the type to do me a kindness a second time."

"The three of you can come and live with me. It'll be like old times. There's no need for you to worry at all. Besides," she dropped her voice to a whisper despite there being no one else there, "it'll be lovely to have my child growing up with yours."

Annie smiled at her. "It would be a bit crowded."

"We'd manage. You'd be doing me a favour. What do I know about having a baby?"

She felt a tremor pass through Annie.

"Everything is changing so fast," Annie said, both puzzlement and fear colouring her voice.

Ellen covered her hands where they rested in her lap and gave them a reassuring squeeze. "Yes, but I think it's all changing for the better, even though that's impossible for you to see right now." She released Annie's hands and lay her own on her stomach. "But remember there is always new life and new hope."

Annie was prevented from saying more as the rest of the mourners began to arrive into the church, some coming up to the front to shake hands and offer their condolences.

Fionn came and hugged them both before sitting in the pew behind them. Before long the church filled up. Ellen looked around but couldn't see Blake among the congregation. Disappointed, she looked up when the door to the sacristy opened. To her utter amazement, Blake and Mr. Shaughnessy hurried out and walked towards them. Father Dempsey and two altar boys came out as Blake slipped into the seat beside her. Looking at him quizzically she saw such tenderness in his eyes that her heart soared with love for him. Mr. Shaughnessy sat behind them, near Fionn. The two sisters turned to acknowledge him. He nodded back at Ellen but then turned a very intense look on Annie, followed by a smile of encouragement and support.

They faced forward again and Blake took Ellen's hand and squeezed it.

Father Dempsey performed the funeral Mass but at the very end broke with tradition. Instead of moving to the coffin to say the final prayers, he went to the pulpit.

"I must ask the indulgence of Mrs. Leahy for a moment while I invite Mr. Travers to say a few words."

There was an audible gasp from the congregation and some uncomfortable shuffling and disapproving grunts.

Ellen looked at Blake in puzzlement, but he gave her a reassuring smile before making his way up to the pulpit.

"I would like to offer my condolences to Mrs. Leahy and her children, and my gratitude for allowing me to speak today." His eloquent voice carried around the church, while hostile feelings were evident on the faces of many. "Having you gathered here allows me the perfect opportunity to speak to you all at once. My name is Blake Travers. Up to now some of you have had dealing with my half-brother, Arthur Travers, who acted as your landlord."

Wary eyes bored into him, but he continued.

"I use the word 'acted' for that is exactly what he did. Arthur was not your rightful landlord and his treatment of some of you has been appalling. He nearly got away with cheating me out of my rightful inheritance, an estate in Bantry and the lands here, all of which belonged to my father and now belong to me."

Again the congregation gasped, especially Annie and Ellen.

"Arthur set himself up as your landlord, claiming he owned this land. My father would have been horrified at Arthur's scheming and his treatment of the people here, as I myself have been horrified. But all that will change now that Arthur has been arrested."

He looked directly at Ellen, seeing her baffled expression.

He continued: "So tenants like Mrs. Leahy here no longer need to live in fear, because I do not do things the way my half-brother did."

Murmurs rippled through the congregation. Someone started to clap, then another and another until it spread throughout the whole church and the sour looks of moments earlier changed into smiles.

"If anyone is having any difficulties with their holdings or rents, you are very welcome to come and speak to me. I hope you will find me a much more reasonable man than my brother. I appreciate being allowed to speak here like this today. I know Arthur caused a lot of worry for the late Mr. Leahy, and I hope that he may rest in peace knowing that his widow has no such worry now. Thank you for your time."

As Blake left the pulpit, Ellen felt a mixture of pride, amazement and joy for Blake, and his new tenants, but most of all confusion.

He resumed his seat beside her. Annie reached across her and squeezed his hand.

"Bless you," she said, her eyes swimming with tears.

"If you will all stand," Father Dempsey invited.

The congregations rose and he said the final prayers.

The church bell pealed slowly as Mick's fellow fishermen carried his coffin out to his final resting place.

Ellen and Annie walked behind it, with Blake and Shaughnessy close behind them.

After the burial, Shaughnessy offered to walk Annie to the public house where everyone was going to gather.

Ellen and Blake walked behind them and Ellen saw the tender way Shaughnessy looked at her sister.

Inside the pub, Ellen stayed by Annie's side and was very quiet as she watched her friends and neighbours come and speak with her. Many of them then went to make Blake's acquaintance. She noticed that Mr. Shaughnessy was also very watchful of her sister.

At one point, when a kindly neighbour had just walked away from Annie and her eyes brimmed with tears, he came straight over to her and asked who was minding the children and if Róisín's tooth had broken through yet.

Every now and then Blake caught Ellen's eye across the room and smiled at her.

When she and Annie were on their own for a moment, Annie asked why she was so quiet.

"It's time for Blake and me to decide about the future. I should have told him about the baby before now," she whispered. "It will look like I want to trap him now that he has all that land and wealth, and nothing could be further from the truth. Now, more than ever, I know how important it is for him to marry someone of his own class – someone who will know how to run that big house in Bantry and be a proper hostess for him."

With eyes wide, Annie looked at her. "Are you going to send him away without telling him about the baby?"

Ellen shook her head. "No, I can't do that. He was nearly cheated out of his inheritance with lies and deceit. I will not do the same to him regarding his child. It's up to him now to make his choices."

They were unable to say any more as another neighbour came to speak to Annie. Ellen's eyes returned to Blake, feeling her love for him intensely.

At that moment Fionn came into the pub and saw her. With a sinking heart he followed her gaze, seeing that it was Blake Travers who had put that look in her eyes. Fionn looked back at Ellen and their eyes locked. Ellen saw the sadness there. She rose and crossed the pub, took his arm and led him outside. Without a word they walked down to the harbour wall and stood looking at the sea.

"It's all right, Ellen," Fionn said. "You don't have to say anything. You warned me yourself that you loved him and I've seen the strength of it back there. There's no fighting something that strong."

Ellen's throat ached with sorrow. "Oh, Fionn, I'm so sorry." She turned and took one of his hands in both of hers, as her tears began to fall. "I love you dearly, but as a treasured friend. And it breaks my heart that I can't return your feelings for me. I wish I could make you happy, but we both know that just isn't possible." Her voice cracked on a sob and he pulled her into his arms.

His own voice was thick with tears as he spoke. "If you value my friendship that much then I promise I won't ever take it from you, Ellen. So no matter what happens from here on, I'll still only be a shout away, always."

Ellen sank further into the strong arms of this beautiful man and sobbed as he rocked her. Still uncertain of the future, she grieved for the companionship and love that Fionn was offering and she was refusing.

After a while, when Ellen's sobs had eased, Fionn cleared his throat and pulled away. With calloused but gentle thumbs he wiped the tears from her face. "Come on, I'll take you back – Annie will be missing you and I don't want to be challenged to a duel at dawn by your man."

Ellen gave a shaky laugh. "Thank you, Fionn."

"Whist now. We'll say no more about it."

Going into the pub together, they could see that some people had left and things were winding down.

Blake was with Annie and looked up curiously at them. Mary, Annie's neighbour, had brought the children in and Annie was cuddling them close. Fionn made his way to the bar, leaving Ellen to go over to them. Though her eyes were obviously red, Blake didn't question her.

"Are you ready to go home, Annie? We'll walk you home, won't we, Blake?"

"No, I'll be fine."

Shaughnessy coughed. "Eh, why don't I walk you home, Mrs.

Leahy, so that Mr. Blake can see your sister home safely?"

"Oh – that's very thoughtful of you, Mr. Shaughnessy," Ellen said. "Is that all right with you, Annie?" She tried to keep the twinkle from her eye.

"It's grand." She turned to Shaughnessy. "Thank you, Daniel."

"Here, let me take Róisín for you," he said, taking the baby from her arms as naturally as if he did it every day. Annie took Michael's hand and, after saying their goodbyes, they left the public house.

Ellen and Blake followed them out and a look passed between them as they watched the pair walk up the hill, Shaughnessy keeping a respectful distance between him and Annie as he chatted away to the two children.

"Well, well," Blake said, "I think he has it bad."

Ellen smiled softly. "Let's hope so."

"She couldn't do any better," Blake agree. "He's the most decent man I know."

She and Blake strolled along the road towards her home.

"Can I ask you who that man was and why you were crying?" Blake asked.

"He's a wonderful friend. He wanted to marry me but I refused him because I'm in love with you," she answered.

"Oh." Blake was a little taken back by her directness.

"Now that we are on our own, can you tell me what transpired in Skibbereen?"

He was thrown by the sudden change in topic but knew she needed to hear what had happened, so he told her about the extraordinary events of the past few days.

Abruptly she stopped walking, making him stop too, and she stared at him, trying to take it in. "Thank God for your aunt! It's quite an amazing story."

"I was a trusting fool perhaps, but it never occurred to me that Arthur and the solicitor were dishonest."

Ellen put her hand on his arm. "Yes, you have been trusting, but you're no fool, Blake. To be trusting is a fine thing – it means you believe in the goodness of people."

He squeezed her hand. "Arthur certainly took advantage of my trust. When he got away with it once, he obviously felt he could get away with it a second time. And he very nearly did."

"I'm happy for you, Blake," Ellen said.

They left the road and walked through the field that led down to Ellen's cottage. There was no breeze and all was still. The only sound came from the hem of Ellen's black skirt swishing across the grass. She clung to these moments, not knowing if they soon would be saying a very final goodbye. As they reached the top of the shore she gathered her courage and broke the silence and said what she had to.

"I know that now you are Lord of the Manor it's more important than ever that you marry someone of your own class."

She saw frustration cross his face.

"Not this again, Ellen."

"I could ask you to go, thinking I knew what was best for you, but that choice isn't mine any more. There are other things to be considered." She paused and blew out a steadying breath. "So I want to know what it is you want."

Without hesitation, he said: "I want to marry you."

"Why?" she asked quietly.

"Because I love you, of course. You know this!"

"And I need you to know that I love you too and, if I were to marry you, that it's because I have loved you from the moment I first helped you and —" she took a shaky breath, "not because you are now a wealthy landowner."

Blake laughed. "You know I would never think that — my social standing has always been the barrier for you, not an enticement."

She nodded and held up her hand.

"I cannot change who I am and become a fine lady who wants to live in that house in Bantry."

"I know this too and I know how to get around that."

She frowned at his reply. "Well, I don't know how we can get around it, but I needed to establish that if we were to discuss marriage then it was for love — that I'm not marrying you for your money, and you are not marrying me because I'm carrying your child."

Her heart pounded as he stared at her, not sure he heard correctly. "What?"

She nodded.

Taking his hand she placed it on her stomach and watched as he looked down at it and then up to her eyes again, realisation dawning.

"My sweet Ellen, really?"

"Yes," she whispered as his hand lovingly caressed her still flat stomach.

He laughed and gathered her into his arms. It was the only place Ellen wanted to be.

Reluctantly she pushed back.

"But how can we make this work, Blake?"

Blake stood staring at the sea and her heart beat painfully while he took his time answering.

At last he turned his gaze back to her.

"The estate in Bantry and the lands here mean nothing to me without the knowledge that you would share it all with me, Ellen." He swept his hand around to encompass the cove and the cottage, then spoke softly. "I would never ask you to give all this up. It's as much a part of you as your healing, your eyes, your voice, your hair, and I wouldn't change any of those, so why would I try to change that part either?"

He took her hands in his.

"So I wondered if you would do me the honour of becoming my wife and letting me make this little piece of heaven my home too? If you were agreeable to the idea, I thought we could extend the cottage, add on some more rooms. The estate isn't so far away and I can appoint a new farm manager there, dividing my time between there and here. I think it would be good for the tenants here to have me near to hand some of the time."

Her heart both lurched and danced at his words. "It's a simple life here, Blake, not what you're used to."

"In this case 'simple', means wonderful, mystical, satisfying. And it's what I want more than anything." He could still see doubt in her eyes. "Please say yes, unless you want to see me spend the rest of my days alone, Ellen Cassidy – because it's you or no one."

Ellen gazed into his earnest eyes and saw so much love there. "In that case, yes."

Blake pulled her close again. "My darling Ellen, we'll build lots of rooms for all the children we're going to have!"

Ellen laughed with him. "When Mr. Berkley gave this cottage to my grandmother, little did he know such a grand gentleman would be coming to live in it!"

Blake moved his thumb over her lips and then her cheek. "And little did your grandmother know that her granddaughter would save my life, on this beach that first day, and every day since."

She shook her head in wonder at all that was now possible.

Blake's looked at her intently. "I love you, Ellen Cassidy. Give me your healer's heart and I will treasure it all my life."

Without hesitation she replied: "It's already yours and always will be."

He pressed his lips to hers to seal their promise.

Ellen kissed him back with all her love, as the sound of the sea embraced them both.

If you enjoyed
Rescued by Maria Murphy
why not try these opening chapters
from her debut bestseller?

For the Love of Martha

It is only with the heart that one can see rightly;
What is essential is invisible to the eye.

The Little Prince, by Antoine De Saint-Exupéry

Prologue

All was still as Juliet made her way across the courtyard in the fog and around by the orchard wall. The iron bars of the gate were cold to her touch. She stood for a long moment. The nearby trees looked lifeless in the dull grey light, while those far off were mere shadows where the fog was thickest.

A beep from the phone in her pocket seemed totally out of place, like an insult to the orchard's silence. She switched it off.

Her natural curiosity fought with a feeling of unease, and won, compelling her to push the gate open and step inside. She turned left, as though not of her own volition, and followed the pebbled path. The musty scent of the old, lichen-covered branches hung in the air. The wall ahead turned right, as did the path. Juliet followed it for a few feet and then stopped abruptly. There in front of her was the exact scene she had dreamed – the same group of trees standing on their own section of grass near the wall and to the left of them an old stone bench.

'How can you dream of a place you've never seen before?' she muttered, unnerved.

The sadness she'd felt on waking that morning was back, like a physical weight, while echoes of the sobbing she'd heard in her dream swirled around her. The recall was so vivid that for a moment she thought she could actually hear it. Her eyes darted around, searching for any movement, but there was none. There was no one there.

'Is it you, Martha?' she asked, her breath disturbing the fog. 'Is it your sadness I'm feeling? If so, what made you so sad and why am I the one to feel it now?'

Her words went unanswered, and it got colder. She shivered. With relief she heard a car door close in the yard and she quickly left the orchard.

Chapter 1

BERKSHIRE, ENGLAND, 1888

In hindsight it amazed me that the moment could have carried such insignificance, considering all that was to follow . . .

I picked up another ribbon, held it against my bonnet and examined the contrast in the mirror on the counter. The colour clashed with my auburn hair.

'What about this yellow one, Martha?' Mrs. Beckett the shopkeeper said, laying it next to the others.

As I reached for it, I was distracted by the raised voice of another customer and the excitement in her tone.

'There he is now,' she exclaimed, as she and two other ladies moved closer to the window, their bustles bobbing and twitching as they leant forward, jostling for position.

I got a fleeting glimpse of a horse and rider passing on the street, leaving me with the impression of height and broad shoulders in a dark frock coat and hat. But I did not see the face.

I turned back to Mrs. Beckett, my eyebrows raised in question at the fuss.

'That's the new doctor,' she informed me. 'And I must say he is a wonder, especially for one so young. Easy on the eyes too, I don't mind saying. For twenty years, old Doc Johnson couldn't give me any relief for these aching knees of mine. But Dr. Adams there, he gave me an ointment that eased them straight away. Mind you, he told me that if I lost a little weight that would make them even better. "Not likely," I told him, "and I married to the best baker in all of Berkshire!".'

She guffawed, her hands resting on her ample waist. Her mirth was contagious and I laughed too.

'It's a long time since I had a slim figure like yours,' she said.

'Thank you,' I smiled, then held up another ribbon.

'Ah, there you go,' she said. 'That colour is perfect. Pretty as a picture!'

Was I pretty, I wondered, looking at the familiar reflection. Well, my father had always said that I had eyes that were alive with laughter. They were sober now, and the same blue as the ribbon I held. My nose was straight, my cheekbones high, and my chin neither too sharp nor too round. I ended this contemplation with a shrug, turned from the mirror and took some coins from the purse hanging from my wrist.

'I'll take it,' I said.

Mrs Beckett nodded her approval and wrapped the ribbon in paper.

'Give my regards to Mrs Pershaw,' she said, handing it across to me.

'I will. Thank you and good day.'

Stepping out into the bright August sunshine, I waited for two carts to pass before crossing Main Street.

As it happened I had to walk by the new doctor's house and surgery. The memory of another doctor, only months before, telling me that my father was dying was fresh in my mind, so I had no desire to meet this one or any other member of the medical profession either.

Leaving the village I walked along the lane, trying to ignore the familiar pain of my father's absence. Although I missed him every day, I was determined to keep my spirits up. It was what he, who had been a great lover of life, would have wanted.

Twenty minutes later I walked through the gates of View Manor and headed up the driveway, still marvelling at my good fortune to be living in such a grand mansion, in such beautiful parkland.

Yes, I was very fortunate. On that pleasant thought, I gave a little skip as I rounded the corner of the west wing, and came upon my cousin, Helena Pershaw, sitting at a table on the terrace outside the open doors to the drawing room.

'Martha,' she called as the maid put down a tray in front of her, 'you are just in time for lemonade!'

'I was on my way to the nursery,' I said.

'Sit for a moment. Lily will bring Beatrice down shortly.' Ice tinkled against glass as she lifted the jug.

I sat near her, wishing that day dresses with high collars and long sleeves had never been invented. After removing my bonnet, I took a welcome sip of the chilled drink.

'Did you purchase anything?' she asked.

Before I could reply Beatrice appeared, her tiny hand gripping the maid's. Letting go, she ran into Helena's arms. There was a great likeness between mother and daughter, their two blonde heads pressed close together, one neatly coiffed with a pleat at her neck and the other covered in bouncing curls.

'Thank you, Lily.' Helena dismissed the maid with a smile.

'Did you have a nice nap, Beatrice?' I asked.

She nodded, jumped down from her mother's lap, ran to me for a hug, and then began a hopping game around the cracks in the paving.

'You are so good with her,' Helena said.

'She is very bright for three and a half,' I said.

Helena smiled at the compliment.

'You have become a good friend to me, Martha. I hope you are happy.'

'Oh yes, Cousin, very happy,' I rushed to reassure her. 'Having no other living relatives but you, I shudder at the thought of what might have become of me after Father's death if you had not invited me to live with you as Beatrice's governess. I cannot thank you enough.'

Helena smiled, reached out, and gave my hand a gentle squeeze. 'Your home is with us now.'

I relaxed in quiet contentment. A bee droned past, the scent of roses lingered on the warm air.

Beatrice soon grew bored with her game and wandered over to a low wall where she sat to watch a spider make a web. I was only eighteen and yet the simple freedoms of childhood seemed a very long time ago.

'My throat is sore.' Beatrice's voice broke into my thoughts.

Concerned, I went and hunkered down in front of her. My hand went to her forehead, but to my relief it was cool to the touch.

'Can I see where it hurts?' I asked, tilting up her chin.

Obligingly she opened her mouth and pointed into it with a small finger.

Helena was now beside us. 'Well?' she asked anxiously.

'It is a little red,' I told her, 'but she doesn't have a fever.'

'Good,' Helena said. 'Keep a watchful eye on her for the rest of the day, Martha.'

'Of course.'

I led Beatrice over to my chair.

'How about sucking on a little bit of ice?' I suggested.

Her curls bounced as she nodded.

The ice seemed to soothe her and within minutes she was off my lap and jumping again. After a while I took her down into the garden while Helena did some sewing.

In the nursery, a few hours later, Beatrice refused to eat her supper, saying again that her throat was sore. Her forehead was now warmer.

'All right,' I said, in a mock stern voice. 'I will let you go to bed tonight without supper, but just this once. Now, into your nightgown!'

She laughed but it turned into a cough and, lacking her usual spirit, she let me get her ready for bed. Seeing a faint rash on her chest, I fetched Helena. She came to Beatrice's room already dressed for dinner in a sapphire-blue gown. The diamonds at her neck shimmered in the evening light as she leaned over her daughter.

'Her fever is still not very high but a rash should never be ignored,' she said. 'I think we should send for the doctor.'

'Best to be safe,' I agreed.

'Oh, I wish James was back from Italy!'

So I was going to meet the new doctor after all, I thought as I went downstairs to send one of the servants to fetch him from the village. I hoped he was worthy of the praises Mrs. Becket had showered on him earlier that day.

Chapter 2

LONDON 2010

Juliet pushed the door shut with her elbow before bending at the knees to shrug off the shoulder-strap of her camera-equipment bag onto the floor. She slung the tote bag down beside it before continuing into the open-plan living space. Sighing with the pleasure of being home, she just stood for a moment to admire the apartment, the clean lines of steel and wood in the kitchen area, the polished wooden floor and glass coffee table in the living area. Some people thought it a bit severe, even sterile, but she needed its simplicity to soothe her after the busyness and unpredictability of life on an assignment.

Her one concession to cosiness was a deep crimson armchair which her mother had bought her as a housewarming gift the previous year. The sight of it made her smile and, after making a cup of coffee, she settled into it with a sigh, curling her long legs under her. She dialled her mother's number and fiddled with the ends of her short blonde hair while waiting for her to answer.

Frances Holmes picked up after three rings.

'Hello?'

'Hi, Mum, it's me.'

'Hello, love. How are you? How was your trip?'

'Amazing –'

'That's great, pet,' Frances cut in. 'I've been waiting for you to ring. I need to ask you a favour.'

Juliet was surprised at the interruption. Her mother was usually anxious to hear every detail of her trips.

Frances continued. 'Can you house-sit an apartment in Florence for two weeks, starting Saturday?'

'What? But I'm just home! I can't go travelling again so soon.'

'That was work, dear – this would be a lovely holiday for you. You work too hard and don't take enough time for yourself.'

'I'm taking time for myself right now,' Juliet replied, smiling and pressing further back into the comfort of the chair. She could hear the hum of London traffic from across the park below her window, and found it soothing.

Using the pause as an opportunity to press her case, Frances continued. 'I can't get away from the practice at the moment because our other paediatrician went into labour two months early. I simply can't leave them in the lurch here. But I promised a friend of mine that I'd be in Italy on Saturday to mind her apartment, and I don't want to let her down.'

'But it's Wednesday already. I'll have the debriefing at work and other stuff, not to mention unpacking and laundry,' Juliet protested.

'Black combats and white T-shirts are not exactly what you wear when on holiday in Italy. You won't be needing them.'

Juliet glanced over at her discarded bags. 'So why does your friend need someone to house-sit her apartment in Verona anyway?'

'Florence,' her mother corrected, 'and her name is Elizabeth, Elizabeth Pershaw. She used to be in my book club up to five years ago before she moved to live permanently in Florence. We've kept up the friendship since. But now she's going to America for a month and she doesn't like to leave the apartment empty. So she insisted I would be doing her a favour if I stayed there for two weeks to keep an eye on the place, water her plants etc.'

'Why can't Dad go instead?'

'Work on the new orthopaedic wing has gone to tender at last and he has to be around to oversee that.'

'If she's going away for a month, why does she need me for only two weeks?'

'Apparently her son is going to spend the second fortnight there.' She paused. 'Come on, think about it – Italy in June – the wine, the food, all that lush vegetation. It will be completely different from the dry heat of Africa.'

Juliet was immediately transported back. 'Oh, Mum, I got some fabulous shots. There was this magnificent lioness and her cubs and we got up so close. I took some beauties of them. They'll definitely be in next month's issue.'

Juliet felt the thrill again as she spent the next few minutes filling her mother in on her latest photo shoot.

'The sunsets there are everything people say they are – absolutely magnificent!' she enthused.

'I'm sure, but I worry constantly about you when you're away working. It'll be a relief to know you're in such a civilised spot as Florence for a change.'

She was successfully reeling Juliet in.

'I don't think Rob has a new assignment lined up for me for a few weeks. I suppose I could ask for a couple of weeks off. I hadn't even thought of holiday plans.'

'Thanks, love. I'll call Elizabeth straight away and then I'll change the name for the flight. I'll email you details.' There was a pause. 'I suppose you could take Russell with you.'

'I'm not seeing him any more. I finished it before I left for Africa. It just wasn't working.'

'Of course it wasn't working. You weren't suited at all.'

'I thought you liked him.'

'I did but there was no magic between you.'

'You always say that.'

'Well, there wasn't. Your eyes didn't light up when he came into the room.'

'Like with you and Dad.'

'Still,' her mother sighed contentedly. 'After all these years.'

Juliet pictured them as she had often seen them – her father grabbing her mother in the kitchen and dancing her around to a slow song on the radio, she with her apron on and some cooking utensil in her hand. She would pretend to bat him away at first, saying the dinner would be ruined, but then she would snuggle in close and they would be lost in their own world until the song finished.

Juliet came back to the present as Frances spoke again.

'Don't settle for anything less than magic, my love.'

'You must be the only mother in the world who doesn't mention ticking clocks to their unmarried twenty-nine-year-old daughters.'

'There's still plenty of time, don't worry. Just don't fall for some Italian who will want you to live over there with him and his *mamma*. Seriously, you'll have a lovely time. I'm so disappointed I can't go.'

'Maybe it's what I need. It'll be good to travel without the team for a change. It's been a while since I've taken any photographs simply as a tourist.'

'Great, that's settled. Now go pack some girly clothes and don't forget to check your emails later for all the details.'

'Wait! Don't do anything until I fix things at work. I'll text you.'

They hung up.

Juliet continued to sit, watching the trees moving in a squally shower. Even though it was the beginning of June, it looked like a day in October. English summers seemed to be getting worse each year, she thought, so a couple of sunny weeks in Italy might be very nice indeed. She began to feel that familiar kick of excitement at the thought of going to a new place, but this time without the accompanying rush of adrenaline at the possible dangers that would be encountered. Yes, an uneventful two weeks was definitely gaining in appeal.

She pressed the speed dial on her mobile for her editor at the wildlife magazine she worked for.

'You did good, Juliet. The photos you sent through are wonderful, and I've seen the outline of Jack's article. It's going to make a very good feature.'

'Sorry they were a couple of days late. We had trouble with the sat phone.'

'No problem.'

'Well, while you're in such a great mood, will you give me two weeks off?'

'Starting when?'

'I need to travel on Saturday.'

'Okay, well, if we bring the meeting forward to Friday morning, work through the day, and if we can all agree on which pics work best, then, yes, you can have your two weeks.'

'That's great, Rob, thanks. See you Friday.'

Well, it seems that's decided then, Juliet thought, hanging up. A quick text to her mother confirmed that she would go.

She went to the bedroom and threw open her wardrobe doors.

There was nothing suitable there. It had been a few years since she had taken a real holiday and she didn't have anything pretty in there, certainly nothing suitable for a stylish city like Florence. Obviously she was going to have to fit a bit of shopping into the next two days too.

'I'll think about it tomorrow,' she said out loud and, suddenly overcome with fatigue, she got ready for bed.

If you enjoyed this sample from
For the Love of Martha by Maria Murphy,
why not order the full book online
@ www.poolbeg.com